PRAISE FOR *THE EDGE OF WORLDS*

"The venerated pulp spirit in science fiction and fantasy has dwindled since the golden age of the 1920s to '50s. Yet an atavistic craving for adventure remains, and it is this need that Wells's books in general and the Raksura books in particular satisfy. The stories are straightforward adventure, but what makes Wells's 'new pulp' feel fresh is its refusal to take the easier storytelling routes of its forebears. Rather than thinly veil an existing human society as alien others, for example, Wells—a master world builder—creates a multicultural world of humanized monsters . . . The result is breathtakingly surprising and fun. So for readers who missed earlier entry points to this delightful series, now is the time to get on board."
—*The New York Times*

"That rarity—a completely unique and stunning fantasy world."
—Hugo Award-winning author Elizabeth Bear, author of *Karen Memory*

"A feast for the imagination . . . As a fan of the series, I really enjoyed *The Edge of Worlds*. The ending left me pumped for the next book and I can't wait to see what happens next. The Three Worlds is one of my favorite places to escape to, and this book delivers."
—*Roqoo Depot*, 5/5

"With sure-handed prose, Martha Wells provides unforgettable characters, gripping action, and fantastical vision. An addictive mix."
—Carol Berg, author of the Rai-Kirah series

"The Three Worlds is unlike any other fantasy world I've ever encountered. It's wildly imaginative and beautifully depicted."
—*The Illustrated Page*

"An irresistible tour-de-force of excellent storytelling and fine characterization . . . I consider *The Edge of Worlds* to be one of the most addictive and entertaining fantasy novels of the year."
—*Rising Shadow*

"Four novels and a host of stories in, Wells' command and depiction of the Raksura and her world are better than ever. Far from mindless sock-em action, The Edge of Worlds provide conflicts with stakes, with choices, and illuminate the inner lives of Moon and the rest of the characters."
—*The Skiffy and Fanty Show*

PRAISE FOR MARTHA WELLS
AND THE BOOKS OF THE RAKSURA

The Cloud Roads

"[Wells's Raksura books] are dense, and complex, with truly amazing worldbuilding, and non-human characters who are quite genuinely alien, yet still comprehensible and sympathetic. The characters, particularly the protagonist, Moon, are compelling and flawed and likable. The plots are solid and fast moving. But it's the world that . . . just, wow! There is a depth and breadth and sheer alienness here that I have rarely seen in any novel. Shape-shifters, flying ships, city-trees, six kazillion sentient races, floating islands, and on and on and on."
—Kelly McCullough, author of the WebMage series and the Fallen Blade novels

"*The Cloud Roads* has wildly original worldbuilding, diverse and engaging characters, and a thrilling adventure plot. It's that rarest of fantasies: fresh and surprising, with a story that doesn't go where ten thousand others have gone before. I can't wait for my next chance to visit the Three Worlds!"
—N. K. Jemisin, author of *The Hundred Thousand Kingdoms*

"It reminds me of the SF/F fantasy I read as a teen, long before YA was categorized. Those books explored adult concepts without 'adult content'; the complexity of morality and the potential, uncaring harshness of life. This story's conclusion satisfies on all those counts as well as leaving me eager for the sequel."
—Juliet E. McKenna, *Interzone*

"There's so much to like here: multiple sapient species sharing a world (or NOT sharing) with complex gender roles, wildly differing societies, and varying technologies. This is rigorous fantasy without the trappings of European medievalism. And most of all, it's riveting storytelling."
—Steven Gould, author of *Jumper* and *7th Sigma*

"Martha Wells's books always make me remember why I love to read. In *The Cloud Roads*, she invents yet another rich and astonishingly detailed setting, where many races and cultures uneasily co-exist in a world constantly threatened by soulless predators. But the vivid world-building and nonstop action really serve as a backdrop for the heart

of the novel—the universal human themes of loneliness, loss, and the powerful drive to find somewhere to belong."
—Sharon Shinn, author of *Troubled Waters*

"I loved this book. This has Wells's signature worldbuilding and wholly real character development, and her wry voice shines through. I can't even explain how real the world felt, in which each race and city and culture had such well-drawn back story that they lived on even outside the main plot."
—Patrice Sarath, author of *Gordath Wood* and *Red Gold Bridge*

The Serpent Sea

"With these books Wells is writing at the top of her game, and given their breadth, originality, and complexity, this series is showing indications it could become one of the landmark series of the genre."
—*Adventures Fantastic*

"Wells remains a compelling storyteller whose clear prose, goal-driven plotting, and witty, companionable characters should win her fans among those who enjoy the works of writers such as John Scalzi and Lois McMaster Bujold."
—Matt Denault, *Strange Horizons*

"A worthy sequel to *The Cloud Roads* and it features all of the strengths (fantastic world-building, great story, awesome characters) of that first novel. It is so easy to fall in love with this series and the reasons are manifold."
—*The Book Smugglers*

The Siren Depths

"I really loved Book 3, which wound up as my favorite book of the trilogy . . . I'll be pushing it on everybody who loves great writing, ornate worlds and wonderfully-drawn nonhuman characters."
—Rachel Neumeier, author of *Lord of the Changing Winds* and *Black Dog*

"*The Siren Depths* has more of what I've come to love about the Books of the Raksura—a compelling story, great world-building in a unique setting, and lovable characters with very realistic problems. In my opinion, it's also the most satisfying installment in the series."
—*Fantasy Café*

"Truly inventive and stunningly imaginative world-building perfectly melded with vivid, engaging characters make the Books of the Raksura one of my all-time favorite science-fiction series."
—Kate Elliott, author of The Spiritwalker Trilogy

Stories of the Raksura: Volume One

"Wells is adept at suggesting a long, complex history for her world with economy . . . Longtime fans and new readers alike will enjoy Wells's deft touch with characterization and the fantastic."
—*Publishers Weekly*

"The worldbuilding and characters in these stories are as wonderful as the novels and I had no difficulty immersing myself into Wells's world and societies again."
—*SF Signal*

Stories of the Raksura: Volume Two

"Immensely pleasing . . . the shorter stories still encompass everything that makes the novels so satisfying, from the daily interactions between Raksura to the incredible creatures, mysteries and landscapes of the Three Worlds, and if Martha Wells were to never write anything other than Raksura stories from now on, as much as I love her other work, I can't say I'd complain."
—*A Dribble of Ink*

"I wonderfully enjoyed these stories . . . I urge readers with any interest in secondary world fantasy who have not done so to pick up *The Cloud Roads* and begin there and work your way to this volume. And then, like me, you can hope and wait for future volumes set in Wells's rich and endlessly entertaining world, peoples and characters."
—Paul Weimer, *Skiffy and Fanty*

The HARBORS
OF THE SUN

THE HARBORS OF THE SUN

MARTHA WELLS

Night Shade Books
NEW YORK

Night Shade books may be purchased in bulk at special discounts for sales promotion, corporate gifts, fund-raising, or educational purposes. Special editions can also be created to specifications. For details, contact the Special Sales Department, Night Shade Books, 307 West 36th Street, 11th Floor, New York, NY 10018 or info@skyhorsepublishing.com.

Night Shade Books® is a registered trademark of Skyhorse Publishing, Inc. ®, a Delaware corporation.

Visit our website at www.nightshadebooks.com.

10 9 8 7 6 5 4 3 2 1

Library of Congress Cataloging-in-Publication Data

Names: Wells, Martha, author.
Title: The harbors of the sun / Martha Wells.
Description: New York : Night Shade Books, [2017]
Identifiers: LCCN 2016038948 | ISBN 9781597808910 (hardback)
Subjects: LCSH: Paranormal fiction. | BISAC: FICTION / Fantasy / Epic. | FICTION / Fantasy / General. | FICTION / Fantasy / Paranormal. | GSAFD: Fantasy fiction.
Classification: LCC PS3573.E4932 H37 2017 | DDC 813/.54—dc23
LC record available at https://lccn.loc.gov/2016038948

Edited by Jeremy Lassen
Cover Art by Yukari Masuike
Cover Design by Lesley Worrell

Printed in the United States of America

The HARBORS
OF THE SUN

CHAPTER ONE

Bramble woke with Merit's hand on her forehead. He whispered, "It's all right."

She took in a lungful of scent, nearly all unfamiliar. The only source of light was a hole in the roof. From the sense of movement and height they were no longer on the groundling sunsailer; this was a flying boat. "It is not all right," she growled. She winced and the motion sent spikes of pain through her head; even the small amount of light was too much. She could tell it was just her and Merit in a small enclosed chamber. "Where are the others? Where's Jade?"

Merit's voice went raw with fear. "I don't know." He cleared his throat, an effort at control, then more evenly said, "I think it's just us."

Bramble opened her eyes, for a heartbeat frozen in terror. Leaving the court and traveling far across the Three Worlds was one thing when you were accompanied by a queen, her consort, your line-grandfather, and a clutchful of warriors. It was like a court in miniature, and therefore reassuring. But for two lone Arbora, it was a horrifying nightmare. She forced her pounding heart to calm, and managed to ask in an almost normal voice, "What happened?"

Merit wet his lips, looking up toward the opening. "We've been stolen."

Arbora don't get stolen, Bramble wanted to say, *that doesn't happen*. Courts always had enough of their own Arbora to deal with, there was no reason to covet anyone else's. And Arbora wouldn't permit that kind of bad behavior anyway. Then she belatedly remembered who did steal Arbora, and her throat went tight. "Fell?"

"No, no," Merit said quickly and Bramble breathed again. "There's no Fell stench." He shuddered and Bramble reached up and squeezed his wrist. Merit had been captured by Fell once, not so many turns ago during the attack on the old colony. "It was the Hians who came for Vendoin. That's who brought the water. They used Fell poison on us."

"The Hians?" That just didn't make any sense. Bramble squinted at Merit and realized what she had thought were shadows from the dim light were actually the faint outline of his scales, showing on the brown of his groundling skin. It was the outward sign of the poison, deadly to Fell and not much better to Raksura. She lifted her arm and squinted at her own scale pattern, the darker lines on the brown so strange to see. She tried to shift, reaching for her other form; her stomach did a painful loop, but nothing else happened. "Why is it Hians? What do they want?"

Merit's voice was bleak. "I don't know."

With Merit's help, Bramble pushed herself into a sitting position. They clung to each other, both weak and shaky, the poison doing something intermittently painful to Bramble's insides. She knew the stories that said groundlings would drink the poison and then let Fell eat them so it would kill the Fell. She had never understood it; now after personal experience with how sick it made you, she was starting to see how the idea of being eaten by a Fell might seem like a sweet relief.

"The poison was in the food they gave us on the sunsailer," Bramble said. That part seemed obvious. Fell poison was odorless and the taste was mild, easily disguised by spices. "That means the others are poisoned too."

"What about the Kish-Jandera?" Merit said. "They wouldn't just let the Hians steal us."

"No. No, they wouldn't. They were afraid at first, but they liked us. They wouldn't . . ." Bramble couldn't talk anymore. The others, the Jandera, everyone else on the sunsailer might be dead. That was the only way she could see that this made sense.

The small chamber had only the one opening in the ceiling, covered by a grill of some material that was close to bone in texture, but not at all brittle. Merit had already tried to break it and demonstrated his lack of success for Bramble. Hanging from it and swinging wildly didn't even make it creak. When Bramble could stand without her stomach trying to jump out of her body, they both tried their strength against it, but it wouldn't budge.

The walls were of the dense moss, like Callumkal's flying boat, though Bramble had explored every pace of it during their long trip to the sel-Selatra and found no chambers like this one. There was no light except for the dim illumination falling through the roof opening, and Merit wasn't able to make anything glow. The poison must affect his mentor abilities as well as their shifting. It was not a reassuring thought.

At least there was a ceramic jar of water and another empty container for their latrine. After what felt like forever, a Hian came to drop a basket of fruit through the grill, while several more Hians stood around with Kishan fire weapons. Merit tried to speak to them in Altanic, but the Hians wouldn't answer. Bramble whispered in Raksuran, "Remember, they don't know we speak Kedaic."

"You think that still matters?" Merit asked, staring warily up at the Hians.

"It's the only advantage we have," Bramble reminded him.

The fruit was dried, some kind of ground fruit they didn't recognize, but they forced themselves to eat it. They were Arbora Raksura, not Aeriat, but they still needed meat to live. Bramble thought that would probably be the least of their problems. She asked Merit, "How long does the Fell poison last?"

"It depends on how much they gave us." He hunched his shoulders uneasily. "They can always put more in the water and keep us like this indefinitely."

Bramble hissed. They might die of that first, before they figured out why the Hians wanted them.

The wind rose high enough to make the boat tremble, then died away again. Bramble realized she hadn't been able to scent the sea since waking. The air wasn't fresh, and she and Merit now smelled badly enough that it was obscuring more subtle odors, but she thought she could detect hints of greenery. Which meant they were traveling over land and had been for some time.

"It's been days." She turned to Merit, shocked by the realization. "Since they took us. Days." And no one had come flying after them. Her heart wanted to sink and she refused to let it. *The others can't be dead. They can't be.*

Merit admitted reluctantly, "Yes. Several days, maybe more. I remember being given water. I'm sure someone picked me up and carried me, at some point. I don't think we were put in this cage until they decided to let us wake up."

She frowned. "Why didn't you tell me?" As her nausea faded her brain was starting to work again, and she knew she needed as much information as possible.

He shook his head. "What's the point? It's my fault we're here. I should have seen this." His voice trembled and he buried his face in his hands. "My scrying was useless. If the others are dead it's my fault."

Bramble had to nip that bud right now. She made her voice hard, and as queen-like as it was possible for a short round Arbora hunter to sound. "Merit, we don't have the luxury for things to be anybody's fault. We have to be ready to act."

Merit lifted his head and glared at her, which was the result Bramble had been going for.

Then a door must have opened somewhere because Bramble suddenly caught a confusing blend of new scents. Voices and steps sounded near, getting closer. She leapt to her feet, her shoulder slamming into Merit's as he did the same. They stood under the grill, near the dim shaft of light from above. "It's Delin!" he whispered harshly.

Bramble caught Delin's scent and drew it in. There was something sour in his sweat, not unlike the Fell poison. But if he was here, the others must be too. *They're coming to rescue us*, she thought, her heart pounding. She couldn't catch any hint of Raksura but it might just be lost in her and Merit's too-strong unwashed musk.

Bramble heard the steps of at least four groundlings. They stopped nearby and Delin said anxiously, "Bramble, Merit, you are there?" He spoke Raksuran, and his voice was hoarse and strained.

"We're here," Merit called back. Bramble stepped to the side, angling to see. Delin stood at the edge of the opening. He was small and slim like all Golden Islanders, his gold skin weathered and worn like an old tree. All Islanders had straight white hair, but now Delin's was ragged and unkempt, and his long beard was in disarray. It was hard to make out details in the bad light, but she thought his cheeks and the soft flesh under his eyes were sunken, a sign of illness. She wanted to growl aloud in disappointment. This wasn't a rescue; he was a prisoner too.

"Speak Kedaic," an unfamiliar voice ordered.

"They don't understand it," Delin protested, in Kedaic.

Merit squeezed Bramble's wrist, and she bit back a quiet hiss of triumph. When Jade had told them at the beginning of the trip that they would pretend not to understand the western trade language of Kedaic, Bramble had thought it was a lot of trouble for not much return, especially once the expedition groundlings had seemed so trustworthy. Moon had thought it necessary, but then Moon was the most suspicious person Bramble had ever met.

Now it was proving more than handy. And it didn't escape her that Delin had just reminded them of it. Whatever was happening, Delin was still on their side.

The unfamiliar voice said, "I don't know that I believe you. Vendoin said not to trust you."

Bramble looked at Merit to share the outrage, and Merit rolled his eyes.

Delin was clearly thinking along the same path. He said, dryly, "Since Vendoin betrayed and poisoned me and my friends, and stole myself and Callumkal away to hold us prisoner, you will understand why I am uninterested in her opinions."

So just Callumkal and Delin, no one else, Bramble thought. She didn't know whether to be relieved or newly terrified. If Jade and the others weren't here, where were they? What had happened to the sunsailer and Rorra and the rest of the Kishan crew?

There was a slight hesitation, and the voice said, "Do they understand Altanic? Speak to them in that."

Delin switched to that trade language to say, "Are you well?"

"We're all right," Merit said, in careful Altanic. "They gave us Fell poison and we still can't shift. Are the others here?" Bramble nodded approval of the question, knowing it would add veracity to the Raksura-can't-speak-Kedaic fiction.

Delin answered, "No. Vendoin says they were left on the sunsailer. Perhaps I believe her."

Bramble almost bit through her lip in anxiety.

"Are you all right?" Merit asked. "You smell like you don't feel well."

Bramble heard the Hians react to the question, as if they found it unsettling. Delin said, "Vendoin added a mixture to the supplies sent down to the sunsailer, a combination of Fell poison and some other simple that made us all unconscious. It has made me quite ill, but I recover."

Bramble drew breath to speak, but Delin added, "I know your sister Bramble is very afraid, but you must reassure her, so she does not panic and make herself ill too, you understand."

Bramble let the breath out, startled. *Ah, I think I see.* She nudged a nonplussed Merit, who said doubtfully, "I'll try." She nudged him again and he added, "She's very upset. What do they want with us?"

Speaking Kedaic, the other voice interrupted, "That's enough."

In the same language, rapidly, Delin said, "But surely I should be allowed to tell them that we go south to another place of the foundation builders, and I have no notion yet why Vendoin has betrayed us—"

"No, that's enough."

Bramble barely heard the rustling, the protests as Delin was pulled away. "Why?" Merit whispered. "Why is this happening? What do they want?"

Bramble swallowed down bile and tried to remember everything Vendoin and Callumkal and the others had said about the foundation builders. "The Hians knew things about the city the Kishan didn't." The Hians could see in colors that eluded both the Kish-Jandera and the Raksura. Vendoin had said she was translating all the writing on the walls, but they had only had her word for it, and now they knew her word was nothing. "Maybe there was a map to this other foundation builder place. Vendoin wanted it for the Hians, and not the Kish-Jandera, and she stole Callumkal and Delin, and us, to help her get inside it." That presupposed a lot of things, the main one being that the new city would be sealed like the sea-mount city. It also presupposed that Vendoin valued Merit and Bramble's contribution to opening that city, which was not an impression that Bramble had had before.

Merit said, "We don't know that the others are all right. Delin didn't see what happened either."

Bramble turned away. Her mind was racing and she needed to settle herself and get down to some serious thinking. "We have to get away and find them."

Merit hissed in frustration. "How? We can't even shift! I can't even make light!"

"I don't know, not yet." Except Bramble knew she wasn't Merit's sister, not the way the Altanic word meant, and that she wasn't afraid, not the way the Hians would think, not the paralyzing fear of helpless prey. Delin knew that as well as she did; he was preparing the Hians for something, the way Arbora would prepare the ground of a garden for planting. "Delin is trying to give us an opportunity. We just have to wait to see what we can do with it."

CHAPTER TWO

The Port of Gwalish Mar

Sleeping in swamps was always difficult. The brackish mud was too cool against Moon's scales to be comfortable, and every time he managed to doze off, something crawled over him. The clouds of insects sheltering in the tall grass weren't much interested in Raksura, but the ugly little things that looked like fish with legs had sharp teeth and were annoyingly persistent. Moon had always found sleeping in his scaled form awkward and not restful, but the distractions made it nearly impossible.

Fortunately for his temper, the sky was finally darkening toward evening. Moon shoved himself up out of the mud and slid through the sharp grass blades and over to a much larger puddle. He found a knot of driftwood near the edge and chunked it in. "Stone, wake up."

Bubbles broke the muddy surface, then a big dark scaled tail whipped up and took a swing at Moon. He dodged and went to find a less muddy place to clean off in.

He waded through the waist-deep grass out to one of the pools where the sea entered the wetlands. Sitting on his heels in the cool salt-water, he scrubbed the sticky mud off his scales with handfuls of sand. The empty sea stretched out, the evening sky was indigo and purple, and the quarter moon gleamed on the water. The breeze held saltwater and the intense green scent of the wetland grasses, leavened with various flowers and laced with bird scat and dead fish. All the groundling shipping that he had spotted throughout the afternoon, both surface sailing ships and flying boats, had already made port.

Moon glanced around again out of habit, even though nothing could see him except for a few tall spindly shore birds striding away through the shallows. Then he shifted.

His wings, tail, spines, and black scales flowed away into his soft-skinned form. Anyone watching would now see a tall lean groundling, with dark bronze skin and dark hair. He was dressed in light pants cut off at the knee and a loose brown shirt, the kind of clothes some groundlings wore for sailing or other work. It wouldn't draw attention in most of the groundling ports Moon had visited, but this wasn't exactly a groundling port. He felt the wind lift his hair and scratched at the back of his neck where he hadn't managed to get all the mud out of his spines.

With no warning, Stone stepped out of the grass. Moon twitched in spite of himself. Stone was in his groundling form now too, with gray skin and hair, in battered clothes much like Moon's, and a pack slung across his shoulder. He was somehow already dry and mostly clean, despite having been buried in a mud wallow for most of the afternoon. Clearly not in any better a mood than Moon was, he said, "What's taking you so long?"

"I'm waiting for you." Moon hissed at him and followed him back through the grass.

The port that lay just beyond the wetland was far enough from the protected Imperial Kish territories to be wary of Fell. Since Raksuran consorts were almost always mistaken for Fell by uninformed groundlings, approaching it by air in the late afternoon daylight had been impossible. Also, it had been several long days and nights of flight across the archipelago to the mainland coast, and they had needed a few hours rest. If their quarry had come here, they were already too late to catch them; the best they hoped for was some confirmation that they were on the right track.

They slogged through the weeds until they came to a seawall constructed of huge chunks of sandy-colored rock. It was nearly fifty paces tall, and reminded Moon of the ancient roadways in the east and down in the Abascene peninsula. Following Stone, Moon clambered up, the rough texture of the rock still holding the day's heat and warm against the hard soles of his feet.

At the top Moon saw the lights of the port, though it was already dark enough not to be able to make out much detail. But Rorra had described it well enough for Moon to know what they were looking at.

A long curve of lights marked the dock area where the sea-going ships would tie up, though many lay at anchor in the protected harbor. Just past the docks were tall dome-shapes dotted with light that weren't made of stone or metal or wood, but were a kind of resin excreted by tame creatures that sounded like a combination of herdbeast grasseaters and skylings. The domes were used as dwellings and warehouses for cargo. Past them were clusters of tall spindly metal structures that looked like giant flowers; those were docks for flying boats. Between them a mutli-storied web of bridges and walkways and suspended structures linked the stalks for the groundling crews and formed an upper city for the skylings.

They made their way along the seawall as it sloped down slightly until it was only twelve or so paces above the muddy ground. When it turned toward the harbor, Moon and Stone climbed down and headed in toward the domes.

Moon tasted the air and winced. Groundling cities held a myriad of different scents, but this place had a bitter undertone of predator musk that confirmed all of Rorra's warnings. It also made the skin of Moon's fingertips itch, an urge to flex the claws he didn't have in this form.

The area around the nearest dome was lit by tall lamps hanging from metal poles. The dangling glass bubbles were filled with the darting, glowing flickers of trapped insects. More light spilled out of a large round door, and figures moved inside.

It was too far from the flying boat docks to be useful to them, so Moon meant to pass it by. But as they crossed the circle of light, a shape came rumbling out toward them.

It was large and thick, with heavy muscles in its arms and legs, and slick light green skin. Its head was a rounded lump set directly on its shoulders, and its nose and wide mouth were equally compressed, as if it was designed not to give an enemy anything to get a grip on. Its hands were big and clawed, and bone spikes stood out all over its body, along its arms, on its shoulders and the top of its head. Moon thought they were inserted, not natural, since there was bruising on the skin around them. It was wearing a harness of fishskin with various sharp metal implements attached to it and a bone armor plate over its genitals. From the webbing on its feet, Moon guessed it was a swampling.

It advanced on them, making a gargling noise Moon realized was a laugh. In gravelly Kedaic, it said, "Soft skins. You know what we do with soft skins here?"

Stone stopped and tilted his head to regard the swampling with his one good eye. The other eye was clouded, and had been from birth; Moon had never been sure how well Stone could see out of it. Stone said, easily, "No. What do you think I'll do when I find out?"

Moon winced and rubbed his temple, and said in Raksuran, "Don't." They had been traveling hard, Stone doing the flying so they could move as fast as possible, feeding on nothing but the fish Moon could catch during the brief rests when they found an uninhabited island or a sandbar. If Stone's temper snapped, it would just make this harder.

To the swampling, Stone said, "Wait." He turned to Moon and said in Raksuran, "'Don't' what? You're the one with the temper."

Moon folded his arms. "You're senile and delusional." Admittedly, Moon wasn't exactly in a good mood either.

"After him, you're next." Stone turned back to the swampling. "Now what do you want?"

The swampling hesitated, rocking on its heels, the blades on its harness jingling. It had clearly expected them to be afraid. That they weren't implied its estimation of their ability to defend themselves was incorrect, possibly fatally so. But it rallied and said, "There's nothing but trouble for softskins here."

Stone said, "Good, that's exactly how we like it."

Moon snarled in irritation and asked the swampling, "Is there a resting place for flying boat crews?"

The swampling looked from Moon to Stone. Stone seemed to be taking up far more room than could be accounted for by the size of his groundling body. The swampling stepped back and pointed. "They mostly stay on the hive masts, and the webs."

That was no help. Moon suppressed a hiss of frustration. They didn't have time to search the whole upper city.

Stone eyed the swampling a moment more, then stepped past it and walked on into the darkness. As Moon followed, the swampling made a last attempt to dominate the encounter and called after them, "Careful. Somebody might get eaten."

"Not just now. Maybe later," Stone called back.

Moon hissed. "That's not funny."

Stone glanced at him. Moon couldn't read his expression in the dark, but he was fairly sure he was getting that annoyed look again.

There were broad pathways of hard-packed dirt between the domes, and no real attempt to light the way. The other structures seemed makeshift at best: shacks and lean-tos made of driftwood and fragments of large insect carapaces, probably from the same creatures who made the resin for the domes. Huddled figures sat outside, watching the foot traffic pass. The scents were intense, bitter and smoky and rotten and sweet, and Moon could identify few of them. Stone didn't react, but then Stone didn't react to a lot of things. Though his senses were far more acute than Moon's, he was able to filter out scents and sounds much more effectively.

They found their way through a cluster of domes, most rowdy with small crowds of various species of swampling and other scaled groundlings. Like the first swampling had said, Moon didn't see any groundlings with soft skin. No one approached them, and most ignored them, but Moon caught one or two watching them with a possessive intensity. It made his back teeth ache and his prey reflex twitch. He hoped he and Stone could do their business and get out of here without killing anybody. He said in Raksuran, "Maybe we should have done this in daylight."

"No, it wasn't worth the risk." Stone sounded less irritable. "The last thing we need is for some ally of the Hians to figure out that we're on the right trail."

Moon hoped they were on the right trail. When they had left the others, Lithe's visions had still been indicating movement.

They came to the area where the giant stalks of the flying boat docks towered up. Squinting, Moon saw several boats anchored on each of the nearest, tied off to the elaborate flower structures that extended out to partially enclose their hulls. The upper city stretched overhead, the complicated webs of cable and platforms dotted with light. Voices and the sounds of movement drifted down.

They could safely ignore the bladder boats, which were kept aloft by giant inflated air bladders and were much slower and more difficult to steer than the others. There were several kinds of craft Moon didn't recognize, and some spiky shapes that might be made from the same material as the giant insect carapaces. But on the third flower stalk were three Kishan-made boats, grown from the moss that converted sunlight to the power that allowed them to fly. But none was the right shape and all were much smaller than their quarry.

An armor-plated form staggered toward them in the dimness, then staggered rapidly away as Stone growled low enough to make Moon's bones vibrate. Moon felt pretty certain that if the Hians had stopped here, they wouldn't have left the upper city. Even with Kishan fire weapons, this place was too dangerous.

Below the nearest stalk lay one of the structures made from the nearly complete carapace of a giant beetle-like insect. The scents and the smoke drifting out was foul, and a few swamplings had collapsed outside. Some big scaled groundlings stood near the door, watching Stone and Moon.

The predator scent was getting stronger. "We need to move," Moon said. It was getting harder to control his prey reflex. "Or we could shift and kill everybody in town." The longer he was here the more attractive the second option became.

"We wouldn't have to kill everybody." Stone eyed the group near the carapace. It was hard to tell if he was joking. He turned back to the docking stalk. "Let's see if there's any rational people in the upper levels."

A ramp curved up the first stalk. There were cage-like structures on the sides, which was disturbing, until Moon realized they were climbing bars, basically a staircase without steps, clearly meant for races other than the swamplings or scaled groundlings. More predators watched from below, though no one tried to follow them.

The ramp was gritty underfoot and they followed it up two turns to the first flower structure standing out from the main stalk. Small bulbs of light lit the interior, the glowing insects flickering inside. More climbing racks filled the space, leading up to smaller rooms tucked in among the curving petals. On the floor of the chamber lay bags for supplies and some baskets. As Moon and Stone climbed closer, the miasma of the town faded a little and was alleviated by a strong scent of clean fur and fruit.

The sources of the clean fur scent hung from the climbing bars. They were long limbed, long bodied, with narrow heads and large eyes in shades of yellow and green. Their hands had spidery, nimble fingers, and surprisingly, so did their feet. They must be a treeling race, not intended for the ground. Moon realized the small metal frames with the straps lying among the other supplies might be meant to help them walk on flat surfaces, like the way Rorra's boots worked.

As they drew level with the chamber, a treeling uncoiled from the frame, head lifting to stare at them in what seemed to be surprise. "What are you doing here?" it said in Kedaic. Its voice was rough and rippling, suggesting a throat with an unusual texture.

Moon had a bad moment, thinking that it had been warned by the Hians and recognized them, before it added, "The Ilmarish hate soft skins. It's dangerous for you to walk on the ground."

"We're not as soft as we look," Stone said. "It's not dangerous for you?"

"We're the only Lisitae who trade with them," the treeling said. "They can't afford to chase us away." Moon wasn't sure if that was the name of the race, a family, or another city. It continued, "Why are you here? Are you traders? You should go to the upper city. It's not as dangerous there."

"We're looking for someone," Moon said. "Are there any Kishan flying boats from Hia Iserae in the docks?"

Stone added, "With Hians aboard. They're about our size, but look like they have rock armor in patches on their skin."

The treeling blinked, then leaned back and spoke to the others hanging in the upper frames. Moon caught the words "Hia Iserae."

A smaller one with darker fur peeled itself off the frame and hung upside down to say, "Better check with the portmaster." The treeling swayed toward them, sniffing thoughtfully. "Why do you want to know?"

Stone said, "They stole something from our flying boat, back in Kish-Jandera." That had the virtue of being true, though it had happened on the fringe of the ocean deeps. Two more Lisitae swung down to listen, their wide eyes fixed on Moon and Stone. It would have been disturbing, except there was just something non-threatening in their attitude. Or maybe it was the long languorous limbs and the fluffy fur. "Where's the portmaster?"

"In the upper city, toward the fifth stand over, that way. The one with the ktarki flyer. It has a loop, like this." One long furred limb made a gesture. "The portmaster's structure is large and round, with a light at the peak of the roof."

"Thank you," Stone told them.

"Go up!" one called as they turned back to the ramp. "Stay away from the ground!"

They followed the ramp up. On the ground below, a group of predators stared at them, intently following their progress. Moon was too occupied by his trail of thought to snarl at them. "So did the Hians plan to stop here all along? And if not, why stop?"

Large Kishan flying boats could carry a lot of food and water. This was why Jade and Malachite meant to search other potential directions and sightings of Hian flying boats; there just wasn't a good reason for the Hians to come to this port, and even Lithe had been afraid her vision was wrong.

Stone rumbled under his breath, but it was thoughtful rumbling, not irritated rumbling. "Either something went wrong with their boat, or someone was waiting for them here," he said.

They reached the point on the stalk where a bridge led off the ramp and into the walkways of the upper city. The maze of structures extended up several levels overhead. Some were just awnings stretched over platforms, others had driftwood walls and thatched roofs, and many were secreted bulbs, like the domes down on the ground.

The further they walked, the more activity there was, and the more variety among the races. Moon saw more treelings, some furred and some with shiny scaled hides. There were tall, willowy groundlings with long limbs and narrow skulls that curved back. They wore draperies that concealed much of their bodies, and there was something about their delicate appearance that was deceptive. Other soft-skinned ground-lings were blue like the Serican traders in the east, or a dark brown, similar to the Kish-Jandera. Music, mostly drums and other staccato instruments, vibrated through the metal and plank walkway.

There was too much activity for Moon and Stone to draw attention. Some groundlings glanced up to watch them pass, but most were too occupied with speaking to each other or with moving goods along the walkways. Some platforms acted as gathering places, and some seemed to be caravanserai and depots for supplies. From the scents of cooked meat and spiced oils, some were selling food.

Stone veered off toward one and Moon stopped to wait without protest. Cooked groundling food wasn't that filling, but it might stop Stone from ripping apart the next predator-swampling that looked at them funny.

Standing out of the way beside a heavy support cable, Moon caught movement overhead and nearly shifted. It was only a big skyling, climbing along a web of rope above. It was hard to get a good look at it in the intermittent light, but the body was rounded, with reflective shells and multiple hands that gripped the supporting bars of the web. Some smaller skylings that looked a little like the eastern Dwei buzzed along after it.

Stone returned, slipping past a noisy party of furred groundlings. He shoved a packet of greased paper at Moon. "Hold this."

It was full of fried dumplings. Moon scented sugar dough and his stomach growled. Stone took another packet out from under his arm and poked at it tentatively. "What's that one?" Moon asked, hoping it was meat.

"I don't know, I asked for some of everything they had." Stone tasted it and shrugged. "It's bug paste." As he tucked it away in his pack, he tilted his head toward the far side of the walkway. "Did you see that?"

Moon spotted the little turret. It extended out and up from the other structures, with a distinctive muzzle sticking out of the top. It was an emplacement for something like a Kishan fire weapon, part of the port's defenses against the Fell.

They started off again, following another party of assorted ground-lings, and shared the dumplings. A few were filled with more bug paste, the shell fragments and tiny wings scratchy in Moon's throat, but the others had spicy sweet root centers or chopped fish.

Then Moon spotted a round peaked roof with a blue light atop it. A number of skylings of different sizes and shapes slept on the roof and the web structure above it. Stone had stopped to taste the air speculatively at the walkway to another food place. Moon nudged him. "There."

They made their way to the little bridge that led to the portmaster's house. It was a couple of levels tall, with open galleries allowing a view into the dimly lit interior. A few figures moved around inside and a dark blue groundling guarded the bridge, along with something wearing a lot of clothes and a shell over its head. Hoping it might be possible to skip meeting with a figure as official as a portmaster, Moon said, "We're looking for a Kishan flying boat from Hia Iserae, with a Hian crew. We were told to ask here if one had been in dock."

The blue groundling turned to consult the shellhead, who gestured for them to follow it and started across the bridge. Moon groaned under his breath and followed with Stone.

They stepped onto the lower gallery. The high ceilings let the cool breeze off the sea sweep through. The outer portion was occupied by smaller versions of the tall slim groundlings with the elongated curving heads. They all fled inside at Moon and Stone's approach. The shellhead ignored the effect they were having on the house's inhabitants and led them up a ramp to the second level.

A sling chair hung from the roof and sitting in it was a curved skull groundling, only this one was tall, probably a few heads taller than Moon when standing. Moon wasn't sure if it was female or male or some other gender. The concealing robes, all in different shades of blue, didn't reveal any hint. Moon was guessing this was the portmaster. Smaller versions of it were seated around on multi-colored cushions, apparently partaking of something that looked like smoke in glass bowls.

The shellhead addressed the tall groundling briefly in a deep voice, using a language Moon didn't recognize. Then it turned and said in Kedaic, "Be seated, the portmaster will speak to you."

Moon really didn't want to sit down, he just wanted to ask their question, get an answer or not, and get out of here. His hesitation wasn't obvious to anyone except Stone, who elbowed him hard in the ribs. They both sat down on the bare wood floor, and Moon pulled the pack off his shoulder in order to look like they had all the time in the Three Worlds.

The portmaster said, "What are you?" Its voice was light and high, and it spoke the Kedaic so fluidly and musically that it sounded like a different version of the language.

In some cultures, the question would have been offensive to the point of being a tacit invitation to violence, while in others, it might be the normal way to open a conversation with strangers. There was no way to tell which, so Moon just said, "We're from the east, from the far end of the Abascene Peninsula." This was true in one way, at least. It was where the Indigo Cloud court's old colony had been, and where Moon had lived most of his life before Stone had found him.

The portmaster tilted its head in a way that Moon wanted to read as predatory. "But you look for Kishan craft?"

This close to the Imperial Kish borders, with ships from all along the coast passing through, the portmaster had to know they didn't look much like the groundlings from the Jandera cities. But lots of different kinds of people, groundling and otherwise, lived in Kish. Again, it was hard to tell the portmaster's attitude. "We were traveling with friends from Kish-Jandera. Hians traveling in a Kishan flying boat stole something from us, and we were told they came here."

The others tittered and whispered to each other. On a Raksura, the portmaster's expression would have been described as arch, except Moon would have slammed a Raksura across the room by now. It said, "Stole what?"

It clearly didn't believe them, and Moon could understand why if not sympathize. He and Stone looked like people who traveled on foot and slept in the dirt, not like people who traveled on flying boats with cargo valuable enough to steal. But there was nothing else he could do but keep trying. He took a deep breath to weave a better lie, when Stone said, "People. They stole people."

The room went silent. The sudden focused attention made Moon want to twitch. Stone continued, "From our friends, they stole a father and a grandfather. From us, a grandson and a granddaughter."

Everyone looked at the portmaster. It held up one graceful hand. One of the little ones jumped up and Moon braced himself to move. But it went to a doorway into an interior room and returned almost immediately with what looked like a stack of thin plates of wood. As it carried the stack to the portmaster and held it up, Moon realized it was a record keeping system.

The portmaster leaned over the stack, turned the first plate over, and ran a finger across it. It said, "A ship listing its origin as Hia Iserae docked at stalk gal-alan, in the fourth position from the top, two days ago. They left the same night." It made an open-handed gesture. "That is all we know here. If you go to that stalk and ask, there may be more information to be had."

Stone was already standing and Moon shouldered his pack again and pushed to his feet. Stone said, "Which one is gal-alan?"

The one with the record stack handed it off to another helper and said, "I'll show you."

It walked with them down to the bridge back to the main walkway, and pointed. "Three stalks to the north, facing out from the sea."

It darted back into the structure before Moon could say thank you. He followed Stone back to the walkway. "How did you know that would work?"

Stone glanced at him. "You mean telling the truth?"

Moon nodded. Stone just looked at him. "What?" Moon demanded.

Stone sighed and slung an arm around Moon's shoulders. "Nothing."

They made their way over the walkways toward the gal-alan stalk, and Moon tried to make plans. They should have enough metal trading bits to buy more food before they left. It would have been nice to buy lodging too, and sleep somewhere not covered with sand or mud for a few hours, but he didn't know if they had the time to lose.

That was assuming they could find someone to confirm the direction the Hians had left in. If they couldn't, they would have to wait for the others and see if Lithe had a new direction, or if a real horticultural had been found to trace the Hians.

They reached the stalk, having to shoulder their way through a loud, excited gathering of spindly skylings with what looked like flowers sprouting from their heads who were all apparently intoxicated. Moon gently moved a flower antennae out of his face and squeezed past onto the bridge that led over to the stalk. There were two flying boats docked in the upper portions, one made of the same mossy material as a Kishan boat, but much smaller, and the other resembling a spindly ball of spider web. Below them, docked as far from the others as possible, was an air bladder-style boat.

They crossed over to the relative quiet of the stalk's platform. A ramp with climbing bars curved up to the berths above and another led below. "Fourth position from the top is down here, next to that bladder-boat," Moon said, and started down.

"I hate bladder-boats," Stone said.

The last bladder-boat people they had run into had been hostile and far too eager to shoot their projectile weapons at Raksura. Maybe it had something to do with the general unreliability of air bladders as methods of transportation.

First they followed the curved walkway into the empty berth the Hians had used. The flower shape formed a partial roof overhead, and the empty space for docking was an open oval meant for the boat to fit into. It was a little cramped for a Kishan ship the size of the one belonging to the Hians, but it must be worth it to dock in partial shelter. There was nothing left in the folds of the flower that formed little rooms, no signs of previous occupation, not even any trash left behind. Moon crouched down and sniffed close to the floor, while Stone paced around and tasted the air.

Moon sat back finally, shaking his head. They were closer to the ground here and the bitter miasma that came from the swamplings' part of the city covered any subtle odors.

Stone grimaced in annoyance and headed out of the berth, and Moon pushed to his feet to follow.

They traced the stalk's ramp around to the bladder-boat's berth and found a groundling curled up in front of the opening to the dock. It had very white skin, and patches of silver-blue hair, and was dressed in light silky fabrics. They stood there for a moment, but it didn't move.

"Is it dead?" Moon started to say, and it suddenly sat bolt upright with a yelp.

Moon twitched, startled, though Stone didn't. The little groundling curled up in a protective ball, staring at them with huge aquamarine eyes. It said something in a language Moon didn't understand.

Stone asked it, "Do you speak Kedaic? Or Altanic?"

It blinked at them, then said in Kedaic, "Are you thieves?"

"Do we look like thieves?" Stone said, deadpan. "That's a little insulting."

Still wary, it edged toward the door. "Sorry, you startled me. I'm supposed to be guarding the ramp."

"We're not thieves." Moon just wanted to get this over with. He didn't think this groundling would have any information, and they would have to head back to meet the others and lose any advantage they might have had. "The portmaster sent us here. We're looking for any news about a Kishan-made flying boat that docked here two days ago, with Hians aboard. They were in the next berth on this level."

The groundling's narrow shoulders relaxed a little. It rubbed the flat triangle of its nose and yawned. "Yes, I saw that ship. It traded cargo with another Kishan ship that was docked up top and then left."

"Traded cargo?" Moon hadn't been expecting that.

"Which way did it go?" Stone added.

"Don't know." It looked from Stone to Moon. "I didn't see it leave."

Stone looked away, obviously controlling the urge to growl in frustration. Moon wondered about that cargo. Maybe they had the wrong Hian flying boat, and this one was just a group of traders. Maybe Vendoin's boat had docked somewhere else in the city and had lied about its origin to the portmaster, or Lithe's augury had been wrong and it hadn't stopped here at all. He said, "What cargo did they trade?"

"I didn't see it." The groundling leaned against the doorframe, relaxing more as it became increasingly clear that Moon and Stone really were here for information. "They went back and forth a lot, kept us awake through our rest day."

Moon considered the possibilities. "So all you saw was a bunch of Hians going back and forth between the two berths." Stone glanced at him, gray brows drawing together.

"Heard, mostly." The groundling made an elaborate gesture with its stick-like arms, then added, "But why would they do that except to exchange cargo?"

Moon was certain they had been exchanging something. Stone said, "How long was the first Hian boat here? The one that was docked in the upper part of the stalk."

"I don't know." It rubbed its nose again, thoughtfully. "It was here when we arrived. I guess they were waiting for the second Hian ship, to exchange cargo."

Moon asked, "Did you see it leave? The first ship, the one that was waiting for the second one."

The groundling made another gesture. "It went south."

Moon switched to Raksuran to say to Stone, "They switched flying boats."

"Huh," Stone commented. He asked the groundling, "Where was it docked, the flying boat they traded cargo with?"

The groundling pointed upward. "The first berth on the second tier, the one facing the sea."

Stone was already halfway around the curve of the ramp. Moon said, "Sorry we woke you," and followed.

The Kish-Jandera and the Hians could track the moss used in the motivators of their water sailers and flying boats; it was how the Hians had found Callumkal's sunsailer out in the Ocean's fringe. The sunsailer's horticultural shaman had been killed during the Hians' attack, but Lithe and the surviving Jandera navigator had been able to cobble together a tracking liquid so they could follow the Hians toward the coast. But the range wasn't limitless and it had given out by the time the sunsailer reached the archipelago, leaving them with only a general direction and Lithe's visions to guide them. The Hians had obviously planned ahead to foil any attempt to track them, with the second flying boat waiting here.

In his pack Moon carried another piece of Kishan moss, a sensible precaution Jade had insisted on. Once Kalam found a Kishan horticultural, the others could find them if anything went wrong and they missed the meeting at the swampling port.

Stone reached the ramp and stopped so abruptly that Moon bumped into his back. "What?" he demanded.

Stone tasted the air. His mouth twisted into a growl. "Fell."

Moon hissed in startled reflex, then glanced back at the bridge to the bladder-boat's berth to make sure the groundling hadn't heard. "How close?"

"Somewhere nearby, on the ground." Stone started down the ramp. "I'll keep them occupied. Make sure the Hians didn't leave anything behind in that berth."

Moon considered telling him to be careful but there was no point in that. He started up the ramp at a run. They knew at least one flight of Fell had followed the sunsailer, maybe two. Or maybe one was following the other flight. Moon snarled under his breath, frustrated at himself. It was his fault one of those flights was still taking an interest in them, but there was nothing he could do about it now.

The climbing racks were tempting, but Moon didn't want to shift yet. Some races had even better night vision than Raksura and he still didn't want to chance being seen, not until he had checked this last berth.

He passed up through the darkness to the upper tier of flying boat docks, where two of the ramps led to empty flowers and one was guarded by a furred groundling sleeping in the shadows of the doorway. There was no sound of movement from the berths, but the wind played with something light and metal and jangly, maybe attached to one of the boats. On the next tier all three berths were empty and he went to the one facing the sea.

At first glance, there was again nothing left behind, not so much as a discarded fruit rind or muddy footprint. Moon paced around impatiently, sniffing the walls and floor, trying to be thorough even though he wanted to rejoin Stone. Then he glanced up at the petals where they curved over the berth. There was something up there, just a dark shadow on the edge of the metal.

Moon hesitated, but this berth was facing out and away from the hanging city structure, and as long as he stayed inside it, nothing could see him from below. He shifted and the change flowed over him, his skin turning to dark scales, spines growing from his head and back, claws from his hands and feet, and the weight of his furled wings settling on his back.

He crouched and leapt, caught the edge of a petal with the claws of one hand and one foot, and leaned in for a closer look. The dark substance on the metal was moss, scraped from the hull of a Kishan flying boat. Moon used his free hand to carefully collect it. It was from the upper hull, not from a motivator, so he didn't know if the usual Kishan method of detecting the boat's direction would work on it. But it was worth a try, and it might help Lithe with her scrying.

He dropped to the floor, shifted back to groundling, and dug one-handed in the pack until he found his spare shirt. He carefully wiped the moss off his hand, rolled the shirt into a ball to protect it, and tucked it away.

Moon went down the ramp at a run and stopped just above the last level to taste the air. The Fell taint was faint, and he didn't hear any screaming from the ground or the upper city.

He started around the last curve and saw the base of the stalk, lit with only a few flickering insect lights amid the carapace huts. A crowd of swamplings and an assortment of other groundlings who stunk of predator gathered in the cleared area, watching something. Moon followed the faint trace of Fell stink to the crowd.

He found Stone standing with folded arms, on the outskirts of the group. The swamplings had loosely surrounded a big soft-skinned groundling, who was paying no attention to them and looking up toward the tops of the docking stalks. It was taller and wider than Moon, and probably male. His skin was pale and it was hard to tell if it was tinged with any other color under the insect-lights. His face was boney and heavy, his hair dark and tied back in braids. He wore nothing but a short wrap of fabric around his waist, held up by a belt of braided cord.

Moon stared, looked blankly at Stone, and stared at the figure again. Bare feet, no weapons, no pack, clothing little suited for travel even in this climate. And the casual disregard of the swamplings and other predators that could only mean it was far more dangerous than they were. He looked again at the pale, colorless skin, the blocky brow. Baffled, he said, "A kethel?"

Stone's expression was somewhere between incredulous and homicidal. "Have you ever seen a kethel wear clothes?"

Moon was still trying to get past the braided hair. He had seen kethel wear collars or chains around their necks, probably given to them by rulers or their progenitor. He wasn't even sure a kethel understood how to disguise itself as a groundling, unless a ruler had told it to. But what ruler would tell it to braid . . . "The half-Fell queen," Moon said, and the words came out in a growl.

Just then the kethel turned and met Moon's gaze. It froze.

Moon stalked forward, a snarl building in his throat. Stone had already slipped away through the crowd of distracted swamplings, circling to come up on the kethel from behind.

The kethel hesitated, lowered its head in indecision, then bared its teeth at Moon. Its fangs had been filed or cut back somehow, so they weren't piercing its lower lip.

Moon said, in Raksuran, "You're following us."

The kethel glared. "Consort." It slid a wary glance back toward Stone. "Old consort." Its voice was deep and rough, and it spoke Raksuran. It added, "She sent me."

"What does she want?" Moon said. He took the last step forward, so he was easily within its arm's reach. Major kethel were far stronger even in their groundling form than a consort or a warrior, but with Stone ready to gut it, Moon figured it was worth taking the chance. His back teeth were aching and the skin on his fingertips itched with the urge to shift. "We're not drugged now."

It dropped its gaze with a flicker of unease. "She helps you."

Moon had never seen a kethel talk for long before a ruler took over its mind and voice. He kept waiting for that to happen. It spoke the Raksuran words with an odd accent, as if it had learned the language from someone who could barely speak it.

"Helps us?" Moon hissed a laugh. "We know what kind of 'help' Fell give Raksura."

The kethel's gaze lifted briefly. "Help you find the weapon."

Moon gritted his teeth. "Why?" It was his fault the Fell-born queen knew about the weapon, the dangerous artifact from the foundation builder city. He had been drugged and sick and panicked when he told her about it, but that was no excuse and it was like a stab from a claw every time he thought of it.

Moon had been half-aware of a swampling in his peripheral vision, now it stalked aggressively toward them. "You softskins—"

Moon turned on it and let loose the snarl of thwarted fury he had been withholding, in time with the kethel's deep warning growl. The swampling flailed, fell on its backside, and scrambled away. The watching crowd flinched and edged back.

Moon met the kethel's gaze. It said, "Weapon. Other Fell want it."

"Help by leaving us alone."

"Other Fell won't leave you alone," the kethel said. "They follow too. She warns you."

Stone stepped between them suddenly, shouldering Moon away a pace. The kethel fell back a few steps, lowering its head, turning its gaze away. Stone eyed it, his expression revealing nothing. He said to Moon, "We need to go."

Moon didn't care what happened to the stupid swamplings and their predator friends, but the fate of the groundlings and skylings in the bustling upper city worried him. He asked the kethel, "You think you're going to feed on this city?"

The kethel grimaced and showed its fangs again. "We don't eat groundlings."

Stone rocked on his heels toward it and the kethel fell back another step. It said, again, "She warns you. She helps you," and turned away.

The swamplings, proving they weren't incapable of learning, scattered as it strode off through the crowd.

Watching it disappear into the shadows, Moon said, "You believe that? That the half-Fell flight won't attack the city?"

Stone snorted. "No." Then he added, "Maybe. But if it was telling the truth about the other Fell flight following us too . . ."

Moon hissed a breath, trying to think how to warn the city without lengthy explanations and the risk of being exposed as shapeshifters who would look exactly like Fell to everyone here. *It's not like we have to come back here.* "We can make sure the city's prepared for Fell."

Stone followed that thought immediately. His brows quirked as he considered it, then he sighed. "I wanted some of those rice ball things at that other food place we passed."

"You should have got some while we were there." Moon glanced around. The swamplings gathered in a rough circle, clearly having some sort of debate as to whether to rush the strangers or just keep staring at them. The sensible ones casually wandered off into the shadows. This was the edge of the port and Moon and Stone had a clear path to the sky on the far side of the stalk, away from the fire weapon emplacements in the upper city. Moon didn't see anyone on the ground with projectile weapons. "Ready?"

Stone stepped back and shifted. His form flowed into existence, large dark wings lifted and spread. Moon turned and flung himself at the swamplings, shifting in mid leap. The predators scattered and cried out as he bounced off the ground and snapped his wings out. Moon landed on the climbing rack of a stalk and paused to watch Stone.

As a line-grandfather, Stone's winged form was far bigger than Moon's; tip to tip his wings were three times the size of Moon's twenty pace span. Raksuran queens and consorts grew larger and stronger as they grew older, and Stone was very old, and very strong. He was also hard to see, though that had nothing to do with the flicker of the inadequate insect lights. It was something to do with being a line-grandfather that made his form seem nebulous, terrifyingly so for groundlings. It was as if you could only see him in pieces; razor sharp spines lifting above the dark shape of his head, huge gnarled claws flexing as he left the ground. All combined into something huge, dark, and frightening. Moon was used to it, and now hardly noticed it, but the screaming and running told him that it was having the desired effect on the swamplings.

Everyone here would believe they had seen a major kethel and a ruler, if not a dozen major kethels and rulers. The city would have time to ready its defenses if the Fell were on the way.

Moon swung to the next climbing rack and leapt into the air, flapping to gain height and get away from the bridges of the upper city. Stone swept past him as he caught the wind, and Moon banked to follow him.

CHAPTER THREE

At the port of isl-Maharat, on the Selatran Rim

It was early evening and Jade stood alone on the deck of the sunsailer, waiting and watching the docks of the busy groundling port. The sun had still been up when Kalam and Rorra and others from the sunsailer's crew had gone to meet with the local Kish leaders, to tell them about the Hians' betrayal and ask for help in finding them. Now it was after dark, and they still hadn't returned.

Jade wished she could talk to Niran and Diar, see what they thought about this delay, but the Golden Islander wind-ship had gone to tether at a docking tower a short distance inland. She was starting to wonder how difficult this place would be to escape from if it came to that.

The city was obviously huge, the buildings of the harbor all made of white stone and curved and twisted like shells, glowing with interior light. They were built atop a series of terraces from the harbor level all the way to the cliff tops, like a massive set of stairs. More terraces extended out and became bridges, enclosing and sheltering the harbor. Groundlings moved along the walkways and ramps between tiers and the docks, all going about their business, but the multi-leveled bridges that curved over the harbor's entrance were beginning to feel like a trap. Jade was drowning in strange scents, from the dead fish smell that clung to the dock pilings to the combined miasma of all the strange groundling bodies. The constant movement of the other sailing craft at the crowded docks was endlessly distracting, making her prey reflex twitch.

She was in her Arbora form, to keep from drawing attention with her wings. Most of the others were inside resting, but Briar and Deft, one of Malachite's warriors, were on watch, sitting atop the sunsailer's cabin in their groundling forms. Looking over the harbor, Jade thought, *I don't know how Moon endured places like this for most of his life*. The city was interesting to look at, but Jade couldn't forget that it was heavily protected from the Fell by large fire weapon placements, and that all those groundlings in pretty fabrics and jewelry would be just as happy to use their weapons on Raksura.

It would be a relief to get in the air and track the rumors of Hian flying boats they had heard from other Kishan craft, and to rejoin Moon and Stone at the swampling port. And to prove to herself that she wasn't an idiot to let the two consorts go off on their own, even with a piece of Kishan moss. Jade would feel better about that precaution once they managed to secure the help of another Kishan horticultural to track the moss and help search for the Hians. She suppressed another growl of impatience. Why was this taking so long? Didn't the stupid groundlings in this city understand they had to hurry?

Then Briar called down from atop the cabin, "Jade, they're coming back."

Jade spotted the groundlings passing through the light from a tall metal lamp shaped like a giant seabird. They were all over the port, a warm white glow falling from their spread wings onto the walkways and bridges. Chime had been out on deck earlier drawing them for the Arbora and Delin. But it was only Rorra and Kalam who were returning; they had taken with them Esankel and Rasal, the most senior surviving members of the sunsailer's crew.

Rorra limped as she came down the dock. It was a bad sign; Rorra was a sealing, and one of her legs ended in a fin, and the other had been badly damaged until only a stump remained. She had to wear special boots to allow her to walk on land, but while they seemed clunky and awkward, she normally didn't limp unless she was exhausted.

Jade leaned down to give her a hand up the boarding ladder. Rorra had lightly scaled, pale green skin, and loose patches of flesh on either side of her throat that had once been gills. She wore heavy dark clothes and a Jandera harness, to hold her various weapons and devices. Jade caught a trace of Rorra's distinctive scent, and remembered to filter out pheromones. It was a communication scent to sealings, but it could trigger aggressive impulses and other unfortunate effects on Raksura and even some groundlings.

Rorra nodded in gratitude as she climbed onto the deck. "Are you all right?" Jade asked.

Rorra pushed her gray braids back and frowned toward the city. She frowned all the time, and between that and her communication scent, it could be hard to read her emotions. After traveling with her, and nearly getting killed a few times with her, Jade was used to it. Rorra said, grimly, "It didn't go well."

Kalam pulled himself up the ladder behind her, saying, "I sent Esankel and Rasal to hire a horticultural. Rasal, she knows this port, and Esankel, she knows what to ask, to judge if the horticultural is good enough to track the moss samples. I had to come back here to warn the others."

"'Warn?" Jade said.

Kalam took a sharp anxious breath. "I need to tell the crew—Those who don't want to go with us must stay here. Some of them must stay with the ship, but others will want to return to Kedmar. I have to send someone—" He started to turn away.

Jade caught his wrist and pulled him back to face her. "Rorra can talk to the crew. You need to tell me what happened." She wasn't as good at recognizing the difference between a young groundling and an older one the way Moon was, and the fact that Kalam was only recently considered an adult wasn't always obvious. It was obvious now, though. Kalam was Janderan, and to Jade's eye almost identical to the species called Janderi, except Janderi were shorter and more thickly built where Janderan tended to be tall and lean. His hair was short and tightly curled and he had tough, reddish-brown skin with the texture of rough pebbled rock. Like the rest of the Kish-Jandera crew, he wore an open coat of a richly textured fabric over loose pants and sandals.

Rorra made a gesture of agreement and started away down the deck. Kalam said, "We'll need to take the wind-ship after the Hians."

30

It was faster than a Kishan flying boat anyway, as far as Jade could tell. She didn't think that was the problem. She said, "What did the Kishan leaders say to you?"

Kalam seemed to brace himself. "They don't believe me. Us. Any of us."

Jade felt her spines try to lift and forced them back to neutral. She said, "What? They think all of you are lying? Making it up? At what point is that a rational thing to do?"

Kalam's voice shook a little and this time Jade read the emotion he was struggling with as suppressed rage. "They think it's some private quarrel. They think we're fighting over 'scholarly nonsense.'"

Jade felt her jaw go tight. "They think you lie about your dead." She let go of Kalam's wrist so she wouldn't squeeze too hard.

"They think we had some battle with the Hians, over the artifacts from the city." He hesitated, then reluctantly admitted, "They didn't believe Esankel or Rasal because they're Janderi. I'm the only high-ranking Janderan left. It isn't like that in Kedmar, where we live, but this is a provincial city, mostly Janderan, and they know the Hians as friendly traders. If Magrim, or Kellimdar, had survived . . ." He made a frustrated gesture. "I don't know if they think I'm lying or deluded."

The Hians had killed Magrim outright, to keep him from using his skill as a horticultural to track their flying boat, and Jade had felt certain that Vendoin was also responsible for Kellimdar's death. He had been given the same poison as the Kish who had survived, but there was nothing to show that something else hadn't been forced down his throat once he was unconscious. Kellimdar was on the same level of authority as Callumkal, and if he had been with Kalam to support him and second his accusation of Vendoin and the Hians, they probably wouldn't be having this conversation. She began, "We need to get out of here before they—"

Then Malachite was suddenly standing beside them.

Kalam flinched, and Jade managed not to hiss. Malachite was a head taller than Jade and broader in the shoulder, and it should have been impossible for her to approach so closely without Jade knowing. Yet here she was.

Jade said, "You heard all that?" *Of course she heard all that.* Malachite's scales were a dark green, webbed over with a layer of scar tissue that obscured her web of secondary color, and she faded into the shadows. All queens could keep other consorts, warriors, and Arbora from shifting, but Jade had never encountered a queen who could use her mental connections to other Raksura in the ways Malachite could. She had never encountered another queen who had needed to do what Malachite had done to save her court.

Malachite moved one spine in a way Jade knew by now meant assent. All Malachite's concentrated attention was on Kalam. "Do they know there are Raksura here?"

"Yes." Kalam was a little accustomed to Malachite by now, and Raksura in general, and managed to bear the scrutiny. "I had to tell them, to explain what had happened. I told them about the Fell, too. Not the half-Fell," he added hastily. "I didn't know how to explain it, and Rorra thought it best not to, that it would just confuse them."

Good for Rorra, Jade thought. They were in enough trouble as it was. "We need to get out of here."

"Not through the groundling city," Malachite said. She tilted her head toward Jade. "We'll fly out to sea, toward the barrier islands we passed, and the wind-ship can meet us there."

Jade managed not to say that she had thought of that already. She turned to call up to Briar, "Go tell the warriors to get ready. Tell them to leave nothing behind, we won't be coming back to this boat. We're going to the Golden Isles wind-ship."

Briar jumped down to the walkway and headed for the nearest hatch, and Kalam's shoulders slumped in relief. Maybe he had nursed a suspicious fear that the Raksura would desert him, too.

Since the Hians had betrayed them, things had been tense with Kalam. He was Callumkal's son, and young to be facing the abduction of his parent and the responsibility for trying to get help from the other Kish-Jandera. The deaths of the crew who hadn't survived the poison had been hard enough for him. It had just made the situation worse to find out that the foundation builder artifact that the Hians had plotted to steal had been brought aboard the sunsailer by the Raksura, even if it was inadvertent. Then Jade had had to tell him that most of the Raksura could speak Kedaic, that she had ordered the others to deliberately deceive the Kish-Jandera because she hadn't trusted Callumkal's motives. That hadn't been an easy conversation.

It had been better before Moon and Stone had left; Kalam trusted Moon more than he did her.

Now Jade met his gaze and said, "We'll find your father, Kalam. And Delin, and Bramble and Merit. I swear to you I'll be standing with you when we find the Hians."

Kalam looked away for an instant, to gather himself. He conquered the emotion, then said firmly, "I'll tell Rorra. I need to give the crew their travel funds, buy supplies for the wind-ship. We have to hurry. I'll send Sarandel to Niran and Diar at the air docks to tell them where to meet us—" He headed down the deck.

Jade faced Malachite, who looked out over the harbor, eyes narrowed. Jade had been around her enough not to take the lack of attention as an insult. Malachite was not a normal queen anymore than Moon was a normal consort. Malachite said, "Is there time for his preparations?"

Jade said, "I think so. It sounds as if the Kishan here underestimate him so much they think he'll sit here on this boat and keep begging them for help." She had never wanted to count on aid from Kish, the way Rorra and the other groundlings had. After the Hians' betrayal, Jade hadn't wanted to count on anything but her own warriors and the Golden Islanders, who were proven allies with their own stake in finding the Hians. "The sooner we can get away from here, the sooner we can catch up to Moon and Stone at the swampling port."

Malachite tilted her head to eye her. "You expected me to object to that."

Jade had been surprised when Malachite agreed to the plan; sending two consorts off alone to scout after murderous groundlings in strange territory was so unheard of as to be impossible for most Raksura to contemplate. Moon should be back at the colony with his clutch, guarded by warriors and Arbora. Stone, as a line-grandfather, had more license for his behavior, but Jade felt sure no one in any Raksuran court had ever contemplated this much license. But they didn't have a choice.

Jade knew Moon had come to see Malachite as a powerful ally, but she still wasn't sure how Malachite saw him. Their relationship was different from anything between a birthqueen and the only surviving consort of her last clutch ought to be. For most of his life Moon had thought his birthcourt had been wiped out. *No, for most of his life Moon hadn't had a clue that anything like a court existed,* she reminded herself. Jade said, "It did surprise me, but then I don't know what you think about anything, least of all my consort."

Malachite moved her spines so slightly Jade wasn't sure if it was indicating anything or they had been stirred by the breeze. "At the moment Moon's experience is far more valuable than his ability to breed, and we do not have the luxury of pretending that he is anything other than what he is."

Jade reminded herself that from Malachite that wasn't an insult. She forced her spines and claws to relax, and made herself say, evenly, "I'm glad we're in agreement on that."

South of Gwalish Mar

Some distance outside the port city, Moon and Stone found a ruined statue that was so worn by weather and vines all you could see was that it had four legs and was crouching. Though the body was protected a little by the heavy growth of trees around it, the head was above the canopy and had worn down to a featureless ball. A cavity that had been knocked in its chest at some point made a good place to rest. It was padded with turns worth of palm leaves and rotting vegetation, and Moon was so exhausted he slept the rest of the night curled against Stone's side.

He woke at dawn, and crawled out of their nest to sit on the edge of the cavity. The air was cool and damp, laced with the scent of the sea and the swampling city. Stone was still deeply asleep, and Moon felt bleary and half-conscious. It was a sure sign they were both short on food.

He wondered how close the others were, if they had reached the mainland yet, if they had gotten help from the Kish the way Kalam hoped. Every instinct said he and Stone were close behind the Hians, that they needed to keep moving. He hoped Jade didn't regret sending them ahead.

Moon had spent the last night before they had left with Jade, Chime, and Balm, up on the roof of the wind-ship's stern cabin. It held the ship's cistern, and was far enough away from the steering cabin and the sleeping areas down in the hull for relative privacy. Not that Raksura in general cared much about privacy for sex, but Moon still did, and he had been around Golden Islanders and Jandera enough by now to know that they appreciated it too. It didn't help that his mother was on this wind-ship somewhere, with Shade and Lithe and the rest of the warriors. Stone, at least, had snuck off down to the sunsailer to see Rorra.

It had been quiet then with not much movement except for the few warriors taking their turn at watch. Jade was sitting up, still in her Arbora form, looking into the distance as the wind pulled at her frills. Moon lay on his side next to her, Chime pressed against his back and half wrapped around him, mostly asleep. Balm lay curled on Jade's other side, dozing. Jade's tail coiled around Moon's arm, and he ran his fingers down the tiny frills along its length. He could tell her thoughts were weighing on her, and to distract her he said, "You can't see land yet, can you?"

It was partly a joke; Rorra had calculated that they were still some distance from the coast.

Jade tilted her head toward him, but didn't take her gaze off the dark horizon. "It's a long way. Are you sure you don't want to wait another day at least?"

Moon had recovered from the Fell poison and had had nothing to do but rest and reflect on all his mistakes as they made their way back toward Kish. The urge to go after the Hians had been burning in him, he couldn't bear to wait another day. "I'm sure." Because it was easier to blame it on Stone, he added, "It's been hard enough convincing Stone to wait this long."

Jade had bared her fangs. "I should never have let any of you come on this trip to begin with. Especially the Arbora."

Balm's eyes were open, her brow furrowed worriedly. From Jade's tone, she was about to go back to the conversation they had already had many times, where Jade tried to take sole responsibility for everything that had gone wrong since they left the court. What made it worse was that it inevitably led to the other conversation, the one where they talked about what might be happening to Merit and Bramble. If Moon dwelled on that too much, the mix of fury and fear made it hard to think, let alone plan.

Moon nudged Chime gently until Chime woke enough to nip his ear and let him go, rolling over and sinking back into sleep. Moon released Jade's tail and rolled over to nuzzle her hip.

Jade said, "I know you're trying to distract me."

It would be the last distraction until they found the Hians, so Moon had meant to make it count. Then Jade had growled and dragged him into her lap, and he had tried to make her forget everything that had gone wrong.

Now Moon missed her, and missed the others, in a way that felt like a knot of pain in his chest. He shook away the memories, then stretched, shifted, and leapt out of the cave to hunt.

He found a swampy stretch of water not far from the statue's left rear foot. It was surrounded by ferns, and the deceptively still pool was filled with large armored lizards. He killed one, carried it back for Stone, and found it gone by the time he got back with a second one.

Moon ate the tail of the second lizard, left the rest for Stone, and went up on top of the statue's head where shallow basins had formed and collected rainwater. He sat on his heels and started to clean the blood and flesh out of his claws.

The sky was clear with few clouds, and the wind was light but steady. He spotted a few flying boats in the distance, two leaving the city but another one coming in. It meant that for now at least there had been no Fell attack.

Stone's big dark shape flew past. He circled around and dropped down onto the statue's head, then shifted to groundling and wandered over to sit beside the puddle.

Moon watched the blood spiral through the water. "I'm guessing you don't think we should wait for the others."

Stone rolled one shoulder and scratched under his arm. "What, are you worried about what Jade will think?"

Moon gave him a glare. "Yes. That doesn't mean I don't think we should keep going." Flying boats tended to take a direction and stick to it, not having to navigate around anything except mountains. If the boat hadn't been cautious enough to change direction once it was out of sight of the city, they still had a good chance to catch it.

"If we hadn't come ahead and found that moss on the berth, it would have dried out by the time the others got here. And there would have been nobody to tell us about the second Hian ship and the switch." Stone squinted into the distance. "I don't want to take a chance on missing something else."

Moon took the waterskins out of his pack and started to fill them from a clean puddle. "We need to leave the Hian moss for the others. We can put it in a bundle with some of the moss they're using to track us, and hide it in that hole we slept in, that should work." He sat back on his heels, glancing around. "We need to mark the top of this statue to help them find it. Something that won't draw attention if another flying boat spots it, but that they'll know is from us. It can't be writing, because the Fell might see it. And it can't be anything that might get blown away by the wind—"

Stone said, "You sound like an Arbora."

Moon knew this was Stone trying to start a fight to relieve tension. He shrugged his spines, knowing it would be more irritating than anything he could think of saying.

Arbora liked to talk and they liked to figure things out, which often meant their favorite pastime was to analyze every aspect of a situation from every angle. It also meant that they were very good at coming up with solutions to problems. Which was why Bramble and Merit, with Delin and finally Chime, had been able to discover the way into the foundation builder city.

Stone, faced with Moon's refusal to argue, said, "Draw a flying boat on it."

That . . . would work. Moon turned the fastener on the last water-skin and dug the inkstone and paper out of his pack. He handed it to Stone to write the message. After a couple of turns of intermittent study, Moon could read Raksuran well enough but his writing was terrible. They were going to need some rocks to scratch the drawing on the statue's head. He tried not think about how Jade would react when she found out that not only had they flown ahead instead of waiting, but that a kethel from the Fellborn queen's flight was following them.

By the time Moon came back with a rock that made a satisfactory dark scratch through the statue's weathered coating, Stone had filled a page with the elegantly flowing oblongs of Raksuran writing. Stone made a bundle of it and the mosses in a cloth waterproofed with mountain-tree sap, then went down to hide it in the cave where they had slept. Moon's drawing skills weren't much better than his writing, but he got started with the rock.

When Stone returned, Moon said, "You think Bramble and Merit—" He hesitated, not wanting to finish that sentence. The Hians had taken them as hostages, but Moon had been afraid they would decide that since they had Merit, they didn't need Bramble. He was also afraid Bramble would lose her temper, try to kill the Hians, and be killed herself. Or that the artifact would require some test to prove it would kill Fell, and the Hians might use it on Bramble or Merit or both of them. There were so many things to be afraid of at the moment he couldn't pick just one.

"Bramble's smart," Stone said, handing Moon a fresh rock. "Just because she's never had to use her brains for manipulating Hians doesn't mean she can't do it."

"Manipulating," Moon said, thinking about it. Vendoin, the Hian leader who had been plotting this apparently since she had first left Hia Iserae for the Kish-Jandera city of Kedmar to work with Callumkal, was a master manipulator. As Kalam had said, she had known him and his father for turns, since Kalam was a child. But they were Janderan and Bramble was a Raksura. More importantly, she was an Arbora. "Vendoin never did think any of us were that smart, did she."

"No. She thought we were smart animals, not smart people." Stone stood to survey Moon's handiwork. He indicated the drawing with one toe. "What's that?"

"That" was meant to be a fan-folded sail on a wind-ship's central mast, except it looked nothing like the image in Moon's head and he had no idea how to make it any better. He said, "Guess."

Stone sighed, like Moon was the one being a problem. "Ready?"

Moon pushed to his feet and shouldered the pack. They were going south on the random word of a sleepy bladder-boat groundling, and their own theory that the Hians had switched flying boats to keep a Kish horticultural from tracking them. It was a risk, and they were gambling for the lives of their friends.

Stone walked to where the statue's head started to curve down, shifted, and leapt into the air. Just before Moon followed, he caught a hint of Fell stench in the wind, a reminder that they weren't the only ones searching for the Hians.

CHAPTER FOUR

As they waited, stuck in their cage, Bramble considered Delin's hint that she should pretend to be weak, and decided to give the Hians some proof of it. She would stop eating.

Merit wasn't keen on it when she informed him of this decision, but mentors always thought they knew everything, particularly mentors who were younger than you. He said, "And if you just die, what then?"

"I won't do it right away, that would be stupid." Someone might connect it with Delin's visit and suspect a trick. "I'll eat less, gradually, each time they feed us. I don't know if they'll notice, but if I need to pretend to be sick later, it'll add—" She waved a hand. "Verisimilitude."

Merit sighed. He sat back against the mossy wall of their prison, small and tired. He had been trying to augur but had admitted that either the Fell poison was still interfering with his sight or the situation was so confused right now there was nothing to see. The scale pattern was fading from their skin, but slowly, and they still couldn't shift. "Maybe I should do it instead."

"They aren't going to let you near them," Bramble explained, almost patiently. "Vendoin saw too much of what you can do."

"She saw you, too." Merit sounded sulky, more like a fledgling warrior than an adult mentor. Bramble decided to save pointing that out for the moment when they needed a violent argument to clear the air.

"Vendoin saw me making sure everyone ate, and had clean bedding," she explained. "She saw me putting up the tent. She saw me with you and Delin figuring out the way into the city, but she didn't see how much I helped. That was bad, I shouldn't have done that, but we didn't know what she was then. At least she didn't see it from close up. She thinks I'm a—" She lowered her voice, because the Raksuran language had no real word for this, and she didn't know if Altanic did either. She said in Kedaic, "—servant."

Merit frowned. "What is that?"

"Someone who does things for someone else, like wash their clothes and bring the food—"

"Everybody does those things."

Bramble tried to explain. "For yourself, not for other people."

"Of course you do it for other people." Merit was clearly exasperated. "If you're doing it for yourself you might as well do it for everybody nearby who needs it at the time."

"Royal Aeriat don't do it."

Now Merit was scandalized. "If we let the queens and the consorts do things like that, everyone would laugh at us! Even lazy warriors wouldn't let that happen. What kind of shit court would let—"

"Merit, shut up and let me talk," Bramble growled. "It's a thing for groundlings, that's why we don't have a word for it." You could serve someone in Raksuran, like you might serve tea or food, but it didn't mean the same thing in Kedaic. It was like the way the Raksuran word "lazy" didn't have a case for Arbora, only warriors. "It's what Vendoin thinks I am. Magrim and Esankel thought so too, but they asked me about it, and I tried to explain how the court doesn't work like a Jandera settlement. They understood, but I doubt they ever explained it to Vendoin."

Merit shook his head, still confused. "But the warriors were helping you. I wasn't, very much, because I was busy."

"Vendoin didn't see much of that. And she's . . ." Bramble didn't know quite how to explain it. "She's not a very agile thinker. Not like us and Delin, the way we talk about things and change our minds. Once she gets an idea, she doesn't change her mind about it." Bramble thought it was a sad way to be. If you weren't entertaining a dozen different possibilities and probabilities at once, what was there to think about?

"I can see that." Merit let out his breath and leaned his head back against the wall. "So how does this help us?"

"Some groundlings look down on the ones who are servants, and think they do all the work because they're inferior. Hians do, Esankel told me that." Bramble grinned, baring her teeth. "It means Vendoin thinks I'm weak, and not smart."

Merit was still frowning. "I'm not sure you're right about this. I understand that you think you can trick her, but . . . Even if we get out of this cage, and let Delin and Callumkal out of their cages, wherever they are, we can't fly, Bramble. We could steal some of those flying packs, but the Hians would just chase us, or shoot us with the fire weapons. We can't go fast enough to get away from them, like Aeriat could. We're stuck on this boat."

Bramble slumped back. That was the flaw in her plan. Merit continued, "Though if we did try to get away, the Hians would have to stop while they were catching us. That would give the others more time to find us."

Without discussing it, they had both decided to pretend the others had survived and were hunting for them. Mostly because the alternative was unthinkable.

Merit added, regretfully, "It's not like we can kill all the Hians."

Bramble blinked, struck by the perfect simplicity of the idea. It was an idea still, not a plan. It wouldn't be a plan until she could figure out some things, and make contact with Delin again. And most importantly, trick the Hians into letting her out. She said softly, "It's not like they have poison on board."

Merit turned to stare at her, and hissed in speculation.

The letting out part came sooner than Bramble expected, but it wasn't any trick of hers and Merit's that did it.

Bramble knew it was evening, could feel the sun sinking into the horizon somewhere outside the confines of the flying boat, when several Hians came to the edge of the opening and said that Vendoin wanted to speak to her. There was a great deal of reassurance that she wouldn't be hurt, and Bramble pretended, hopefully convincingly, that she needed it. She protested the fact that Merit wasn't allowed to come with her, but the Hians said it must be only her.

Merit squeezed her wrist as the Hians opened the grill and Bramble leaned against him reassuringly. She knew he didn't want to be left alone. *It'll be all right*, she thought. *I promise.*

She let the Hians drop a rope ladder for her to climb up, because she wanted to look weak. Even in her groundling form, she could have made the leap from the floor to the opening, but that was the last thing she wanted the Hians to realize.

She climbed out into a room with walls and floor of tightly woven moss, just like their cage. Beams like stems arched overhead. The lights were dim, smaller versions of the globes that had been used on Callumkal's flying boat. Those had been filled with luminescent fluids that had supposedly come from sea creatures.

Five Hians confronted her, three standing down the wide corridor with fire weapons. Bramble tried to look downcast and sick, and suspected her effort wouldn't have convinced a Raksura for a moment. She knew she didn't look very good. Her shirt and pants had been clean when she had taken them out of her pack days ago on the sunsailer, but now they were stained and smelled like sickness. There had been barely enough water for her and Merit to wash their hands and faces, let alone clean their clothes.

One Hian pointed down the corridor, indicating that Bramble should come with her. She obeyed, walking with the Hian as the other three followed. They looked much the same as those who had arrived on the sunsailer with Bemadin, though Bramble found it difficult to tell them apart. Arbora were short compared to Aeriat, often wide or round, and always sturdy. The Hians were muscular in a different way, with long arms and legs, and their silver gray skin marked with patches of a rough armored rock-like hide, with one large patch on their heads. Their eyes were wide but their noses were barely visible, and their clothes were short skirts and tunics of a light material, as if their bare skin didn't need as much protection as soft groundling skin usually did. Bramble had never much noticed Vendoin's personal scent, which had tended to disappear under the stronger scents of the Rak-sura, the Kish-Jandera, and Rorra's sealing scent. In the confines of the corridor it was easier to smell them, but there was still not much that was distinctive, and even the cool moss scent of the flying boat tended to drown them out.

They took her up a set of steep stairs, down a winding corridor of closed doors, then up another set of stairs. This brought them into a wide foyer, and they led her through an open door into a large common room.

It had the bones of a Kishan craft, with padded benches back against the walls. There was no pedestal stove in the center for holding heated material, but there was a bare spot in the deck where it looked as if one had been removed. Large windows in the far wall looked out into an evening sky in shades of purple and blue. There were distant unfa-miliar mountains, and she could just catch a glimpse of green treetops.

The Hians had added more furniture, some padded chair-couch things that Vendoin, Bemadin, and another Hian half-lay on. Bemadin had led the Hians in the flying boat that had found the sunsailer; it was her gifts of food that had poisoned everyone aboard. Bramble didn't recognize the third Hian sitting with her and Vendoin. Others stood around the room, like warriors in attendance on queens. Except in a court everyone would get to sit down eventually but that didn't look like it was going to happen here.

A little table stood in front of Vendoin's seat, and it had something on it that looked like a gray, striated rock. Maybe it was some sort of food? A careful taste of the air told Bramble nothing, but she caught a familiar scent. Then one of the Hians stepped aside so she could see Delin, seated on a stool among the attendants. He quirked a brow at her; Bramble sucked her cheeks in to try to look ill and hunched her shoulders to seem smaller.

In Altanic, Vendoin said, "It's all right, Bramble. We won't harm you. I just want to ask you some questions."

Bramble had been calm up till now, but something about the sound of Vendoin's voice, the confidence, the self-satisfaction, made her skin want to crawl off her body and her fingers ache. For once the Fell poison worked for her, keeping her from shifting, making it easier to control her temper. She stilled the growl in her throat and nodded. "I understand."

"Bramble is an Arbora," Vendoin said to Bemadin and the other Hian sitting with them, in Kedaic. "The Raksura servant class."

Bramble didn't react. It was a relief that her speculation was right. It would have been highly embarrassing to have explained it all so passionately to Merit only to find she was completely wrong.

Also in Kedaic, Bemadin said, "You should have gotten one of the others, the winged ones."

"I took what I could get." Vendoin had always been hard for Bramble to read, far more so than Delin or Niran or any of the Jandera, but Bramble got the impression she was not happy with Bemadin.

The strange Hian seated beside them said, "There is no reason to enjoy this so much. Your power over these people has changed you."

Bramble kept her gaze on the deck and forced herself not to react, but it was difficult. She let herself look up and saw Bemadin turn partially away from Vendoin and the other Hian, something stiff in her posture. Bramble wasn't sure what it meant. Then Bemadin said in Kedaic, "I apologize."

Vendoin said hurriedly, "We will speak of this later."

Delin had taken the whole exchange in with polite attention. "We have not been introduced," he said to the strange Hian. "I am Delin-Evran-lindel, of the Golden Isles. This is Bramble of the Court of Indigo Cloud. She does not speak Kedaic, only Altanic. We have two other friends here, Merit of the Court of Indigo Cloud and Callumkal, Master Scholar of the Conclave of the Janderan."

The new Hian said in Altanic, "I am Lavinat, and I am afraid I cannot be your ally."

Delin gave her a nod. "It is a pleasant change to have that out in the open at the first meeting."

Bramble had to bite the inside of her cheek.

Obviously trying to ignore Delin, Vendoin explained to Lavinat, "The winged ones would be too difficult to control. The two I selected are more malleable, though the little male has some arcane powers and must be more carefully guarded."

Bramble slid a look at Delin, and saw by the set of his mouth an expression that in a Raksura she would have described as an attempt to conceal contemptuous amusement. He said in Kedaic, "You fear they will still find you, even though you have changed to a different flying craft so that the Jandera can't track the moss in the motivator."

That's not good, Bramble thought, not letting her expression change. She hadn't noticed the difference, since the only thing she had seen of the flying boat that had come to the sunsailer was the bottom of its hull.

Vendoin ignored Delin again, turning back to Bramble and switching to Altanic to say, "My friends are very curious about your people, Bramble."

Bramble didn't have any idea how to respond to that and keep up her guise as cowed and subdued. She knit her brows, trying to look hesitant, and asked, "Why did you take us prisoner?"

"I wonder this as well," Delin said.

Bemadin and Lavinat looked at Vendoin. Instead of answering the question, Vendoin said, "We are told that the Fell are the natural enemies of the Raksura. But we are also told that the Raksura and the Fell are the same species."

Bramble let her expression show confusion. It was easy, because she couldn't tell where this was going. "We come from the same species. But we aren't the same." *You idiots*, she added mentally.

"Is it possible that a handful of Raksura could drive off a whole flight of Fell?"

Bramble lifted her chin. It depended on the number of rulers and kethel, and how badly they wanted to eat the groundlings aboard the sunsailer, and if any of the Kish-Jandera had been conscious enough to use their weapons. But Bramble said, "Yes. You saw the Aeriat fight them at the foundation builder city." She could see from Delin's expression he didn't understand the purpose of the questions, either.

Vendoin seemed satisfied with her answer. "Bramble, if you were to promise me to behave as a good guest, could I believe you?"

Bramble hesitated, knowing that a quick yes was as good as a *no, I will kill you as soon as I have the slightest chance*. Torn between behaving in a believable way but not trying to seem too intelligent, she said, slowly, "What do you mean by 'good guest?'"

"That you will do as you are told, and not attempt to leave our hospitality. Then you might be given some more freedom to move about the ship, and to help Delin." Vendoin fixed her opaque gaze on him. "He has said that his health is failing, though there was no sign of this on the expedition."

Delin regarded her steadily. "I was much exhausted by our trip through the enclosed city. The poison and drugs did nothing to make my condition any better. I am an old man, by my species' standards."

Looking at Delin, Bramble wasn't entirely sure he was lying. She said, "You should let Merit help him."

Vendoin said, "We have our own physician. If I allow you to move about the ship, to help Delin, would you take another drug mixture without protest?"

Bramble went still. She wanted to growl but she kept her gaze on the deck. Delin stiffened and said sharply, "That is not necessary. You will harm them if you poison them again."

"It will harm them if we have to use our weapons on them," Vendoin spoke to him in Kedaic. "It would be better if you urged her to cooperate."

Delin's lip curled, like he was about to snarl.

Bramble felt like she had walked herself and Merit into a trap, but . . . *No, if they want to poison you again, they'll do it. They don't care about your permission.* This was a test, obviously. She knew what Vendoin wanted her to do, but her instinct was to bargain. She had a growing sense that Vendoin liked to think herself right about everything, and Bramble hoped that worked in their favor. She made her voice low and hesitant, and said, "I want to help Delin, and I could promise to be good if . . . If I understood why you took us?"

Bemadin glanced at the rock on the table, as if it had something to do with the question. *Huh,* Bramble thought. Maybe it wasn't a rock, maybe it was an artifact, stolen from the foundation builder city.

"If you cooperate, explanations might be forthcoming," Vendoin said.

That weak promise wasn't worth another dose of poison, but Bramble couldn't think of any other way to bargain or stall. She set her back teeth and made her voice sad, and said, "I'll cooperate."

"Bramble . . ." Delin began. She flashed a glance at him and he shook his head in helpless dismay. *If Vendoin does what she says, it'll be worth it*, Bramble told herself.

Vendoin said, "Well. We will see. You may go back to Merit now."

Bramble managed to look humble and grateful, and not bare her teeth and think about what it would be like to tear at a living person's throat.

Bramble followed the Hians back down to the cage. The one who seemed to be the leader gestured at the opening in the floor and said, "Please."

Bramble hesitated, and asked, "Will Vendoin keep her promise, if we take the poison?" She didn't much care about the response, she just wanted to get this particular Hian accustomed to speaking to them.

The Hian looked uncertain, and said, "I—If Vendoin meant what she said, she will surely do it."

That wasn't exactly an enthusiastic yes. Bramble said, "What is your name?"

The Hian hesitated again. Bramble thought for a long moment she wouldn't answer. Then she said, "I'm Aldoan."

Bramble said, "I'm Bramble," and climbed down into the cage.

As Aldoan and the other Hians fastened the grill overhead, Merit bounced with impatience. "Well?"

Bramble motioned for him to be quiet, waiting as the Hians' footsteps moved away on the floor above. She described the first part of the conversation, then winced in anticipation of Merit's reaction. "Then . . . Vendoin asked me if we would take Fell poison again, willingly, and I said yes."

Merit stared at her. "Uh. Why?"

"Because that's the plan. Make them trust us."

"It's not the plan," Merit pointed out. "It's *a* plan. A bad plan."

Bramble took his wrists, trying to persuade him. "Delin is pretending to be ill. Or maybe is really ill. Vendoin thinks I'm a servant. And I think she wants to tell us where we're going, what she's doing. She wants to brag. I need more opportunities and we can't get them in here. I'm right about this, Merit."

Merit pulled away, and paced back and forth across the chamber. But he said, "I know we don't have a choice. They'll give the poison to us anyway, whether we agree or not, and this way, maybe we can make them think we're not dangerous. But . . ." He stopped, and rubbed his hands over his face. "I hate letting them think we're . . . cooperating. I want to kill them."

Bramble wanted to kill them so badly she could almost taste Hian blood. But she knew trying would be their last act, only to be done when they had exhausted all hope of escape. "That's why we're Arbora, not Aeriat." She didn't think a warrior could keep their temper in this situation. "Aeriat wouldn't be able to do this."

"Moon might," Merit said.

Bramble conceded the point. The court had always realized that Moon, living as a solitary for most of his life, was not a normal consort. It wasn't until Bramble had seen him in life or death situations that she had really begun to understand what that meant. She still wasn't sure she understood the entirety of it, but she did believe Moon was capable of almost anything. "Moon's been in a lot of strange situations."

Merit took a sharp breath. "I hope he's still alive. I hope the Hians didn't—"

"Something made it sound like they had to leave the sunsailer in a hurry." Bramble was thinking of Vendoin's reaction to the remark about not getting a winged Raksura. She was holding onto that hope with all her claws. "Maybe because the others were waking up."

Steps moved down the corridor above and she hissed softly for silence, even though they had been speaking Raksuran. The steps drew closer, and Aldoan leaned over the opening to say in Altanic, "I have the medicine. Will you take it?"

Merit made a soundless snarl at the blatant misuse of the Altanic word "medicine." Bramble lifted her brows at him. After a moment, he nodded reluctantly. She called up to Aldoan, "Yes, we'll take it."

CHAPTER FIVE

Chime was in the big main cabin of Niran and Diar's wind-ship, watching as Dranam the Janderi horticultural tried to find the Hians.

Dranam sat on the deck of the cabin, leaning over two open pottery containers of acrid fluid and the strands of moss growing inside them. A fabric map was spread on the floor and Chime crouched on the other side of it, with Lithe and Shade beside him. Niran, too impatient to sit down, leaned on the wall near the doorway.

Chime tried not to breathe too loudly and distract Dranam. Kalam had hired her at the port of isl-Maharat where they had left the sunsailer, and she wasn't used to Raksura yet. Chime wasn't certain Kalam had told her she would be traveling on a Golden Isles wind-ship with a group of shapeshifters. Before this, she probably hadn't known what Raksura were, or that they, unlike Fell, didn't eat groundlings. Chime wasn't entirely sure she believed that now, despite how unafraid the Golden Islander crew was. But since she seemed to be trying as hard as she could to help them, maybe her personal beliefs didn't matter.

Kalam and Rorra had come aboard the wind-ship, leaving the rest of the crew in the port to get transport back to Kish-Jandera. The plan was for Esankel and Rasal and the others to ask for help from the local leaders in Kedmar, who knew them and Callumkal and would hopefully be more inclined to listen to their story. It would be nice if that happened, but Chime wasn't counting on it.

Dranam sat back, frowning at the first jar. To Chime's eye she was almost identical to Kalam, with short curly hair and dark red-brown skin, except that she was a Janderi and therefore shorter and more thickly built. Her dark coat was open across her chest, revealing the four breasts that marked her as female. Dranam said, "I still can't detect the Hian ship. The distance must be too great for the moss. But that at least tells us that it isn't coming back toward the coast." She traced a line on the map with one finger. "I think we should keep going south, the direction of the last clear sighting, until your scouts return with news."

Niran stepped forward to look at the map. His golden brow furrowed and he didn't look pleased, but then he seldom did, especially since finding out that his grandfather had been stolen. "A number of trading ports are marked along that coast. Some are built around foundation builder ruins, according to Kalam."

Lithe's expression was doubtful. "I think we need to look inland."

Niran nodded absently, still studying the map. "Your guess is better than mine," he admitted.

Shade asked, "The second fragment?"

Draman's shoulders hunched in reflex, though Shade had spoken softly, and he was sitting there in his groundling form, slender and lovely, dressed in a plain blue shirt and pants. He looked more like a warrior than a consort, his only jewelry copper wristbands and an anklet. His skin was the pale white of a Fell ruler, but his eyes were green and his hair dark, and his sharp-featured profile was just enough like Moon's to make Chime's heart twist.

They shouldn't have told her he was half-Fell, Chime thought, a little sourly. Rorra and Kalam seemed to have no fear of Shade, but then they had met him aboard the sunsailer when he had arrived with Malachite and their other rescuers, and had seen how he had helped care for the poisoned crew. They hadn't had much time to think about the fact that Shade and Lithe's mother was a Fell progenitor, and by the time they had, it must have seemed a minor consideration compared to everything else that had happened.

Lithe, whose groundling form had dark copper skin and a halo of dark hair, looked like nothing other than a small Arbora. Dranam didn't seem quite as nervous around her. But then Lithe never shifted when the groundlings were around if she could help it, so Dranam might not fully realize Lithe was also a Raksura.

Dranam tapped a point on the map, and in a mostly steady voice, said, "That's the sample the two . . . consorts took with them." She stumbled over the Raksuran word. "It's here, to the south of this port."

At least Moon and Stone had a moss sample so Dranam could follow their progress. And find their bodies when they were killed by something, but Chime was trying not to think about that part. As a line-grandfather, Stone had traveled the Three Worlds on his own, and so had Moon. They were the best suited to the task. *Keep telling yourself that*, he thought sourly. Jade and Balm, and Malachite, had also gone off scouting in different directions, to follow sightings of flying boats supposedly crewed by Hians that had left isl-Maharat before them. Chime was left to sit here on the wind-ship with the others, nursing his frazzled nerves.

"South of the port?" Niran asked. "Not at the port?"

"It's not exact," Chime reminded him. Niran had lived with Raksura long enough to understand how scrying and augury worked, but he kept wanting the horticultural direction-sensing to be as right as his magnetic stones were when they pointed south, and it just didn't work like that.

"That's right," Dranam said, though Chime couldn't tell if she appreciated the support or not. "The sample just gives us the direction. We won't be sure of their position until they move a more significant distance, or we get closer."

Lithe looked up at Niran. "We should keep going southwest, at least until we hear from Malachite and Jade."

Niran grimaced, and tied his long white hair back up in his scarf. "This delay is frustrating. It gives Grandfather more time to annoy the Hians into killing him."

Trying to be reassuring, Chime said, "Delin is very sneaky. And—I don't mean that in a bad way. He just might be able to get away from the Hians on his own. Especially with Bramble and Merit to help him and Callumkal."

Niran made a weary gesture. "Perhaps. I should be accustomed to worrying about him, but the waiting wears on me." He sighed. "At least the lying carrion-eaters don't know where we are either, yet." The problem was, of course, that bringing that moss fragment aboard so that Dranam could try to pick up the track of the Hians' flying boat meant the Hians could also pick up the track of the wind-ship.

Niran went along the passage to climb the steps to the steering cabin, as Dranam fastened the lids on the jars and got up to carry them back to the rack where they were stored. Helping her with that task just made her more nervous, so Chime sat back on his heels. He had nothing to do but wait. At least the warriors could guard the wind-ship and the Golden Islander crew could clean and tend it.

Lithe rubbed her face wearily, and Shade gave her a nudge to the shoulder. "Remember to rest, and eat," he said. Like Merit, Lithe would scry herself unconscious if you let her. *I hope Merit's alive,* Chime thought bleakly.

"I will," Lithe promised. "As long as you do too."

"I'll make some tea," Chime said, and got up to go to the wind-ship's little heating hearth. It was set back in a cubby, a square metal box carefully insulated from the deck and walls by squares of thick polished stone. Though Chime knew just how hard it was to set a wind-ship on fire; the plant fiber that looked so much like wood was much tougher than it appeared. This main room was where the crew had their meals, and a long low table, stools, and seating cushions were pushed back against the far wall now to make it easier to spread out the big maps.

Chime found the pack where the Raksuran tea was kept and filled the Islander's oddly-shaped version of a kettle from the water cask. Shade got up to fish the embossed metal cups out of the storage chest, though as a consort he wasn't supposed to do little tasks. Or do anything, really. Chime hesitated, not feeling he knew Shade well enough to tell him not to. Then Flicker arrived, shouldered Shade aside and gathered up the cups. Shade complained, "There's no one here to see. It's like being at home."

Flicker frowned at him. "Go sit down."

Amused, Lithe patted the mat beside her, and Shade stamped over and dropped down to sit like an annoyed fledgling.

Flicker gave Chime a sideways look, as if gauging his reaction. Keeping his voice low, Chime said sympathetically, "Moon isn't good at being a consort, either."

An instant later he regretted it, realizing Flicker could take it as an insult. He felt as if he had shoved his whole tail into his mouth. But Flicker nodded in relief and said, "It's important for him to follow etiquette, when we're away from the court. Because if he doesn't act like a consort then someone might . . . You know."

Someone might not treat him like one, Chime finished. It was even more important for Shade than it was for Moon. Insults bothered Moon more than he liked to admit, but he was so practiced at dealing with them it was hard to tell. Shade, gently raised but without Moon's impeccable bloodline, shouldn't have to deal with it at all.

Chime filled the cups with Flicker's help, and they carried them over to Shade and Lithe. Once Chime was seated, holding the fragrant cup under his nose, Shade said, hesitantly, "You haven't sensed anything? Like you do sometimes?"

Chime didn't wince. The warriors kept asking this question, though Shade managed to make his inquiry sound wistful rather than as if Chime was failing as a . . . as whatever Chime was now. "No. I've tried but . . . It's never been a matter of trying, if that makes sense. It just happens, usually around groundling magic."

Flicker asked carefully, "So that's really true, about you? That you were born an Arbora?"

"It's true," Chime said and shrugged helplessly. At the old eastern colony, Chime had shifted one morning and found himself a warrior. He had lost all the mentor skills, the ability to heal and augur, to produce heat and light out of minerals and plants. But he had also gained some odd sensory abilities. It was a strange situation that Indigo Cloud had mostly become accustomed to over the past few turns, but it was hard to explain to other courts. It was almost impossible to explain it to groundlings, who usually found Raksura difficult to cope with or understand. Shade, who must have been in the position occasionally of being difficult to explain, just nodded glumly.

"It's a colony response to disease, a drop in Aeriat births, lack of food, other bad influences." Lithe took a drink of tea and gave Chime a sympathetic smile. "It's natural, just very uncommon."

Then Lien, one of the Golden Islander crew, leaned her head in the door and said, "Jade and Balm are returning! The lookouts just spotted them!"

Jade and Balm had been flying all night, stopping only for brief rests. The morning had dawned clear and now they flew over low hills, covered with some unpleasantly spiky and thorny vegetation, punctuated by tall clumps of multicolored fungi and ferns. The only visible sign of groundling habitation was the occasional canal, constructed of wide stone troughs standing on pylons just above the vegetation. Some had been damaged, the flowing water leaking out through holes and cracks, or blocked by debris. A few were whole, the water unimpeded. On one Jade had seen a small groundling boat with sails, traveling down it like a caravan on one of the raised stone roads to the east.

It would have been an easier flight if they had been returning with good news, but at least they had bitter impatience to spur them on.

"If Malachite didn't find them either," Balm said, as they shared a waterskin at a rest stop on a bare hill, "that means Moon and Stone are going the right direction." Balm had probably kept Jade from flying herself to death; in Jade's current mood, she wouldn't have heeded the signs of weakness from her own body, but she didn't want to hurt Balm. Queens could fly faster than warriors, even the strongest female warriors, but with two of them, they could take turns sleeping and hunting, a much more practical way to travel and better suited to the effort of such a long sustained flight. "That's reassuring."

"That's terrifying," Jade corrected. She was tired and her mood was sour. As a line-grandfather, Stone was supposed to be the sensible one, though the idea of Stone preventing Moon from doing anything rash was hilarious if you knew either of them. "They're bad enough on their own. Together they're worse than Malachite."

Balm snorted a laugh, and then had to wipe water off her face. She was wearing her groundling form to rest, and Jade could clearly see her bloodline resemblance to their birthqueen, Pearl. Queens never gave up their fangs and claws and the closest they could get to a groundling form was a softer version of the Arbora's scaled form, but Pearl's features were echoed in the sharpness of Balm's profile. Balm's groundling skin was a dark bronze, her hair a dark honey color, and like all Raksuran warriors she was tall and all lean muscle. Jade had always wondered if Balm was what she would have looked like if she had been born a warrior. Shaking the water droplets off her hand, Balm said, "If Malachite finds the Hians, she won't wait for us."

"We're lucky Malachite acknowledges that I exist." Jade sighed in exasperation, pushed to her feet, and held out a hand to Balm. "Let's go."

By the time Jade and Balm circled down to land on the wind-ship, Chime, with Kalam, Rorra, and Niran, stood on the bow deck, watching impatiently. Root, Briar, and River perched up on the nearest cabin roof. The Opal Night warriors, waiting for Malachite's return, gathered towards the stern, with one sitting up atop the mast in the look-out's basket.

"Well?" Chime said as Jade lit on the railing. "Were we right?" Root hopped down from the cabin roof, his spines twitching with impatience.

"No." Jade furled her wings and hopped down to the deck, as Balm landed a few paces away. "We were right about the flying boat with Hian traders heading northeast, but we were able to get close enough to see the crew were all other species. It wasn't Vendoin."

Kalam looked away, out over the plain, controlling any reaction. Niran swore. Rorra, more practical, just unfolded the wooden plates of a map. She said, "Malachite isn't back yet, but Lithe says the signs are still pointing strongly toward the southwest. It's suggestive that Dranam tracked Moon and Stone moving south of the port."

Jade felt frustration spike her as if she had flown into a thorn tree. Moon and Stone had agreed to wait if they found anything, or if they lost the trail. But had she really expected them to abide by that? Or had she counted on them to disobey her and rescue the Arbora, so she could still look like a proper queen who would never send consorts into danger?

"If Moon and Stone find them, will they try to follow on their own?" Kalam asked, turning to face Jade.

More angry at herself than anyone else, Jade controlled her spines and said, honestly, "I would like to believe that if they pick up the

Hians' trail, they'll wait for us. But knowing them, they may follow the Hians and take the first opportunity to rescue the others."

Kalam nodded, almost trembling with nervous anxiety. Niran put a hand on his shoulder and steered him down the deck. "Come and help me tell Diar the news. She can't leave the steering mechanism and if she has to wait much longer she will turn furious."

Kalam went without protest, though it was clearly more an opportunity for Kalam to conquer his emotions in private than to appease Diar, who was as calm under adversity as her grandfather Delin.

Rorra looked from Jade to Chime, who was still bouncing impatiently. She said, "I'll get the other map," and followed Niran and Kalam away.

Rorra was right, Kalam and Niran weren't the only ones disappointed at the lack of news. Chime said, anxiously, "You think Moon and Stone are following the Hians."

"They know to be careful," Jade said. They knew to be careful; whether they actually would or not was another question. Jade saw Balm lean heavily on the railing and told her, "Go in and get some rest."

"I know you don't think you do, but you actually need rest too," Balm told her, but pushed off the railing and started down the deck. "I just wish this boat could move faster."

Standing by the cabin door, his spines drooping as he watched them, Root said, "I don't understand why we can't push it."

Chime grimaced and said, "It. Doesn't. Work. Like. That." His voice was tense with barely contained irritation.

Jade suppressed a spine lift of exasperation. Obviously, while she and Balm had been absent, the other warriors hadn't been handling the tension very well.

"You know, just let him try." That, unexpectedly, was River. He jumped down from the cabin roof to take Root's wrist and pull him toward the stern of the boat. "Come on, let's go to the back and you can push on the boat."

It made Jade think about poor Branch, River's clutchmate, who had been killed by the Fell just before the attack on Indigo Cloud's old eastern colony. Maybe River could help Root deal with Song's death. She said, "Briar, go with them and make sure River doesn't hurt himself." The scars of the deep claw slashes that had cut through his scales were healing but still visible.

Briar, perched on the roof of the steering cabin, uncoiled and dropped to the deck to follow River and Root. Her spines drooped. Briar was another one who thought this was all her fault, but she had reacted with depression instead of anger. Jade thought, *I should have sent her and Chime off with Moon and Stone. Then they'd be so busy trying to keep up they wouldn't have any time to think.* Mostly at the moment she wished she didn't have any time to think, particularly about whatever Moon and Stone were doing, what might be happening to Bramble and Merit, and to Delin and Callumkal. With the other warriors out of earshot, she said, "Chime. Take a deep breath."

"I know." Chime was in his groundling form, probably because he understood all too well just how dangerously tense he was. He buried his hands in his hair and groaned. "I know they're afraid and worried. I just can't . . . listen to it anymore."

Jade squeezed his wrist. "It'll be all right."

Chime said mournfully, "It might not be."

Jade sighed, and pulled him close to press her cheek against his. "I know. Don't say that to the others."

She drew back and Chime took a sharp breath and nodded. "You'd better rest, too," he said, and she let him draw her down the deck toward the cabin door.

The Opal Night warriors, led by Rise, had organized a hunt and brought in enough game to feed all the Raksura, so instead of dried meat and bread, Jade and Balm each had half a grasseater. The hides were covered with short sharp hairs, as hard as metal, possibly due to the spiky vegetation the creatures must feed on. Rise cautioned them about it before leaving them to eat in peace on the stern deck.

"They're very efficient," Jade commented to Balm, meaning the Opal Night warriors. It had been a couple of turns since she had been at the Opal Night colony, and she had forgotten how they made Indigo Cloud look like a disorganized mess. She tried not to resent it.

"It makes a nice change." Balm grinned at her. "I could get used to it."

Jade pushed her over and Balm rolled on the deck. She landed on her back and looked up at the cabin roof. "Root, are you hungry?"

Jade glanced up but Root had already disappeared. "Is he all right?" she asked Balm.

Balm rolled back to a crouch to continue eating. "I don't know," she sighed.

After the meal they went down to their sleeping cabin in the hold to rest. After a brief nap, Jade was almost coherent again when the warrior on watch called out, "It's Malachite!"

Balm was still deeply asleep, and Jade didn't wake her when she climbed out of the blankets. She leapt up the stairs and stopped at the railing to watch the small shape in the distance grow gradually larger.

Shade, Lithe, Rise and the rest of the Opal Night warriors had gathered by the time Malachite drew near enough to make out detail. Flicker, Shade's warrior, whispered, "Does she look mad?"

This nonsensical remark was apparently a running joke. Lithe smiled, the other warriors flicked spines in amusement. Shade snorted and gave Flicker a nudge to the shoulder.

Malachite cupped her wings and lit on the railing, compensating for the wind and the speed of the wind-ship with irritating ease. "Did you find the Hians?" Jade asked, as Malachite furled her wings. At least Malachite's complete indifference to the customs of Raksuran politeness meant Jade didn't have to waste time greeting her.

"No." She stepped down to the deck. She glanced in the direction of Shade and the others, not so much a greeting as checking to make sure they were all still alive and present. "But I found something else. You need to come with me."

CHAPTER SIX

Jade followed Malachite out over the plain, towards the foothills in the distance.

The territory was even more inhospitable, and the occasional groundling canal curved away from this direction. Jade was glad she had had the chance to eat and rest briefly; when Malachite had said to follow her, she had meant now, immediately, and the reason was urgent.

Malachite had said, "I scented Fell. They've been following us at a distance, probably all the way from the coast. They've dug in around these hills. Once the wind-ship reaches the end of these plains, they'll move again."

Jade had squinted into the distance. "How do we approach them?"

Malachite said, "We fly in," and leapt into the air.

Jade hissed, looked around at Chime, Niran, and the others. They were all staring, startled and uncertain. She said, "Keep moving. We'll catch up."

"Take care!" Niran had shouted after her.

Now they came in low to approach the hills at an angle, sweeping across the stretch of dry sandy ground where the land sloped up. "They'll see us," Jade called out.

Malachite didn't respond, and Jade snarled to herself, *I suppose that's the point*.

As they crested the top of the first hill, Jade caught a glimpse of a camp nestled below, where dark shapes moved between makeshift shelters. It was such an odd sight, she thought she had imagined it.

Malachite clearly had no intention of being unobserved. She made a slow circle over the encampment as Jade followed her.

The dakti scouts must have seen them but none took to the air. The Fell had dug into the sandy ground between the outcrops in the base of the hills, creating shallow caves and rough lean-tos made of brush. Dakti peered out from around the rocks, and there were three large pale figures just inside the shadow of a cave. Even from this height, they were clearly kethel in their groundling forms. Jade spotted rough fire pits and the outline of a latrine area. Piles of bones lay nearby, but the broken skulls matched those of the grasseaters the Opal Night warriors had hunted in the plain.

It hadn't been her imagination. *It is an encampment, like the Arbora would make,* she thought. Not exactly like; Arbora would have arranged it so it was invisible from the air. But this wasn't something Fell did. Everything in a flight was geared toward the comfort of the rulers and the progenitor. Those shelters and firepits had been built for the dakti and the kethel.

Malachite finished her leisurely pass and slid across the wind, then dropped to land on a flat rock. Jade followed and landed next to her. Malachite furled her wings and just stood there. Jade did the same, and wondered if they were about to be attacked by the entire flight. It would certainly be a dramatic way to die. She doubted Moon and Balm and all the others would see it that way.

Finally Jade had to break the silence. "The kethel dug caves in the sand. I didn't know Fell did that." At least one large flight had used a giant sac, made from the kethels' secretions, as a kind of shelter, but according to Moon, even it had used fragments of stolen groundling-made ships as supports. It was far more common for Fell to use the ruined remnants of other species' settlements for shelter, usually while feeding on the other species.

"They don't," Malachite said.

Jade tightened her jaw. The urge to disturb that impermeable exterior was hard to fight. "So this is the flight of the half-Fell queen. You want to see her. You want to make sure she isn't one of your consort's fledglings." Queens could see bloodline resemblances that were invisible even to other Raksura; Jade had seen the Fellborn queen only once, briefly, and in the dark. She hadn't noticed any resemblance to Moon or his clutchmate Celadon, or to Shade, but she might have missed it.

Malachite turned to stare down at Jade and whatever temporary amity there had been between them snapped like a cord. It was as if Jade stood out here not with another Raksuran queen, but with a predator, pitiless and filled with silent rage.

Jade didn't change her expression, didn't give in to the temptation to snarl or hiss, refused to let her spines flare. *You asked for this*, she told herself.

A Fell flight had destroyed the eastern branch of Opal Night, killed much of the court, and taken away prisoners for forced breeding. Malachite had destroyed the flight to retrieve them, but not in time to save her consort. She had managed to save Shade and Lithe and the other half-Fell babies. Jade could imagine the thought that she might have missed one, that a fledgling might have been taken away to another Fell flight, would haunt her.

Stone had said that for Malachite that turns-old disaster had happened yesterday, was still happening, would always be happening. Jade should have remembered that. She said, "Moon said the half-Fell queen was young, almost still a fledgling herself. She couldn't be from your consort's bloodline."

Malachite gave no sign that Jade could read, not one spine dip or tail twitch. But suddenly the deadly stillness was gone, and it was like the person poured back into the predator's shell. Malachite said, "Moon may have been mistaken. He hasn't had much chance to observe fledgling queens as they mature."

Jade kept her spines neutral, glad Balm hadn't been here to see that. She would have heard about it for the rest of her life.

From the camp, two figures leapt into the air, a ruler and a dakti. *No, not a ruler,* Jade thought grimly as the two shapes circled down. *A queen.*

The Fellborn queen and a dakti landed a dozen paces away, at the edge of the rock. The queen had the Fell crest and the Raksuran spines, but her scales were matte black, like a ruler or a Raksuran consort. Looking closely, Jade saw she had the contrasting color pattern of a queen, but it was in a lighter shade of black, barely visible.

Jade slid a glance at Malachite. She couldn't see a bloodline resemblance between the Fellborn queen and any of the surviving issue of Dusk, Malachite's consort. Malachite dipped one spine in a negative, actually making the gesture broad enough for Jade to read. Jade felt all the relief that Malachite wouldn't show. *That's one less thing to worry about.*

There was nothing different about the dakti, at least as far as Jade could see or scent. Dakti were half the size of an adult warrior, with armored plates on their backs and shoulders in place of scales. Their jaws were oddly long with the double row of fangs exposed. This one crouched at the Fellborn queen's feet, watching them warily. *No, it is different,* Jade thought. She had never seen a dakti with that much intelligent awareness in its eyes.

"You found us," the queen said. She spoke Raksuran. Her gaze went from Jade to Malachite and back. "We thought we were hiding."

Malachite said nothing. Jade set her jaw. She suspected she was going to have to be the one to do all the talking, probably right up until Malachite abruptly decided to change the plan, whatever it was. Jade said, "You followed us here from the sel-Selatra."

The Fellborn queen dropped her gaze and dragged her foot claws across the rock. The dakti studied them with doubt and suspicion. The queen said, "We were going the same way."

Jade tilted her head, resisting the urge to show her fangs. "Do you mean to attack us?"

The queen looked up at her, spines flicking. "No." Then she shifted. Her form flowed into a figure who could have been mistaken for a Raksuran warrior. But her skin was bone white, like the groundling form of a Fell ruler, like Shade, and her dark hair was long and straight. But unlike Shade, there were patches of dark scales on her cheeks, down her neck and shoulders. She still had her frills, but they were heavier than Jade's, with a texture more like hair. It was like a queen's Arbora form blended with a ruler's groundling form. She wore a loose dark tunic, patched and stained around the hem. She said, "Is this what you look like when you change?"

"No," Jade said.

"Will you show me?"

Jade's spines wanted to lift and she forced them back into a neutral angle. "No."

The queen's brow furrowed. "Why?"

Moon had been right, it was oddly like talking to a fledgling. A frighteningly strong fledgling with dakti and kethel at her call. Jade drew breath to answer, but Malachite said, "Did they name you?"

The Fell queen flinched, staring at Malachite. The dakti edged closer to her knee and its wings fluttered nervously.

Jade stared at Malachite, frowning. The Fell queen acted as if she had forgotten Malachite was there, or somehow never seen her. Jade knew Malachite could make herself so unobtrusive she seemed to disappear. This was the first time it had occurred to her that Malachite might actually be able to effectively disappear, by somehow using the same ability that allowed a queen to connect with her court and to keep any Aeriat and Arbora from shifting. *No, that's not it. The Fellborn queen saw her, I saw her look at Malachite.* But had Malachite been able to make the Fellborn queen forget she was there?

Watching Malachite with suspicion now, the Fell queen didn't answer.

She said, "I'm Malachite of Opal Night. That is Jade of Indigo Cloud. What are you called?"

Jade had a twinge at the idea of Fell knowing her name and her court's name. Hearing your name spoken by Fell was never a good thing, though concealing it from them was nearly impossible.

The silence held for so long Jade didn't think the Fellborn queen would answer. Then she said, "Consolation. The . . . The flight doesn't have a name. Yet."

Jade's chest went tight. She threw another glance at Malachite, unable to help herself. Apparently unmoved, Malachite said, "Who gave you that name?"

"The consort. Our consort." Consolation hesitated. "Is it a good name?"

He loved her, Jade thought, and suppressed a hiss. "Consolation" wasn't a name for hatred or irony or even wry regret. Jade wanted to ask what the consort's name was, if he had said what court he came from, but she reminded herself that it was in the past, that he was as dead as the progenitor who had stolen him, and there was nothing they could do about it now. If she thought about what life had been like for him in a Fell flight for who knew how many turns, she wouldn't be able to keep her temper and somebody was going to die. She couldn't imagine what Malachite was feeling under her impenetrable expression.

Malachite said, "Yes, it's a good name. The progenitor let him raise you."

Consolation drew her foot claws over the rock again. "She had to. The others didn't know how to take care of me." She tilted her head to study Malachite. "A mistake. She made mistakes."

"You killed her," Malachite said, still even and expressionless. "What about the rulers?"

"I didn't kill the older ones." She looked down at the dakti. It grimaced at her. She looked up again and said, "Someone else did that."

The dakti and kethel, Jade thought. The progenitor had made mistakes all right.

Consolation looked from Jade to Malachite, eyes narrow. "You're a queen too?" she said.

Startled, Jade realized that she must have been the first Raksuran queen that Consolation had ever seen, that night outside the foundation builder city. That she and Malachite were different enough that it might be confusing to unaccustomed eyes. Malachite said, "Yes."

Still crouching, the dakti nudged Consolation's knee. Consolation twitched at the reminder and said, "Why do you want to talk now? You didn't before."

Jade countered, "Why are you still following us?"

"Because you're here." Consolation seemed to think it was obvious. "Why are you here? Why didn't you go back to the Reaches? He said the groundlings took a weapon out of the old sea city, is that why?"

Rage burned in Jade's chest at the reminder that this deceptively naive queen had tried to steal Moon off the sunsailer. Would have stolen him, if River and Rorra hadn't delayed her long enough for Malachite to arrive.

Malachite said nothing, and Jade forced herself to answer, "That was true."

Then Malachite said, "They stole two of our Arbora, and two of our groundlings."

Jade managed to control her reaction down to a tail lash. It couldn't be a good idea to give that much information to Fell, but Malachite apparently didn't care.

Consolation frowned at the ground again. "I saw that. Some of that. I didn't understand it." The dakti nudged her again and she stepped out of its reach.

"You did understand it," Malachite said. Her head tilted. "You tried to steal the consort."

Consolation's head jerked up to meet her gaze, as if that slight change in tone had been a shout. "Not like that," she said. She was angry, and the sheer audacity of that made Jade's fury rise until she could taste blood in her throat. But Consolation said, "We need help. We need someone to tell us things. The young rulers are useless. Our consort died. We need . . ." She looked from Jade to Malachite again, and let the words die away, as if it was just occurring to her that two Raksuran queens might not react well to talk of stealing consorts, whatever the reason. The dakti tugged belatedly on her ankle.

Malachite said, "You wanted a consort to help you rule the flight."

"There's a lot I don't know," Consolation muttered, and kicked at a drift of sand. She said suddenly, "The other Fell hate us. They want to use us to fight you, like back at the sea city."

"Where is that flight?" Jade asked. The last thing they needed was another Fell flight involved in this. "We know you fought them."

"They're here somewhere," Consolation admitted. "Their rulers told the rest of the Fell what happened." She hesitated, then finished, "The Fell think everything that's wrong is because of you. That it was all a big trick." The dakti stared at her in apparent shock. "What?" she asked it. "What do we owe the Fell? They hate us."

66

Jade didn't understand. "What's all a big trick?"

"Me, and the others." She indicated the dakti with her foot. Malachite's gaze went to it and it huddled in on itself, covering its face with a wing. Consolation said, "That it was a trick to make us."

"A trick," Malachite repeated. Her spines didn't move, but it was as if the air around her had gotten colder. Jade's fangs itched in reaction. For once, she knew what Malachite was thinking. All that pain the Fell had caused, the consorts and Arbora stolen for forced breeding, the courts destroyed, the fate of the crossbred offspring not strong enough to survive. *A trick.*

Apparently oblivious to Malachite's reaction, Consolation said, "Making Fell who are part Raksura just gets flights killed, and there's never any advantage, like was promised."

"We weren't the ones who promised them," Jade said, part of her attention on Malachite. She couldn't decide if an explosion was imminent or not. She had always thought that Malachite's self-control was more daunting than her rage, but she might be about to be proved wrong. "Raksura had nothing to do with it."

Consolation watched them, the breeze stirring her frills, her brow furrowing as if it was just occurring to her that something was wrong. Jade's jaw hurt from gritting her teeth. She wasn't certain what Malachite wanted from this meeting, if she was asking the right questions, if there was any point to this. In a small voice, Consolation said, "That's what they think."

Jade snarled, mostly at herself. She thought they had heard everything they needed to hear. "We should go."

She was surprised when Malachite lifted one spine in agreement and turned away.

"No," Consolation said, startled. "Stay!"

The dakti tugged on Consolation's ankle again. *It's afraid she'll fly off with us,* Jade realized suddenly.

Then Malachite whipped around, hissing in a breath to taste the air. The abrupt movement made Jade flinch back a pace. Consolation leapt back and ducked. The dakti almost fell off the outcrop.

Malachite tilted her head, and said to Consolation, "If this is a clumsy attempt at a trap, none of you will live to regret it."

Jade tasted the air, but Fell stench was already heavy through these hills. She threw a glance at Consolation, who just looked confused. "What trap?" Consolation said.

Suddenly a dark shape appeared over the hill from the camp. It was the size of an adolescent warrior, its limbs still gawky and its wing control awkward. It made a keening sound of alarm as it dropped to a landing on the outcrop down from Consolation and the dakti. It called out to her in the Fell language, and that was when Jade realized it was a young ruler. Consolation shifted into her winged form, and said, "He hears the Fell. The other Fell. They're coming."

The dakti made a squawk of alarm, and said in a low gravelly voice, "He's not here. What do we do?"

Then Jade caught fresh Fell stench on the wind, coming from the northeast. Another flight was coming. She snarled, "If you planned this—"

"No," Consolation growled at her. "Not a trap. They hate us because they know we fought the flight at the old sea city." She glared up at the sky, gathering herself to leap. "They think we're allies with you."

Malachite said, "Stop."

Consolation froze, then shook out her spines and stared at Malachite in confusion. "What?"

Malachite said, "Don't take to the air yet. Wait until their kethel are overhead. I'll take the first one."

"I know." Consolation backed away. The dakti and the ruler scrambled down the outcrop. "I know what to do. I just forgot, because I was mad." She whirled around and bounced up, snapped her wings out for one powerful flap, and then dove behind the hill.

Jade turned to Malachite, incredulous. "We're going to help them fight off a Fell flight."

Malachite didn't take her gaze off the sky. "I am."

A growl rose in Jade's throat. She shouldn't have been surprised. The bloodline resemblance between Moon and Malachite was particularly strong, though Moon couldn't see it. *And you have five of them back home in the nurseries*, she reminded herself.

The first kethel swept into sight, then two more not far behind. They were the largest Fell, and always the first sent to attack. The lead one was probably half the size of the Golden Isles wind-ship, the other two a little smaller. Like all Fell, their armored scales were a deep unreflective black, but they had distinctive halos of horns protecting their heads.

They were flying far too close together. Jade bared her teeth. "They don't think much of the half-Fell." Bunching like that might be a good tactic for approaching groundlings, but not for fighting in the air. Perhaps they were relying on surprise; Fell weren't good scent hunters, and if Malachite and Jade hadn't been here, the half-Fell flight might have been taken unawares.

Malachite moved one spine. "They wouldn't. The progenitors and the rulers think of these half-Fell as something to be used against us. It's a mistake." She spared Jade a glance. "Perhaps their penultimate mistake."

This time when Malachite crouched to leap, Jade matched her and they burst into the air together.

Malachite hit the first, largest kethel in the throat. Jade struck its shoulder and scrambled up past the horns, going for its eyes. She had known Malachite's size and strength gave her an advantage, and she had seen how fast she was in battle. But it was still a shock that by the time Jade reached the kethel's head, dark blood fountained up from its throat and its wings flapped in frantic alarm. Jade shoved off it, twisted away from a wild grab by the second kethel, then landed on its back. She spared a glance down and saw the half-Fell flight rise out of the hills in a black cloud.

Malachite was so fast, leaving so much carnage in her wake, it was hard for Jade to find targets. She caught glimpses of Consolation tearing through the other flight's rulers, and her dakti and kethel attacking in a smart, coordinated fashion completely at odds with the way Fell usually fought. By the time Jade ripped open her kethel's eyes, got knocked sideways from a tail slap by another one, recovered to claw up two rulers, and shredded a half dozen dakti, the attacking flight was in confused retreat.

Malachite shot past and Jade followed her to circle down to land on a hilltop.

As Jade's claws hit the sparse grass, Malachite dropped two severed ruler's heads and shook her claws to get the blood off. It was usually important to sever and bury the rulers' heads, to keep the rest of the flight from being drawn to them. Since the rest of the flight already knew exactly what had happened to their missing rulers, Jade supposed Malachite had only done it to make a point.

As if she needed to, Jade thought. Two of the attacking kethel lay sprawled in the lee of a hill, and the rocky ground was dotted with the corpses of dakti.

The half-Fell circled now, the kethel staying in the air to watch the other flight retreat, while the dakti and rulers started to land back at their camp.

This whole fight should have been impossible. You couldn't ally with Fell. It was impossible to ally with a being that didn't see you as anything except prey. But none of the half-Fell flight had even tried to use the confusion to strike at Jade or Malachite.

Jade spotted Consolation circling down toward them. She told Malachite, "We have to get back to the wind-ship." The Fell had been coming from the wrong direction to have found it, but they couldn't take any chances.

Malachite flicked blood off her spines and turned away.

Consolation cupped her wings to land down the hill, and called out, "You're still leaving?"

Malachite paused to look back at her. "We have to return to others who travel with us. We care for each other the way you care for your flight."

Consolation hesitated, spines signaling confusion, but so erratically it was hard to tell if the gesture was intentional. Then she said, "I'll keep following you." It should have sounded like a threat, but it had the air of a stubborn fledgling refusing to obey their teachers.

Jade heard Malachite say, "I'm counting on it," just before she followed her into the air.

The sun was starting to sink into the horizon by the time they came within sight of the wind-ship again. Jade hissed with relief to see it floating along undisturbed, Islanders on the deck and the glint of scales from the warriors on watch atop the cabins and the mast. But she wanted a private conversation with Malachite, and the ship would be no place to have it.

One of the raised water channels was below. Jade dipped her wings toward Malachite, then turned down toward it. As Malachite followed her, Jade landed on top of a supporting pylon, not far above the water.

The channel was thirty or so paces wide, the water clean except for windblown dirt and the thick purple leaves of the vegetation around it. Patterns and unreadable writing were carved on the channel's bottom, faded with age. Jade let her gaze follow it, trying to get her thoughts in order. This was not going to be an easy conversation, at least for her.

Malachite landed neatly on the rim of the channel, her dark foot claws curving around it. "We can use the half-Fell to our advantage," she said, as if continuing a conversation they had already been having. "If the Fell are as agitated as Consolation said, the half-Fell flight may deflect their attention."

It wasn't going to get any better, so Jade blurted, "How did you—You made Consolation forget you were there."

Malachite stared at her, the only sound the lap of water in the channel.

Jade persisted, "I know you can do that to other Raksura. You can do it to Fell?"

Malachite said, finally, "It's possible."

"Can you hear them?"

"No." Malachite stood there like a statue. Then she added, "It's unnecessary."

"You can make them hear you." It had finally started to come together for Jade. All the different things she had noticed herself. The brief accounts she had heard about the destruction of Opal Night's eastern colony, the rescue of the prisoners taken away by the Fell. What Malachite must have done to rescue those prisoners. Hearing how Consolation had killed her progenitor and taken over the flight, and how the dakti or kethel or both had turned on the older rulers, had finally made Jade understand. She asked, "Is that how you killed the Fell that attacked your colony? You got inside the progenitor's mind. Without her, the rulers couldn't make the kethel and dakti obey."

Malachite looked down, but it didn't feel as if she was avoiding Jade's gaze. She touched the water with one claw tip and watched the minute change in the flow. She said, "I made her obey me, and it broke her control over the flight. Many of them killed each other." She looked up, pinning Jade with her gaze again. "They were not adept at functioning without her. And she had made the dakti and kethel hate each other very much."

Jade moved her spines in understanding. "Teach me how."

Malachite's head tilted. It wasn't quite amusement, and it wasn't quite a threat. "It isn't something that can be taught. Not entirely."

Jade felt the burn of disappointment. "Are you sure?" She realized an instant later it was a stupid question, a fledgling's impatient question, but Malachite didn't react to it anymore than she would have if Jade had said something intelligent.

"You have to want it very badly." Malachite looked away into the distance, toward where the flying boat would be by now. "But you must be careful of what you want."

"I don't want it," Jade said honestly. "But I might need it."

Malachite's tail twitched once. "I hope you don't," she said, and then turned and launched herself into the air.

Chapter Seven

The Court of Indigo Cloud, in the Reaches

The arrival of Celadon, the sister queen of Opal Night, and her two hundred warriors went better than Heart had expected.

Celadon had been greeted formally by Pearl, then taken up to the queens' hall for tea and to meet Ember. Since Opal Night was already a bloodline ally, Heart and the other chiefs of the Arbora castes had stayed in the greeting hall to help with sorting warriors and supplies.

Indigo Cloud's colony tree was large enough to take in a much bigger group than this without crowding, and most of the preparations had revolved around cleaning out unused bowers and getting the lights and heating stones ready. The teachers had been sorting the food stores and bringing in everything ready to harvest, with the hunters working hard to bring in more game to preserve. Even though Malachite had said her warriors would be prepared to do their own hunting, they still had to be ready to supply a number of meals. They had also warned the Kek, the people who lived under the roots of the colony tree on the floor of the Reaches, and made every other preparation for Fell attack that anyone could think of. Heart just hoped it would be enough.

Watching with Blossom as the strange warriors streamed in through the greeting hall entrance, Heart felt an odd combination of dismay and relief. Indigo Cloud had never had this many visitors in its entire history, at least as far as their still existing records said, and it was daunting. But if the attack did come the way the visions had suggested, the Fell were going to get an unpleasant surprise.

Vine, who stood nearby, said, "They're showing off. They're not really this organized all the time."

Heart snorted. He was clearly jealous. "Keep telling yourself that," Blossom told him, unsympathetic.

The Opal Night warriors all seemed to be on the large side, with strong lean muscles and good conformation. Heart could tell they spent a lot of time in the air, a lot of time hauling and carrying, and maybe fighting, too. It was a contrast to the Emerald Twilight warriors Heart had seen, who all seemed very sleek and well-fed and strong, but not this intimidating. And each group that entered was well-behaved, jostling each other good-humoredly. They all stopped to stare up in admiration at the tree's great well. The enormous space spiraled up through the trunk, with balconies and round doorways leading off into the upper levels. They pointed out the curving stairways and the carved pillars, and the waterfall dropping dramatically down to its pool.

Floret, Aura, and Selene managed the influx, greeting the warriors rapidly and sending the different groups off with an Arbora soldier or teacher to take them to their quarters. The Opal Night warriors caught on to this system immediately, with one from each group going to join the crowd around the three female Indigo Cloud warriors and politely shifting to groundling to wait for their attention, while the others dumped their packs on the floor and settled down to wait. The younger Indigo Cloud warriors who weren't on patrol or helping Floret were gathered on the balconies, watching and, Heart hoped, learning some decorum. So far none of them had made any trouble, but maybe that was because Blossom kept catching the gaze of her warrior clutchmate Fair and making motions indicating that if he and his friends started anything that she would finish it.

A group of smaller, rounder figures entered next and Heart stared in surprise. "They brought Arbora!"

"That's a relief." Blossom craned her neck to see the newcomers. "We can use the help."

The Arbora seemed pleased to be here, regarding the greeting hall with approval as they shed their packs. One saw Heart and Blossom and came forward, the warriors parting for him respectfully. Heart went to meet him, Vine and Blossom following her. As the stranger reached her, he said, "I'm Auburn, mentor of Opal Night."

It was even better that Opal Night had brought another mentor. Heart named herself, Blossom, and Vine, and said, "All of you are welcome here." That was especially true; Arbora of different courts didn't get a chance to meet much, except on the occasional trading visit.

Auburn thanked her politely, and added, "I wanted to ask after the warrior Chime, who visited at Opal Night with us once."

Blossom said, "Chime isn't here. He went with the sister queen's party to the sel-Selatra."

Auburn took that in with a worried expression. "I hope they are all well."

"So do we," Heart admitted. "The waiting hasn't been easy."

Vine leaned in to ask, "How did so many warriors move so fast?"

Auburn turned to him, explaining, "Small groups of warriors travel ahead, carrying some of the hunters and a mentor. They prepare camps, and hunt for game, so food and places to rest are ready when the larger groups come through. We've done this before on a small scale, but never with quite so many warriors. The mentors had to consult the old *Suspended Forest Travels and Recorded Court Movements*. Not a book anyone has much reason to look at nowadays, but very helpful." He glanced around. "I should get back to the others and help move the supplies."

Blossom kicked Heart in the ankle and Heart said hurriedly, "I hope you and the other Arbora will join us in the teachers' hall later."

Auburn thanked her for the invitation, and returned to the Opal Night Arbora.

Heart turned to Blossom, who spread her hands helplessly. Blossom said, "Don't look at me, I've never heard of a court moving that many warriors, let alone like that."

Vine asked hopefully, "Do we have that book?"

Heart sighed. It was obviously not only the Indigo Cloud warriors who were going to feel inadequate during this visit. "I've never heard of it. We should probably try to trade for a copy." Much of the court's library had been lost during the chaos of the long journey from the Reaches so many turns ago. Heart and the other mentors and teachers were still coming to the realization of just how much must have been left behind along the way.

Blossom gave Vine a poke. "Floret's glaring at you."

Heart looked. Floret was glaring and would have been flicking spines if she wasn't in her groundling form. Vine muttered, "All she had to do was ask, I've been standing right here," and went off to join her.

"Aeriat," Blossom sighed. "Sometimes I wonder what our ancestors were thinking."

Heart absently agreed to this sentiment, much expressed among older Arbora. "I just hope they're all settled by the time the other queens get here." The messengers had been sent just after Malachite had left to follow Jade and the others. With Indigo Cloud and Opal Night both experiencing the dreams and visions, it had been obvious it was time to convince the other courts the danger was real. But the messengers had brought back the news that the mentors of Emerald Twilight, Sunset Water, and some other allies had begun to have similar visions. Arranging the meeting of the queens at Indigo Cloud had been easier than anyone had anticipated.

Now the only problem was Pearl. She had seemed to agree that a meeting of allied queens was a good idea, but Heart knew from experience how quickly Pearl could change her mind. And just because Pearl thought something was a good idea didn't mean she actually wanted to do it. "How do you think this will go?"

Blossom said slowly, "That depends on what kind of day Pearl is having, doesn't it? If she's down, it'll be a disaster. But you know, she's been better since the day we got here, and even better than that since Jade had a healthy clutch. So the chances are good."

Heart hated relying on luck. Flower, the mentor who had taught her, who had been so important in the fight to bring the court here to safety, had tried over and over again to help Pearl. *It's melancholia,* Flower had told her, *there's nothing to be done but wait and hope.* It was the product of Pearl's consort Rain's death, the death of so many clutches, of Pearl's sister queen, all the others, from the illness and misfortune that had haunted the old colony. Being away from the Fell influence on the old court had helped immeasurably, but Pearl was . . . still Pearl.

And Heart didn't know how much help Celadon was going to be. "I wish Jade was here."

Blossom leaned against her shoulder in brief comfort. "Me, too," she said, and went off to help the soldiers show the waiting Arbora to their guest quarters.

South, the Drylands

They had been flying all night, taking advantage of a strong south wind, and Moon was relieved when Stone circled down to the valley. It wasn't an ideal place to stop and rest, but at least it was there.

The terrain was mostly barren sandy ground with sparse grass, punctuated by low rises and some scrub brush and one lone tree. Moon came in low, tasting the air and catching the scents of dryland flowers and sand.

Stone dropped to the ground not far from the tree. Instead of shifting, he threw himself down and proceeded to make a dust wallow. Moon landed nearby and furled his wings, surveying the valley while Stone cleaned his scales. There was no open water source nearby, not much grazing, and the tree had a forbiddingly spiky canopy, which meant there would be few if any grasseaters and predators, except those traveling through to somewhere else.

Moon got the waterskin out of his pack for a drink, thinking that their next stop would have to be at a water source. Putting the stopper back in, he faced the single spiky tree. Then he went still. At some point, the tree had moved.

The branches above the ball of thorns pointed toward Moon and Stone and the sand wallow now. Something gleamed at the end of each spike. Whatever it was, it hadn't been there before either, but perhaps the reflective surface had been concealed inside the bud-like structures that surrounded them, like eyelids. Exactly like eyelids. "Stone."

Rolling in the dust wallow, Stone stopped, looked, and after a moment flicked his spines in dismissal.

Moon backed away from the tree cautiously. They had seen tree-creatures before and Moon always found them a little disconcerting. Their branches were almost like tentacles and he expected them to burst up out of the ground and attack him, even though so far it hadn't happened. There was always a first time.

There were no bones or other remnants of hunting around the tree, or even in the rest of the valley, and there was no predator musk. Moon was still glad the dust wallow was some distance away.

Finally Stone finished, shook the dust off, and shifted to his groundling form. Moon took his own dust bath, then shifted and managed not to groan out loud. His back was sore, an ache that spread out down his arms and legs, though they had been riding the wind most of the time. If they were on the wrong track, it was all a waste of time, a waste of effort.

"Do you think we're going the right way?" he asked Stone, mostly just to make conversation.

"I did three days ago," Stone admitted, stretched out in the sandy wallow.

"Do you think we should have waited for the others?"

"No."

It was a moot point, anyway. If they were on the wrong path, and the others were on the right one, they wouldn't be able to find the wind-ship. But Moon missed them, even though he knew Jade would probably want to kill him by now.

Stone said, "Come over here and lie down. Otherwise we'll never catch anything."

Moon realized he had been standing there a while, absently scratching the back of his neck and staring at nothing. He sighed and went over to lie down in the sand wallow with Stone.

The sand was warm on his abused muscles and he dozed off, listening to the wind in the grass. After a time, Stone elbowed him. "We've got something."

Moon slit his eyes just enough to spot the shape arrowing down at them out of the cloudless blue sky. "Is it one of those birds again? The last one tasted like dead leaves."

"You'll eat what I catch and like it." Then Stone growled in irritation. "It's a damn flower-head."

Moon snarled tiredly. "I thought we flew out of their range."

Stone hissed. "It's probably lost."

The creature stooping on them was roughly the size of an Arbora, with a head shaped like a rounded, multi-petaled flower, a little like an aster. It had the brains of an aster, too. As it neared them, Stone twitched out of the wallow and shifted. Moon didn't bother.

Flapping wildly, the flower-head tried to stop mid-air, managed not to slam into Stone but lost control and hit the ground. It skidded about fifty paces through the sand and grass and landed near Moon. Moon sat up and told it, "Piss off."

It scrambled back and cowered, which was even more annoying. But you couldn't eat something that talked, no matter how stupid it was, and there was no point in killing it otherwise. Stone shifted to his groundling form and ambled back to the sand wallow.

The flower-head said, in bad Altanic, "What are you?"

Moon growled, "None of your business."

It backed away a few steps, and hesitated. Moon hissed, preparing to shift and snarl, but it said, "Do you know which way the big river is?"

Stupid as rocks, Moon thought, and said, "It's north, that way." He pointed.

The flower-head turned, ran a few steps flapping, and awkwardly launched itself again. Stone sprawled in the wallow and sighed. "I told you it was lost."

Moon didn't dignify that with a response and stretched out in the sand again. This method of hunting while resting sometimes didn't work, but when it did, it saved a lot of time.

The flower-head had caused enough commotion that it took a while to lure anything else down. Both Moon and Stone were able to get a short nap in before a large bird finally took the bait and dove on them.

It wasn't a big meal, but it was enough to keep them going until they reached better country. Moon sat on his heels in the grass and tossed the last cracked bone away. Stone had finished eating and was rolling in the dust wallow again, getting ready to leave. Moon stood and stretched and looked across the valley.

A figure walked toward them across the grassy plain. It was coming from upwind, but Moon knew what it was. *This is the most crowded empty valley in the Three Worlds,* he thought sourly. He said, "Stone."

Stone turned to look, then hissed out an angry breath.

We knew they were probably following us, Moon thought. *Or it was following us.* He just hadn't expected a kethel to be so good at it.

Stone tasted the air, then shifted to his groundling form. His bared fangs weren't any less intimidating. "It's just the one. If there were more, I'd scent them."

"So it spotted us and went down in the hills. I didn't think their eyesight was that good." The uneasy sensation of being stalked made Moon's spines want to twitch. "This thing is smart." It was hard to believe it wasn't half-Raksura. But maybe this was what happened when a half-Raksura trained a kethel to hunt.

It stopped a good distance away, far enough to have time to shift if they tried to rush it. It looked much the same as it had in the swampling port, though its pale skin was coated with a layer of dust and sweat. Its braids were frazzled and it was still wearing a loose wrap around its waist. So it hadn't just done that to blend in better with the groundlings around the port, Moon realized. Or that hadn't been the only reason. As if they were travelers who encountered each other all the time, it pointed back toward the hills. "There's water back there. A little stream under a rock."

Stone stood silently, radiating suppressed fury. Knowing he was going to have to do the talking, Moon asked, "What do you want?"

The kethel scratched under one of its braids. "To help you."

Moon set his jaw. "Stop saying that. We know it's not true."

The kethel appeared to give up on that point, at least for now, and eyed the dust wallow. "What were you doing?"

"It's none of your business." You would think the middle of nowhere would be safe from intrusive questions.

Stone hissed and turned to grab his pack. "Stop talking to it."

"I can help you," the kethel said. "Find the groundling weapon—"

Stone shouldered the pack and used the motion to whip around and shift to his winged form. But the kethel anticipated it and shifted almost in the same instant. Moon crouched to leap but the kethel bounced backward in a move Moon had only seen Aeriat use, putting distance between it and Stone. It bounced again, snapped its wings out, and flapped toward the hills. It wasn't wearing a collar, Moon noticed.

Stone snarled in frustration and stirred like he was thinking of giving chase.

"Don't be an idiot," Moon yelled at him, "it's just trying to lead you into a trap." The rest of the half-Fell flight might be just past those distant hills.

Stone's spines rippled, but he turned and leapt into the air. Moon crouched and leapt after him, flapping up through the dust storm Stone's wings caused. He was relieved to see Stone head south, back on the route they thought the Hians had taken.

Hoped the Hians had taken. Moon had the grim thought, *At least the kethel thinks we're going the right direction.*

CHAPTER EIGHT

The new dose of poison seemed even worse, and Bramble was only vaguely conscious for a time. When she began to fully wake, miserably sick again, she decided it was time to implement her plan. They had no guarantee that Vendoin would keep her promise, and Bramble felt it would be better strategy to force the issue.

Merit leaned over her. "Bramble?"

She whispered to him, "Pretend I'm sick, like you have to take care of me."

He frowned blearily and put a hand on her forehead. "You are sick."

She groaned for effect and pushed his hand away. "Don't try to put me in a healing sleep, you idiot." She didn't think he could do it under the effect of the Fell poison, but she didn't want to take any chances.

"You said take care—Right, right, I get it," Merit grumbled, and crawled away to the water container.

It took most of the day, while Merit begged the Hians above their cage for help and Bramble groaned and made gagging noises. Merit's voice grew increasingly frustrated and weary, and parts of Bramble's body went numb from lying down so long. By the time Aldoan finally appeared in the late evening, Bramble was ready to groan for real.

Peering down through the mesh covering, Aldoan told Merit, "You are a healer. Why can't you help her?"

"The Fell poison. It hasn't worn off yet and it stops me from healing her. And I don't have anything to make a simple for her." Merit leaned against the wall, his slump of exhaustion convincing because most of it was real. The Hians had lowered a basket of food a while ago but neither of them had eaten. It was fruit and some bread-like stuff, not very tempting, even if they weren't both nauseous.

There was a long silence, then Aldoan walked away. Merit slid down to sit on the floor, scrubbing his hands through his hair. "It didn't work," he said in Raksuran.

Bramble groaned. She thought they still had a chance, but she didn't want to wreck it by talking.

After what seemed a long wait, Aldoan returned, and said, "We will take her to our physician."

Merit, sitting beside Bramble, squeezed her wrist in triumph.

Bramble staggered and stumbled down the hall, forcing one of the Hians to guide and help her. With her eyes half-closed she noted the sequence of corridors and stairs along the way. They led her into a cabin two levels above their cage and deposited her on a padded bench. Bramble fell over and curled up as the Hians retreated. She heard them take positions just outside the doorway.

A Hian leaned over her and said in slow, careful Altanic, "I am a physician. I will try to make you well."

Bramble tried to look both frightened and hopeful. She didn't want to seem so sick that she couldn't recover quickly if that seemed a more effective strategy.

To the Hian healer's credit, she felt Bramble's stomach and looked into her eyes and mouth, and seemed to be actually trying to figure out if she was injured anywhere, or if she showed signs of more serious sickness. Finally she said, "It may be internal distress from the mixtures you have been given. I will make a new mixture which should help."

Bramble watched her sort through some small wooden and glass containers in an untidy heap on the workbench. Bowls of plain brown pottery, a pestle, and some tiny cups meant for measuring lay there too. A door in the wall was open to another attached room, and it seemed to contain most of the healer's supplies, still in wrapped bundles or stacked in light wooden boxes. Above the pile, several waterskins hung from pegs in the wall. Bramble tasted the air but there were too many acrid mixed scents to identify individual odors. The skins were labeled in a language she couldn't read, but whatever they contained was in large portions, unlike the jars the healer sorted through now. Bramble memorized each label.

The healer stepped away from her workbench and slid the door to the other room shut, cutting off Bramble's view. Then she brought the draft. Bramble decided there might still be more to learn here, and she flatly refused to drink it.

Steps sounded in the corridor, and she heard the Hians on watch shuffle away from the door. Then she heard Vendoin's voice.

Speaking Kedaic, Vendoin asked the healer, "Is she truly ill?"

"Yes, I think so," the healer replied in the same language. "Too much of the drug, perhaps, causing stomach pain. She has no difficulty breathing—"

Vendoin cut that off. "Give her a draft for it."

"What does it matter?" Bemadin asked.

Bramble managed not to react. That would have quashed any doubts that the Hians eventually intended to kill them, if she had had any.

Vendoin ignored Bemadin. "Well?" she asked the healer.

"I'm trying," the healer said, with what sounded to Bramble like carefully forced patience. "She won't take it. Perhaps if the other one could be brought—"

"No, it's too much of a risk," Vendoin interrupted again. There was no mention of Vendoin's promise to let them out of the cage if they took the second dose of poison willingly, which wasn't a surprise.

"I can't make her take it," the healer said. She must have seen something in Vendoin's manner that told her that answer wasn't acceptable. She said, "Perhaps she would take it from the Janderan."

Vendoin made a noise that Bramble interpreted as derision. "He has refused to help us so far."

"I don't understand these people," Bemadin said. "This will save uncounted lives. It's a risk to us more than to the Jandera."

Obviously they weren't speaking of giving Bramble a simple any-more. Her heart beat faster with the knowledge that she might be about to find out why the Hians had betrayed the expedition. But then Vendoin said impatiently, "They don't understand. I need to get back to work on the translation."

Vendoin and Bemadin were leaving. Bramble sat up on one elbow and, making her voice weak and hoarse and as pitiful as possible, said in Altanic, "You promised if we took the poison willingly, we could help Delin. Please let me see Delin."

In Kedaic, Vendoin said, "Very well. Take her to the easterner's prison. Perhaps it will make him more cooperative." She added in Altanic, "They will take you to Delin, Bramble."

"And Merit?" Bramble said, feeling as if her gambit had gone terribly awry.

"No, just you," Vendoin said, and she and Bemadin walked away.

Bramble hesitated. She didn't want to be separated from Merit. Particularly after forming the theory that Vendoin might want to test the artifact on Raksura before she went off to find Fell. But she had to take the chance.

Bramble drank the draught, to the Physician's relief, and slowly climbed to her feet. Aldoan and the other armed Hians led her away down the corridor.

Trying to remember to sound weak despite her urgency, Bramble asked Aldoan, "Will you tell Merit I'm with Delin? I don't want him to think—To be afraid I—"

Aldoan seemed uncomfortable, but said, "I'll tell him."

Seizing the moment, Bramble said, "I'm just afraid Merit will be lonely. We're not meant to be alone."

Aldoan tried to be reassuring, though it was clear she didn't believe her own words. "You will not be far away. Perhaps Vendoin will let us take you to visit him."

They reached Delin's cage, which was an interior room with a door that had been reinforced with metal strips. Two Hians stood outside.

Delin was happy to see Bramble, and anxiously helped her sit on the padded bench. Once Aldoan was gone and the door locked again, she told him in Raksuran, "I'm not really sick, it's just the poison again. I wanted to get to you, but I had to leave Merit alone." Guilt stung at her like biting insects. She didn't know what Merit would think when they didn't bring her back. She hoped Aldoan kept her word and told him what had happened.

Delin patted her hand. "Merit will surely understand. Perhaps we can agitate for him to be brought here as well."

Maybe he was right. Vendoin had seemed to give into her on a whim; maybe all Bramble had to do was ask at the right moment. At least this cage was better. It had padded benches against two walls, and a cabinet with a basin inside, drying cloths, and a container for a latrine. The Hians had also given Delin some writing materials, which was more than they had given Bramble and Merit. Bramble thought one of the pens might make a stabbing weapon for a groundling, but with the Hians' armored skin, it probably wouldn't do much but antagonize them. If they let the poison wear off, then Bramble would have her claws, but that wouldn't do much against a Kishan fire weapon.

They had also given Delin far more water and he said it was changed twice a day, so the first thing Bramble did was use a wet cloth to give herself a quick bath. As she scrubbed under her shirt, she said, "I heard Vendoin and Bemadin talking. They want Callumkal to help them with something, but he won't."

Delin's brow furrowed. "You heard no more details?"

"Only that it would save uncounted lives, but it's a risk, mostly to the Hians? And Vendoin was working on a translation of something, she didn't say what." She wrung the cloth out. "They didn't ask you?"

"No. Not yet." Delin threaded his fingers through his beard, something he did when he was thinking. "I wish I knew why they took me, then, if they didn't mean to make me help them. Perhaps Vendoin changed her mind, at some point? Or could there be another reason."

"Delin . . ." Bramble's eyes narrowed. "Do you know what they want?"

Delin hesitated for a long moment, and Bramble could read guilt in his expression, even without spines. He said finally, "I fear so."

Bramble sat down on a stool so he didn't have to look up at her. "You know so."

Delin's mouth twisted as he hesitated. He said reluctantly, "On the sunsailer, when all were resting and Vendoin was in the steering cabin, I looked through the translations that she had done from the inscriptions in the city. I did not trust her and I felt she might be lying. I found one translation among her papers which was older, on a much worn paper, that she had clearly brought with her. It spoke of a hidden weapon, and a warning, an exhortation not to take it to the place where it can be used for it was ill-made and would destroy their children and allies as well as enemies."

"A weapon. What weapon?" He met her gaze, and then Bramble knew. She shook her head. "Not the artifact. That can't be it."

It had lain in a chamber in the ruined foundation builder city, protected by spells designed to let only the forerunners, or their descendants, find it. It had drawn the Raksura to it, tricked them into bringing it to the sunsailer. From the spells on it they had known it was dangerous, that it was something that should have been buried in the city forever. They had planned to drop it into the ocean deeps. But then the Hians had come. *Surely that's not the weapon,* Bramble thought, dismayed, *we can't be that unlucky.*

Delin made a weary gesture. "There was no description, no way to make certain. But the artifact was so carefully guarded, to make sure no one but a foundation builder or forerunner's descendent could reach it. I feared it was the case. And Bramble, forgive me, I feared to tell you and the other Raksura of it because I thought you might wish to use it against the Fell, and I thought it was best to heed the warning."

His expression was so bleak, it frightened Bramble. "I don't think we would have used it."

"Perhaps." Delin made a weary gesture. "Vendoin has not said why she betrayed us, but I think the artifact must be the reason. That she knew of it all along, and made use of Callumkal's expedition to reach it. I believe she is taking it and us to this place where it can be used."

It was bound to be another foundation builder city, and the thought made Bramble's skin twitch. And she still didn't understand Vendoin's motives. "But they already have Kishan fire weapons. What makes this weapon so special?"

Delin shook his head helplessly. "A good question. The writing about the weapon said 'destroy children and allies as well as enemies.' Perhaps it creates a poison, or some other effect against those two species but no others?"

"So who are the 'enemies and allies and children?'" This kind of story logic game was Bramble's favorite when played around the hearth with other Arbora. Playing it in earnest wasn't nearly so fun. "The allies could be the forerunners." She hissed in dismay. "And we're their children, Raksura and Fell."

"It's a strong possibility. Callumkal and many other Kishan scholars believe the Jandera and others native to the Kish lowlands are descended in some way from the foundation builders. This weapon might be used to kill half the inhabitants of Imperial Kish. If the goal is to use it against the Fell, then it would have to be used carefully." Delin made a baffled gesture. "But again, the same could be said for Kishan fire weapons, which will kill just about anything they are pointed at."

Bramble's throat was dry. "Maybe they took me and Merit to test it on us. If it kills us, it'll kill Fell."

They stared at each other for a long moment. Delin took her hand, and said, "I fear this, Bramble."

South of Port Gwalish Mar

Chime sat atop the wind-ship's cabin, taking his turn at watch. It was late afternoon, and they were flying over heavy jungle and rolling hills, the air humid and heavy. Finding the message cache from Moon and Stone had been a sharp moment of relief in the long days of tension and waiting, and he was still reveling in it. The certainty that they were going in the right direction, and the new moss sample to follow, had lightened the burden of everyone on the wind-ship.

Briar jumped up on the cabin roof to take his place, and Chime hopped to the deck to head down the stairs and into the main cabin.

River and Rorra were there, and she was saying, "We're going faster than it seems. I've been calculating it and the flying island stones that this wind-ship uses to travel give it considerably more speed than a Kishan moss craft."

Chime eyed River, reluctantly curious. It sounded as if River had actually expressed impatience over their progress. Chime still disliked

River and always would, but River had tried to save Moon from the Fellborn queen and got his scales ripped open in the process. River saw Chime staring at him, sneered, and looked away. Chime snorted in derisive amusement, more as a reflex than anything else. It was the only way he and River ever interacted.

"Especially over land," Rorra finished. She noticed Chime's expression, looked from him to River and back, then shook her head. "And the Kishan say I'm hard to get along with."

"That's probably why you like us," Chime told her. "Niran's like that, too. Did Dranam say if they're still going in the same direction?" He had missed the last check of the moss samples during his turn on watch.

"The moss is showing that both samples, the Hians, and Moon and Stone's, are still heading toward the south." Rorra frowned in frustration. "I just wish it showed what they were doing."

Chime just hoped Moon and Stone hadn't been led astray and that it was the right flying boat. Jade hadn't exactly been pleased that the two consorts were continuing on alone instead of waiting for the windship to catch up to them. Not pleased, but not exactly surprised, either. Chime felt the same way. There was no telling how Malachite felt.

Rorra said, "I'm going to see if Diar needs a break," and went out, her boots clumping on the light wood of the stairs.

River turned to follow her, then hesitated. He looked at Chime and said, "Have you talked to Root lately?"

Chime had been so certain that River was about to insult him that it took him a long moment to understand what River had actually said. Wary of a trick, Chime said, "Uh, no. Why?"

River looked away, the still-raw scar from his injuries puckering the bronze groundling skin of his neck and collarbone. "He's acting strange."

Chime had a moment to realize it was odd that he hadn't talked to Root. Root never seemed to be in the sleeping cabin when anyone else was, or when they gathered to eat or go over the maps with Rorra and Kalam and the Islanders. Whenever Chime came to eat, it seemed Root was always just leaving. He might be spending time with the Opal Night warriors, but . . . maybe not. "Did you tell Jade?"

River hissed impatiently. "She's got enough to worry about."

That was true. Chime said, "I'll talk to him."

River stamped out without an acknowledgement.

Chime rubbed his face and sighed. Root was still on watch now, and it would be better to catch him when he came in to rest.

It was depressing how days of anxious waiting and worry could make you just as exhausted as days of long-distance flying. He thought about making tea, or getting his writing materials out of his pack and taking some notes. But it was probably better to try to sleep while he could.

Some of the others were sleeping out on top of one of the sun-warmed cabin rooftops. But it reminded Chime too much of other trips with Moon, and just made his absence hurt more. He turned to go to the sleeping cabin instead.

Then from the deck above someone yelled, "Fell! Fell are coming!"

Already shifting, every nerve on edge, Chime bolted upstairs to the deck. He paused in the shelter at the top, but the sky was not full of kethel and dakti. Stepping out cautiously onto the deck, he found River and Rorra there with Jade, Balm, and Niran. More Golden Islanders stood near the rail, already armed with the small Kishan fire weapons. Rorra carried her weapon cradled in her arms. Kalam hurried out on deck, his own fire weapon slung across his back.

Chime couldn't spot Fell anywhere. The sky was deep blue and laced with light clouds. In the green forest below, tall trees were wreathed with purple and blue flowering vines, with rocky outcrops emerging occasionally to tower over the foliage.

Sweep, perched on the rail, amended his warning to, "Some Fell are coming! Two Fell!"

Chime squinted and finally saw the two dark shapes approaching. River hissed and muttered, "Idiot."

Chime agreed, but he wasn't going to say so out loud, mostly because it would mean publicly agreeing with River.

The other Opal Night warriors gathered on the deck and atop the cabins. Shade came up from the stern and stood beside Chime. He was still in his groundling form but Chime was relieved to have him so solidly nearby.

Which was odd. If two turns ago someone had told Chime that a half-Fell Raksura would be a reassuring presence to him, he would have thought they were making an unfunny joke.

Then Jade said, "It's the Fellborn queen, and a dakti." She told Niran, "Don't use the weapons."

Niran turned to the young Islanders and snapped, "Put those things down. You hardly know how to use them."

The Golden Islanders hadn't used the Kishan fire weapons before, since it took a Jandera horticultural to keep them supplied with the moss they needed to work, and Kalam had said that horticulturals didn't venture outside Kishan territory without permission from Kishan elders. Apparently Kalam had broken some rule by talking Dranam into coming with them. Niran and Diar had both been uneasy about it, but had finally agreed.

The young Golden Islanders stepped back and lowered the weapons, still uneasy.

"Why are they here?" Chime said, and tried to stop his spines from twitching nervously. "Just the two of them? Is it a trap?" He wanted to make absolutely certain everyone knew it could be a trap.

"They want help from us," Jade said. She bared her teeth in distracted irritation. "Maybe they're going to ask again."

A thump on the deck so faint as to be nearly soundless made Chime flinch. It was Malachite, who must have been coiled up somewhere out of sight. She said, "Shade, go inside with Lithe. I don't want them to see you yet."

Shade stirred a little, but didn't protest. He turned to go down below deck again. As Flicker started to follow him, Shade told him softly, "No, it's all right, stay up here."

Flicker came back to stand beside Chime, bouncing a little nervously.

The Fellborn queen circled down to land on an outcrop some distance from the boat, and the single dakti swept over her twice before it dropped down beside her.

Malachite stepped up onto the rail, her foot claws wrapping around the wood, her intention clear. Jade told her, "I'm coming with you."

Balm said, "Not alone. Chime's right, it could be a trap."

Chime said hurriedly, "They know you and Malachite came out alone to talk to them before—"

Malachite said, "Bring some of your warriors, then," and dropped off the railing.

Rise bounded up the stairs from the hold just in time to see her go. She hissed in exasperation. Jade leapt to the rail and told Rise, "Stay here, guard the boat. Balm, River, Chime, come with me." Then she hesitated. "River, you can stay. Briar—"

As Chime followed Balm to the railing he remembered the last time River had seen the Fell queen she had been trying to gut him. Balancing on the rail, Chime made sure his spines weren't flaring in nervous fear.

"No, I can do it," River said quickly.

Jade flicked a spine in agreement and River leapt to the railing beside Balm and Chime.

Niran said, "We'll stop and wait for you."

Jade said, "Are you sure?" and Chime knew she was weighing the possibility of this being an attempt to attack the wind-ship versus an attempt to separate the queens and attack both them and the wind-ship at the same time.

Niran, obviously following this trail of thought, said, "We can't out-fly them. It's better to be stationary if we have to use these unnatural weapons."

Chime saw Kalam grimace in irritation, but he didn't argue. Kalam and Niran apparently disagreed on a lot of things you would think groundlings would agree on. Considering how long it had taken Niran to become reconciled to the existence of Raksura, Chime wasn't surprised he had problems with Kishan too.

Jade acknowledged Niran's statement with a spine lift. She told the warriors, "Don't leave this boat, no matter what happens."

There were spine twitches of assent all around, and Jade flung herself off the rail. Balm and River dove after her, and Chime braced himself and followed.

It was a short flight and within moments they were dropping down to land on the outcrop. Malachite and Jade faced the Fell queen and the dakti. River half-turned away where he could watch their backs and keep an eye on the wind-ship. Chime wished he had thought of that first. Then Balm gestured for him to move to Jade's flank and he carefully eased into that position.

The Fell queen had shifted to a groundling form and looked less frightening than Chime was expecting, but maybe that was a product of all the time spent with Shade and Lithe. Jade had said her name was Consolation, an uneasy reminder of the poor consort who had given it to her. Thinking of Moon or any other consort Chime had ever known in that position made him shake with fury. She stared at them all curiously, and he found himself evading direct eye contact. He didn't want his anger to antagonize her. Not until they found out what she wanted, anyway.

Malachite, staring at the Fell queen, said nothing. The dakti twitched uneasily and settled closer to Consolation's feet. Jade was the one who spoke first. "What do you want here?"

"To warn you," Consolation said. "The Fell are going to the Reaches. To kill Raksura."

Chime froze, dread and rage gathering in his chest. Jade's spines snapped to neutral. Balm hissed and River flinched. With her usual opaque calm, Malachite said, "Where in the Reaches?"

"I don't know." Consolation tried to step away from the dakti and it wrapped a clawed hand around her ankle. She told Malachite, "I know they know where a court is. They found it out from the same groundlings that knew about the old groundling city in the sea. They want to take it, and make the Raksura there tell them where the other courts are."

Jade hissed out a breath and her spines started to lift. Horrified, Chime thought, *It's Indigo Cloud. It has to be*. They knew the Fell had managed to influence a Kishan who had known about Callumkal's trip to the foundation builder city. If that groundling had learned the direction that Callumkal's flying boat had taken into the Reaches, the Fell could use that to find the Indigo Cloud colony tree.

Jade forced her spines down. "When are they—How many—"

Consolation's brow furrowed, clearly aware how the news affected them. "Three flights, moving west now. But slowly, waiting for a fourth. Maybe more. Maybe two more."

"How does she know?" Chime leaned toward Jade and whispered, "If she's had contact with other Fell, do they know about us?"

Jade asked, "How do you know this?"

Consolation frowned at her, and frowned at Chime behind her, as if not pleased that he had thought to ask. Chime hissed and fought the urge to move behind Balm. Consolation said, "The two younger rulers can still hear them. The other Fell. They heard the call." She added, looking at Chime, "The Fell don't know you're following the Hians. I think. I don't know if they know."

Malachite tilted her head. If she had looked at Chime like that, he would have flung himself down on the ground. Malachite said, "And why tell us?"

Consolation waved her arms. "Because we aren't Fell. I don't know what we are. But it's not Fell." She tossed her head, an odd gesture, not Raksuran or Fell, as if deliberately emphasizing her differences. "I want help. You can help us. I need to know things—"

Jade must have reached her limit. Her spines flared and she spat, "Help? Like you tried to get from my consort?"

Consolation flinched. Chime knew this was bad, that Jade should try to emulate the icy iron of Malachite's calm. That this was Jade's panic and fear coming out as anger and they didn't have time for it. But he couldn't help feeling a jolt of satisfaction at seeing the Fell queen flinch.

The dakti's head turned to look up at Consolation, and it said, "I told you so." Chime stared at it in astonishment. He had never heard a dakti speak in its own voice before and he had had no idea they could sound that . . . sensible.

"It was a mistake," Consolation snapped.

Jade bared her fangs. "You make a lot of mistakes."

Consolation hissed, "I know that!"

Then Malachite said, "Enough."

Her tone made Chime recoil as if something had punched him in the chest. Jade twitched and Consolation froze, then stared warily at Malachite.

Malachite stepped forward and Consolation edged back, the dakti with her. Malachite said, "You came here with an offer. If you want our help in exchange for this information, I tell you it is not enough." She bared her teeth and Chime felt all his spines involuntarily drop. "Your people have killed too many of us for that to be enough."

"I know." Consolation seemed to gather herself, and with obvious effort she lifted her head to meet Malachite's hard gaze. "I offer swift travel. I have two kethel who can take you to the Reaches to warn the courts twice as fast as you can fly."

Chime's stomach wanted to turn at the thought. He had spent time in a sac while a Fell flight traveled and the stench still haunted his dreams. But if Consolation really meant it . . .

Malachite's tail moved in a long slow thoughtful lash that was somehow more intimidating than a growl. "Not twice as fast as I can fly."

"But without stopping," Consolation said. "The kethel slow, the dakti fly down and hunt, and bring them food and water to eat on the wing, and then they fly fast again."

Jade bared her teeth. "What kind of food?"

"Grasseaters!" Consolation glared at her. "The gleaners were a mistake. No more mistakes!" With a quick glance at Malachite, she added, "Besides, you'll be there, to make sure we do it right."

Jade looked at Malachite. Chime thought, *it could work.* If they could trust a Fellborn queen. If the whole thing wasn't a trap. Malachite said, "And in return you want help. Instructions in how to lead your flight."

Consolation tossed her head again. "From you, or someone. Anyone." The dakti nudged her. "And a place. A place to live. A good one in the Reaches somewhere." The dakti nudged her again and muttered inaudibly. She added, "There's caves in trees there. Good ones. The consort told us that."

Jade took a sharp breath, as if her first instinct was to refuse outright. Maybe her second instinct, too. But Chime could understand the impulse behind that request. Knowing something of what Moon had gone through before Stone had found him, he could understand it all too well. And he wondered if this had been a story Consolation's consort sire had told, a fantasy of killing the progenitor and the other Fell and escaping back to the Reaches with his clutch, to find safety in some isolated mountain-tree. The consort was dead, but Consolation and the others must have held onto that fantasy.

And Chime couldn't help the thought that if there was any queen powerful enough to make that happen, it was Malachite.

Malachite said, "We need to speak of this. Give us a moment."

Consolation stared at her blankly, not understanding, until Jade said impatiently, "Go over there and let us talk alone."

Consolation shifted and Chime managed not to hiss. She turned and spread her wings to hop down from the outcrop. The dakti scrambled in the loose rocks to follow her, clearly as afraid to be left alone with the Raksura as Chime would be with the Fell.

Malachite turned to Jade. "Celadon and her warriors will be at Indigo Cloud by now," she said. "They and the rest of the Reaches will still need to be warned."

The thought of all those Opal Night warriors at Indigo Cloud was the only thing that let Chime keep his fear in check. Balm reached over and squeezed his wrist, and River threw a worried glance at the queens.

Looking up at Malachite, Jade said, "Thank you." Her spines moved in chagrin, and she added, "For thinking of sending the warriors. For talking Pearl into accepting Opal Night's help."

Malachite was still deep in thought, and didn't twitch a spine. "You have my primary bloodline. Our courts are joined together, whether either of us likes it or not."

"I like it." Jade's spines dipped, as if she was well aware she sounded awkward and defensive rather than grateful. "Should we take her offer? Can we believe her?"

"We can believe her." Malachite stared into the distance and her tail moved a little. "The Fell have been stirred for turns by promises of weapons and magic in hidden forerunner cities."

Jade grimaced in dismay. "Now they hear of Raksura helping groundlings to enter a sealed, ruined city."

"They must think we have the weapon," Chime finished her thought, the words out before he knew he was going to say them. Malachite turned the full intensity of her gaze on him and he forced himself not to twitch too violently. "The Fell went there hoping for a weapon. They must think we took it and that we're going to use it on them." Telling them that the Raksura didn't have it, had no idea how to make it work, or even if it really was a weapon, wouldn't help. Fell lied about everything and would hardly credit the idea that Raksura might be telling the truth.

Malachite's attention returned to Jade. "As he says. I will take some of my warriors and go with the half-Fell to the Reaches, to warn Pearl and Celadon. You stay with the groundlings and find the Hians. I'll leave you five warriors, and Shade and Lithe as well. Shade, in case there are forerunner doors that need to be opened, and Lithe, if you need a mentor to help find the Hians."

And she doesn't want the Fellborn queen to see them, Chime thought. He managed not to say it aloud.

Jade didn't bare her teeth but from her tone Chime knew she wanted to. "What if it's a trap?"

As if it was obvious, as if they were talking about whether the weather would be good for flying or not, Malachite said, "Then I'll kill them all."

Chime controlled a spine twitch and exchanged a glance with Balm. River seemed reluctantly impressed.

Malachite was already turning away to face the Fell queen.

"We've got to hurry, too," Chime whispered, half to himself. Catch up with Moon and Stone, rescue Bramble, Merit, Delin and Callumkal. Or there might be nothing to come home to.

CHAPTER NINE

B ramble and Delin came up with a plan, sort of. She asked him, "Do you think we can get Vendoin to let us see Callumkal?"

"It would be a relief to know for certain that he lives." Delin tapped a pen absently against the deck. "I have asked before, but have had no success."

"You might have to trade her something." Bramble was reluctant to suggest this. Mostly because she could think of too many ways it could go horribly wrong. The Fell poison's scale pattern had finally faded from her skin and she had been able to shift for the first time in what felt like forever. The Hians had to realize this and she was terrified they would decide to give her more poison. But they couldn't just sit here huddled in Delin's cage hoping no one hurt them. "I think you need to maybe hint that you might help the Hians with whatever they're doing, if they'll let us all go."

Delin's golden brow furrowed as he considered it. "What if she agrees? Or pretends to agree, as is more likely?"

"Don't help her. But if you could get her to tell you what she knows about the artifact . . ." Bramble flicked her fingers. "We'd have her talking, at least. Once she's talking, she might say more than she means."

The next time Aldoan came with their food, Delin dropped the hint that he might be more amenable if Vendoin asked. A few hours later, as the long day was stretching into afternoon, Aldoan reappeared and told Delin that Vendoin wanted to talk.

"Bramble will come with me." Delin stood and tugged a tangle out of his long white hair.

Aldoan hesitated. "Vendoin did not say—"

"It will save you the trouble of guarding us separately." Delin stepped to the doorway and waited expectantly.

After a moment of indecision, Aldoan gave in, and she led them away down the corridor.

They went forward along the curving corridor toward the steering cabin, trailed by Hians with fire weapons. But this time Aldoan turned into the wide passage that ran below the steering cabin, and led them to a room just off it. Delin stopped in the doorway and Bramble peeked over his shoulder.

It was a workroom, the stem-beams that supported the ceiling arching to give it more height. There were shelves and cabinets built against the moss walls, holding all sorts of ceramic jars, bound stacks of paper, rolls of paper protected by leather or wooden covers, and small devices made out of metal and glass that must be tools of some kind.

Vendoin stood beside a table in the center, where a scatter of papers lay next to a gray rock. The rock, the one Bramble had seen with Vendoin, Bemadin, and Lavinat up in the flying boat's common room. Bramble tried not to react. Vendoin glanced up and didn't seem surprised to see Bramble. Vendoin said, "Aldoan said you wished to speak to me. But perhaps you left it too late."

"Perhaps I did," Delin said, unperturbed. "It is a fine day; I appreciate the walk about the ship."

Vendoin's mouth shaped something that Bramble, back on the sunsailer, would have confidently interpreted as a smile. Now she wasn't so sure. Vendoin said, "What do you make of this, then?"

Delin stepped into the room and moved to the table. Bramble followed, glancing back to note that Aldoan and the others stayed in the corridor. She stopped a few paces to one side of Delin, and got enough of a glance at the papers to see it was a translation into Kedaic. The other language looked like the glyphs of the foundation builder writing they had seen in the escarpment city. Delin frowned down at it. "Another translation of a builder work? From the city?"

He spoke Altanic, and Vendoin answered in the same language, "No. The inscriptions in the city were all fairly utilitarian, though interesting in their way. The foundation builders enjoining visitors to dock their craft correctly is still a work of poetry to modern Kish. They were useful to Callumkal only because he wished to reconstruct more of the language."

Delin flicked a grim look at her. "Which you had already reconstructed in Hia Iserae, and simply withheld."

She made a throwaway gesture, as if it was of no importance. "Have you ever encountered a reference to a forerunner place that indicated some sort of transportation, or transference, took place there? Something to do with the docking of ships, perhaps."

Delin's expression was thoughtful. Bramble's armpit itched and she was sweating under her ragged shirt, but she was afraid to move, to distract Delin. He said, "This is something you need to know in order to use your new weapon?"

Bramble controlled a wince. She wasn't sure that Delin should have revealed how much they knew, not yet.

Vendoin inclined her head, as if conceding a point, but Bramble thought she had just tensed with surprise. "You knew of it, then. You were after it too?"

On the other hand, it was nice to have confirmation that their suspicions were right.

Delin said, "I learned of it from your own writings, which I took from your bag before we left the sea-mount city. I suspected you of deception, but not that you would attack us with poisons." He added, "If you let me speak to Callumkal, I will answer your questions about the forerunners."

"Hmm." Vendoin clearly wasn't certain if she believed him. "But surely you wish to know how I learned about the weapon." She put her hand on the rock. With a rasping sound it moved, expanding, pieces of it fanning out like folded paper. Bramble couldn't help a twitch; though she knew better, a rock that moved was too much like a disguised predator, and part of her wanted to snatch up Delin and flee out of the room.

Delin eyed Vendoin. "You have arcane powers."

"No. But there are Hian practioners who can move rock the way Jandera horticulturals can manipulate the sun moss. This fact is not commonly known, but is handy for examining buried foundation builder sites."

"Not commonly known," Delin repeated. "You have concealed these abilities from your own Kish allies."

Vendoin was impatient. "Do you wish to see it or not?"

Delin leaned forward. Bramble stood on her tiptoes to see. The inside of the rock was inscribed with more of the foundation builder writing, etched deep into its surface. Vendoin said, "This was found in the ruins beneath Hia Iserae. There are hundreds of them, containing different writings, most referencing places we can't identify or species with names we have no record of, filled with words we can't translate. They are correspondence, messages sent from other foundation builder sites to Hia Iserae."

Delin looked up at her, eyes narrowed. "The message in this rock spoke of the artifact." Bramble heard the faint tremor in his voice that he couldn't control, the thrill of scholarly excitement.

"It described it, and the city where it was hidden. But there was no way to discover where that city was, though there were indications it lay somewhere in the sel-Selatra." Vendoin touched the rock and it twisted and folded itself closed. "Until we heard of Callumkal's map. Will you answer my question now?"

Delin said, "Perhaps I and Callumkal together will be able to answer."

Vendoin sighed. "I can trade you knowledge. The imprisoned creature your Raksuran friends found in the underwater forerunner city; would you like to know what it was, and why it was there?"

Bramble's eyes went wide, though she managed not to gasp. Delin went still and she could have sworn his scent changed, he was so shocked. And greedy. Vendoin had known exactly what to offer. Then he wet his lips and said, "You cannot know that for certain. There are theories—"

"When I first read your account, I recognized it. There were passages in the Hia Iserae message-stones which could only refer to it." Vendoin lifted a hand. "It was a weapon as well."

Delin glanced at Bramble, his brow furrowed. "A weapon? That being?"

It could be true, Bramble thought, turning this new information over. From what Jade, Moon, and Chime had described, the thing had been as deadly to the Fell as it was to Raksura and groundlings.

Vendoin said, "A weapon, bred by one of the enemies the forerunners and foundation builders united against. It was there to be studied, so the forerunners could understand it." She nodded at Delin's expression of consternation. "The creature was described in detail, though again there was nothing to tell us its location. But the depiction in your monograph was too exact to be referring to anything else."

Delin watched her, the conflict in his expression obvious. Bramble caught Delin's eye and nodded, just slightly. It was worth the risk.

He eyed Vendoin. "After questioning the Raksura about the forerunner city they were able to briefly examine, I could conclude only that the forerunners must have craft that could travel below the water, as well as the means of building beneath it. As we saw demonstrated in the foundation builder city. That is all I know of the forerunners' method of transportation. I have encountered no writings that mention it in connection with them." He shrugged. "In short, I have no answer. I know far less of the forerunners than you know of the foundation builders."

The moment stretched as Vendoin met his gaze, then she looked at the papers again. "Perhaps later you'll wish you had been of more help to me."

"Perhaps," Delin said.

Once Aldoan took them back to their cage-room and locked the door on them again, Delin said, "That went badly."

Bramble had to agree.

CHAPTER TEN

Moon and Stone flew southwest, making brief stops only to rest and hunt, or when they came across anyone who might have seen a Kishan flying boat pass. This country was fairly empty and there weren't many opportunities, which was for the best, since it usually required them to waste time pretending to be groundlings.

The latest confirmation that they were still going in the right direction came from a party of furred groundlings moving slowly along on the back of a giant armored herdbeast. Their leisurely method of transportation had given them plenty of opportunity to watch the flying boat go by.

There hadn't been any more sign of the kethel, but Moon had an itch in his back teeth that told him it was out there somewhere, still following them. Whenever they stopped, Stone stared toward the north, growling a little.

The cloudbank Moon had spotted to the south never broke up. And he was certain it was getting bigger, like flying toward a mountain growing in the distance. He had decided it must be a large collection of flying islands. They had passed several and used a couple as spots to sleep a little. All were fairly small, some with broken towers or ruined remnants of walls still visible above the encroaching greenery. There had been a number of different flying island people, of a variety of species. They were all gone now, as far as Moon knew, their flying archipelagos nothing but fragmented remains.

But the next flying island they came across was different. From a distance it looked like a mass of trees with light-colored trunks and light green leaves, as thickly clustered together as grass, with a sweet green scent. Up close, it still looked like that, and flying under it, Moon found there was apparently no island, just the matted tangled roots.

He banked up to see Stone had landed on the edge. Stone shifted to groundling to squeeze through the trunks into the glade's interior. Moon dipped down again to light on one of the outermost trees and hook his claws in the roots. Large dead trees, and some failed saplings, had their roots still trapped in the matrix. Moon furled his wings and carefully pulled himself up and in.

He slipped between the trunks as birds chattered overhead, stepping over holes in the root mass where he could look straight down to the ground far below. The sweet scent was clean and piercing, like a mountain-tree almost, but sharper.

He found Stone in a small open clearing, drinking from a deep rainwater basin formed where a trunk had fallen. Moon crouched on the edge to scoop up some water. When he was done, he sat back and said, "What kind of flying island is this?"

"A cloud forest." Stone wiped the water off his face. "I'd heard of them but never seen one before."

Moon looked around again. The leafy canopies were open enough that the sun fell through, bathing the whole grove in a warm light. There were smaller trees and more saplings here, as if the forest must grow from its center and push outward. It was too bad they hadn't encountered it later; it would have made a good place to sleep for a while. "Is that what we're seeing to the south? That big thing that looks like a cloud bank?" If it was one mass, and not a collection of fragments and heavy clouds, it was far larger than any other flying island Moon had ever seen.

Stone shrugged. "I've heard stories about a giant flying island you can see from the far south. I didn't think they were true. It was called the walls, or the cloudwall, or something like that."

Moon mentally sorted it under "things with no explanation that were interesting to look at and not particularly dangerous." He stretched his back, taking a deep breath of the cloud forest's scent. He thought about shifting to groundling, but Stone was probably going to want to leave in a moment and it wouldn't be worth it. Just then Stone grunted and started to push to his feet.

The birdsong abruptly dropped in volume.

Moon clamped his jaw against a hiss. Stone went still, head cocked to listen. There was no stench of Fell in the light wind, and none in the forest. Stone stepped soundlessly over the rotting trunk, and turned to slide between the two nearest trees. Moon eased to his feet and followed.

The moss and winding roots didn't creak as they moved toward the edge, but the low nervous rustle of birds and flying lizards made Moon's spines want to twitch. They reached the outer circle of large trees. The view was nothing but empty blue sky and the rolling, brushy green hills below, and the wind came straight at them from the northwest. Keeping his voice to a low whisper, Stone said, "Probably Fell. We need to split them." He jerked his head. "You go out the other side."

Moon twitched his spines in agreement and ducked back through the trees. This was bad, but could still be survivable. The Fell must be angling up toward them from downwind. They would have spotted Moon and Stone sometime after dawn and been waiting for them to stop to rest. It probably meant there weren't that many, maybe just a small scouting party. They wouldn't want to fight inside the cloud forest but they wouldn't be sure exactly where Moon and Stone would come out.

Moon reached the outer fringe of the forest, stepped between the trees, and spotted three dakti riding the wind high above. He flung himself out into the air, extended one wing and twisted as if he had fouled the other one.

The dakti took the bait and dropped on him. At the last instant, Moon snapped his other wing out, caught the wind and used it to slide under the forest. He caught a dangling root and contracted his body, tucking himself up and out of sight.

Two dakti shot past but one tried to follow him under the roots and blundered in right beneath him. Moon fell on it, shredded its right wing, dropped it, then dove on the other two. He caught one as it foolishly tried to come up at him and ripped its chest open. The other fled, flapping madly, and that was when he heard the crashing and growling from the far side of the forest.

Moon snarled, forgot the dakti and flapped up toward the roots. He found an opening in the forest floor and wriggled through, clawed his way past roots and moss. Dodging between the narrow trunks, the roots vibrated under his feet and the trees ahead shook and thrashed as something struggled just at the edge of the forest. Moon swung up into the canopy for a better view. He spotted Stone and snarled in horror.

Stone was in his winged form but something had fallen on him, a huge thing like a sticky web that had trapped his left wing and half his body against the dead trees on the outer edge. A kethel flapped just above him, swiped at Stone as he struggled to free himself.

Moon leapt from tree to tree then jumped down into the under-story, dangerously close to the thrashing body. Moon lunged in and ripped at the sticky net with his claws. This close he saw it had been made from a sac, the substance that the kethel could secrete to carry dakti or rulers. It was caught all through the dead trees and there was no way he could shred it fast enough—

Something hit his back and bounced him off the nearest tree. He fell onto the moss and rolled to see three more dakti clawing their way toward him, jaws gaping with laughter. But the trees were too close together for them to come at him at once, and one shouldered the others aside to be the first to leap on him. That was a big mistake.

Moon caught its shoulders, yanked it forward, spread his jaw to its fullest extent and bit its face and muzzle off. He flung the still-twitching body into the second one, who tried to retreat but wedged its body against a tree long enough to get its chest ripped open. The third fled but Moon caught it in the dead trees at the fringe, slammed it down between the roots and snapped its neck. The dead roots cracked and broke under the force of the blow, and Moon realized this was how he could free Stone.

He shoved through the trunks to where Stone's left foot was trapped in the sac-net, then started to claw and rip at the brittle roots of the two nearest dead trees. Without the root connection to the rest of the forest, the trees started to sway and topple. Stone must have felt the give; he jerked his foot and the trees ripped out and dragged half a dozen others with them.

Stone dropped and twisted, the sac stretching, strands snapping. The kethel caught the edge of the forest with one clawed foot to swipe at Stone's face. Moon was close enough to see the collar of skulls around its neck, all groundlings, different shapes and sizes, some so recent rotting skin was still attached.

Another dark body loomed over them, blotting out the light.

Moon looked up at another kethel and thought, *well, we're dead now*.

Then it slammed down atop the first kethel, yanked it off its perch and dragged it away. Stone twisted out of the sac-net as they fell past him. The two struggling kethel dropped out of sight under the bulk of the forest.

Moon leapt into the air as Stone wheeled away. He flapped until he caught the wind and then looked back over his shoulder. The two kethel fell, locked in combat. The kethel who had helped them had to be the one from the half-Fell flight. It was the same size and wore no collar.

Three smaller figures darted away in the opposite direction, fleeing the battle. It was a ruler and two dakti.

Ahead, Stone growled. Moon turned back and they flew south and away.

They flew until the cloud forest was out of sight. The terrain below was spidered with river channels running through shallow gorges, steep and inhospitable for groundlings. It was shaded by the occasional tall slender tree with a single layer of delicate canopy, spread like a parasol. Moon tried to signal Stone to land, and finally Stone circled down.

Stone landed on a rocky island that broke a wide channel into a short waterfall. He perched on the rock, then shifted to groundling and collapsed face down. Moon hit the rock, frantic, and shifted to lose his claws as he crouched to examine Stone. He didn't see the big wounds he was afraid of, just streaks of blood from scratches on Stone's arms and back. Then Stone croaked, "Left shoulder's dislocated."

Moon hissed, rolled him over, and shoved the shoulder back into place. Stone snarled as it clicked into the socket, then gasped in relief. He blinked and yawned. "Yeah, that's better."

"How did you fly like that?" Moon demanded. The wing joins used different muscles, but still.

"Not very well," Stone admitted.

Moon pulled Stone's pack around and dug in it. He pulled out a paper-wrapped packet and sniffed it. "You're still carrying around the bug paste?"

Stone worked his shoulder carefully, his jaw set against the pain. "Obviously."

Moon snarled in frustration, shoved it back in the pack, and dug out the half-full waterskin to hand to Stone. He took the empty one to the edge of the island to fill it. *This is stupid*, he thought. *We can't keep doing this.* They were relying on luck and the word of a bladder-boat groundling that they were even on the trail of the right flying boat. And that shitting kethel was still following them.

Moon splashed water on his face and felt the sting of claw slashes and bruises he hadn't noticed until now. He sat back and looked at Stone.

Stone was watching him, the waterskin on his chest. "We're not stopping."

It wasn't nearly as satisfying to hiss in groundling form, and Moon was more exhausted now than frustrated. "We don't even know if we're going in the right direction."

"We do, because the Fell are going this way."

"They could be following us."

"Then where are they?" Stone lifted his brows. He sat up with a groan, cradling his arm, and jerked his chin toward the empty sky. "That was the flight's rear guard. The rest of them are ahead of us. They sent scouts ahead and spotted the Hians."

He had a point. Moon rubbed his eyes and tabled the decision for the moment. He was suddenly hungry, and knew it was probably just nerves more than anything else. "That other kethel, that was the one the half-Fell queen sent. Which means the rest of the half-Fell flight has to be out here somewhere. They're following us, fighting the other Fell."

"Not necessarily." Stone shrugged and winced. "It might be just that one kethel."

"So it's competing with the other Fell to see who gets us?"

"Maybe." Stone squinted at the empty sky again. "We need to get going."

"No. I'm going to hunt, we're going to eat, then we'll find a place to sleep until dark." At the far side of the pool below the waterfall, large silvery fish wove through the reeds and water flowers, and there were cracks and crevices in the rock that could make a good hiding place if he could find one wide enough.

He expected Stone to argue, but Stone gave him a sideways look and a slight smile. "And then we'll get going."

Moon snarled in frustration again, mostly at himself this time, shifted, and jumped into the water.

He managed to get enough fish for both of them before the school fled the pool, then helped Stone up to a crevice in the cliff that was big enough to lie down in. Stone slept, but Moon sat up just inside the cover of the overhanging rock, dozing off and on and watching the sky.

Before the sun set he spotted a lone kethel, crossing back and forth across the clouds, searching for them.

Malachite and the others left at sunset. Chime watched with horrified fascination as the Fellborn queen's three kethel built the sac from the secretions of pouches in their winged forms. It was far smaller than the huge sac Chime had seen before, maybe thirty paces across at most. Two kethel lifted it between them and most of the dakti and the rulers climbed inside. Malachite, her warriors, the Fellborn queen, and a few dakti rode the two kethel, with the third flying alongside. The idea was to switch out periodically with the riders inside the sac and rest, with the third kethel spelling one of the two others, so that the flight could be in continuous motion.

"Good luck," Chime had said to Rise, Malachite's lead warrior.

He had thought he was doing a good job of hiding how appalled he was, but she had smiled ruefully. "Believe it or not, this is not the oddest thing I've done with Malachite."

Malachite had chosen five Opal Night warriors to remain behind, and Chime stood with them in the stern, watching worriedly as the flight vanished into the clouds. Saffron was one of them, and Chime found himself exchanging a horrified expression with her. He didn't particularly like Saffron, and they didn't agree on a lot, but they were as one on this point. The Fell sac they had been trapped in together had been a terrible experience, and Chime couldn't imagine climbing into one voluntarily.

And he would have never thought he would miss Malachite, but with her and so many warriors gone, the wind-ship felt far more vulnerable.

Chime turned and realized he stood next to Root. The news about the threat to Indigo Cloud and the Reaches had struck everyone so hard, and preparations for Malachite and the others to leave had been so urgent, Chime hadn't gotten a chance to talk to him yet.

There was something about the way Root stood there, his spines drooping a little, that made Chime think that River's concern wasn't misplaced. Not that Chime expected Root to be happy, but . . . "Are you all right?"

Root didn't react, his gaze on the shapes fading into the dusk. "I'm fine."

He didn't sound fine. He didn't sound like himself at all. "That's good, because nobody else is," Chime said, hoping to provoke a reaction.

It did. Root turned to face him, his expression grim and unfamiliar. "We shouldn't have left Song's body behind."

It was as abrupt as a sudden slap. The memory of Song's face, twisted and slack with death, was too vivid still and Chime winced, controlling a snarl. He swallowed his temper and made his voice calm. "We had to, Root."

The Kishan had left their dead behind, too. They had buried them all on a small island in the archipelago off the coast of Kish, barely more than a sandbar. The Kish were afraid the dead would bring disease in the warm weather, and Chime couldn't blame them. Indigo Cloud had left its dead before, when the court had had to flee the eastern colony and they had burned the remains of all those killed in the Fell attack. It was never easy, it was never right. But there was no choice.

"We brought Flower back with us," Root said, stubborn and angry.

"It isn't a far comparison," Chime said. Root knew that as well as he did. They had had a queen's urn to carry her in, and they had been on the freshwater sea, with a boat to take them near the shores of the Reaches, and not so many days of flight from home. Without Flower they wouldn't have had that home; burying her in the tree had been a symbolic act.

Root looked away, his throat working. Then he shifted and leapt to the cabin roof, so fast Chime stumbled backward. Saffron caught his arm to steady him. "What was that about?" she asked.

"He's hurt, and he has to take it out on someone," Chime told her. That was all he wanted to say in front of the Opal Night warriors. He just hoped Root could control himself.

CHAPTER ELEVEN

It was morning when Bramble and Delin were taken down the corridor and up to the common room.

Through the large glass-shielded windows, Bramble could see the blue morning sky. Vendoin, Bemadin, and Lavinat sat on a bench, while several other Hians stood in attendance. Bramble hadn't seen or heard anything of Lavinat since that first meeting in this room, and had almost forgotten her. But her presence here again seemed to show that she was important, though what her place was on this boat or in Vendoin's plans, Bramble had no idea.

A young Hian male knelt by a low table, using a ladle to combine the contents of various jars into a set of three cups, then he stood and carried the tray to Vendoin, kneeling to offer it to her. There was something about it that Bramble found unnerving and alien. She flicked a quick look at Delin, and saw his expression was closed and neutral, almost as enigmatic as Stone at his best.

Vendoin must have seen Bramble staring, because she asked in Altanic, "Your males do not serve your females this way?"

"Not that way," Bramble said. She wasn't sure why it made the back of her neck itch, as if the spines she didn't have in this form wanted to twitch in discomfort. Consorts made tea for their own queens and each other, informally. Except for Moon, who would do it for anybody unless you stopped him, and Stone, who as a line-grandfather did as he wanted. During formal meetings with other courts, Arbora generally tried to make the tea, since it was important to get it exactly right. But this was different somehow. It didn't help that Vendoin was critically watching her discomfort.

With an edge to his voice, Delin said, "I don't mean to interrupt your entertainment, but perhaps you could tell us what you want of us."

Vendoin motioned them forward, indicating a stool near the table. There was only one stool, and Delin glanced at Bramble. She nodded at him to take it and he sat down with a sigh. Bramble stood behind him and realized she had a better view through the windows from this angle and could see that the flying boat was coming to a stop above a settlement.

It lay in a wide valley with a shallow river winding through that sparkled in the morning sunlight. Steep, rounded, forested hills stuck up out of the otherwise flat terrain, placed at random on either side of the bends of the river and sprinkled across the valley. The groundlings had mostly built their dwellings atop or in the sides of the hills, which were carved with pathways and stairs. Bridges joined the hills, and the ground around them was covered with colorful tents, apparently a market or trading area to receive the traffic from the docks along the river and the two elevated stone trade roads that curved in from the surrounding forest.

Before this trip, Bramble had only heard about large groundling settlements from Moon, and it was still exciting to see one, even under these circumstances. Groundlings moved on all the pathways and bridges, and big flat boats were moored at the river docks or moved slowly with the current.

Vendoin said, "You see we have stopped above a trading town, the last for some distance. We're well past the borders of Kish now."

That was discouraging. Bramble knew they had traveled a long way, far outside the bounds of any map she had ever seen, but at least she knew groundlings from Kish. She didn't know if they were still alive or not, but it felt like Kish was the last familiar thing left in her world outside this flying boat.

Delin said, "That would mean something to me if I knew where we were going."

Vendoin made a gesture, as if accepting that fact. "If only you had some information of use to me, perhaps I could be more forthcoming."

Impatiently, Bemadin said, "Why play this game? We will have help soon and we no longer need him or the Janderan."

Vendoin eyed Bemadin without favor. Then Lavinat said, "What Bemadin said is true, we have stopped here to find another scholar to help us."

Bemadin's glance at Lavinat seemed wary. Vendoin stiffened, as if Lavinat had insulted her somehow. The first time Bramble had seen them together, it had been obvious they weren't in accord. It seemed like the division between them had grown worse over the journey; Bramble hoped it was something she and Delin could take advantage of.

Delin's brow furrowed. "Do I know this scholar?"

Vendoin looked at Lavinat, as if waiting for her to answer, then said, "She is a great scholar of the foundation builders, but has not lived in Kish for some time."

Delin smiled a little. "Does she know she is to help you or will you steal her as well?"

Bramble thought that if Vendoin had been a Raksura, she would have hissed and rattled. Vendoin started to say, "That is not—"

Someone shouted from down the corridor behind Bramble, a wordless yell of alarm. She whipped around just as the deck rocked under her feet. *It's Jade and Stone and Moon and the others*, she thought in fierce joy. *They found us!*

Then she caught the scent carried in on the air from the corridor and shifted almost before her mind processed what it was. Fell stench. Sick, she blurted out, "Delin, it's the Fell!"

She had spoken in Raksuran, but Hians in the corridor shouted the warning in their own language. Bemadin leapt up and ran from the room, calling out orders. Vendoin and Lavinat bolted after her, and Aldoan and the other Hian guards followed in a desperate rush. Delin shoved to his feet, knocking his stool aside in his haste. "Bramble—" His eyes were wide.

She stepped to him and caught his wrist. She didn't want to risk being separated from him. Opposing impulses to hide and to fight warred in her chest. It was an Arbora's duty to protect others and hide, and an Arbora's instinct to fight. There was no queen or consort or older Arbora here to resolve that inner conflict.

Then Delin said in Raksuran, "Bramble, should we try to escape? If they have lifting packs aboard—We must find Merit and Callumkal—"

Bramble twitched and was able to think again. Yes, they had to use the confusion to get to the others. "Come on."

She went out and up the corridor, tugging Delin along. Several cabinets lined the wall and Bramble stopped to fling them all open and Delin hurried to help. But there were no flying packs stored inside. Hissing, Bramble led the way to the nearest stairs. The Jandera had worn the harnesses for the packs all the time on their flying boat, and the packs themselves had been stored away in every cubby Bramble had ever looked into. The Hians didn't do that, maybe because the skin between their armored patches was irritated by the harnesses. Or maybe they just didn't care as much about survival as the Jandera did. "We'll get Merit first. Do you have any idea where Callumkal is?"

"I have not heard him since we moved to this ship," Delin said, his voice unsteady with exertion. "I think he must be on the far side, away from our room."

They passed a window and Bramble caught a glimpse of dakti diving away from the flying boat. She felt a stab of despair; they might escape right into the mouths of the Fell.

Bramble plunged down the stairs, Delin hurrying after her. The boat rocked abruptly to the right and Bramble bounced off the wall. Delin hung on to the railing and she staggered, her claws catching on the soft surface of the deck. Multiple thumps shuddered through the deck, and she knew someone was operating the boat's big fire weapons. Out of the corner of her eye she caught motion in the cross-corridor and hauled Delin back under the stairs.

Aldoan and another Hian trotted past, Aldoan carrying something and holding it out from her body like it was a poisonous fruit.

It was a dull, silver-colored metal cage with a jagged piece of dark crystal suspended inside it.

Bramble hissed under her breath. It was the artifact, the weapon.

Aldoan and the other Hian went through the outer hatch, letting the heavier door bang behind them as they ran out.

Delin gripped Bramble's arm. He said, "That was it, the artifact—They must mean to use it against the Fell."

Bramble leapt to the nearest crystal-covered window with a view of the deck.

Over the hills of the city, dark bodies shot through the air. Bramble spotted more dakti and two kethel. Light and sound burst from the top of a hill not far away; a Kishan fire weapon must be mounted atop it somewhere.

Bramble dragged her gaze down toward the Hians on the deck. Vendoin held the artifact now. She spoke to Lavinat, but the glass in the window muffled sound too much for Bramble to make out the words. From their gestures and posture they seemed to be disagreeing about something. Vendoin turned impatiently to Aldoan and handed the artifact back to her. Aldoan turned toward the hatch and Bramble started to duck.

The Fell ruler hit the deck barely three paces away from Aldoan. It slashed through the two armed Hians in the way, bounced forward, snatched Aldoan, and flung itself off the boat.

Delin made a strangled noise of horror. Bramble's snarl was soundless, vibrating in her chest. It struck her suddenly that no matter how much she hated the Hians for everything they had done, this was not something that should happen. Not to them and not to anyone. It was too late for the armed Hians to fire their weapons, even as a mercy killing. The ruler carried Aldoan toward the outer edge of the city, so fast Bramble was sure only her eyes could track it. *And now the Fell have the artifact.* She hoped they didn't know what it was.

She turned away from the doorway and grabbed Delin's wrist to pull him with her. Nothing had changed, they had to escape now.

She made it two steps down the corridor when the deck suddenly leapt up and struck her in the face.

Bramble woozily contemplated the curve of the moss ceiling. Her whole body ached, especially her joints. She groaned, and realized the rush of noise was her ears ringing. Delin must have rolled her over, because he was leaning over her, eyes wide with dismay, shouting her name.

She tried to lift her hand and flail at him to stop. They couldn't let the Hians know they were here. Then she saw two Hians stagger by behind Delin and groaned again. *Well, piss on it. We're too late.* She tried to ask what had happened, but couldn't get her mouth to form the words in her head.

Delin patted her face, as if trying to rouse her. Bramble realized she had shifted, that she was in her groundling form now. She tried to tell him she was all right but again no sound came out of her throat. It occurred to her that she was very much not all right.

Delin twisted to speak to someone she couldn't see. "What is this? What has happened?" He sounded frightened. Bramble had never heard Delin sound really frightened before, and it turned her insides to ice.

A Hian stepped in to lean over her. It was Lavinat. "It was the weapon," she told Delin. "It affects the Raksura as well as the Fell, as we expected. I think we will find it affects other races, any who descend in some way from the foundation builders or forerunners. There was a good reason why they chose to hide the weapon instead of use it."

"This I suspected," Delin said impatiently. "But Bramble was so far from it . . ."

Lavinat made a gesture of dismissal. "Vendoin knows less of it than she believes. She hoped the scholar who lives here could tell her more." She added bitterly, "Aldoan obviously discovered how to get some use of it in a moment of extremis. If she lives, she can tell us."

Delin looked down at Bramble, his face etched with fear and anger. "I don't understand. Why this concealment, and abduction, and violence? If it is a weapon against the Fell surely no one could object to obtaining and using it? If it is carefully directed, the Raksura would not be harmed. There are no Fell flights near Raksuran colonies." He glared up at Lavinat again. "Why did the foundation builders fear using it?"

Lavinat eyed him. "You haven't guessed? Vendoin feared you had. The artifact is only one component of the weapon. The bulk of it lies somewhere else, somewhere nearby on the coast, if Vendoin is right. It is meant to kill on a large scale. Our scholars believe if this artifact is united with the rest of the device, it will destroy all the Fell on this part of the continent, from the far west to the eastern end of the Abascene peninsula."

Bramble couldn't take it in. It was like listening to a story read from a book. Surely this couldn't be real. She was Bramble, an Arbora hunter of great skill from the Indigo Cloud Court. People like her hunted and worked and made art and had sex with their friends and at some point had a clutch or two or three on their way to old age. They didn't become witnesses to the end of their world.

Delin's face flushed a dark gold in distress. "That includes all the Reaches. All of Kish. The Jandera think they descend from the foundation builders . . ."

"As do other races within and outside the Imperial Kish borders." Lavinat tilted her head in wry inquiry. "Would you have helped Vendoin if she had asked?"

"No." His lips curled in revulsion.

"Then she was right," Lavinat said, as Bramble saw the world go dark and drop away.

CHAPTER TWELVE

As Moon and Stone flew, the cloudwall still didn't seem to change, except with the play of light and shadow. The rolling hills of the forest under them began to grow wider and deeper, like the swells of a sea of trees.

Then Stone abruptly turned, slipped sideways, and dropped down toward the ground. It was so abrupt, Moon's heart went tight with dismay. Stone had said he was recovered from his injuries, but Stone lied a lot.

Moon followed him down, already mentally scrambling for alternative plans, and dropped down onto the rocky ground beside him as Stone shifted to groundling. "What is it?" Moon demanded. "What's wrong?"

Instead of answering, Stone climbed the nearest outcrop. A large tree with fringed leaves perched atop it and birds clacked angrily at them from the branches. Stone tasted the air and said, "Fell and death, from upwind."

Moon furled his wings and bounced up onto the rock beside him. "I can't scent it yet."

"It's coming from the south." Stone shifted and leapt, his wings brushing the tree branches as he flapped upward. Moon shook the stirred moss out of his frills and leapt after him.

After some hard flying, Moon started to catch the scent too. Stone was right, it was Fell stench, a taint on the clean wind, and growing steadily heavier. But it was accompanied by the growing sweet-sour stink of rot. So much that it almost overpowered the Fell stench. It was odd. In Moon's experience, the strength of the scents should be reversed. Fell ate most of their kills. The remnants they would have left behind wouldn't have an odor this strong.

The sky was mostly clear, with some clouds gathered toward the west where a small rainstorm fell. Moon scented wood smoke before the rising trails of it became visible. They were approaching a groundling settlement. Or what was left of one.

Finally he caught sight of it, built atop a series of steep hills overlooking the wide bends of a shallow river. Two different trade roads wound through the forested hills toward it. The roads had been elevated some twenty to thirty paces off the ground, supported by large carved stone blocks, similar to those Moon had been familiar with in the east. It meant this spot had been a major nexus of travel for more turns than anyone could remember.

Stone leading the way, they dropped out of the air while they still had a hill and tall forest for cover. Approaching on foot and in groundling form was a frustratingly slow necessity, though at least when they reached the first raised, stone-paved trade road they were able to run without wading through brush and high grass. The stench of Fell and death-rot was almost choking the air now, and scavenger birds circled overhead.

The road took them over two bends of the river toward the settlement. Tall, evenly rounded hills dotted the river valley, the slopes covered with low buildings, the pathways and staircases winding upward shaded by trees. On the valley floor between the hills it was all tents and light wooden structures. Flags and other symbols, some variants of ones that Moon was familiar with from the east, hung from poles along the road and near the river docks, telling travelers everything they needed to know, from what shelter and food were available to which kinds of goods trading was done here.

The wind brought the faint sound of agitated voices and Moon saw groundlings still moving among the tent pathways and up the stairs on the hills. Most were short, hairless, with a dull green skin tone. There were far too many groundlings still alive for the aftermath of a Fell attack. *This doesn't make sense*, Moon thought.

Then Stone stopped, staring at something. Moon caught up and looked down to see a black scaled arm lying in the dust on the ancient paving stones. His first horrified thought was that it was Raksura, but the scales and claws were wrong. "It's a Fell ruler's arm," he said.

Stone's brow was furrowed. "Right." He looked up and tasted the air again. "Come on."

Next it was a join with a leathery dakti wing still attached, then a ruler's torso, then more dakti limbs, then a kethel's foot, and more, all rotting in their own congealed blood, surrounded by buzzing insects and the small ground-scavenging lizards. It was impossible to tell what had killed them. Some groundlings had weapons that could cause things to explode, but it was usually accompanied by fire, and Moon couldn't scent any burned flesh. There was no sign of damage from Kishan-style fire weapons.

"A little more than a day," Stone said, judging the time the bodies lay on the road by the carrion insects and the smell of rot. "Maybe yesterday morning. Must be the flight that was ahead of us."

Moon hadn't seen any remnants that suggested this was the flight controlled by the Fell-born queen. He felt a little relief about that. Seeing dismembered Fell was puzzling but not horrific. He didn't want to see dismembered Fell-Raksuran crossbreeds, no matter how mad he was at them.

They reached a place where a ramp had been constructed to allow travelers to leave the trade road. As they climbed down, it was clear the exploding Fell phenomenon was not confined to the old road. Groundlings gathered dead Fell pieces and dumped them in piles in the city's outskirts, clearly making ready to burn them. Many of the groundlings stumbled with exhaustion, and others carried jugs of water for the workers. Everyone was busy and no one paid attention to the two astonished travelers. Moon said, "What did . . . How did . . ." That was all he could manage.

Stone shook his head, and started away from the burial piles toward the nearest tents.

Moon followed, noting signs that a battle had taken place. Some tents closer in had collapsed, and one had caught fire, its canvas and poles now a smoking heap. Everywhere there was disarray, broken pottery, smashed carts, confused herdbeasts wandering the streets, groundlings who were injured or in obvious distress. There was also some damage to the structures on the hills. The greenery and trees made it hard to see, but Moon spotted a collapsed terrace on the nearest, and on another bricks and roof tiles had spilled down, blocking a stairway.

But most of the groundlings are alive and the Fell are dead, Moon thought. There were Kishan fire weapon emplacements on the hills, but the Fell hadn't been burned. That was the part that didn't make sense.

Stone wound his way through the tents with his usual lack of concern in strange groundling places, heading for an open plaza. More groundlings gathered there, some of the stocky green-skinned ones and some who were skinny and light blue-gray and looked as if they were wearing their skeletons on the outside. They were clearly distressed, talking to each other in a high-pitched language Moon didn't understand, and letting out occasional wails. The cause was obvious: groundling bodies had been laid out on the hard-packed earth of the plaza. The motionless forms had been covered by blankets to protect them from the carrion birds and lizards.

Stone stopped beside a green-skinned groundling, and asked in Kedaic, "What happened?"

The groundling looked up at him. Her head was narrow and almost square, and her eyes large and lidless. She said, "The Fell came here before the last sunset, and attacked, but then they died in the sky. They dropped." She gestured toward the rows of bodies. "But when we came out of hiding, we found all the Jandera traders dead, with no mark upon them. The Viatl think they're next." She wiped at her face, conveying exhaustion and anger. "They panic."

The Jandera, Moon thought, startled. *You thought it didn't make sense before.*

Stone stepped toward the bodies and Moon couldn't help a hiss of caution. Stone ignored it. He knelt by the first motionless form and pulled the blanket back.

It was a Janderan woman, her dark leathery skin unmarked, eyes open and staring, sunken and clouded with death. The skeletal Viatl and the others all went quiet, watching Stone. Moon eyed them but it was clear they were hoping the stranger had answers.

Stone leaned close to study her, to sniff and examine her mouth and eyes. Then he shook his head and tugged the blanket back over her. Stone pushed to his feet and said, "Tell the Viatl that if it hasn't happened by now, it probably won't happen."

There was a startled murmur from the green-skinned groundlings. "It's sickness?" one asked.

Stone said, "No, I think it's something the Fell did."

Another turned to speak to the Viatl, who greeted the information with confusion. Some wailed in relief, while others seemed understandably unwilling to put much trust in the word of some random person from the trade road.

Stone came back to Moon. In Raksuran, Moon said, "You know what this is?"

"No. But it's not doing them any good to panic." Stone looked across the plaza. "We need to find out if the Hians were here."

He was right; this was a puzzle, and it was too much of a coincidence that it had happened on the route they thought the Hians followed. "Somebody would have noticed their flying boat."

Stone frowned. "How do you know that?"

Moon sighed. How Stone had traveled all over the east without picking up on these things continually irritated him. He said, "The trading flags. They have two sets, one near the ground, and one on those tall poles. The ones on the poles have to be for flying boats."

The caravanserai that maintained the trading flags was in as much disarray as the rest of the town. It was carved in the base of the hill nearest the river docks, on the side facing toward the water. There were pens for draft beasts and tents on the flat ground below it, and a wide set of stairs led up to the entrance. Big windows and a balcony overlooked the river, and it was full of traders and locals, sitting on carpets made of woven reeds and trying to ease their shattered nerves with intoxicants and talk. The place stank of fear and the inhabitants were jumpy and suspicious, far more so than the locals outside who were hauling bodies and trying to calm the Viatl.

From picking up snatches of conversation, Moon managed to glean the information that the green-skinned locals were called the Bikuru. This town was an important rest stop for traders, with the nearest cities being some distance away, and the country not being much inhabited.

Asking after the proprietor of the caravanserai led Moon and Stone back outside and around the base of the hill, where a collection of tents forming the better part of the grain trading market had collapsed under the weight of a very dead kethel torso. The Bikuru proprietor was helping to drag it free of the debris and seemed to welcome the distraction of answering questions.

Stone asked her, "There were Hian traders at the last place we stopped, meaning to meet a flying boat somewhere along here. Was there a flying boat here before the Fell attack?"

The proprietor said, "No traders like that came to the caravanserai. But there was a ship of the air of Kish. It fled when the Fell appeared."

One of the groundlings sitting beside the debris looked a little like the slender Coastals of Than-Serest. It said, "No, the airship stayed. I was trapped under a collapsed tent in the market, and I saw it was there when we crawled out. We were all looking up to see if the Fell were really gone."

The proprietor made an arms wide gesture, her equivalent of a shrug. "There were no mails for a ship to take, so it was here for trade or passengers."

"Mails?" Moon asked.

"Messages. For ships." The proprietor pointed up at the trade flag poles standing high above the river docks. "They take and leave from the poles."

Moon shaded his eyes. Now that he looked, he saw there were baskets atop the poles, just below the flags, with ropes attached so they could be hauled up and down.

"Were the Fell chasing the boat?" Stone asked. Moon thought that question was a little too pointed, and nudged him in the back. Stone ignored him.

"Chasing it here?" The Coastal made a neutral gesture. "Maybe? But the craft gave no warning. It stopped, like it meant to take on or drop passengers. I didn't see it go."

"Did it use its fire weapons on the Fell?" Stone asked.

"Not that we saw," the proprietor said. She gestured at the kethel. "But in the end it wasn't needed, I suppose."

Moon pulled Stone away a few steps, and said in Raksuran, "Why didn't they use their weapons?"

Stone said, "Somebody used something. The Fell didn't fall out of the sky for no reason."

"And the Jandera—" Moon stopped. He had a terrible thought. Hians had reason to fear Jandera, since they had stolen Callumkal. "You don't think . . . this was the artifact. This is what it can do. This is why Vendoin wanted it."

From Stone's expression he had already thought of that. "It would make sense. The Fell heard it was a weapon, but they got that from the Hians. They didn't know what kind of weapon it was."

"Vendoin said it would be cruel to tell us what it was." Cold settled in Moon's stomach as all the wider implications hit him. "If it could do this to a Fell flight, it could do it to a Raksuran court."

Stone's jaw tightened, as he tried to hold back a hiss or growl that would frighten the nearby groundlings. "That would explain a lot."

"This is our fault." Moon looked down and wiped the grit from his eyes to give himself time to think. It didn't help. Song, Magrim, Kellim-dar, the three others on the sunsailer who hadn't survived the poison. It had been bad enough before the Hians had killed a group of harmless Jandera traders for fear of pursuit. "We brought the shitting thing out of the city for them." Now the Hians could do anything with it.

Stone ruffled his hair sympathetically, then said, "Stop it."

Moon twitched, an urge to self-consciously settle the spines of his other form. "We're only barely more than a day behind them and we don't know if they're still going south. Or why they stopped here."

Stone didn't answer, until Moon looked up. Stone's expression was somewhere between resigned and grimly amused. He said, "I've got nothing else to do."

Past the smashed tent a voice rose in anguish, speaking in Altanic, "But how were killed the Jandera? Why dead them?"

The Coastal shook its head, its crest shivering with the motion. "And who is next?"

Stone turned back to the proprietor and said, "Are there any Kish living here who weren't Jandera traders? Any Hians?"

Following the proprietor's directions, they climbed the stairs that wound up one of the hills, past the stone houses and the twining limbs of small determined shade trees and flowering bushes. There was less confusion up here, most of the inhabitants still huddling inside the sturdy structures. An array of small colorful birds sang and called as if nothing had happened.

They followed the staircase around and up, past an open terrace where potted garden plants had been toppled when dead dakti limbs had fallen on them, and up again. The houses had little archways marking the paths that led to their doors, most wound with vines or other greenery. They found the one with the symbol on it that the caravanserai proprietor had told them to look for. It led to a square doorway in a chunky stone façade, sheltered by the branches of a leaning fringe tree. Moon heard movement inside as they approached, and cautiously stopped short of the door. "Hello?"

A small Bikuru emerged, her large eyes curious. Stone said, "We're looking for the Hian scholar."

She lifted her hands helplessly. "All dead."

Moon hadn't expected that. He glanced at Stone, and asked the Bikuru, "It was the Fell?"

"Just dead," the Bikuru said. She motioned for them to come in, and they passed through a cool stone foyer and into a larger room. Windows were carved in the rock but shaded by the greenery outside, letting in a cool breeze. Pieces of wooden furniture and a woven rug had been pushed aside so the Bikuru could lay out four bodies.

All four were Hians, three small enough to be children. Their clothes weren't torn and there was no blood; it looked as if they had just fallen down dead, exactly like the Jandera.

Another groundling sat on the far side of the room, a willowy one with white hair and blue-gray skin, very thin, with long boney ridges along its arms and hands. It was shaking, making distressed noises. "We came to see the scholar," Stone said. "What happened? Was it the Fell?"

"I don't know." It looked up at them with gray eyes. Its Kedaic was much better than the Bikuru's. "She was outside when the Fell came, but there are no wounds! And the younglings were in here."

Moon wasn't sure what to ask. "Was she expecting visitors from the flying boat? Other Hians, maybe?"

It buried its face in its hands, made a distressed noise, then pushed to its feet and ran out of the room.

Stone hissed under his breath. The others were staring at them and Moon said in Raksuran, "We better go."

Stone grimaced agreement. But as they turned for the door, one of the Bikuru said, "Why are you here?"

On impulse Moon decided on a version close to the truth. It had worked for Stone in the swampling city. "We're looking for the Hians who were on the flying boat. We thought they wanted to meet with the scholar who lived here."

The Bikuru stepped out into the foyer with them. "The ship of Kish left after the Fell died. They had devices that allowed them to lift up and down. Kish have these. You have seen?"

She meant the flying packs. Moon said, "Yes, with the harnesses?"

"Yes. Some came from the ship in that fashion. I did not see them, but Ile-res said she saw them leave the house, and now the scholar's writings are gone." The Bikuru watched them carefully, critically. "Do you know why they did this?"

That one Moon could answer honestly. "No."

Stone added, "They stole from us, too. They're thieves."

The Bikuru watched them a moment more, but Moon got the feeling she believed them. "Most of the scholar's writings are not here. They are at the scriptorium on the tier below."

Stone lifted his brows. "Her writings about what?"

"Her ancestors. The ancestors of all of Kish. They had a city out that way somewhere, near the sea." She made a vague gesture toward the south. "Under the cloudwall, in poetic terms."

"Are the writings in Kedaic?" Moon asked, though he wasn't hopeful. Kedaic was primarily a trade language, made up of words from other Kishan languages. He didn't think it was something most scholars would use.

The Bikuru seemed bemused by the question, but answered, "Not Kedaic. I have not seen myself, but the scholar was partial to Kish-Kenar, and would write in High Isra, or Kenarae, perhaps."

Someone in the house wailed again, and the Bikuru gestured a hurried farewell and went inside.

Stone made a thoughtful noise and started back down the path. Moon said, "So we know what they were here for. We just don't know if they got it." It didn't sound like the Hians had had much time to go through the scholar's papers after they killed her and her family. If the writings they wanted were stored in the scriptorium, they hadn't realized it.

Stone said, "I don't suppose you read High Isra or Kenarae, because I don't."

"No." Moon doubted they would be able to figure it out, whatever it was, even if they could read the scholar's books. That was a job for a mentor, or for Delin and Callumkal . . . Moon stopped on the steps. "You think that's why they took Delin and Callumkal? Because Vendoin knew they were going to have to come here, and get something from this scholar that she needed help to understand?"

Stone hadn't stopped, and Moon had to hurry to catch up with him. Stone said, "That, or she didn't want them with us when we followed her and found this place. We've wasted enough time here. We need to get in the air again."

"There's one more thing we can do," Moon said. "I want to leave a mail."

They stopped at the caravanserai on their way out of town. Stone wrote a message and Moon added a bit of the tracking moss to it to guide

Kalam's horticultural here. Then one of the proprietor's assistants folded it up in a waterproofed cloth packet, labeled it with Niran's and Diar's names and hauled it to the top of a mail pole with a flag indicating urgency.

Once that was done, they walked out of town toward the road. Moon looked up at the forest, wondering if there were any loose herd-beasts there or if they should wait until they spotted some wild gras-seaters. Someone else was on the road now, another traveler standing on the raised stone surface and staring toward the town. Staring toward them . . . Moon stopped abruptly. "That's a kethel."

"That's our kethel," Stone said after a moment.

Moon had had time to spot the kilt and the braided hair. He suppressed the urge to shift. They couldn't do it here, not in front of this shocked and reeling town. He started for the road. "It's not ours, I don't want a kethel."

But by the time they reached the ramp up to the elevated road, the kethel had vanished. Moon balanced on the nearest pylon, staring into the sandy hills and the tall fringed trees, alert for any sign of movement.

"Moon, come here." Stone was looking at something on the road's weather beaten surface. Reluctantly, Moon stepped down and went to join him.

It was an arrow, scratched into the dust of the pavement, pointing south.

Moon and Stone flew the rest of the day, crossing low hills dotted with large serene umbrella trees, shading little colonies of what Moon had first thought were small mammals. When they landed at dusk, the little creatures turned out to be plants, able to uproot themselves and walk slowly away from the Raksuran intruders. Between the trees were small ponds and streams, lit by iridescent water grass, and Moon was able to catch a few fish.

While Stone was eating, Moon stood in the shallows of a stream, staring at the glowing grass between his foot claws, lost in thought, until the walking plants decided he was harmless and returned. He missed his clutch so much it felt like a physical ache.

Then he felt something change, something different in the shadows under the tall umbrella trees. His spines lifted and he tilted his head to listen. Behind him, Stone was suddenly on his feet.

Then Moon caught the scent and swallowed a growl. Stone stepped up beside him and snarled, then said, "Come out of there."

There was a silent pause, then Moon sensed something moving in the shadows. The kethel stepped out of the dark onto the iridescent grass near the stream.

Moon hissed. "Stop following us, or we'll kill you."

It said, "If I didn't follow you, you'd be dead in the flying trees."

It had a point, which just made Moon that much more frustrated. Stone took a casual step toward it. It ducked its head and looked at the ground, but didn't back away. "What do you want?" Stone said, frustration under the growl in his voice.

"I told you, to help you," it said. In the dimming light, it was hard to read its expression. Reading a Fell ruler's expression was useless, since Moon thought it was rare that they used facial expressions to communicate with each other. Mostly they used them to fool and entrap groundlings. The kethel, which didn't interact with groundlings, might be different, but with the shadows concealing its deep-set eyes, it was hard to tell.

Stone hissed out a breath and said, "Where are the others?"

The kethel said, "No others. I sent the dakti back to her long ago. To tell her that I followed you."

"Her" had to be the half-Fell queen. Moon asked, "Where is she?"

The kethel turned its face up to the sunset sky, and Moon had a moment of trepidation that it was about to say "here." The kethel said, "With the others. On the plain, nearer to the sea."

Stone eyed him thoughtfully. "But what is she doing now? Why did she send you ahead?"

The kethel looked down, its lips pursing stubbornly.

"The rulers won't let you tell us," Moon said.

It made a noise of contempt. "Rulers."

Moon turned to look incredulously at Stone and found Stone looking incredulously at him. Moon said, "I know your flight has rulers. I saw them at the island."

"The rulers are young. She—" It faced them suddenly. Moon hissed and flinched back. Stone's growl made the tree beside them tremble and release a shower of puffy white seed pods.

The kethel took a hasty step back. It said, "She killed the progenitor."

The half-Fell queen had said that too, and Moon believed it. He just wasn't certain he could believe this kethel was operating under its own will, with nothing to tell it what to do but its own judgment. "There's no voice in your head. Nothing making you talk."

The kethel said only, "No," but something in its voice suggested controlled irritation.

"Since when?" Stone said, "When did she kill the progenitor?"

"Long ago." The kethel watched them, as if trying to gauge their reaction. It took all of Moon's concentration not to let his scales twitch uncontrollably. Stone was staring at it with a concentrated intensity that finally made the kethel look away. Then it said, "You tell stories?"

Moon let himself twitch. It was a relief. Stone cocked his head and said, "What?"

The kethel slid a careful glance at him. "The other consort told stories."

Stone hissed out a breath, and Moon belatedly realized what the kethel meant. He snarled, "We don't want to hear about how the consort your flight captured and forced to mate with your progenitor passed the time while being tortured."

The kethel looked away again. If it had been a Raksura, Moon would have said it was disappointed. "I just thought you have stories."

Stone considered it for a long time. Then he said, "Tell us your story, and we'll tell you a story."

Moon's jaw tightened. He said to Stone, "By *we*, you mean you."

Stone ignored him. "Tell us about her, your Queen."

The kethel seemed to struggle with itself, the emotion almost hidden under what must be a deliberate effort at expressional stoicism. Moon had thought it might be young, though he had no idea how kethel aged. Now he was certain it was young. It said, reluctantly, "I was too small. But she wouldn't let the others kill me. I was hers. There was us, and the dakti that were born with her. Some other dakti that were too small, or too different. And our consort. He called her Consolation."

"He named her," Stone said, his voice giving away nothing. Moon felt his spines ripple uneasily.

The kethel hesitated, as if uncertain how to react, then it continued, "Then our consort died and she said that some time she would be big enough to kill the progenitor. The progenitor didn't fear her. The rulers were there, they protect the progenitor. But the progenitor forgot me, and I grew big too. I killed the rulers, and she killed the progenitor. Our dakti helped."

Moon looked away, watching the sparkling water weeds move with the current. Stone said, "What about the others?"

"We killed some, but the others are friends now." The kethel added, "Now you tell a story." It tilted its head toward them, clearly hopeful.

Stone rubbed his face. Then he turned and took a couple of paces away to sit down on a thick tree root.

The kethel threw a wary look at Moon, then sat where it was on the iridescent grass. Moon moved a few paces down the stream, where he would be in a good position to attack if the kethel flung itself at Stone. As he sat on his heels on the bank, Stone began, "This is a story of Solace and Sable, when they went to trade with cloud people in the far east valleys . . ."

Later, Moon and Stone went to rest in the curving bowl-shape of a parasol tree's crown. It was high and difficult to reach, so a predator would be unable to approach without shaking the whole tree.

They were both in their groundling forms, sheltered by the inward-curving leaves. Moon curled up and tucked himself in under Stone's arm, and Stone didn't comment. His face pressed against Stone's ribcage, Moon said, "We can't believe anything it says. That's not a half-Fell. That's a shitting kethel."

Stone made a noise of agreement. After a time, he said, "That's the third Fell flight we've heard of that was destroyed because it made Fell-Raksuran crossbreeds. Plus a couple more, if you count the flights that were destroyed because another flight made Fell-Raksuran crossbreeds."

"I noticed that." Moon was tracking the presence of the kethel by scent and sound, knowing it was about thirty paces from the base of their tree. It was sleeping next to the stream where they had talked. "You'd think the Fell would pass the word around and stop doing it."

"I think it's a little late for that." Stone scratched his chest. The insects left them alone but the tree pollen was thick in here. "Lithe and Shade said they and the others at Opal Night couldn't hear the Fell. Shade couldn't hear that thing in the forerunner city that was speaking to the Fell."

Moon saw where that thought was going. "So maybe some Fell-Raksuran crossbreeds can't hear the progenitor, even when they're raised as Fell, so the progenitor can't control them. The progenitors are so used to having absolute control over the flight, they don't realize it until it's too late."

"And something happened when the Fellborn queen took in that baby kethel," Stone added. "The progenitor lost control over it."

Consolation, Moon thought. The captive consort who had sired her must have had very few choices, but Moon couldn't imagine the progenitor had forced him to name his offspring. "Don't call it a baby," he said. He had enough problems handling all of this. Stone didn't reply, and after a moment Moon added, "The Fellborn queen is maybe more queen than Fell. Maybe . . . It sounds like what Malachite did to destroy the flight that attacked Opal Night's eastern colony. She took control of the progenitor."

Stone let out a frustrated sigh. "Go to sleep."

Jade stood in the hold of the wind-ship, contemplating the meal of dried fruit and grain that the Golden Islanders were preparing. The sun was setting and she was going to have to try to sleep, though it was the last thing she wanted to do. She was so tense it took effort just to keep her spines from flaring.

Most of the others were already asleep, except for the warriors outside on watch. Or at least she hoped they were asleep. Since Malachite had left with Consolation and the half-Fell flight, they had all had nothing to do but worry about what might be happening in the Reaches. It almost overwhelmed her worry for Moon and Stone. Almost. But she wasn't angry at the Reaches for racing off alone into unknown territory knowing it was being followed by Fell, which added a whole different level to the emotion.

Along with Shade and Lithe, Malachite had left them with five of her warriors, Flicker, Saffron, Flash, Spark, and Deft. Jade had sent the whole bunch hunting early this morning, and then made them and her own warriors eat their fill. They had to stay fed and rested, ready for flight at any moment, in case they came upon the Hians or the Fell found them. Now she needed to take her own advice. She grimaced to herself, admitting it was unlikely.

Diar had warned them that the maps indicated a nearby groundling trading town in the forested hills, so Jade couldn't even do a fast flight around the wind-ship to work off some of her nerves. Dranam had said the tracking moss for Moon and Stone had split again, so they must have left another message somewhere in the town. Jade just hoped the horticultural could locate it quickly; if they were delayed by a long search, her last nerve would snap.

Lithe wandered in from the corridor, a shawl wrapped around her shoulders, but she looked wide awake. "Anything?" Jade asked her.

Lithe shook her head, frustrated and weary. "I keep seeing the sea breaking on a beach, and having the feeling that we should hurry. And I can't tell if the latter part is from the vision or just common sense." They both spoke Altanic, for the benefit of the Golden Islanders in the cabin, but the groundlings were more interested in preparing the meal than listening. Probably because Jade and Lithe had been having this same conversation for the past few days. "I'm still not getting anything about the Reaches, either."

That might be good news, Jade thought. It might mean Malachite still had time to beat the Fell there.

Lithe added, "I was going to make tea. Would you like some?"

"You should try to get some rest," Jade said. She didn't expect Lithe to listen. It felt like she had been telling mentors to rest all her life and none of them ever listened. They were as bad as feral consorts and line-grandfathers.

"So should you." Lithe smothered a yawn. "And I need to be awake, so I can have more useless visions."

Those words pricked a memory, and Jade said, "You know, Merit kept getting visions of the sea, when we were close to the foundation builder city and he had trouble scrying—"

Then River leaned in the doorway and said, "Jade? Something's wrong ahead. Rorra said to get you."

Jade hissed and whipped out of the cabin. She passed River on the steps up to the deck.

Outside the breeze carried the scent of running water, greenery, and wood smoke with something foul under it. *Rotting flesh*, Jade realized, startled. The fires were consuming dead bodies. She went first to the rail and saw they approached a groundling settlement built across a series of tall hills or mounds, set between the curve of a river and two raised stone trade roads. The sun was sinking past the horizon, turning the clouds cloaking the huge flying island formation to the south every shade of gold.

The flicker of fire seemed to be mostly on the outskirts of the town, but it was in orderly rows. Lights gleamed in windows and doorways in the hills and in the tents below. Boats and barges were tied up at the river docks. Jade tasted the air deeply. There might be some Fell stench, but it was too faint to be nearby, or buried under the harsh wood smoke.

She reached the steering cabin and found Rorra and Niran. Diar was in the bow, focusing a distance-glass on the town. "Was it a Fell attack?" Niran asked her. "Can you smell them?"

"A little, maybe. They're not here now," Jade said, concentrating on the scents, trying to sort them out. "And if they were here, I don't know why so many groundlings are still alive."

Rorra's expression was tight with worry. "Maybe Moon and Stone drove the Fell away."

Jade imagined the two of them taking on a whole Fell flight and suppressed a growl of unease. If they had fought the flight and one of them had been captured, and that was why the moss showed a split again . . .

Diar turned away from the bow. "We'll know soon. There are trade flags for a caravanserai, and I think I see message poles." She explained to Jade, "We saw these in Kish. Messages are tied to the tops of the poles to make it easy for flying craft to collect them. If the consorts left us a message, it may be there."

"Yes, it's a handy system," Rorra added.

"I will recommend it for ports in the east, if we survive long enough to return there," Niran said.

Diar sighed. "My sibling the optimist."

Jade turned at a faint sound. Lithe had followed her to the steering cabin. The mentor stood, one hand on the wall, and the dying sunlight made her eyes into white reflective pools. No, that wasn't the light, that was a mentor caught in a vision. Jade said softly, "Lithe? What do you see?"

Lithe hissed out a slow breath. "Fast," she said. Then she shook herself and blinked, her eyes a soft brown again. "We need to move fast. We have to get to the coast before—Before something happens." She grimaced. "I don't know what."

Niran turned the steering device and the wind-ship angled down to the message poles.

CHAPTER THIRTEEN

The Court of Indigo Cloud in The Reaches

Frost was hiding in the little chamber adjacent to the queens' hall, the one consorts were supposed to wait in before they went out to greet visiting royal Aeriat. Her plan worked well, until Ember came down the steps from the upper passage and there was nowhere to go.

He stopped, startled to see her. "Frost, what are you doing here?"

Disgruntled, Frost said, "I'm waiting for the queens." She realized Ember must also use this room as a quick private route down from his bower in the consorts' level to Pearl's. She should have thought of that. He was dressed for the greeting, in a sleeveless dark blue shirt and pants of the best silky cloth Indigo Cloud could produce, with armbands, a heavy gold bracelet, anklets, and gold chains with sunstones braided through his hair.

"Why?" he said, eyes narrowing suspiciously.

Frost stirred mutinously. Ember wasn't First Consort like Moon, but being rude to him would definitely fall under the category of something an immature fledgling would do, and not a daughter queen ready for responsibilities. And he was always nice, and she didn't want to be rude. But she knew he would tell her to go back to the nurseries. She said, unwillingly, "Jade's not here and there's no other sister or daughter queens."

Ember folded his arms. "You were just going to walk in on a formal meeting of queens making an alliance to defend the Reaches and demand to participate?"

Put in those terms, it did sound bad. "I wasn't going to jump out at them. I was going to wait until Pearl came out, and then ask her." She had meant to do it just before the other queens came in, when it was too late to order her to leave without causing a disturbance. Looking up at Ember's disapproving expression, Frost decided not to explain that part. "Pearl can't meet them alone. We'll look bad."

Ember pointed out, "Celadon is here."

Frost knew that. It was the flaw in her otherwise carefully thought out reasoning. She said, "She doesn't live here. She's Malachite's daughter queen, not Pearl's." Of course, Frost wasn't, either. The bloodline tie through Moon made Celadon more part of Indigo Cloud than Frost. But Sky Copper and everyone in it was dead, and Frost would be a daughter queen of Indigo Cloud. Frost added, "I live here."

Ember studied her a moment. "You know it's a bad idea to surprise Pearl."

Frost didn't know that. She didn't see Pearl much, except when Pearl came to the nurseries to visit the new clutches. "I like surprises," Frost said.

"Grown-up queens usually don't," Ember said.

Frost flicked her spines, glumly resigned. Maybe it hadn't been a very good idea. Then Ember added, "You should ask her if you can be present. Come on."

He took her wrist and walked her out into the queens' hall. The teachers Dream and Bead stood near the hearth, studying the arrangement of the cushions and the tea service with critical eyes. They were too occupied to notice Ember and Frost. Which was good, because Frost's spines had started to flick nervously and if they saw that they would tell Rill and no one would believe she was grown enough to be a real daughter queen.

Ember led her into Pearl's bower. Some warriors were there, and so was Gold, the teacher who was best at making jewelry. She was sorting through a pile of polished gems with silver settings, choosing pieces for

Pearl to wear. Pearl was curled on a cushion near the hearth. Everyone looked up at Ember and Frost.

The first time Frost had seen Pearl was burned into her brain, when Moon had told them to run and Frost had known the Fell would kill him, when suddenly Pearl and Jade had slammed down out of the sky to rescue them all. But seeing her here, resting in her bower with warriors and Arbora in attendance, Frost remembered being brought to her birthqueen's bower to listen to the Arbora read stories, and the scents came back to her, of the court and the members of their mingled blood-lines who she would never see again. She couldn't do anything but stand there and hold on to Ember. He nudged her forward, gently.

Frost gathered herself. "Reigning queen, I—" Her voice came out high and squeaky, and she had to force it lower. "I want to be at the meeting with you. Jade isn't here. I want to be—Like a daughter queen." She gave up and stood there miserably. The prepared speech in her head sounded much better; she had no idea how it had come out that way.

Everyone looked at Pearl. Her spines flicked in annoyance, which Frost didn't think was a good sign. She looked over Frost's head, at Ember, then down at Frost. Frost's spines tensed and she braced herself.

Then Pearl said, "Your behavior has not always warranted such favors."

Frost felt her spines sink. Then Pearl added, "But Blossom has told me how much you've improved. If you can keep quiet, and speak only when you're spoken to, you may stay."

So not long later, Frost sat on a cushion next to Celadon, with Bone, Heart, Bell, and Knell, all watching Pearl as they waited for the other queens. Frost's frills were still wet because once Pearl had given her permission to stay, Gold had hauled Frost over to the bathing pool at the back of Pearl's bower and made her wash all over. Mindful of staying on her best behavior, Frost hadn't even protested that she was already clean. Frost had put on all her good jewelry back in the nurseries, but

Gold had made her take off two bracelets and had quickly polished the copper disks of her necklace for her. Then Gold had hugged her and whispered, "Your first time at a formal greeting! It's so exciting!"

Frost was beginning to realize how lucky she was that Ember had caught her. It was better to have this given to her instead of trying to take it. Once the other queens came, she would have to move over to sit with the Arbora, but Celadon had said Frost could sit with her until they arrived.

The lights caught the polished blue stones of Celadon's belt and necklace, and the deep green of her scales. She had three warriors with her, who waited in the back of the hall with Floret and the Indigo Cloud warriors. Celadon's close resemblance to Moon was reassuring and Frost had already met her in the nurseries when Ember had brought her down to visit the new royal clutch. Celadon said, "I was much older than you when I went to my first formal meeting."

Frost tried not to show how gratifying that was. "Was there a war with the Fell?"

"No." Celadon's spines flicked a little in amusement. "It was about trading ball fruit." She looked down at Frost and said a little cautiously, "The Fell war happened when I was much younger."

Frost said, "Moon told us. They came and killed everyone. It happened to us, too."

Celadon squeezed her wrist. "It will never happen again."

Frost's spines flicked and her throat went dry suddenly. *It won't, it won't happen again*, she thought fiercely. She was bigger now, and she could fight them if they came to the nurseries. She leaned against Celadon's solid warmth and thought, *never again*.

Bone was saying to Pearl, "Don't forget to talk about supplies."

Pearl tilted her head toward him. "Somehow I'll manage to recall it, being reminded of it every other breath."

Then Coil came in and whispered to Floret, and she told Pearl, "The other queens are coming."

Frost had moved over to sit with the Arbora, and not long later, she was suppressing the urge to yawn. After getting through the greetings, they had been talking about supplies, the way Bone had wanted, and how many warriors each court would send to defend the Reaches. Frost hadn't seen any of the queens before, except Zephyr of Sunset Water, who had come several times for trade visits. She was an older sister queen, with a strong build, her scales amber webbed with green. Flame of Ocean Winter sat beside her, and had light green scales with a silver web. Tempest of Emerald Twilight was the most intimidating, but also the youngest, the same age as Jade, with light blue scales and a gold web.

Then Pearl said, "If a Fell flight truly means to attack, we have to meet them outside the Reaches."

Flame's and Zephyr's spines flicked in surprise. Celadon said, "I agree."

Tempest tilted her head toward Celadon. Frost knew why; even she could tell Celadon and Pearl must have talked about this earlier. Tempest said, "I don't. It would be giving up our advantage."

Pearl said, "Our advantage is their advantage. We can't pin them down in the Reaches. There's too good a chance they can get past us and reach a colony."

Tempest's spines flicked. "They don't know the fringe the way we do."

Celadon put in, "Opal Night doesn't know the eastern fringe. Does Emerald Twilight?"

The end of Tempest's tail curled in ironic amusement. "We know it better than Fell who have never been here."

Then Pearl said, "Which of you has had a colony taken from you by the Fell?"

The words dropped into a sudden silence. Everyone's spines went still. Frost's throat was suddenly almost too tight to swallow.

Pearl's voice was hard and cold. "I have stood in a room filled with my dead Arbora and warriors. I will not do that again. Indigo Cloud will meet the Fell outside the Reaches."

Celadon locked gazes with Tempest. *Celadon doesn't like her,* Frost realized. And not in the way queens and other Aeriat sometimes disliked each other for no reason. Celadon said, "In this, Opal Night and Indigo Cloud are as one."

Tempest's calm was tinged with contempt. "Opal Night and Indigo Cloud appear to be one in other things, too."

Celadon's head tilted slowly. "Oh?"

Pearl seemed more amused than angry. She cocked her spines inquiringly. "Yes, please explain. We always await Emerald Twilight's pronouncements with the greatest of interest."

Frost saw Bone bury his face in his hands.

Tempest said to her, "When Indigo Cloud made its way back to the Reaches, it spread the word about the Fell's new trick of capturing Arbora and consorts to breed with." Her gaze went to Celadon again. "That Opal Night retrieved and kept the issue of these acts was a fact it shared only with Indigo Cloud."

Frost leaned over to Bell and whispered, "Nobody's supposed to know that."

"We know," Bell whispered grimly, and squeezed her wrist.

Knell muttered, "Idiot warriors can't keep their mouths shut . . ." Heart poked him in the side and hissed, "Shut up!"

Pearl glanced at Celadon, her spines tilted in ironic comment. *Pearl knew this would happen and warned her, but Celadon didn't think it would,* Frost interpreted, and was startled by how certain she was that she was right.

Celadon sat there in silence until Frost's scales prickled with nerves. Then Celadon bared her fangs and said, "This is none of Emerald Twilight's concern."

Frost conquered the urge to leap up and bare her own fangs at Tempest, but it wasn't easy.

Tempest's eyes narrowed in a glare. "Since the Fell are attacking the eastern Reaches, it has become my concern."

Pearl flicked her spines again, in agreement so polite Frost suspected it meant something else entirely. "Emerald Twilight has so many concerns, it must be a trial to keep up with them."

Tempest transferred her glare from Celadon to Pearl.

Flame leaned forward. "Wait, what happened?"

Her voice tinged with acid, Pearl said, "It's common knowledge that Opal Night's eastern colony was attacked, and that Malachite returned here with the survivors to seize control of the mother colony after she destroyed the Fell flight. But the Fell had performed this 'trick,' as Emerald Twilight calls it, on their prisoners, and Malachite rescued the children as well."

Flame exchanged a look with Zephyr, and asked, "But this doesn't affect the royal bloodlines of either Indigo Cloud or Opal Night?"

"It does not," Celadon said, her gaze not leaving Tempest.

Flame sat back, her brow furrowed. Zephyr said, "This is strange to hear. But is Emerald Twilight suggesting that this is the reason for the Fell attack?"

Tempest looked as if she wanted to suggest it, but couldn't justify it. She said, "It needs to be discussed, and Opal Night and Indigo Cloud have given no sign they intended to reveal that it had happened."

Celadon said, "It is no one else's concern."

Pearl said, "No, if Emerald Twilight wishes to discuss it, we should discuss it. Let's put off any decisions on how to meet the Fell attack, of what preparations our Arbora should make, of where to station our warriors—"

Tempest's spines trembled and the expression she turned on Pearl made Frost want to hiss.

Zephyr tilted her head, but she was smiling. She said, "That's told us." As Pearl and Tempest tilted their heads toward her, she said, "Perhaps it's best to return to the discussion of whether to meet the Fell outside the Reaches or not."

Frost was listening so intently she didn't realize the sound echoing up from the greeting hall was noisier than it should be. Heart and Bell twitched uneasily, Bone cocked his head to listen, frowning, and Knell half-turned away, as if he meant to stand.

Then Aura shot up over the edge of the hall and landed on the floor. Floret's expression was horrified. This was a huge breach of etiquette. But Aura shifted to groundling and blurted, "Pearl, I'm sorry to interrupt, but Malachite is here."

Celadon looked startled and hopeful, and Pearl's spines flicked in agitation. She said, "In the greeting hall with her warriors?"

Aura said, "Yes, I mean, I think she's right behind—"

Then a great dark shape flung itself over the edge and onto the hall floor. Aura skittered out of the way as Malachite strode forward.

Frost stared. She had been formally presented to Malachite when the Opal Night queen had stopped here on her way to join Jade and Moon, but this was a shock. This Malachite was a completely different person than the one who had sat in the nurseries with fledglings curled around her arms and Arbora babies playing with her tail.

Pearl and the other queens stood. Pearl's spines were tense as she said, "What news of Jade? She's with you?"

Malachite paced forward. "No, but I left her well."

Pearl's spines twitched in relief, and Frost bounced excitedly. If Jade was well, all the others must be all right too.

But Malachite said, "I returned because the Fell are massing in the wetlands to the east, preparing to come here. There are at least five flights so far, perhaps one more."

Bell gasped, and the other Arbora growled. Frost felt a snarl build up in her chest, squelching the first wave of panic.

"You've seen the Fell for yourself?" Flame sounded aghast. "The auguries were true?"

"I have. I—" Malachite's gaze fell on Tempest, and she stopped.

Celadon looked from Malachite to Tempest, and her spines twitched in alarm. "Malachite—" she began.

Malachite said, "Emerald Twilight has no place here."

Tempest's spines flared. "We are the chief court of the eastern Reaches. The defense of this territory has always fallen—"

Malachite stepped forward, and was suddenly a pace from Tempest, towering over her. Frost stared, wide-eyed. She hadn't even seen Malachite move. The Opal Night warriors tensed, looking to Celadon for orders. The Emerald Twilight warriors twitched nervously. The others, Sunset Water and Ocean Winter and Indigo Cloud all looked at Floret. Floret's expression was appalled.

Malachite snarled, "Go back and tell your birthqueen to send another daughter. You insult me and this court with your presence."

"You don't command me," Tempest snarled back, but Frost thought it was an effort for her to keep her spines up. It wasn't fear, or not all fear. It was as if Malachite was doing something that was forcing Tempest back . . .

Malachite bared an impressive array of fangs and Frost's heart thumped.

Then Pearl shoved Tempest away and stepped in front of Malachite. Spines flared, she snarled, "Not here. Not now."

Frost's insides seized up, her throat closed on a squeak of alarm. Bell grabbed her arm, bracing to snatch her out of danger. The Indigo Cloud warriors all twitched in reaction; Floret held up a hand, the gesture telling them to hold back, her snarl soundless. Bone, Knell, and Heart all rocked up into a crouch, bracing to defend Pearl.

Malachite stared down at Pearl long enough for Frost's lungs to run out of air. Malachite didn't loom over Pearl the way she had Tempest, but she was taller than Pearl, her shoulders broader, her whole body more powerful.

Then Malachite whipped away, turning to face the wall.

Everyone flinched except Pearl. She tilted her head toward Tempest and bared her fangs. Tempest bared hers back, but briefly, then paced away to stand with Zephyr. Celadon took a step away, her spines rippling to shed tension. Pearl said, "Emerald Twilight will stay."

Then Malachite turned back to face Pearl and said, "We have a few days, maybe more, to prepare. You mean to meet them in the open?"

Bone hissed out a breath in relief, and Heart and Knell sank back onto their cushions. Bell squeezed Frost's wrist and relaxed. Frost started to breathe again.

As if nothing had happened, Pearl said, "Yes, that was my intention." She turned and walked back deliberately to her cushion and took an unhurried seat, her tail curling around her feet. "We were discussing it just now."

Zephyr and Flame sat down again, then Tempest, who was doing a good job of keeping her spines neutral, though she couldn't quite stop her tail from snapping. One of the Opal Night warriors brought a cushion for Malachite, putting it next to Celadon. Celadon sat, and then Malachite took her seat, as unhurriedly as Pearl had.

Pearl glanced at Floret. Floret took a deep breath, then moved to the hearth. She poured a cup of tea, carried it over and set it in front of Malachite, then retreated to the other warriors. Sage and Drift stared at her in admiration.

Mostly still unruffled, Zephyr said, "With only a few days to prepare, I don't see how we can meet them in the Reaches. It will be quicker to assemble our warriors in the fringe."

Flame said, "Ocean Winter agrees."

They were looking at Tempest. She flicked a spine, but said, "The presence of the Fell in the wetlands presents a compelling argument for swift movement. If the other queens are in agreement, then Emerald Twilight will support this plan."

Malachite's claws contracted, but she didn't otherwise react.

Frost could sense the Arbora holding their breath, but instead of poking Tempest again, Pearl just turned to Bone and said, "We have a hunting shelter close to the fringe that can be used as a resting point, if it can be made ready quickly enough."

"It can be done," Bone said. His voice came out even and calm, but Frost could see the pulse still racing at his throat. "With a group of thirty or so Arbora, we can dig out more shelters and supply it for our warriors. There are other usable platforms nearby."

Zephyr settled herself more comfortably on her cushion. "We should have several resting points, at intervals. Is there a map?"

Floret jerked her head at Coil, who leapt to fetch the map and carry it to Zephyr. Frost saw Vine take a deep breath and lean against Sage, who shook his head incredulously. Heart rubbed her face, and reached for the forgotten pot to refill the Arbora's cups. Bell gave Frost a one-armed hug and she had to fight down the impulse to climb into his lap. If she did that, Pearl would never think she was old enough to attend a meeting again, not until Frost was older than Jade.

Celadon watched Malachite carefully, and after a moment Malachite picked up the tea cup and drank. Celadon reached over and squeezed Malachite's free wrist.

Frost tried to pay attention for the rest of the meeting, but after that, it was almost dull, with all the talk being about how many warriors would go where and when, and what the Arbora needed to do to prepare.

Finally the talk was finished. Zephyr and Flame and Tempest would leave immediately to go to their courts and pass the alarm, and get their warriors ready. When they had left the queens' hall, Malachite turned to Pearl and said, "I have much to tell you and Celadon and it must be done in private."

Pearl flicked her spines in acknowledgement. "We'll go to my bower. We won't be overheard there."

Celadon said, "If food could be brought . . ."

"Of course." Pearl made a gesture to the Arbora, as she got to her feet.

As Celadon led Malachite away and the Opal Night warriors followed Floret, Knell leaned over to Bell, and whispered, "Food is a good idea. I don't know what that was about, but the long flight probably didn't help."

Bell nodded grimly, and waved Coil over to ask him to take the request down to the teachers' hall. As the Arbora got to their feet, Frost went to where Pearl stood by the hearth. Pearl absently looked down at the map, flicking her spines. Frost wrapped her hand around Pearl's much bigger wrist. Pearl glanced down at her, spines and brow quirked in inquiry. Frost said, "I thought you were going to fight Malachite."

Pearl flicked a spine dismissively. "We're not friends, but our primary bloodlines are blended in Jade and Moon's royal clutch. We can't fight."

Maybe, but Frost knew from everyone else's reaction that something terrible might have happened. She said, "You can't fight Tempest either, because of Ember."

"No matter how tempting," Pearl agreed.

Heart stepped up beside them, and Frost took her wrist too. Still looking at the map, Pearl said, "You should be down there telling the others to prepare."

"In a moment," Heart said. "What did Tempest do? Why did Malachite react like that?"

Now that Heart mentioned it, Frost wondered about it too. Tempest had been mad about Shade and Lithe coming to Indigo Cloud, which was none of her business, but Malachite hadn't been here when Tempest had said that.

Pearl's spines tilted in exasperation. "Tempest took Moon to Opal Night, when Malachite wanted him returned to her. There was some incident before the greeting took place, and Onyx, Malachite's sister queen, ordered Tempest to leave the court at her consort's request. It was done in a hurry, before Malachite had a chance to get scent of it and make it worse. So I suppose she's been saving that up since then."

Heart hissed out a breath. "That's not good, Pearl."

Pearl tilted her head at her. "It's entertaining, but you're right, the courts can't afford these quarrels now."

"That's bad, getting thrown out of a court," Frost said. It was mildly amazing to her that fully grown queens could still do things that got them in trouble. And not made-to-feel-guilty-by-Arbora trouble but serious fight-with-another-queen trouble.

"I suspect being thrown out of Opal Night is more common than not." Pearl gave Frost a nudge. "Now go with Heart and Bell. It's time you were back in the nurseries."

Near the Southern Coast and the Cloudwalls

Now Moon and Stone had a kethel flying with them. Moon was trying not to think about what Jade would say about their choices and ability to make decisions and sense of survival. It didn't help that he agreed with her.

With the Hians' boat not far ahead, they flew through the day and late into the night, stopping only briefly to rest. The kethel kept pace with them easily, but having followed kethel before, Moon was unsurprised. It wasn't like rulers or a progenitor would have had a great deal of concern for the kethels' wellbeing. They probably killed the ones who couldn't keep up and used them to feed the rest of the flight. He had seen a Fell nest made with part of a kethel's carcass once, and for the first time wondered how that would affect a thinking being. He doubted it was done with the same reverence as when Reaches Raksura placed their dead in pockets in a colony tree so the wood would eventually grow around them.

It gave him something to think about on the long flight at least. The terrain below was starting to flatten out, the hills softening into long rises and shallow valleys, with clusters of tall fringe trees and other foliage so thick along the occasional meandering streams that it nearly concealed the sparkle of moving water from view. The wind was only a little cooler, but it carried the faint distant scent of the sea.

It was the next morning, at first lightening of the sky, when Stone suddenly slipped off the wind and fell sideways toward the ground. Moon almost fouled a wing in surprise, thinking Stone had passed out. But as he came around, he saw Stone control the fall with one economical flap and come in for a neat landing near a big stand of trees.

Moon dove down to light beside him as Stone shifted to groundling. "What is it?" he demanded. Once on the ground, he realized the stand of trees, their purple-gray trunks entwined like huge vines, seemed to be independently mobile and watching them with little round dark spots that were probably eyes. Moon tasted the air, but picked up no traces of predator musk. Still, this was not a place that Stone would have normally chosen to stop at. "Are you all right?"

Stone jerked his head toward the south, as the kethel dropped into the tall grass about forty paces away and shifted to its groundling form. "I spotted a flying boat ahead. Didn't want them to see us. If they've got those distance-glasses, they might be able to pick us up, even this far away."

Moon hissed, startled. After all this searching, they might finally have found their goal. "Could you tell if it was the Hians?"

The kethel approached, throwing a wary glance toward the tree-creature. It looked like it was farming fungi and other crops on its own branches. Moon still kept one eye on it, just in case it decided to object to their proximity.

Stone snorted in exasperation. "Not yet. We're going to have to hang way back, and try to catch up after dark."

"I told you the truth," the kethel said pointedly.

Stone eyed it. "So you did. Let's see what you can do to earn your next story."

Bramble didn't remember much of what happened next. She came back to herself lying on the padded bench in Delin's room, tucked into blankets, with Delin sitting on a stool beside her. She said, "Merit?"

"He is well," Delin said. "The hull protected him, and he was not affected as you were."

She squeezed her eyes shut, and remembered she had asked him that before. Several times before. She opened her eyes and shoved herself upright. Delin almost fell off his stool, startled. He said, "You are better?"

"Yes." Bramble ran a hand through her hair. Her scalp itched with sweat, and she could tell from the way her shirt stuck unpleasantly to her skin that she had been lying here inert for some time, at least a day. Maybe more than two days. She remembered the Fell. "Did Aldoan figure out how to make the artifact kill the Fell? Did it kill all the Fell? Do the Fell have the artifact? I can tell we're stopped, are we where we were going, did you find out?"

Delin buried his face in his hands. "Oh, Bramble, I feared you were lost to us."

Bramble stared at him, and it dawned on her how exhausted he looked. She remembered again that he wasn't just a funny-looking Arbora who couldn't shift. He was a groundling who wouldn't get stronger as he got older. She pulled him half onto the bench in an awkward hug. "I'm sorry I scared you."

"As if it was your fault." He pulled away, wiping his eyes on his sleeve. "Aldoan is dead. The Fell were all killed, or fled. Vendoin went down with some others in their levitation packs and retrieved the artifact, and Aldoan's body, but she did not bring back with her the scholar she said they had stopped there to meet. They do not know why the artifact worked; they found it still in Aldoan's hands, and no marks of injury on her body. We traveled for three days at speed and we stopped here late this afternoon. They asked me to help them make the artifact work, and said if I did not, they would injure you and Merit. I said I would help them."

"Right." Bramble took it all in. Aldoan, who had always seemed so uncomfortable with the role of captor, had somehow made the artifact work, and died for it. "Are we near the foundation builder place where the rest of the weapon is supposed to be?"

"We must be, but no one has come to take me there." Delin lifted his hands. "I am glad of the respite, for time to think of some way out of this."

Bramble rolled her shoulders, shifted to make certain she could, then shifted back to her soft-skinned form. "We need to go back to the original plan."

Delin nodded. "Which one was that?"

"The one I didn't tell you about." She took a sharp breath. The one that probably wasn't survivable, at least for her. "The one where you distract the healer, while I get into her room and find a poison."

The Court of Indigo Cloud

"You promised them what?" Pearl said to Malachite. "Have you lost your mind?"

Ember controlled a wince. He saw Celadon, seated across the hearth, confine her reaction to a blink. Crouched on the fur beside him, Heart let out a near-silent breath that might have been a repressed hiss. Bell twitched and Knell went still. Bone's sigh was more annoyed than anything else.

Malachite didn't move a spine. She said, "I value your plain-speaking."

"Are you trying to be funny?" Pearl said.

They were in Pearl's bower, with only the two reigning queens, Celadon, and the Arbora present. Floret and Vine were casually loitering outside the bower's doorway, making sure no one else came near enough to overhear. Ember had been a little horrified at the idea of having a private meeting with such a prominent queen in Pearl's bower; he was glad the Arbora had already come through this morning and taken the blankets to air, and rearranged the cushions and the kettle, pot, and tea cups for maximum effect. But having heard what Malachite had wanted to tell Pearl, Ember was glad of the privacy and the precautions. The other news that Malachite had brought had been horrifying enough: Song dead, and Bramble and Merit taken captive by groundlings.

Pearl continued, "You've promised these half-Fell a home in the Reaches. How am I supposed to convince the other queens to allow this?"

"I haven't promised it yet, but I will," Malachite said. She was as still as the statue above the queens' hall, but Ember wasn't reassured by that. Her stillness felt unpredictable, like a predator that could change its mind and strike at any moment. The fact that Pearl was utterly indifferent to the effect was not reassuring. Malachite added, "And you've handled the other queens well so far."

Pearl tilted her head, clearly suspecting irony. "Gathering together to fight off a Fell attack is one thing. They would have to be idiots not to agree to act."

Celadon leaned forward. "We need the help of the Fellborn queen. If we can find out which progenitor is leading the others, it could save many lives—"

"You don't need to explain your mad plan to me." Pearl's spines almost rattled in frustration. She said to Malachite, "You realize I am ill-suited to this role that you've foisted on me. The other queens dislike me almost as much as I dislike them."

"You are better suited to it than I am." This time Malachite did move a spine, and Ember was a little astonished to read amusement in it.

"A rock is better suited than you are." Pearl coiled her tail around, considering the problem. "We need to speak to Zephyr first. Sunset Water has the closest old bloodline ties to us and she is not unreasonable."

Malachite said, "You dislike her less than the others."

Ember bit his lip to hold back an involuntary and undignified facial expression. The Arbora controlled their reactions well, though Ember thought he heard a suspiciously sharp exhalation from Knell. This whole situation was terrifying. Malachite had seen the Fell flights gathering in the wetlands outside the Reaches. It was real, it was happening, it was no longer just a vision. What Pearl and Malachite decided here might save or doom so many courts in the eastern Reaches. So much depended on the cooperation of two queens not known for cooperating with anybody, including their own bloodlines.

It should have been a disaster, except Pearl and Malachite seemed to be getting along fine.

Pearl's eyes narrowed. "I may need something to make our alliance stronger. Zephyr's intimated that another bloodline alliance with us to strengthen the previous one would be welcomed. Our royal fledglings and the Sky Copper clutch are too young to decide what they want to eat, let alone choose future mates."

Ember cleared his throat gently, and Pearl flicked her claws toward him. He said, "Sunset Water has two unattached daughter queens. There's a secondary bloodline with at least two consorts just reaching maturity, and maybe one more soon."

Malachite lifted a claw toward Celadon, who said, "We have several unattached consorts and queens in Opal Night, including myself and Ivory, a daughter queen of Onyx's bloodline. We can agree to open negotiations on that point."

Malachite said, "This privilege would extend only to Sunset Water." Pearl's spine flick of acknowledgement was unconcerned. Ember breathed easier now that that was settled. Then Malachite said, "I know you didn't want Shade and Lithe to enter Indigo Cloud, that it was your consort's intervention that allowed them in."

Ember froze. Malachite hadn't glanced in his direction once but he suddenly felt as if he was a grasseater surrounded by predators. Heart hissed in a breath and Bone, Bell, and Knell went still. Celadon's glance at Malachite was a combination of appalled and annoyed.

Pearl was the only one unperturbed. She said, "I know you know. I didn't want the last consort of your bloodline in my court either, and look where that got me."

Bone made a muffled noise and covered his face with his hands. Everyone else was still frozen.

Malachite moved that one spine again to the slight angle that just might be indicating amusement, but she kept her gaze locked on Pearl. Finally Pearl made an annoyed hiss. She said, "I don't like surprises. Bone, the one groaning under his breath over there, will attest to that. Next time you want to fundamentally change the nature of Raksuran life in the Reaches, have your warriors bring me a letter first and give me time to think about it."

The silence stretched. Then Malachite said, "Agreed."

Ember took a much needed breath, and he saw Heart squeeze her eyes shut in relief. Continuing on as if nothing had happened, Malachite said, "Will you be able to deal with the Fellborn queen?"

"Oh, I'm well used to being forced into decisions against my own better judgment." Pearl flicked her claws. "It will all be for nothing if your mad plan doesn't work."

There might have been a tinge of irony in Malachite's voice. "It isn't my mad plan. It was the Fellborn queen's."

Pearl snorted. "I'm sure she thinks it is."

Chapter Fourteen

The sun was setting and the wind carried the scent of the sea when Moon and Stone reached the flying boat.

They took cover in the cliffs above the wide sweep of a bay. Huddled behind a crag of rock, craning his neck to get a view of the shore, Moon said, "At least it's not another sealed city."

A metal ruin stretched from the beach at the cliffs' base out into the shallow water. Tall skinny pylons of different heights supported a series of metal rings, some connected by narrow girders. The metal was dark with age, covered by verdigris, and parts had broken away. Below, stairs led up from the sand to a great stone causeway, a couple of hundred paces wide at least, that extended out into the bay. The pylons that supported it stood in the water or were planted atop rocky outcrops, the waves swirling around them. The causeway was clearly meant to lead to some enormous structure, but nothing was left of it. The end was sheared off and hung out over the empty bay.

Their quarry was suspended in the air above the beach, just to the right of the ruin. The cloudwall loomed on the horizon, wreathed with concealing clouds; there were blue shapes just barely visible that might be mountain peaks, but that was the only discernible detail.

Stone climbed up beside Moon, the gray of his groundling form blending into the rock. He said, "Whatever they're looking for, it's got to be up in these cliffs."

"Maybe," Moon said. Gaps in the cliff face above the beach held collapsed walls, bridges, terraces, and ruined buildings. But Moon didn't see any sign that the Hians had sent out exploring parties. "Or underwater, a part of the ruin that fell into the bay."

Their kethel had landed some distance below them and shifted to its groundling form. It huddled in between the rocks, its gaze going from the Hian boat to Moon and Stone, as if it was wondering what they were going to do. Moon was wondering that himself.

Moon turned and slid down a little, looking out over the shallow valley behind the cliff. There wasn't much sign of current or ancient habitation among the tall grasses and marshy ponds. The only thing Moon could see that might indicate more ruins were tall mounds of dirt, too rounded to be natural.

Moon doubted the Hians would come out of their boat to explore now, with the shadows lengthening toward evening. His first impulse was to attack at once, before the Hians had a chance to do whatever they had come here to do. But the Kishan fire weapon emplacements and the smaller handheld versions the crew would undoubtedly be armed with were a problem he couldn't figure any way around.

Below in the valley one of the mounds shuddered and began to drag itself slowly through the tall grass. A flurry of flying creatures, either large insects or lizards, fluttered into the air, apparently coming out of openings in the moving mound. Some settled back atop its surface, others circled above it. Moon nudged Stone. "What's that?"

Stone turned to look, and shrugged. "I've seen smaller ones, back towards the Reaches. The flying things nest inside the big living rock thing. I don't know if they're supposed to be in there, or if they're parasites."

Moon flicked his spines. Either possibility was creepy, though since Raksura made their colonies inside living mountain-trees, he supposed he couldn't object. "We can't wait for the others. We don't know how far they are behind us, or if they got our messages."

Stone grimaced. "I know that." After a moment he added, "Maybe we could talk the kethel into drawing their fire."

The kethel looked toward them, its big brow furrowed.

Moon didn't think the kethel was that stupid. And they just couldn't trust it for a vital role in their plan. "The Hians wouldn't have to use fire. They've got that weapon." He didn't want to end up in pieces, like the Fell in the river trading town.

But Stone was right, they did need a distraction. Moon looked at the big insects again, buzzing in a lazy circle above their hosts. Another mound rippled awake, disgorged another burst of insects, then started to move ponderously toward the streams and marshes at the far end of the valley. Others slowly began to follow. The swarm of disturbed insect-lizards was like a huge dark cloud, big enough for at least two Raksura to get lost in, easily. It was too bad it wasn't on the other side of the cliff, down on the beach. "What do those things eat?" Not the hosts, or the creatures would be devoured by now. "Why are they in this valley?"

Stone's brow furrowed, and he turned to regard the swarm. "Not grasseaters. There's none near here. Probably bugs, since they come out at night. Probably have to fly around to all the marshes to get enough."

Moon considered. "I wonder if they'd want bug paste." They still had the packet of it from the swampling city.

Stone tilted his head. "There's a thought."

Bramble braced herself as Delin banged on the door of his cage. One of the Hians opened it. Delin said, "She is awake, and I need to take her to the physician."

The Hian said, "She should stay here."

Delin gestured in frustration. "The physician must examine her before she collapses again!"

Bramble choked out a moan and clutched her stomach, letting herself half-fall against the wall. The Hian stared at her, then stared at Delin. Delin said, "You saw what happened to Aldoan. The effect may be delayed. Bramble could die."

The Hian hesitated, then gestured for them to follow her down the corridor. The other Hian on watch at their door followed.

When Bramble had first seen the hanging waterskins in the healer's room, she had committed all the labels to memory. She had written them down on a piece of paper from Delin's small stock and fortunately he had recognized the glyphs. He said, "This is a variant of the scholar's notation of Kedmar, that is used in the library." He tapped one. "From the indicators for predator and eradication, I surmise this one could be the simple we know as Fell poison. But this one has indicators for liquid and danger. It's the only one with such a notation." He met her gaze, his expression serious. "That's the one we need."

Bramble held that image in her memory as they approached the healer's room. "Is she there?" Delin called out. "If she is not there, we will wait inside. Bramble can't walk back and forth in this condition!"

Exasperated, one of the Hians said, "You were the one who wanted her to walk here in the first place—"

As Bramble had hoped, the healer stepped out into the corridor. "What's wrong?" She was clearly startled to see Bramble on her feet. "Are you better? You should be lying down."

"I wanted you to examine her," Delin said as they reached the doorway. "She seems much better, but has strange pains."

Bramble gripped the door frame, screwing her face up into a grimace as if she was about to be sick. "Can I sit down?"

The healer motioned to her. "Yes, go ahead—"

"Perhaps it's the weather here," Delin said. "I confess, I have felt lately as if the air is thick and difficult to breathe." As the healer turned toward him, clearly alarmed by that statement, Bramble slipped inside the room and sat down heavily on the bench. The waterskins hadn't been moved, and her heart thumped in relief. Delin stepped sideways and the healer moved with him, trying to peer into his eyes. As the healer's back blocked the doorway from view, Bramble leapt across to the waterskins.

Bramble found the one Delin had chosen and took it down. She sniffed the bone cap and got a trace of acridity but no definite odor. *This has to be right.*

Bramble pressed the skin to her stomach, steeled herself, and shifted. She took the bag with her, the way she could take clothing and jewelry. She had never carried something as big as the waterskin with her through a shift. It caused a distinctly odd warm sensation in her chest. She took a sharp breath and stepped out into the corridor.

The startled healer blinked down at Bramble's scaled form. The other Hians tensed warily, and one half-lifted her fire weapon. Bramble said to the healer, "I feel better this way, not as sick."

"Ah, I suppose that makes sense—" the healer began.

Delin cried out, staggered sideways, and collapsed against the nearest Hian. She tried to catch him but he jerked out of her hold and fell to the floor. He clutched his chest, his eyes rolling back in his head, and jerked his legs as if having a seizure. Trying to get to him, the healer shoved past the other Hians. With their attention diverted, Bramble said, "I'll get help!" and darted down the corridor.

She was lucky that the healer's room was near the stern of the ship. She dropped down the nearest stairwell, heard voices in the corridor, and jumped up to flatten herself against the stem-like beam that crossed the ceiling. She pressed against the moss and didn't breathe as two Hians passed beneath her. She couldn't tell if she was just imagining the waterskin's phantom weight against her scales. She hoped the fact that it was poison wouldn't affect her. Though if it did, there was so much of it, surely she would have dropped dead by now.

The Hians turned into another corridor and Bramble dropped soundlessly to the floor. She skittered around the next two turns, took refuge in an empty room when someone else passed, and made it down the next stairwell.

She avoided the heavily guarded corridor that led down to Merit's cage. She needed a big distraction before she could get him out, though if they were lucky the poison would work fast enough to provide that.

If this boat was like Callumkal's, then the cistern was down a level in a supply hold. Bramble rounded the next corner.

That was when a Hian stepped out of a doorway halfway down the corridor. She was facing away, still sliding the door closed. She wasn't wearing a fire weapon. Bramble bounded forward and leapt.

The Hian turned toward her but didn't have a chance to make more than a strangled yell before Bramble slammed into her. Bramble ripped her claws across the Hian's head and felt them glance off the armor plate. Unexpectedly strong hands clawed at her face, and Bramble stabbed her claws into the Hian's neck. Blood bubbled up and the Hian gasped, the breath strangled in her ruined throat.

The Hian went limp and Bramble let the body drop. She tilted her head to listen. No running footsteps sounded from nearby corridors. The moss walls tended to dampen noise, and there must be no one near enough to hear. Bramble twitched away the blood on her claws and thought, *I need to hurry*.

She pulled the body into a cabin, slid the door closed, and hurried on. Hopefully no one would notice the blood on the soft cork floor, at least not right away. At the next junction she found the narrow stairs down to the lower level. At the bottom was a corridor with a low ceiling, with larger stem-beams. Just like Callunkal's boat, this was the hold, where the supplies were stored.

Bramble pushed open the first sliding door and slipped inside. The space was dark, crammed with ceramic containers and bundles and boxes, and it smelled grainy and of sweet greens and earthy roots. The smell was enough like the storage chambers in the Indigo Cloud colony tree that homesickness pierced Bramble's heart like a claw. She passed it all by, heading toward the cold wet scent toward the far end.

The big ceramic cistern held the water supply, and also rainwater from collectors that ran up to the top of the flying boat. It had a hatch to the outside where it could be filled and drained. Pipes ran from it to the water flushes in the ship's latrines and the drinking water taps in the cabins. Bramble knew all about it from helping fill the one on Callumkal's boat.

She opened the small cover in the top that allowed the water to be checked for freshness, then shifted to her groundling form. To her relief, the waterskin was still intact, still heavy with the poison.

She pulled the stopper out and dumped the clear liquid into the water. The healer was the only one she regretted, but then the healer was the one who had probably made the poisons Vendoin had used on everyone on the sunsailer.

She hoped Vendoin and Bemadin died in pain.

As she closed the cover, the pipes whooshed as someone used one of the water sources somewhere in the ship. *That's that,* Bramble thought.

She rolled up the empty skin and hid it under a pile of bags, then slipped back out of the hold to the corridor. She leaned against the door, bracing herself. Now she needed to try to release Merit. If there were too many Hians blocking her way to him . . .

Let's see how much damage I can do before they catch me, Bramble thought, and crept up the corridor.

After Moon made a couple of brief experiments, it became obvious that a number of the insect-lizards liked the bug paste enough to follow it anywhere. Fortunately they were indifferent to Raksura in either form, and didn't seem to notice Moon or Stone except to zip out of their way at the last instant. They were only about as long as Moon's forearm, and their mouths were small furry scoops meant for inhaling small bugs, but there were hundreds of them and in combination their tiny sharp claws could have done some damage had they been so inclined.

Watching their preparations in the gathering darkness, the kethel followed Moon and Stone down to the valley. Plowing through the high grass behind them in its groundling form, it asked, "What do I do?"

"Stay back and don't eat anybody," Stone told it.

It didn't seem satisfied with that, but didn't object.

Once night settled over the valley, Moon took flight toward the Hians' boat. He carried Stone in his groundling form, and Stone carried the packet of paste.

A cloud of the insect-lizards followed them up and over the rocks toward the beach, their buzz and whir a dull roar easily covering the sound of Moon's wingbeats.

The bright beams of the distance-lights were created by the same moss that kept the boat aloft and made the Kishan's other tools work. The two lights on the starboard side moved in slow patterns over the cliffs and beach, and the two on the port side crossed the sky, watching for anything approaching by air.

Moon had memorized the pattern earlier, and went down the cliff face to the beach in a series of controlled drops, careful not to outpace their insect escort. He and Stone huddled behind a rock at the edge of the beach as the cloud clustered around them, and one insect-lizard landed on Moon's head. The boat's distance-light passed over them, then hesitated and returned. Stone, jammed between Moon and the rock, breathed, "Don't move."

Moon managed not to, even with the damn insect nuzzling one of his frills. The light made the cloud buzz around even more wildly. Then the beam moved on, the two Raksura hidden by dark rock and silver sand and the flitter of hundreds of iridescent wings.

One distance-light moved down the beach and the other swept over the waves. Moon tightened his hold on Stone and leapt into the air.

That created a vulnerable moment when the rush of air from his wings caused the insects to drop back, but they caught up with him again.

Moon had gauged his angle of approach carefully, and came up under the flying boat's stern. As the next roving distance-light swept past it caught only the cloud of insects trailing him.

Stone was strong enough to hold on to Moon's collar flanges without help, so Moon had both hands free to catch hold of the thick wiry moss of the boat's hull. The boat was stable in the air, and the moss absorbed sound and vibration, so he knew no one had felt his landing.

Stone freed one hand to carefully smear the packet of paste onto the moss, then Moon climbed up the hull away from the now very excited cluster of insects. He stopped well below the boat's rail, and Stone swung around to grip the moss. It made Moon nervous; Stone's groundling form was strong, but it wasn't as if he had claws. "You've got it?" he said, keeping his voice below a bare whisper.

"Yeah, go." Stone started to haul himself up the hull toward the rail.

Moon climbed away toward the bow. He heard a couple of Hians move along the deck, but their steps weren't hurried.

The steering cabin on this boat was in the center section, lifted above the hull to look down on the bow deck, with two levels of wide windows. One small distance-light lit the bow.

The idea was for Moon to look for the prisoners in the front part of the boat and Stone the back, and Moon hung just below the railing, trying to decide how best to get into the cabins. There were no windows in the lower hull, like there had been on Callumkal's flying boat. He sensed movement on the deck and realized he had come too far forward. He swung sideways, then hissed as a flash of bright light blinded him.

Above, someone called out in alarm and more voices echoed her. Moon's luck had just run out. He could have dropped off the boat but getting back up to it without the insect-lizard cloud as cover would be impossible; Stone would be on his own.

Moon made the decision in a heartbeat. If he couldn't help search for the prisoners, he could provide a distraction.

He swung over the railing, shifted in mid-motion, and landed as a groundling in the center of the light on the open deck. As he stood up out of a crouch he heard shouts and startled footsteps outside the circle of illumination. He could just make out the open galleries on either side of the raised steering cabin that would make good vantage points for the Hians. If someone shot him with a fire weapon, this was going to be a short distraction. The weapons had to shoot a small wooden disk first, that allowed the fire to find its target, so Moon would have some warning. If they used the artifact weapon on him, he suspected there would be no warning at all.

Then from somewhere above him, Vendoin's voice spoke in Altanic, "Moon. I didn't expect to see you. I assume the others are with you?"

"I thought you assumed the Fell ate us?" Moon replied in the same language. He placed her location in the steering cabin near a side window or door.

"The moss told us the sunsailer reached the shallows. The others are with you, then?" There was a trace of what might be impatience in her voice. Maybe she didn't want to talk about the chaos of her retreat from the sunsailer.

"They sent me ahead to talk." He knew she wouldn't believe that he was alone, so there was no point in trying to convince her of it.

"That seems unlikely, to me. I know how your queen prizes you."

Moon bared his teeth briefly. "Well, you never really knew us at all, did you. Just like we never knew you."

The silence lasted a beat longer than Moon expected. "So what did your queen send you to say?"

"You didn't talk to the Bikuru who lived near the Hian scholar in the river trade town. They had her maps and writing. Now we have them." If his and Stone's theory was wrong, and Vendoin had been able to find whatever she had wanted in the scholar's house, this was probably the point where Moon would get burned alive.

This time the silence stretched. The lights had drawn swarms of tiny nightbugs, and the insect-lizards from the mounds zipped around just out of range of the illumination. The air was humid and sweat stuck Moon's shirt to his back. His night vision was ruined by the lights, but he tracked the position of the armed Hians watching him from the deck and the platforms off the cabin above by their breathing and the way their bodies blocked the breeze.

Then a door opened in the side of the steering cabin. Vendoin's voice said, "Do not move, Moon. I would dislike killing you."

Moon snorted in derisive amusement. A group of Hians moved out onto the gallery, into the light. Moon had never seen so many handheld fire weapons, even when the Fell had attacked the sunsailer. He recognized Bemadin first, then Vendoin. Then his attention was riveted by the scent of nervous Raksura, and two more Hians dragged Merit forward.

He was in his groundling form. From the way his eyes blinked and his captors seemed to be holding him upright, Moon knew the damp patches on the front of his shirt must be Fell poison, recently forced down his throat. He couldn't see the scale pattern on Merit's skin, but the play of light and shadows might conceal it.

Merit trembled, watching Moon with wide eyes. Moon said, "Bramble, Delin, and Callumkal?"

"All alive and well," Vendoin said, before Merit could answer. "Please speak only Altanic. If you speak to each other in your own language I will have Merit killed."

So Bramble and the others were alive, but maybe not so well. In Altanic, Moon said, "Merit, are you and the others all right?"

"I don't know." His voice was hesitant and a little husky. "I don't know where Bramble is. I haven't seen Delin in—"

Vendoin interrupted, "That's enough."

Moon suppressed a snarl. He hoped that meant they had been held separately on the flying boat, and not that Bramble was dead.

Vendoin said, "Of course you don't have these hypothetical maps and papers with you?"

"Hypothetical?" Moon wondered if this was an attempt to test him. He thought the fact that no one had tried to take him prisoner yet was a good sign. "If you didn't want the scholar's writing why did you stop there to kill her?" He heard Bemadin's sharp breath, and other Hians glanced at Vendoin. He added, "Did you have to kill everyone in the house? The kids, too?"

Her voice tight and harsh, Vendoin said, "We did not kill them."

Another Hian moved uneasily, something uncertain in her body language. This was obviously a topic of some dismay among them. Either there had been disagreement over whether to kill the scholar or not, or . . . Maybe her and her children's deaths had been an accident, somehow. "They were pretty dead when we saw them," Moon said.

"It was unintentional," another Hian said. The Hian added, "I am Lavinat. You speak for the Raksura?"

"I speak for the Indigo Cloud Court, and the families of Delin-Evran-lindel of the Golden Isles and Callumkal of Kish-Jandera." It might help to remind the other Hians that it wasn't just them against the savage Raksura. "How do you unintentionally kill a whole house full of groundlings?"

Vendoin tried to answer and Lavinat spoke over her, "It was the weapon. I assume you know all about it."

Something about Lavinat made Moon wonder if it was still Vendoin who was in charge here. "I know it kills Fell. If that's what you want to do with it, it's none of our concern."

Her voice low, Bemadin said in Kedaic, "Don't bargain with him. They will kill us."

Vendoin ignored her. "Where are the papers you took from the scholar's home?"

"Her friend's home, the Bikuru," Moon corrected. He knew the Hians must have searched the scholar's house. "Stone has them."

Vendoin didn't seem surprised. "He will give them to us in exchange for you."

"Or you could use the weapon and take them off his body," Moon said.

Vendoin said, "We prefer not to waste the weapon."

Then Lavinat stepped forward. "You haven't asked us to release our captives yet. I find that very strange, that you stand here and bargain. As if you are waiting for something to happen."

There was a murmur of confusion from the other Hians.

Moon tilted his head. Lavinat was clever. That could be a problem. Footsteps ran frantically down a corridor somewhere behind the cabin, so it was time to end the conversation anyway. Bemadin glanced at Lavinat, and said, "What does that mean?"

Lavinat said, "It means he's trying to distract us."

Moon flung himself backward and shifted in one motion. Someone shouted and he bounced up off the bow deck just as the wooden disks from fire weapons landed beneath him. The fault of the weapon was that once the disk was fired, the wielder couldn't change the aim. Fire splashed on the deck, rippling across the soft surface as Moon landed on the platform next to the steering cabin. The Hians had already fled back inside, dragging Merit with them. Two armed with fire weapons still stood on the platform. Moon slammed one off, caught the other by the throat, ripped the weapon out of her hands, and tossed her over the side. Then he swung up on top of the cabin roof before any of the Hians inside had a chance to shoot at him.

The tricky part was not giving them time to threaten to kill Merit. Though shooting Merit without injuring any of the Hians near him would have been difficult anyway, as even the small fire weapons had never been meant for close quarters fighting.

Moon rolled across the cabin roof and braced himself on the edge. From here he had a view down into the open cubby against the boat's starboard side, the one that housed the distance-light and the large fire weapon, big enough to repel major kethel. The two Hians at the station looked outward, expecting another attack from the air.

Peripherally aware that a Hian had climbed to the top of a cabin toward the stern and was aiming another bulky fire weapon at him, Moon fit his claw into the first trigger of his stolen weapon and pulled. Wooden disks shot out of the nozzle and landed in the mossy material of the cubby, and on the big fire weapon. The two Hians looked up in horror as Moon hit the second trigger and fire streamed out.

Moon rolled away as the large fire weapon thumped and the whole boat jerked sideways, like a giant fist had punched it. *You can't let them hit each other*, a groundling had told him turns ago, on a trade road within the Kish border, when he had asked why the weapons guarding the camp were spaced so far apart, *nothing else can catch one on fire*. As the boat swung around, the Hian taking aim at him from the other cabin roof staggered and fell. She struck a lower platform railing before vanishing into the darkness on the port side.

Moon rolled back as smoke poured out of the hull. The cubby now hung sideways, connected only by a few broken stem-beams, and the steering cabin windows on that side were shattered. The two Hians in the cubby, their weapon, and the distance-light were nowhere to be seen. He shoved up to a crouch and by pure luck avoided a scatter of wooden disks that hit the spot where he had been lying. He grabbed the top frame of the broken window and swung around to flip himself through.

Moon landed on the steering cabin floor to see the Hians inside either ducking for cover or staring out the starboard window at what remained of the firing cubby. Merit huddled in the back corner, two Hians atop him, though Moon wasn't sure if they were pinning him there or had fallen on him when the weapon exploded.

He grabbed one by the shoulder and the other by the neck and flung them into the group on the far side of the cabin. In his peripheral vision he caught sight of Lavinat crumpled at the base of the wall, but he didn't see Vendoin. He snatched a fallen fire weapon from the floor as Merit flailed to stand. Then he grabbed Merit up and slammed through the door into the inner corridor.

Bramble had to cram herself into a storage cubby not much bigger than her body to hide from the searching Hians, but finally they moved on. She squirmed out, crept back down the stairwell and to the corridor where their cage was.

But when she reached it, it was unguarded and empty. *They moved Merit*, she thought, *obviously, you idiot*, and resisted the urge to rip at the walls. They would be using him as a hostage against her.

She went forward, back to where Delin's cage was. Maybe in the confusion he had been left with only one or two Hians to watch him. But she heard voices in the corridor ahead and hurriedly dropped down a narrow set of stairs. She found herself in a cramped, low-ceilinged corridor, with ceramic containers on either side that stunk so strongly of moss it blotted our every other scent.

She was trapped there for a little time, as Hians crossed back and forth through the stairwell just above. She hissed silently to herself, seething. The poison in the water was not working as quickly as she had hoped.

Then suddenly the whole boat bucked under her feet. Her shoulder hit a container and she bounced off and rolled on the floor. In the stairwell, Hians shouted in dismay and alarm, and their steps pounded away.

Bramble scrambled to her feet and climbed the stairs. The foyer and the connecting corridors were empty now, but she hesitated, unsure which way to go next. She heard a shout from her left and turned right to bolt down that corridor. A Hian shouted again from behind her and she heard the distinctive cough of a fire weapon.

Bramble dove forward and the disks hit the floor, but as she rolled away she caught sight of one stuck to her arm. Horrified, she clawed it off. The Hian strode forward, lifting the weapon.

Then something gray grabbed the Hian from behind. Bramble heard the snap as the Hian's neck broke before the limp body dropped to the floor. And she found herself staring at Stone.

All the breath left Bramble's body in a startled whoosh. His clothes were worn and stained and he smelled like dirt and sweat and home, and she thought she was hallucinating.

Delin peered out from behind him. His eyes were wild but determined. He whispered, "Bramble, we're escaping!"

Stone hissed, "Bramble, get over here!"

She shoved to her feet, staggered, and flung herself at Stone. He caught her, squeezed her briefly, and set her on her feet. "What—How—" she tried to ask. "You found us!"

"Now come on," he said, and he sounded just the way he always did, as if she was a baby playing too long in the nurseries and delaying a meal.

Light-headed with relief, Bramble caught Delin's wrist and followed Stone.

Moon dove down a stairwell and slammed aside two Hians at the bottom. This was an interior corridor with tightly woven moss walls, stem-like beams arching overhead, and light coming from gelatinous globes filled with glowing fluid mounted in ridges in the ceiling.

Merit clutched his collar flanges, gasping, "Moon, Bramble got away, she's somewhere in the boat, that's why they brought me up here, to threaten to kill me so they could catch her, but they couldn't find her—Delin is locked up somewhere—I don't know where Callumkal is—"

"Stone's here, looking for them," Moon told him. Shouting sounded from all directions and the stink of burned moss filled the air. He lifted the weapon and pointed it toward the end of the corridor and the steering cabin, then hit the first trigger to spray wooden disks. The second trigger sent fire streaming after them. It wasn't as good as a big fire weapon; the moss didn't seem to catch but singeing it filled the corridor with acrid smoke.

Merit clinging to him, Moon took the next cross corridor and slammed through the hatch at the end, out onto another platform. Moon turned to trigger the weapon again, aiming back through the hatchway. The burst of fire filled that corridor with smoke. He tried it again, but no more wooden disks came out.

Moon tossed the weapon over the rail and climbed up the wall, pausing at the top for a careful look across the cabin rooftops. No movement, and the remaining distance-light couldn't turn far enough to shine on this area. He slung himself and Merit atop the roof and started toward the stern.

They reached the end of the roof and Moon crouched to see over the edge. The distance-light and fire weapon platform was much lower down on the far end of the stern, and there was another cabin section in the way. If they were quiet, the Hians on that platform shouldn't hear them. He whispered to Merit, "They gave you Fell poison?" The light was bad but he still couldn't see scale markings on Merit's brown skin.

"A little," Merit whispered back. He shivered and wiped his mouth. "I don't think they realized how much I spit back up."

The sound of waves breaking on the beach and on the rocks under the metal causeway was louder. The explosion of the bow's fire weapon must have damaged whatever had held the boat steady on the lines of force that crossed the Three Worlds, and the crosswind had driven it out over the ruin. The hum of the insect-lizards rose, as those driven off by the explosion returned to the lure of the bug paste.

Moon growled under his breath. "Any time, Stone."

Merit whispered, "What are we waiting—" Below, a hatch opened under a stairwell landing. With a faint choked sound, a Hian flew out and over the deck railing, vanishing as she fell into the shadows. "Stone!" Merit gasped.

Moon tightened his grip on Merit and caught the edge of the roof. As three dark figures stepped onto the platform, he swung down to land beside them.

"I couldn't find Callumkal," Stone said. Bramble stood beside him in her scaled form, her spines twitching in agitation and the salty tang of fresh blood on her scales. She and Delin smelled like Merit, a bitter scent of captivity, of confinement and no access to fresh air.

Moon set Merit on his feet and the mentor grabbed Bramble in relief, and wrapped an arm around Delin to pull him into the embrace. The corridor behind them was dark; Stone must have been ripping the liquid lights out of the walls as he went along. Someone called in Kedaic and someone else called back, but it was muffled, at least a couple of corridors over. Stone was saying, "He's somewhere on the level below this one, I could scent him in the draft coming from that direction. The Hians cut off that stairwell and I didn't want to try to get past them with these two."

"We have to get the artifact too," Bramble said in a breathless rush. "I told Stone, it's a weapon, a bad one, worse than anything we thought—"

"Do you know where it is?" Moon asked.

Delin said, "Vendoin has it somewhere."

Stone asked them, "Can Vendoin use it on us?"

Bramble said, "Not yet, she doesn't know how, she has to take it somewhere."

That couldn't be right. Moon said, "But she used it on the Fell at that river town."

Bramble's spines flicked in an urgent negative. "No, Aldoan used it and died. The others don't know how she made it work!"

Moon hesitated. The artifact was important, but they couldn't leave without Callumkal. Moon had no intention of telling Kalam that they had left his father behind. He told Stone, "You take them, get out of here. I'll find Callumkal. Remember to stay away from the stern. That fire weapon can't turn far enough over this way."

Stone bared his teeth in frustration. "Get caught and I will come back and slap you unconscious."

"Right, because otherwise getting caught by these people sounds so attractive," Moon snarled.

Stone snarled back and jumped backward off the boat.

His scaled form flowed into being just in time to disappear into the haze of insect-lizards below. Moon told the others, "You're going to have to jump."

Delin made a faint noise in his throat, then croaked, "I see."

Merit told Delin, "It'll be all right, he'll catch us."

His voice tight, Delin added, "One of you will have to push me."

Moon caught his arm. "Just relax, it'll be fine."

Below, Stone's shape materialized out of the cloud of insects. As he turned sideways, Moon snapped, "Merit, now!"

Merit leapt off the platform. In the dark and the haze of insect movement, Moon didn't see Stone catch him. Several long heartbeats later Stone returned for a second pass with a lighter shape clinging just below his shoulder. "Bramble, you're next."

"No, I should stay here with you." Bramble's voice was hoarse and determined. "I'll help you find Callumkal."

Moon hissed at her, but there was no time to argue. Watching for Stone, he said, "If you jump, I'll give you a clutch whenever you want."

Bramble, clearly braced for snarling and orders, blinked, distracted. "What, really?"

"Really." As Stone appeared in the cloud of insects, Moon gave Bramble a shove. She flailed and fell. Stone caught her neatly in one hand and turned to come around for his next pass.

Delin groaned. "I am not looking forward to this."

Just as Stone appeared below again, a scatter of wooden disks landed on the platform. Moon shoved Delin off with more force than he had originally intended. Then he crouched and flipped down to land on the lower hull just as fire washed the platform above him. The heat warmed his scales and he climbed rapidly, knowing he would blend in with the dark green moss and make a poor target.

He hadn't seen Stone catch Delin, but Stone's big form vanished into the insect cloud with a flip of his tail, so Moon hoped for the best.

Jade rode the wind, scouting ahead with Balm. The sun had set and it was too dark to see much ahead, and they would need to return to the wind-ship soon. At least stretching her wings and fighting the strong salt-scented wind helped keep her anxiety and irritation in check. The last thing Jade needed to do was bite a warrior's head off.

They passed into an open valley where the ground rose up to form rocky hills, all of it shrouded in deep shadow. "We should go back," Balm called.

Jade could feel her spines twitch impatiently. Draman had said they were close, that the two moss samples, the Hians' and Moon and Stone's, had been converging at a point not far ahead. Jade had hoped to find the two consorts before they found the Hians, but flying around aimlessly in the dark wasn't going to help, even though it gave her the illusion of doing something.

She began, "Right, let's—" then she saw the flash of light above the cliffs. She hissed in a startled breath.

Balm slipped sideways in her excitement. "There! That was a—"

"Kishan distance-light," Jade finished as it flashed again. "Go back, warn the wind-ship! I'll wait here."

Balm banked to head back to the others and Jade tilted her wings to land on the rocky crag of the hill overlooking the beach. Finally, their quarry was in sight.

The Hians would be watching the starboard side of the boat, where they had last spotted Raksura, so Moon climbed down, claws sinking into the thick moss, all the way under the hull. The still-working starboard distance-light swept the cloud of insects, catching iridescent reflections off carapaces and wings, as Moon climbed up the port side.

Moon reached the deck and flattened his spines to cautiously poke his head up over the railing. He spotted movement atop a cabin roof; there were Hians up there, but they faced away from him, clearly still expecting him to appear on that side. He wasn't sure whether they had seen Stone or not. They must be aware that their captives were escaping but there was no telling how many Raksura they thought were on the boat.

He eased over the railing and dropped to the deck, then crawled to the nearest hatch and slipped inside. This corridor ran parallel to the deck, and was for the moment empty. Stone had been cut off from the stern stairwell, so Moon went forward, this time trying to make as little noise as possible. Stone had also been hampered by having to stay in his groundling form in order to fit inside the boat, and trying to keep Bramble and Delin from being recaptured. Moon hoped for better luck.

He heard movement and stepped into the nearest door, a cabin with narrow beds and cabinets built into the walls. The footsteps ran past. Moon slipped out and made it to the next stairwell. He crouched at the foot, listening and tasting the air.

The lower corridor and the cross-corridor that branched off the stairwell were empty. Most of the Hians would be up on the decks where they expected the next attack to come from. Moon moved rapidly down the cross-corridor, looking for cabins with sealed and reinforced doors.

The moss scent was strong, especially the further toward the stern he went, nearer to the moss-driven motivator that kept the boat aloft, and Moon had to filter it out of the other scents. Stone had probably been able to find Delin because his senses were so much more acute than Moon's, and because he knew Delin's personal scent. Moon knew Callumkal's, but Janderan and Janderi had skins nearly as tough and thick as scales; they didn't sweat like soft-skinned groundlings, and it made their scent less easy to detect.

But Moon had been close enough to Delin to scent illness on his skin and clothing. He was betting Callumkal wasn't in much better shape.

At the next intersection he caught the bitter scent of recent sickness. He followed it around to another winding corridor. As he started down it he heard movement and voices from the direction of the stern. That had to be the stairwell Stone had found guarded. Moon turned away from it first, but the scent faded. Hissing to himself in irritation he turned back and crept toward the stern. Barely ten paces from the bottom of the stairs he found a door reinforced with embedded bars. Bracing himself, Moon thought, *this is going to have to be fast.* And if it wasn't Callumkal in there, Moon would lose his chance to rescue him.

Moon took hold of a bar, braced his foot against the wall, and yanked it with all his strength. Something snapped inside the door, far too loudly, and half the door came out of the wall. Moon dropped it and flung himself into the room.

Callumkal lay on a padded bench, unconscious and stinking of sickness. A Hian, either guard or nurse, had been sitting on a stool and was just now standing, scrabbling for the fire weapon lying on the floor. Moon snapped out the end of his wing to punch her in the face with the tip. As she fell back against the wall and slid to the floor, Moon snatched up the fire weapon, looped the strap over his arm, and then grabbed Callumkal.

He darted into the corridor and raced away as the Hians from the stairwell shouted the alarm. Callumkal felt like a dead weight in his arms, but there was no time to stop and see if he was breathing. Moon reached the stairwell, slung Callumkal's limp body over one arm, pointed the fire weapon down the corridor and triggered it twice. The fire roared just as the Hians dashed out of the cross-corridor. They retreated in a mad scramble and Moon ran up the stairs.

He reached the landing and heard movement from both corridors in the junction; he was cut off from the outer door on the port side. He went the only way left, and burst out through a hatchway onto the lower bow deck. Vendoin, Bemadin, and the other Hian, Lavinat, stood on the platform just above.

There was a frozen instant where Moon stared at them and they stared at him. Then Lavinat lifted a silver and crystal shape. Moon recognized it instantly. It was the foundation builder weapon, the crystal inside its cage of metal.

He turned to go over the railing but the boat's deck shuddered under him, and he staggered sideways. Looking down he realized the boat was barely twenty paces from the top of one of the ruin's metal rings. The night, which had still been filled with the hum of the insect-lizards, abruptly went quiet as the whole swarm shot away down the beach. So Moon had lost his cover and he and Callumkal were probably about to die anyway, from the foundation builder weapon or the fire weapons of the Hians running across the bow deck toward him. There was no other option, and Moon would rather die in the air, so he crouched and leapt off the boat into the sea wind.

And then everything went black.

CHAPTER FIFTEEN

For a heartbeat the darkness was burning cold and absolute. Then suddenly dim cloudy starlight shone, the wind moving cool and sweet.

Moon clutched at Callumkal, relieved he hadn't dropped him in that strange instant of deprived senses. He tilted his wings to slow and control his fall. The sudden darkness was baffling. He still couldn't see the gleam of waves breaking on the beach, or on the verdigrised metal of the old ruin, or . . . He couldn't hear the waves, either. *That can't be good,* Moon thought, a knot of fear growing in his chest. Something had happened and he wondered if this was what the Fell at the river trading city had felt, right before their bodies had come apart.

But the sky was still there. Faint stars, obscured by far more clouds than there had been when he and Stone had flown to the flying boat. When he looked down, his eyes had adjusted enough to make out a shape below, like the bulb of a giant flower. It was in about the same spot as the edge of the ruin, but it hadn't been there earlier. Wary, he banked sideways away from it.

Overhead, from the direction of the flying boat, Moon heard someone shout in Kedaic, but the voice cut off abruptly. He registered the difference in the air: there was no scent of the sea, and it was dryer and cooler. As his body adjusted to the abrupt change, something told him they were much higher above the ground now, as high as a snow-covered mountaintop, at least. *We moved, we went up,* he realized.

That took a little of the terror of the unknown out of the situation. It must be something the ruin had done, maybe not that different from the forerunner tunnel that had given the sunsailer such a violent exit from the foundation builder city.

His throat dry, Moon took a deep taste of the wind and caught the scent of familiar Raksura.

Moon hissed in relief and adjusted his course, heading toward the scent's origin. Another bulbous shape caught a gleam of light. Something dark moved against it and Moon took the chance and called out, "Stone!"

Bramble's voice, ragged and frightened, answered, "Here!"

Moon dropped toward her and landed on the curve of the bulb, his claws skittering for purchase on the strange soft material. From here he could just see the outline of Stone's dark shape. Guessing that Stone was perched on something, Moon hissed, "Look out, I'm coming down." He jumped, cupping his wings in case the surface was closer or farther than he thought.

He landed on a ledge that felt like smooth rock. He whispered, "Stone, you all right?"

Wings scraped the ground as Stone moved. Delin groaned, and Bramble said, tentatively, "Moon? Where are we?"

"I don't know." Moon edged toward her voice and brushed against the tip of Stone's wing. "I've got Callumkal. He's unconscious." He carefully put Callumkal down on the paving and patted his face, but there was no reaction. At least Callumkal was still breathing. "Delin, are you all right?"

"It's my head," Delin said, thickly, "and my stomach. I'll be well in a moment."

Moon felt the displaced air as Stone shifted to groundling. Stone said, "Something's wrong with Merit."

Moon hissed in dismay. Above them wispy clouds fragmented and more stars shone, just enough light for Moon to make out the shapes of Delin and the Arbora. Stone crouched in front of Merit, who was folded up into as small a ball as possible, his arms wrapped around his head. Bramble huddled nearby and Delin wavered beside her.

As Stone leaned over Merit, Moon turned to face out into the darkness. With the slightly brighter starlight, he saw they were at the edge of a large ruin.

More flower-like blubs stood at different heights across an open space that formed a deep pool of shadow a few hundred paces wide. He tasted the air again, and caught the scents of rock and dust and fresh water, and the more distant hint of greenery and dirt. It was quiet except for faint high-pitch sounds that he could identify as water insects. This had to be a forerunner ruin. Something had happened to the ruin on the beach, it had made some sort of magic and sent them inland, to another ruin on top of a mountain. He remembered Lavinat had been holding the weapon right before he had leapt off the boat, and hissed under his breath. It must have other uses than just killing. *If she caused this . . .* It would be typical.

They needed to get to cover; if the flying boat used its remaining distance-lights, it could find them easily.

Bramble crept up beside him. He felt her tremble against his scales and put his arm around her. She huddled into his side and said, "I thought you were all dead. Vendoin said you weren't, and the way she was so worried about someone coming after her, it didn't make sense if you were. But I was still so afraid."

Moon hesitated, but he felt waiting would be worse. "Song is dead, from the poison the Hians gave us. They killed Magrim, and Kellimdar, too."

Bramble made a noise like all the air had been knocked out of her. Behind him, Delin groaned, and muttered a curse. In a small voice, Bramble said, "Where's Jade?"

"She's following us with the warriors, probably on Niran and Diar's wind-ship." Moon just hoped they hadn't been transported beyond the moss's direction-finding range.

Bramble curled tighter into Moon's side, and Delin said, "Ah. Niran must be beside himself."

"You could say that," Moon admitted. "Diar isn't thrilled about it either."

Behind him, he heard Merit say weakly, "I'm all right, it's just my head. I heard—I thought I heard—I don't know."

Moon felt his spines try to lift. Strange voices in your head while you were in a forerunner ruin were never a good thing. Bramble slipped away from his side to go to Merit. Stone said, "We need to find shelter."

Moon agreed. They had the Hians to worry about, and there might be any number of predators stalking this place. He eased to his feet. "Try to get inside this bulb thing?"

Stone grunted an assent. Bramble said, "I'll carry Callumkal."

It was best, as it would leave Stone free to shift. As Stone helped her sling Callumkal over her shoulder, Moon pulled Delin to his feet, then steered him to Merit. "Delin, take care of Merit."

Delin took Merit's arm and tucked it into his own. "I have him."

Moon followed last as Stone led the way to the wall and then along it. He could see the shape of other structures outlined against the sky, curving up from the ruin's base. Moon wondered if the buildings had sprouted from the floor of the bay somehow, if the whole ruin had lifted up into the sky. No, from the scents they had to be inland.

Ahead, Stone hissed, "Doorway."

They passed under an overhang that blocked the faint light and Moon sensed it was an open cave-like space. His spines twitched with nerves. He didn't scent any living things, but in a strange place anything could be possible. Merit said, "Wait, I think the Fell poison's worn off. I can make a light." He still sounded weak, but the more you were exposed to the poison, the quicker it seemed to wear off. And Merit and Bramble must have been given a lot of it in a fairly short time.

"Are you sure you should?" Bramble asked Merit, her voice raspy with nerves.

"Well, no, but . . ." Merit sounded a bit more like himself. "We need to see."

Delin handed Merit something, and after a moment, it began to gently glow. Moon lifted his wings to block the light, in case anyone was watching from the nearby flying boat. The object was a knotted up head scarf, and either the cloth just couldn't be made to put out much light, or Merit wasn't able to put much power into it. It revealed a pitted stone wall of dark blue, and the edge of a curved doorway. Stone took the scarf and stepped inside, saying, "Wait here."

Moon hissed as the light moved away from the door. He caught a glimpse of a polished dark floor, but that was all. It wasn't a good idea for Stone to go alone, but there wasn't much choice. After some long tense moments when he could hear Bramble's claws click and Callumkal's labored breathing, the light returned. "Come on," Stone whispered.

Moon urged the others forward. They followed Stone inside and up a structure that might be a curving staircase, or a set of shelves, or just an ornamental arrangement of blocks. Whatever it was, it got them to an elevated platform with a round window, looking out under an overhang that would hopefully hide their light from the flying boat.

Stone stuffed the glowing scarf half under his pack to shield it as Moon helped Bramble lower Callumkal to the floor. Moon turned the waterskin and the last of their food out of his pack, then gave the pack to Bramble to pillow Callumkal's head. Delin sank down beside him, and said, "How glad I am to see you, my friends, if I did not make that plain before."

"We're glad to see you, too," Moon said. The platform had pillars partially shielding it from the larger portion of the chamber, giving them some feeling of protection. "Here's food and water."

"Is Song really dead?" Merit asked suddenly. "I heard you tell Bramble—I thought I heard—"

"It's true," Moon said. He was glad it was too dark to read expressions. Bramble reached over to squeeze Merit's wrist.

Stone said, "Drink some water."

Merit shook his head. "I feel sick."

Stone said, "Drink the water anyway," in a tone that didn't leave any option for argument.

Bramble wet a corner of a blanket and patted Callumkal's face. He made a faint breathy noise but didn't wake. "Were they keeping him drugged?" Moon asked.

"We don't know." Delin took a drink from the waterskin and passed it to Merit again. "We were not permitted to see him."

Disjointedly, Delin and Bramble told the story of their captivity, with Merit putting in the occasional detail. Moon listened, and watched Stone, who sat beside a pillar where he had a good view of the dark bowl of the chamber. No one had said "Where are we?" again yet, which Moon was glad of, since he didn't have an answer. The more time he had to think about it, the more worried he got.

He hoped that once dawn broke, they would be able to figure out what had happened. South was still where south had been before the ruin had done whatever it had done, so they must have moved back or forward, and not up or down the coast. Pretty far backward or forward, since beside the lack of sea scent, the air movement was coming from the wrong direction.

"Bramble managed to arrange it so she and I were held together, but poor Merit was alone, as was Callumkal," Delin was saying.

"I'm sorry about that," Bramble told Merit. "It seemed like the best way to try to escape."

"No, that was the plan, I understood," Merit said, absently, his mind clearly on something else. He sounded stronger, as if the effect of whatever had happened was fading. Then he said, "Um."

Moon knew that tone, the one he hated to hear coming from a mentor. He said, "Merit, what's wrong?"

Merit hesitated, and said, "Bramble, do you have a headache?"

"Yes," she said. She added defensively, "It's been a rough day."

Merit continued, "And you feel sick in your stomach, and maybe a little dizzy."

"Yes?" Bramble was uncertain now.

Delin said, "That describes my symptoms perfectly."

"Right." Merit didn't seem pleased to have his guess confirmed. "Moon and Stone?"

Moon had a bad feeling about this. "I'm tired, but not sick." In the faint light, he saw Stone had turned his head to see Merit, the light catching his profile.

Stone said, "I'm fine."

Merit took a sharp breath. "That's what I was afraid of. There's mentor teaching about what happens if an Aeriat has to carry an Arbora high up in the air, much higher than they would normally fly. Like when we went up to the top of the foundation builder city's escarpment. The air is different up there, thinner. Arbora aren't made for going up fast the way Aeriat are. Basically it says an Arbora should be carried up slowly to that height, to give them time to get used to it."

"You didn't mention that at the time," Moon had to say.

"I didn't want to slow us down, and it didn't bother me much. The wind was so bad we didn't go up very fast, anyway," Merit said. "Everyone felt bad afterward."

Stone said, "Merit, get to the point."

"Bramble and Delin and I have the symptoms of going up too fast. I think that's what happened. I think we went up very high, very fast. Higher than the foundation builder city or the top of a sea-mount." Merit lifted his hands, baffled. "And it's cool, but the air isn't thin up here, like it should be on top of a mountain."

"Up where?" Bramble asked. "I mean, what are we sitting on? Is the ruin floating?"

There was nothing above us, Moon thought. *Except the cloudwall. Uh oh.* "It couldn't be the cloudwall," he said. "Could it?"

Delin buried his head in his hands and groaned. "The Cloudwalls, or the World Walls, as they are called sometimes, are seen in the southern regions and said to be seen in the far west, and thought to be a trick of the eye, caused by the light and weather. That is what I've always heard. There are stories of flying boats that try to approach a cloudwall and it seems to recede before them."

"I bet we're on the cloudwall." Stone sighed. He rubbed his eyes and looked out across the dark chamber.

"What's the cloudwall?" Bramble asked, bewildered.

Moon realized she must not have been allowed any kind of view outside the Hians' flying boat. "It's like a giant flying island, or bunch of flying islands, it's hard to tell. It's so high up, we thought we were looking at a cloud bank at first. When we got closer, we could see it was solid but we couldn't tell much more about it." He added, "Before I jumped off the boat with Callumkal, I saw Lavinat with the weapon."

Stone snarled. Merit said, "But why would the weapon take us up here? Unless it's not a weapon after all and Vendoin's been wrong all this time."

"No, it's a weapon," Bramble said. "Delin and I were there when Aldoan used it on the Fell and died. It almost killed me." She twitched uncomfortably. "Vendoin knew she needed to take the weapon somewhere else, to where the rest of it was, and I bet she thought the ruin on the beach was the right place. But if it's going to kill all the Fell and Raksura from here to the eastern end of the Abascene, it needs to be up high. Like casting a net. You get more from a better vantage point."

They all absorbed that in silence. Shocked, Moon said, " . . . what?"

Stone repeated, slowly, "Kill all the Fell and Raksura from here to the Abascene?"

"Yes," Delin said, "that was her plan. That was what she believed this weapon could do. The death of the Fell in the trading city was an accident. She had no intention of using it on a small scale."

Merit said, "But how does—"

Stone snapped, "Quiet."

The others froze. Moon tasted the air and sat up into a crouch, braced to move. After a heartbeat, Stone hissed, "That makes this whole shitting day complete."

"What?" Moon demanded. Then he caught the scent, the trace of Fell stench.

"It's the kethel." Stone shoved to his feet and jumped off the platform.

Moon controlled a growl of annoyance. Of course, the kethel hadn't stayed behind. It had intended to steal the weapon and had probably meant to do it while they were still in the middle of the rescue.

"Kethel?" Bramble whispered. "The Fell are here?"

"A kethel from the flight of the half-Fell queen has been following us," Moon explained wearily. "We told it to stay back off the beach, but it must have followed us into the ruin."

There was silence from the other three. Delin lifted his head to stare blankly at Moon. Merit said finally, "You . . . told . . . it?"

"It's a long story," Moon said.

Below, they heard Stone's voice, too low to catch the words, and the kethel's deeper voice replying. It sounded defensive. Moon rubbed his face. "I didn't know kethel could talk," Bramble said. "Oh, it must be part Raksura?"

"No. It was raised by the Fellborn queen."

"Is Stone going to kill it?" Merit asked hopefully.

"He hasn't so far," Moon said. He thought of trying to explain to the others that it would be weird to do it now, unprovoked, when the kethel had been persistently helpful. It sounded even stranger in his head so he decided not to try. "We're pretty certain the kethel was sent to get the weapon for the Fellborn queen, but it keeps talking to us, and . . . it's a long story."

Stone was returning, and they could hear him say, "—stay down here, or I'll tear your head off." Stone climbed the steps again, snarling in exasperation.

"Where was it?" Moon asked.

"It said it was on the causeway." Stone took a seat. He sounded resigned and furious. "It said everything went dark and it was falling through the air, until it could land on one of these pod-things."

"I need to tell you something," the kethel said from below.

Merit flinched in alarm and edged closer to Moon. "That's a kethel?" Bramble whispered, astonished.

"'Need' or 'want'?" Stone asked.

There was a pause while the kethel thought that over. Then it said, "Another flying boat."

Startled, Moon said, "What?"

"Where?" Stone demanded.

"Another flying boat in the ruin, before the ground went strange." The kethel added, "Is that need or want?"

Moon had the feeling Stone was inadvertently teaching the kethel how to be sarcastic. That wasn't going to work out for anybody.

Stone said, "Where in the ruin?"

"The edge," the kethel repeated. "Back near where I was."

"What did it look like?" Moon asked.

There was a moment of silence. "A boat that flies," the kethel said pointedly.

Stone hissed under his breath. Moon gathered his patience for another try. Then the kethel's head popped up between the pillars suddenly and everyone flinched back. It blinked in the light from the glowing scarf, taking in Merit, Bramble, Delin, and the unconscious Callumkal without any reaction. Merit warily drew back, edging behind Moon. Bramble whispered, "That's not a kethel. That can't be. It's not—"

"It is," Delin whispered back. "His face. The fangs. They have been shortened, but—"

Merit made a noise in his throat and tucked himself against Delin's side.

The kethel seemed to ignore them. It said, "I could show you."

Stone didn't respond immediately. Moon didn't like the idea of having to move the Arbora and Delin in the dark, while following a kethel. Even this kethel.

Then Bramble said, "Oh, there's something I forgot to tell you."

Still watching the kethel, Stone tilted his head toward her. "What?"

"I put poison in the cistern on the Hians' flying boat."

Moon turned to stare at her. "Poison?"

"You managed it?" Delin was startled.

"What poison was it?" Merit asked.

"We're not sure. Delin figured out the symbols on the waterskins but—"

Moon caught her shoulders and turned her to face him. "When did you do this?"

"It wasn't long before you got there," Bramble said. "I don't know if it's had time to work. With everything that happened, they probably weren't thinking much about eating and drinking." She gasped and looked at Callumkal. "You don't think—Maybe that's what made him sick—"

Maybe, but there was no point in worrying about it when there was nothing they could do. Moon said, "No, it's probably the drugs the Hians gave him." He looked toward Stone. "They won't all get it at once, like we did. If everyone who has a drink of water passes out, the others will realize it's in the cistern."

"It depends on how long it takes them to realize it." Stone sounded thoughtful. "Vendoin told you most simples don't work on Hians, so it might not do much to them."

Sounding frustrated, Bramble said, "I was in a hurry, and we didn't know what else to—"

Moon told her, "We're not criticizing you, Bramble. We're trying to think what to do next."

Bramble dropped her head and said miserably, "I had a really hard day."

Moon squeezed her wrist. "It's all right." He still thought the first thing they had to do was find the other flying boat. It could be more Hians, coming to help Vendoin, but he was betting it was Jade and the others. He stood and went to the edge of the platform, crouching to get eyelevel with the kethel. "Will you show me where the other flying boat is?"

Stone shook his head. "No, we can't risk—"

Moon told him, "I'll go alone. We have to find out if it's the wind-ship or not."

Stone glared at him, lifting his brows. Moon hissed, "I know." He knew he was going off alone in the dark with a kethel in a strange place that might be on the cloudwall to look for a possibly non-existent flying boat that might actually be full of Hians instead of their friends.

The kethel looked from Moon to Stone and back. It said, "I'll show you."

Stone turned to meet its gaze. He said, "If you don't come back, I'll come find you."

Stone kept his voice even, but he managed to convey his message. The kethel recoiled a little, and said reproachfully, "We come back, old consort."

"Moon . . ." Bramble whispered in protest. Merit's eyes were huge and Delin's brow furrowed in worry.

"It'll be all right," Moon told them, and leapt down the steps.

The kethel dropped lightly to the floor near him, and went through the door out to the ledge.

Moon followed. His eyes adjusted quickly, and he could see the kethel's outline against the starlit darkness, the light glinting on its pale skin. "Walk or fly?" he said.

"Walk along here. I came this way." The kethel sounded just like a groundling, and Moon reminded himself not to treat it like one. It didn't make sense for it to betray them, at least not until it got a chance to grab the weapon for itself. But just because it didn't make sense didn't mean it wouldn't happen.

As they followed the curve of the pod, the ruin opened up and the starlight illuminated the graceful shape of the flower-pods across the well, where they arced up above the bowl of shadow. Moon still couldn't catch any glimpse of the Hians' flying boat. It must be prudently keeping its lights out, hiding from them. Or from whatever else was here. He tasted the air deeply, but at the moment couldn't scent anything but kethel. He said, "How did you find us?"

The kethel said, "I told old consort I saw you leave the Hian flying boat and fall on the flower thing. We have to go down now."

Moon stopped abruptly as the kethel shifted. Its huge dark shape blotted out the light for an instant and flight reflex almost made Moon fling himself backward off the walkway. But its body flowed forward as it made the jump to the curve of a lower pod. The kethel climbed down the curve to the walkway. It paused there, then shifted back down to its groundling form.

Moon set his jaw and made the leap, landed on the curve and half-climbed half-skittered down the steep surface. The kethel faced toward the flower opening, trying to peer inside. It made a huffing noise that Moon realized was its version of tasting the air. Fell weren't the best trackers; feeding on groundlings trapped in their settlements didn't encourage the development of high level hunting skills. Moon could already tell that if there was anything alive in the darkness under the pod's overhang, it wasn't moving. He didn't feel they were being watched, either. Just to test the kethel, he asked, "Anything there?"

It moved its head back and forth, then turned away from the pod to start down the descending walkway. "Is this the thing in the sky, like the Arbora said?"

So it had been listening to their conversation. "Maybe. Probably."

It made a little sighing noise. "She won't like this."

Moon knew who it meant. As far as the kethel was concerned, there was only one she: Consolation, the Fellborn queen. "What does she want?" He didn't think it would tell him the truth, but he had discovered that following a kethel through the dark in a strange place was easier if it was talking.

There was a hesitation. "To help you."

It seemed to feel sticking to that pat answer was safest. The next pod was just below this one and they could jump down to its walkway without the kethel having to shift. Moon tried, "What does she want in return? The weapon?"

"No." After a moment the kethel answered, "She wants help."

Moon suppressed an annoyed hiss. "She wants someone to tell her how a part-Raksura Fell flight is supposed to live when they aren't Fell anymore. Is she going to keep the flight moving? If you aren't looking for groundling settlements to eat anymore, why move?" He said again, "What does she want?"

The kethel snarled, "She wants a place for us to live." It bit the words off, snorted out a breath, and then said nothing.

It didn't mean to say that, Moon thought. It sounded depressingly true. If the queen was serious about not preying on groundlings anymore, the flight needed to find a place to settle.

Maybe the kethel had been trying to see how sympathetic Moon and Stone were. If the kethel could convince them that Consolation really had sent it to help them, if it could do enough that they felt they owed the flight a debt. *Or it's going to kill us and take the weapon the first chance it gets,* Moon thought. He didn't think there would be a way to tell until it happened.

Bramble was right, it had been a long day. And this had better be their wind-ship with Jade and Malachite aboard. Moon said, "Do you even know how to hunt grasseaters?"

"Yes," the kethel said stiffly.

They crossed over two more pods and Moon began to have some idea of the size and shape of this structure. Without being able to see it in daylight yet, he thought it was like the ruin at the sea's edge, but with all the missing pieces in place. If it was, then the causeway should be somewhere below them.

Then Moon caught a hint of sound, a faint creak. Like the creak of a wind-ship's plant-fiber adjusting itself to the dryer air. He told the kethel, "Stop."

It paused, turning to watch him. Past the edge of the pod, where a large gap between it and the next cast a deep well of shadow, Moon had the sense of something large. He stood still for a moment, listening deeply, squinting to take advantage of the faint starlight. He extended his wings enough to feel the light breeze. Yes, there was something there, blocking the air flow between the two pods. It might be part of the structure, something sitting at an angle where it wasn't catching any light, but somehow Moon doubted it. "There's a boat there, just ahead."

The kethel turned to study the distance between pods. "It moved in and up."

"It's trying to hide from the Hians." *If it's the right boat,* Moon thought. "Go stand downwind."

The kethel didn't grumble, just moved around Moon and down the walkway a little. Moon waited for the air to clear, then tasted it deeply. There was Raksura in the faint breeze, the familiar scents of Indigo Cloud and Opal Night, of one annoyed sealing, and the slightly sour scent of the Golden Islanders' favorite fish paste. He said in relief, "That's it." He turned to the kethel. "Stay here."

"Why?" it asked.

"So my family doesn't kill you on sight," Moon said.

There was a moment of thoughtful silence. "Stay here," the kethel agreed.

Moon moved along the ledge, trying to discern the shape of the wind-ship, and finally made out a deeper shadow against the dark, and the faint gleam of starlight on the glass shield of an unlit lamp. Leaping for the deck would probably be a bad idea; they might have caught scent of the kethel, and had probably heard voices, just too low to recognize. Moon hated to raise his voice when he wasn't certain how close the Hians' flying boat was, but there was no better way to do this. He said, in a tone nearer to his normal voice, "Hey, it's me, Moon."

There was a faint stir of movement from at least two points on the wind-ship. A rustle of scaled wings and a slap of a bare groundling foot on the deck. After a fraught moment, a voice whispered, "Moon? Is that you?"

Relief made his spines twitch. "Briar, it's me. I'm going to jump across to the deck."

There was another flurry of movement and Moon was certain he heard River whisper something and Root reply. He jumped into the air, spread his wings to keep himself aloft, and managed to land on the deck without slamming into a cabin wall.

"Moon?" Chime said from somewhere to his right, then suddenly flung himself into Moon's arms.

Hugging while in scaled form was always tricky. Moon squeezed Chime's shoulders reassuringly and turned his face away from Chime's twitching spines to say, "We've got them, all four of them. They're with Stone."

Chime demanded, "Are they all right?"

"They're fine. Callumkal's sick—"

Kalam's voice said, "My father is ill?" He sounded caught between relief and renewed fear.

Moon turned toward him. "We think they kept giving him that poison they used on us—"

A faint glow appeared near a doorway: Diar with a lamp that was wrapped in filmy cloth to dim its light. "Our Grandfather is well?"

"He's fine," Moon said. "Careful with the lamp. The Hians are here somewhere—"

Then Chime let go of him and stepped away just as Jade grabbed him. Moon shifted to groundling in her arms, and relaxed into her warmth. He had expected to feel relief but he hadn't expected to feel it so intensely he just wanted to fold up on the deck and collapse. He and Stone had been on their own so long, hoping they were going in the right direction, hoping the others had been able to follow as planned, that nothing had happened to them. Jade hugged him hard enough to take his breath, communicating her own fear and anxiety through the scales to skin contact. He took a sharp breath as she pressed her teeth against his neck. Jade pulled back and said, "Do you know what happened? What this place is?"

"Merit thinks we're up on the cloudwall, that island formation." He made himself step back from her. "There's something else I need to tell you right now." There were actually a few things, but he didn't want to blurt them all out in front of the warriors and groundlings.

"What?" Jade said, her voice tight with renewed tension.

"There's a kethel here. From the Fellborn queen's flight. It's been following us."

Jade let her breath out in a hiss, and he heard sharp exclamations from Diar and Kalam. Somewhere down the deck, River muttered, "Oh, that's all we need."

Jade asked, "Do you know where it is?"

Moon said, "It's over there on the ledge. It walked here with me." There was a moment of nonplussed silence. Moon added, "It's a long story."

From the ledge, the kethel's voice said, "Old consort said to come back."

"I know that, be quiet," Moon told it.

There was another moment of silence. Then Chime whispered, "Is that a ruler speaking through him—"

"No, it's just him, it," Moon said. "We need to—"

"Go get the others," Jade finished. She turned toward Diar. "I'll take Balm and Briar."

Diar told her, "If you don't return soon, we'll come after you."

There was a grumble from the ledge. Moon snapped, "What was that?"

"Nothing," the kethel muttered.

Chapter Sixteen

Moon shifted to his scaled form and leapt back to the ledge with Jade. Balm and Briar followed closely behind. Chime followed too, though Moon could practically scent the waves of nervous tension emanating from him. It was because of the kethel, but Moon couldn't tell Chime that it would be all right.

He had explained about the kethel to Jade, quickly and just inside the cabin doorway. She had grabbed his shoulders like she was suppressing the urge to shake him and growled, "Only you and Stone. You knew the Fell were after you."

Moon decided not to tell her about the Fell attack in the cloud forest. "Is Malachite here?" He had no sense of her presence, but with her that didn't necessarily mean anything. She might be standing at his elbow.

Jade hesitated for a bare instant. "She had to take a message to the Reaches. She took some of her warriors with her, but Lithe and Shade and the others stayed with us." She had tugged him back out on deck. "I'll explain later."

It left Moon with the distinct feeling that there was something she needed to tell him that he wasn't going to want to hear.

The kethel backed away a few wary steps as they landed. Moon said, "We'll go back now."

It made a noise of assent and turned to head along the ledge. Jade said, "Wait. There are no rulers anywhere near, telling you what to do?"

"No." It turned to glance at her, starlight catching a glint of reflection in its eyes. "Just me. She sent me to help the consorts."

"That was . . . interesting . . . of her." Jade's voice was hard.

The kethel hunched its shoulders a little and turned to lead the way along the ledge. Beside Moon, Chime's spines twitched in nervous dismay.

They were almost to the next flower-pod when the kethel said, "The queens tell you what to do?"

"Yes," Moon said. The kethel knew that already, so he wasn't certain where this was going.

"Just tell, nothing else?" the kethel said.

Now Moon understood. The kethel was asking if Raksura were controlled by the queens the way kethel and dakti were controlled by progenitors. It was strange to think that Fell, or at least kethel and dakti, might not know much about Raksura at all.

It was a complex question, with an answer Moon wouldn't have understood himself a couple of turns ago. Queens could keep other Raksura from shifting, but it was more than that. There was a connection through and between each bloodline, a subtle pull on the heart that kept the court together or could push it apart. Pearl's pain over her first consort's death had echoed through all of Indigo Cloud for turns before Moon had arrived there. It had weakened the bonds of the court at a time when it was already vulnerable. Malachite's determination had held the remnants of Opal Night's eastern colony together through hardship that should not have been survivable. But that connection didn't compel obedience.

Jade wasn't answering and Moon had no idea how to explain it. He said, "Just telling. There is something else, but not like it is for the Fell."

Chime reached over and squeezed Moon's wrist.

The kethel didn't ask any more questions, and soon they reached the point where the pods curved into the central well. Moon lowered his voice. "Careful through here. We think the Hian boat is in there somewhere."

There hadn't been much time for anything terrible to happen, but Moon was still relieved to reach the doorway and find Stone waiting impatiently for them. The kethel said, "We're back," in what Moon thought was a particularly pointed way.

Stone said, "I see that." He added to Jade, "Glad you found us."

"So am I," she said. "We have a lot to discuss." She would have added more, but Bramble and Merit threw themselves at her.

Balm carried Callumkal, and Moon picked up Delin, despite his protests that he was fine and could walk. Moon ignored that and said, "Diar and Niran are waiting for you."

Delin gave in, holding onto Moon's collar flanges. "They are much agitated?"

"Much," Chime agreed. "We've all been very worried."

They reached the wind-ship without trouble and leapt across to its deck. Moon set Delin on his feet so Niran and Diar could greet him. Delin began, "It was not my intention to cause so much—" before Niran half-smothered him in a hug. Diar said fondly, "We forgive you, grandfather. We're only glad to have you back alive."

Navigating by sound in the dark, Moon followed the others down the steps to the main corridor. It was a relief to step into the warm light of mentor-spelled lamps and the familiar scents of Raksura and Golden Islanders. Ivar-edel, the Golden Islander healer, said to Balm, "Here, bring him this way. We have a bed ready." Balm carried Callumkal down the passage, Kalam following anxiously.

Jade told Bramble and Merit, "Go with Briar. There's a cabin for us at the end of the passage, with water and beds."

The two Arbora stumbled after Briar, and Moon went with Jade and Chime and the others into the big common room, hoping someone was making tea. Shade and Lithe were here, with Rorra, several of the Golden Islander crew, and another Janderi person who must be the horticultural they had intended to bring from the Kishan port. Most of the warriors were still out on the deck, on guard. There were questions, greetings. A pot of something that smelled warm and fishy was on the small stove.

Then everyone went silent. Moon turned. The kethel had followed Stone into the room. Moon was so used to the scent by now, he hadn't realized it was behind them.

Jade turned, saw it, and glared at Stone. He said, "This is not my fault."

The groundlings just looked confused. They would never have seen a kethel in groundling form, and even if they had heard one was here, had led Jade and the others to Stone and the rescued prisoners, they might not have realized this was it. Then Shade shoved past Moon and Jade to confront the kethel, his shape flowing into darkness and then his big scaled form. Moon thought, *Uh oh.*

The kethel stared at Shade. "You are—"

Shade's spines lifted below his crest and his wings flexed and started to extend. He snarled, "I'm a Raksura. You're a dead kethel."

Moon hesitated. He was having trouble believing that he was about to have to put his body between Shade and a kethel, but someone was going to have to do it. Unless of course the kethel attacked Shade, then it was going to be a bloodbath in this cabin, because every Raksura and probably some of the groundlings would leap in to help. Someone bumped against his arm; it was Shade's warrior Flicker, watching in consternation.

But before Moon could do anything, the kethel stepped back and turned away, raising its shoulders protectively. It said, "I don't challenge you. But she is like you. She is our queen. I killed the rulers who challenged her."

Shade stood there, still as a rock. From behind him, Jade said evenly, "Shade. It's all right."

Shade's spines flicked and then started to lower. Flicker went forward and caught his wrist, his spines angled anxiously. Shade pushed Flicker behind him before he stepped back, a move to keep the young warrior out of the kethel's reach. It was a caution Moon approved of. There was no point in being foolishly trusting.

Then Lithe stepped forward, watching the kethel. She said, "I'm like her, too. And I want you to prove to me that there's no ruler controlling you."

The kethel eyed her cautiously. "How?"

Lithe said, "Let me look into your mind."

Jade's spines twitched and then stilled. Moon hadn't known it was possible for a mentor to look into a Fell. He glanced at Chime, who flicked one spine in a gesture of dubious assent. Moon guessed that meant it was theoretically possible, but no one had ever before been in a position to try it and live.

The kethel flinched a little, then bared its teeth. "Not in my head."

Moon knew what it meant. After those cautious questions about how much control over Raksura queens had, it was obvious. He said, "That's not how it works with us. A mentor can't control what you do, or think. She can look into your mind, and see if there's a ruler there hiding from us, but that's all."

The kethel hesitated, then looked at Stone. Stone folded his arms and said, "That's true. Let her look, or leave here and don't come back."

A long fraught moment of silence passed, where Moon saw Rorra rest a hand worriedly on the fire weapon slung over her shoulder. The strange Janderi looked bewildered. Then the kethel said, "Then do it."

Lithe stepped forward. "Sit down." Her voice was hard, she didn't flinch as it stared at her. This was her battle to fight, just as it was Shade's.

"Why?" the kethel asked, eyes narrowing in suspicion.

Stone said flatly, "Because that's the way you do it."

The kethel hesitated again, then sat down heavily on the deck. Lithe stepped forward and crouched in front of it. She looked tiny next to the kethel. Moon was glad Stone stood so close, that he, Jade, and Shade were all in arm's reach. But the kethel just sat there, radiating hostility.

At some point, Delin, Niran, and Diar had come down from the deck and stood in the doorway, watching. Moon was shocked at how bad Delin looked in this light. The gold of his skin was blotchy, and the lines in his face were deeper. He looked smaller. Moon hoped Lithe was able to do this fast, so they could get Delin some food.

Lithe said, "Just look at me."

The kethel met her gaze. Then the stubborn set to its face relaxed and its expression went still.

Chime whispered, "She's got him."

It was always strange to watch, even though Moon had experienced it himself. When a mentor looked into your mind you felt nothing. It sounded like it would be a traumatic process, but it was like falling instantly asleep and then waking again. Keeping his voice low, Moon said, "How did she know she could do it?"

Shade's expression was conflicted. "She's done me, and the others at Opal Night. I guess it's not that different."

After what seemed a long time, long enough for the groundlings to stir uneasily, Lithe sat back. She was frowning. Released, the kethel gasped a breath and stared in confusion. Lithe pushed to her feet, saying, "There's no ruler, no influence."

Rorra eased forward a step. "How can that be? We know the flight has rulers, we've seen them."

Stone eyed the kethel thoughtfully. "It told us it killed the dominant rulers in its flight. I guess that's true."

The kethel looked up, still wary, but the confusion was gone. It climbed to its feet, clearly off-balance. "They were young. The progenitor was dead."

Jade said, "So Consolation sent you here to take the weapon back from the Hians." Moon managed not to react, wondering when exactly Jade had spoken to the Fellborn queen long enough to learn her name. That was probably a part of the thing she had to tell him that she knew he wasn't going to like.

The kethel focused on Jade. "She told you her name."

"She did," Jade said. "We saw her on the way here. She brought us news. But she didn't tell us about you and why you're following our consorts."

"To help you," the kethel said. Then it looked at Lithe, and added, "To get help from you. A place to live. And she sent me to learn from the consorts."

"Learn?" Lithe said.

The kethel said, "If no one who knows things will come live with us, then I need to learn."

There was a moment of silence while everyone digested that. Moon looked helplessly at Stone, who sighed and rubbed his eyes.

Jade hissed out a breath. She told the kethel, "Go up on deck, and wait. We need to talk. And if you touch anyone on this wind-ship, we'll kill you."

The kethel threw a sideways glance at Shade and Lithe again, but Moon thought it seemed relieved at the dismissal. It turned and went out of the room, up the passage to the stairs. There was a shudder of relief, mostly from the groundlings. A Golden Islander at the back of the room sat down heavily. Jade told Balm, "Get the other warriors and watch it, but be careful. Tell them not to get within arm's reach."

Balm flicked her spines in grim assent and followed the kethel. Shade shook himself, shedding tension, and shifted back to his groundling form. Lithe frowned absently at the doorway. She said, "That was a very strange experience."

"That's one way to describe it," Moon told her. He shifted to his groundling form and felt the weight of bruises and sore muscles settle over him. He blinked and scratched his head, trying to shake off the sudden urge to just lie down on the floor and sleep.

Still upset, Shade said, "How do we know it's really from the half-Fell queen's flight? It could be . . ." He folded his arms, uncomfortable. "A spy."

"This is too smart for rulers. They'd never think of something like this," Stone said wearily. "And I doubt a kethel from a normal Fell flight would be able to pull this off. It has to be the half-Fell queen who sent it."

"And the way he—it—talks about her," Moon said. He gave Shade a nudge to the shoulder. "It's not lying about that, at least."

Shade seemed to reluctantly accept that. He put an arm around Lithe's shoulders and she leaned into his side.

Niran helped Delin over to take a seat on a stool, and Diar said, "It presents an interesting problem."

Jade turned to Diar. "If you don't want it on the boat, we'll understand," she said. "But it's here, and I think it's better if we can keep an eye on it."

Diar grimaced, obviously reluctant. "I agree. But it's a complication we don't need."

Delin tugged on Niran's sleeve. "Do you know where we are?"

Niran said, "I took a star sighting when the clouds cleared. We should still be near the southern coast, exactly where we were." He lifted a hand helplessly. "Except of course, we know we must have moved."

"You took a what?" Jade asked.

"Groundlings can look at the stars to tell where they are," Moon told her. "I never knew how it worked." It wasn't something Raksura needed to know.

Delin nodded, absently threading his fingers through his tangled beard. "Then Merit's theory is correct. We were taken up into the air, and are on the cloudwalls."

"The what?" Rorra said, her brow furrowed.

The Janderi woman said, hesitantly, "It's that mass of flying islands, very high in the air, that we saw on the way here. But it's unreachable by flying craft."

Rorra looked aghast. "I thought that was a cloud bank. Cloud-walls are supposed to be mythical. My people called them Cloud Reefs."

Rorra must be rattled. It was the first time Moon had heard her admit that she actually had people, and hadn't just sprang into being as a fully grown adult right before meeting Callumkal and becoming his navigator.

Niran said, "Well, we know it's not mythical now."

"So how do we get back down?" another Golden Islander asked. "Do the lines of force extend this far up? Can we sail along them or will we fall?"

Diar scratched under her head scarf wearily. "Hopefully it will become more apparent in the morning."

"But we cannot leave," Delin said, as a young Golden Islander put a blanket around his shoulders. "We must get the artifact away from the Hians. They brought it here in order to use it to activate some device that they believe is near. The weapon will kill all the Raksura, as well as the Fell, and possibly any other races descended from the forerunners or foundation builders."

Rorra and the Golden Islanders stared at Delin as if they suspected he was out of his mind. Niran said, "Grandfather . . ." He turned to Moon and Stone. "This can't be true?"

Delin said, stiffly, "Do not think I missed your implication that I am delusional."

"I was not implying—" Niran began.

"It's true." Stone cut the argument off. "At least, it's what the Hians told Bramble and Delin."

"That's the other thing we had to tell you," Moon said to Jade. Chime covered his face and groaned.

Jade eyed Moon. "Is there anything else?"

"I think so," Moon admitted. "A lot of things happened. Did you get the message we left at the river trading city?"

"We did, and it was not encouraging," Rorra said. She turned to Delin. "The dead Jandera—Was it the weapon that killed them?"

Delin nodded grimly. "We were very lucky. Bramble was too near, and it almost killed her. If the Hians can use the weapon the way they believe they can—This is why the foundation builders locked it away, only accessible to their allies the forerunners. It does not work the way they intended. It is a terrible mistake."

The silence stretched as everyone absorbed the implications. Jade's spines flared as she thought furiously. She said, "The Fellborn queen couldn't have known about this. Of course, she didn't tell us about sending the kethel after you, either. When Malachite went back to the Reaches with her—"

Moon stared at her. "When she did what?"

Jade turned to him, then her brow furrowed and she looked at Stone. "You two need to rest. So does Delin. Go and take care of Bramble and Merit, and I'll come and tell you about it."

Moon stirred mutinously, but Chime took his arm and dragged him toward the doorway. Behind him, Stone protested, "I have to watch the kethel."

Jade told him, "And you can do that, after you take care of the two Arbora who need you and get some rest."

In the corridor, they passed the cabin where Callumkal lay on a bed of cushions with the Golden Isles healer and Kalam sitting beside him. Kalam had his arms wrapped tightly around himself, as if he might fly apart if he let go. It didn't look good. It would be terrible if they had been too late and rescued Callumkal only to have him die. But at least he would be doing it here, with Kalam and among friends, and not as a prisoner of the Hians.

The next cabin was a larger room, with packs piled up against the far wall and blankets and cushions in mostly neat piles. Briar was in her groundling form, sitting with the two Arbora, looking worried. Merit huddled on a cushion with a blanket wrapped around him, half asleep, and Bramble had wet a cloth from one of the water jars and was giving herself a vigorous bath.

"The consorts need rest," Chime told Briar, in what Moon felt was a far too urgent manner.

"We're fine," Moon told Briar, and sat down next to Merit. Merit leaned against him and Moon put an arm around him. "What is Malachite doing with the Fellborn queen?" he asked Chime. "Why are they going back to the Reaches?"

"I think Jade wants to tell you," Chime said, not quite meeting Moon's gaze.

Stone sat down heavily near Moon. Merit lifted his head, blearily confused. "What? Malachite's not here?"

Moon eyed Chime suspiciously. He wasn't certain if this was one of those "the emergency is over and now Moon needs to start acting like a delicate consort again" moments, or if this was part of the thing that the others knew he really wasn't going to like. He doubted it was the former; there weren't any Raksura here who hadn't already had a chance to be judgy about his behavior.

Briar pushed to her feet. "I'll get some blankets—"

"I'll do it." Bramble dropped the wet cloth and turned to the piles of bedding.

"She won't sit down—" Briar began, waving a hand helplessly at Bramble.

Bramble snapped, "I'm fine! You're not an Arbora, you won't do it right."

In a voice that clearly indicated the need for instant obedience or else, Stone said, "Bramble, I didn't cross half the Three Worlds to argue with you. Come here and sit down."

Bramble froze for an instant, staring. Briar and Chime watched her anxiously. Then she flung herself into Stone's lap and wrapped herself around him. He hugged her close, then asked Briar and Chime, "What do you have to do on this boat to get some tea?"

"I'll get it!" Briar whipped out of the room before Chime could move.

Moon told Chime, "Waiting for Jade to tell us is making it worse, whatever it is. Why did Malachite go back to the Reaches with the Fellborn queen?"

Chime sunk down to sit on the floor, and winced in anticipation of their reaction. "The Fellborn queen told us at least four or five Fell flights, maybe more, are gathering to attack the Reaches."

Moon felt his chest constrict. Merit, still huddled under his arm, went still. He heard Stone let out a slow breath. Bramble made a noise of weary dismay.

Chime said, "We don't know that it's true, except, of course, it matches the visions the mentors had before we left." He shrugged, clearly miserable. "It's not as bad as if there hadn't been any warning. From what Malachite told us, your clutchmate Celadon should be at Indigo Cloud by now, and Pearl agreed to let her bring all those Opal Night warriors. If the other eastern courts are starting to have the visions like Indigo Cloud and Opal Night did . . . They'll be prepared."

It took Moon a moment to fight past the lump of sick dread in his throat. He told himself, *Chime's right, we've known this could happen ever since the shared dream.* Now it was happening. The court should be as prepared as it could get. He put aside all the questions that Chime couldn't possibly have any answers to, and said, "How did the Fellborn queen know?"

"She said she has rulers who can listen to other flights." Chime twitched a little at that uncomfortable thought. "She said the other Fell flights hated them, like the one they followed to the foundation builder city."

Moon bit his lip and looked helplessly at Stone. Stone sighed, and stroked Bramble's hair.

Chime continued, "Malachite found her and her flight when we were coming overland from isl-Maharat, before we got to the swampling port and found your first message." Chime repeated what Jade had told him about the first meeting, then described the second, when the Fellborn queen had come to the wind-ship to warn them.

Stone was frowning. "When did Malachite leave?"

"Five—No, six days ago," Chime said. He massaged his temple, as if trying to make his memory more accurate. "They were flying on a kethel, so they should be traveling much faster than they could on their own."

"A kethel?" Moon said, startled. It was a relief to know Malachite was headed back to the Reaches. Pearl would have a powerful ally. "Not that we can point fingers about that, but . . . A kethel?"

Chime lifted his hands in a sign of resignation. "I know, I know. We were hoping to head back as soon as the Hians were dealt with. Niran and Diar were going to take the Jandera and Rorra to Kedmar for us. But if it's true about the weapon, and, of course, we have to figure out if we're really on the cloudwalls and how to get back from here . . ." He grimaced and added, "Oh, and the Kish in isl-Maharat didn't believe Kalam and Rorra and Esankel and the others about the Hians, so I don't know what's going to happen with that. Maybe nothing."

Moon hissed at the stupidity of it. "Why do they think Kalam and Rorra and the whole crew would lie about something like that? And what about the dead people?"

"They believe it happened, but they think the Jandera got into a fight with the Hians?" Chime shook his head helplessly. "I didn't understand it. Maybe it's a groundling thing."

Moon rubbed his face wearily. Merit had slumped against his side and breathed deeply in sleep.

Chime hesitated, then said, reluctantly, "I don't suppose . . . The weapon. Were the Hians telling the truth about it? It wasn't a lie to frighten us?"

Moon saw Jade step into the doorway, her spines down, listening intently.

Bramble, her face still pressed to Stone's chest, said flatly, "It's the truth. I know it."

Stone grimaced. "From what they told Delin and Bramble, there's no way to tell it who to kill or not kill. The Hians thought it would destroy all the Fell from this coast across Kish and down to the tip of the Abascene peninsula. They knew it would kill all the Raksura too, and the Jandera. The area they're talking about is a big chunk of Kishan territory. But it's worth it to them to kill the Fell."

Bramble stirred, and lifted her head and blinked blearily. "It killed Aldoan, too."

"Who?" Moon asked her.

"The Hian who was holding it, when the Fell grabbed her. At the river trading city. They don't know how she did it, but they think that's how it works when it isn't attached to the rest of it, the part they think is here somewhere. Aldoan must have accidentally made it work because she was so afraid. But she was probably thinking 'kill Fell' not 'kill Fell and all the Jandera in the town and oh, take a swipe at that Bramble back on the flying boat and oh, kill me too while you're at it.'" Bramble rubbed her nose. "So it does kill Hians too. Maybe they're related to the foundation builders, like the Jandera."

Stone frowned and Moon thought of the Hian scholar and her family. It would make more sense than Vendoin killing them.

Jade stepped into the room. "We have to assume it's true. It's too dangerous not to. Once we get the weapon, we'll have to find somewhere to hide it again."

Chime nodded. "A good hiding place."

Then Briar came in with a jug of tea and an armful of ceramic cups. Shade, Lithe, and Flicker followed her in, Rorra and Kalam trailing behind. As Flicker helped her distribute the tea, Moon told the others everything they had been able to find out about the artifact. When he repeated Bramble's description of the message stones and how the Hians had used magic to find them, Kalam was astonished. "I've never heard of the Hians being able to manipulate rock, or anyone able to do that." Kalam turned to Rorra. "Have you?"

Rorra shook her head a little, her frown grim. "It's bizarre, to conceal an ability like that just so no one would suspect they were hiding the discovery of foundation builder ruins."

"Have they fought with the Jandera before?" Chime asked. Moon thought he was trying to make sense of that apparent indifference the Hians had to the possibility of Jandera victims. The indifference to Raksuran victims needed no explanation, but the Jandera were groundlings, not much different from the Hians.

"No." Kalam made a gesture of confusion. "Well, a long time ago, when the Hians were first driven from Hia Majora by the Fell. They wanted the Imperial Conclave to extend the border and protect it, but the Jandera speakers didn't agree. There are mountains in the way, and it would have used up so many moss reserves." He looked painfully baffled. "Could that be it?"

No one had an answer for that. Jade asked Moon, "Chime told you why Malachite left? Are you all right?"

"Uh, no, not really," Moon said honestly. If he wasn't so exhausted, he knew he would have been more upset. Merit was deeply asleep, and Moon lifted him and put him down on the blankets Briar had gotten ready. "Bramble, do you want to lay down here with Merit?"

Stone ruffled her hair. "I'll stay until you fall asleep."

CHAPTER SEVENTEEN

Moon woke with Niran leaning over him, saying, "We found the Hians."

He sat up abruptly and bumped his head on the bench built out from the wall. He had fallen asleep on the floor of their cabin, curled between Jade and Chime. From the light falling through the narrow windows, it was nearing dawn. Bramble and Merit were wound together nearby, still asleep. On the other side of the room, Shade was a lump under the blanket and Lithe yawned and rolled over. Root, Flicker, and some Opal Night warriors were in a pile near the door. Jade, already on her feet and shifted to her winged form, asked, "Where's Stone?"

Niran pointed up. "Sleeping on the roof."

Chime groaned and sat up. Moon managed to reach out in time to catch his head before it hit the bench. "Thanks," Chime croaked, and struggled upright.

Moon climbed to his feet, aware his back was stiff and his throat was raw from the dry air. Niran had turned to point. "Their ship is that way, at the far end of this ruin. River and Spark went atop the masts just before dawn, and were able to spot them."

Jade hissed out a breath. "Let's go say hello."

Not long later, when the sun was just starting to break above the horizon, Moon perched on the back of a flower-pod. Behind him was

Chime, Shade carrying Lithe, and most of the warriors. Stone curled below the pod to keep his larger form out of sight, and Jade had climbed further up to get a better view over the top. They had left River and two of Malachite's warriors behind on the wind-ship with the Arbora and groundlings. Though there had been no scent or sense of anything stalking the wind-ship, there was no point in not being careful.

Speaking of careful, the kethel had followed them, though it hadn't voiced any intention of participating in the fight. It was in its scaled form, tucked behind the next pod, waiting and watching.

Moon peered around the nearest fluted edge, trying to get a better view. The outline of the Hians' flying boat was just visible where it floated above a pod at the far end of the structure. No lights showed in the cabin windows and no one moved on deck.

Moon lifted up a little for a better angle. In the growing light the ruin was even larger than they had thought, with dozens of the huge flower-pods forming a curving forest around the open central area. It looked a little like the docking stalks of the swampling port, and Moon wondered if those had been built in imitation of this strange place. A causeway like the one that had extended out over the bay lay a few hundred paces below, and led to a large building like a pile of domes and spheres. It had obviously been deserted a long time, with scars and jagged holes in its white stone. Bands of carving decorated it, faint colors still visible on the reliefs, and steps led up from the causeway to a large round doorway at its base. Platforms extended out from the sides supporting clumps of vegetation, including a few tall trees with long elegantly curved branches, bare of all but a scattering of leaves.

The building didn't look like it was made of the same material as the flower pods. It looked like someone else had come in after the forerunners and plunked it down. Which was exactly what happened to so many old ruins, everywhere Moon had traveled, new people moving in and adding things to what was already there and using it for new purposes. So maybe it was a little reassuring to see.

Chime, crouched behind Moon, whispered, "How big is this place?"

Moon looked away from the ruin. Far below their perch, the dim morning light gradually revealed a landscape of lush green grass cut through with deep rocky gorges and clouds of mist. Like a plain had been dropped from a height and shattered, with streams of water finding their way through the deep cracks. To the west rose a low range of blue hills. Moon had never seen a flying island this large. "So we really are on the cloudwall," he said, keeping his voice low.

"I didn't want to believe it either," Jade muttered from above. "Get ready. There's no one at the fire weapon stations."

She leapt into the air and snapped her wings out. Moon scrambled up the pod after her. Behind him, wings flapped and claws scratched across the pod as the others took flight toward the Hian boat.

Jade lit on the cabin roof above the nearest fire weapon balcony, on the port side above the stern. Moon landed atop the next cabin over. As the warriors dropped down, Jade made a sharp motion toward the fire weapon stations on either side of the stern. "Two of you get down into those balconies and make sure the Hians don't get near the weapons." Briar climbed into the one on the port side and Saffron motioned for Flicker to take the other.

Shade landed next to Moon and set Lithe on her feet, then Jade leapt over their heads to reach the next cabin roof. Lithe had shifted to her Arbora form, something she only did reluctantly. She still looked like an ordinary Arbora, except her scales were more prominent and were matte black, the color of a consort or a Fell ruler.

Moon leapt forward after Jade and followed her up to the steering cabin. Balm motioned for Root to take the remaining fire weapon station above the bow. The other was just a still-smoking hole in the upper hull, parts of its platform hanging from the ropey vines that must stabilize the boat's exterior walls. Moon turned toward Jade, then realized Root hadn't obeyed, and was still crouched on the cabin roof, as if hoping Balm would tell someone else to guard the remaining weapon. Chime and Saffron were watching the doors in the stern and hadn't noticed.

He wants to go inside with us and kill Hians, Moon thought. He sympathized, but this was no place to argue or disobey Jade and Balm. If a Hian got to one of the big weapons, she could kill anyone still in the air. Balm hissed at Root, who ignored her. When Moon tried to catch his gaze, Root finally turned reluctantly and dropped into the weapon station.

Moon exchanged a frustrated look with Balm. Jade, engaged in hanging upside down to look through the windows into the steering cabin, didn't notice the moment, or pretended not to. She straightened up to whisper, "It's empty." She signaled to the warriors in the stern, then swung down to land on the stairs leading to a hatch. Moon glanced back to make sure Shade and Lithe would stay put on the cabin roof for now. Shade acknowledged him with a flick of spines.

With the fire weapons secured, Stone swept in to circle the boat, then came in low above it. He shifted in midair and dropped lightly onto the roof of the steering cabin. Balm and the other warriors climbed down to enter a hatch in the stern. Moon followed Jade to the stairwell.

He swung down behind her just as she pushed the hatch open. It was made of the same green-gray moss material as the rest of the boat, but reinforced with metal. Moon hadn't had much chance to observe details last night, but had noted how heavily armed this flying boat was compared to Callumkal's.

Just inside a passage curved toward the steering cabin and a set of stairs led down. Light still came from the globes in the ceiling, and Moon couldn't hear any movement. Jade tasted the air and flicked a spine in surprise. "Do you scent that?"

Moon tasted the air again, more deeply. It was so dry and still that it didn't carry a lot of scent, but this time he caught it. It was blood, and burned flesh, and the foul scents when a body voided itself at death. There was more than he expected; he didn't think he and Stone had killed that many Hians. "That's odd," he whispered back.

Almost soundless, Stone stepped through the hatch behind them. He said quietly, "Something's funny with the bottom of the boat."

Jade started down, her foot claws curling silently around the steps. "What do you mean, 'funny?'"

"I mean a chunk of it's missing," Stone clarified. He told Moon, "Where we put the bug paste."

Jade glanced back at them, baffled, then apparently decided not to ask. Moon said, "Does it look like something took a bite out of the boat?" He was wondering if the insect-lizards had been more virulent than they had seemed and had eaten away the moss. Or if it had attracted something bigger.

"It's not a ragged edge," Stone answered. "I think—"

Jade hissed at them to be quiet. She had reached the bottom of the stairs. Ahead the corridor curved around toward the interior of the boat. The scents of death were stronger, the odor of burned flesh mingled with seared moss. As they followed the curve around, Moon saw an open doorway ahead. Jade stepped to the wall to take a cautious look inside, then motioned for Moon and Stone to come forward.

Moon looked over her shoulder into a sleeping room with padded shelves for beds. On the floor three Hians sprawled, all dead, with ugly burn wounds. From their positions it was clear two had been caught by surprise and one had been fleeing into the room.

Jade looked at Moon, scaled brow lifted, as Stone stepped around them to see. They had been killed with Kishan fire weapons; nothing else could do that. Moon said, "It wasn't us."

Jade shook her head slightly. "Then either someone attacked the boat after it got here, or they turned on each other." She stepped away from the door and moved down the corridor. "As if we needed more mysteries. Come on."

Moon followed with Stone, listening carefully, every sense alert. The idea of the Hians turning on each other was hard to imagine, but it was also hard to imagine people living up here who had the same weapons as the Kishan. Had the Hians just been that shocked by the sudden transition to the cloudwall that it made them all go mad? *That couldn't be it,* Moon thought. He was betting it was something Vendoin had done. Maybe some of the crew hadn't been here willingly, and had taken the opportunity to turn on their captors.

They stopped at each room along the corridor, quietly snapping the locks if the doors were fastened. They found more dead Hians, all killed by fire weapons. Stone said, "We need to find Vendoin."

Moon agreed. There had been no shouts, no alarm sounded, so the warriors searching the stern must not have met anyone alive yet either. Jade muttered, "If we can just find the weapon, I'll be happy to leave this boat here to rot."

The corridor ended in a junction with another stairwell, where a wide passage went toward the steering cabin. Another Hian body lay there, collapsed in a heap beside the wall. Jade kicked it over. Though part of the face was burned, Moon had a jolt of unpleasant recognition. He said, "I think that's Bemadin."

Jade flicked a spine in assent, frowning. "With any luck, we'll find Vendoin next." She started up the passage to the steering cabin.

They found a more lavish set of rooms just below it that had to be meant for the Hian leaders. There were thick braided grass rugs, and light silky drapes over the beds, and dishes of a thin glazed pottery with bright metal rims. They split up to search the rooms, looking in every container and cubby, at first certain the artifact would be here somewhere.

Except it wasn't.

Moon opened a roll of paper and found the pages blank, then remembered that Hians could see colors that Raksura couldn't. He shifted to groundling just long enough to run his more sensitive soft-skinned fingers over the top page, and felt the faint indentations in the pressed plant fiber where a pen had left tracks.

From across the passage, Stone said, "In here."

It was a room for storing the devices groundlings used for navigation. Stone stood in front of the open cabinet where the maps were kept, some on wooden panels, others in fabric rolls, and more recent ones sketched on thick paper. Stone had done a quick search, opening all the cabinets and any bags or boxes, even the ones that weren't large enough to hold the artifact. The rock Bramble had described sat in a padded container. Moon ran his hand over it but there were no seams, nothing to indicate there was anything inside.

"Found this." Stone pulled a wooden box out of the cabinet. It was about the right size, empty, with its lid smashed. Stone sniffed it, then shook his head. "Can't tell."

"It could still be aboard," Moon said, but it was beginning to look like whatever had killed the Hians had been after the artifact, too. And while something might have come silently out of the plain during the night, it was far more likely these dead Hians had brought their enemies with them.

Jade came down from the steering cabin, frustration quivering in her spines. "It's not there, either."

They returned to the lower level to check the rooms along the curve of the passage, and found a few more dead Hians, but still no sign of Vendoin. Hissing in frustration, Jade turned down the stairs toward the stern.

This corridor was wider and ran straight through the ship. Jade reached the first junction in one bound, and cocked her head to listen. Catching up with her, Moon heard the faint voices of the warriors. Jade called out, "Balm, did you find anything?"

A flutter of movement came from the stairwell, then Saffron poked her head up through it. "We just found a barricaded door. Something's alive on the other side."

At the bottom of the stairs was a wider junction with two passages and a large door that probably, from Moon's memory of Callumkal's flying boat, went to a common room. Metal bars had been braced across it, keeping it from sliding open. Unlike the sealed door Moon had broken open to free Callumkal, these looked hastily and sloppily shoved into place.

Balm stood beside the door, while Deft and Saffron kept watch on the other passages. Chime crouched on the floor and dug at the moss along the bottom with his claws. Balm told Jade, "We found dead Hians scattered all through here."

Jade moved a spine in acknowledgement. "So did we. Any sign of Vendoin?"

"Not yet." Balm added, "We found bodies in the supply stores, like they'd been forced in there and then killed by fire weapons. The jars and boxes had been dragged around, like someone had removed some supplies. There was a room up on the level above this one where ten Hians were laid out, all with broken necks or like they were smashed against something—"

"Uh," Moon interrupted. "That was us. Probably. When we got the Arbora and the groundlings out."

Saffron twitched her spines but didn't otherwise react. She had seen Moon and Stone fight before. Deft turned to stare, then hastily looked away when Stone met his gaze. Jade flicked a spine impatiently, and Balm continued, "This is the only room we found blocked off like this." She glanced down at Chime.

He sat up and reported, "Still just breathing, no movement."

Moon crouched down with Chime, and helped him pry up another section of moss. "If they locked themselves in last night, and then had some of the water Bramble poisoned, they might be still unconscious." Or the Hians inside could be lying in wait with their fire weapons, a possibility no one needed to mention.

Jade's tail lashed once in decision. "Balm, Saffron, pry the bars off. Don't get in front of the door."

Moon pulled Chime up and out of the way. Balm and Saffron got the first bar off, then the second. They braced themselves as Jade stepped forward. Chime stirred uneasily, and Moon held his breath, every nerve going tight. If one Hian was awake, pointing a weapon at the door . . . Then Jade slammed through the barrier. Balm and Saffron lunged after her.

Something clattered inside, but there was no characteristic whoosh-thump of a fire weapon. Moon pulled Saffron out of the way and looked in.

It was a big common room, with a small square stove for holding heat-spelled moss. Jade had landed on the far wall, and Balm stood in the broken remains of the door. Several Hians sprawled on the floor and one on a padded bench seat, all apparently unconscious. At first glance, none had been wounded, though some had been messily sick. Moon looked for the water source and spotted it on the far wall: a narrow copper-colored pipe, running down from the ceiling and ending in a curved tap with a lever.

Jade leapt down from the wall and used her foot claws to roll the first Hian over. Balm said, "This door was braced from the inside, too." She nudged a stool which had been taken apart and jammed into the door.

Chime leaned in behind Moon. "So these Hians barricaded themselves in here and whoever shot the others blocked the door from the outside, so they couldn't get out? And then left them here?"

"Nice people," Saffron commented succinctly.

Moon looked around but there was nowhere to conceal anything, no containers or cabinets, and the Hians' light clothing left no hiding places. The artifact's continued absence was making his back teeth itch. It was gone for a reason, and it wasn't going to be a good reason.

Jade prodded another unconscious body with a foot. "Tie them up. And collect any of those small fire weapons you find. We'll take some onto the wind-ship and dump the rest overboard."

Chime said, "So where did the people who did this go?"

Stone said, "I think I have an idea about that."

While the warriors continued to search for the artifact, Moon and Jade followed Stone to the bottom of the boat, finding a single small stairwell that led down. The hull curved in here, and there were no cabins, just cubbies and storage racks mostly filled with moss canisters and the supplies for making moss grow. A heavy acrid scent clouded the air.

Then the passage ended in a narrow circular stair, and Moon caught the scent of outside air laced with death. A slow draft drifted up the stairwell. Stone crouched to look. "This is it," he said, and started down the steps.

Below was another dead Hian, with fire weapon wounds in her chest and the side of her face. The fire had actually burnt away the armor plate on her skin.

Stone had already stepped past her and stood beside an open section in the floor. "This wasn't here last night."

Moon stepped to the edge. The opening looked down on the curving stem of the nearest pod and the rising mist that concealed the bottom of the ruin. He crouched down to stick his head through.

"Careful," Jade said.

He felt her hand in his frills, ready to jerk him back. "There's nothing down here," he said. He could see the hull on either side, where it extended down to frame a whole section of the flying boat that just wasn't here anymore. Stone was right, this was the spot they had put the bug paste on, but it hadn't been eaten away by anything. He drew back to look up at Stone. "So there was a separate piece of the boat here?"

Stone nodded. "Has to be. And the missing Hians are on it."

"How could that happen?" Jade's expression was baffled. "A piece of the boat couldn't fly by itself, not unless it had a motivator . . ." She trailed off. "Unless it did have a motivator."

Moon had a sudden realization. "The little flying boat on the island, the one that the Fellborn queen stole. Maybe it was like this, part of a bigger flying boat. Callumkal must have left it there for Kellimdar and the others when he went back to Kish-Jandera for help."

Jade snarled, "No one told us these damn things could come apart." She controlled her spines. "We need to find the artifact. If it's not here, and it probably isn't, at least Dranam can still track the smaller boat. It's made of the same moss as this one."

Looking thoughtfully down toward the misty expanse below, Stone added, "At least they left some Hians to tell us what happened."

When the captive Hians started to wake, Jade sent Flicker, Deft, and Saffron back to the wind-ship to report to Diar and Niran. Shade and Lithe came down inside the boat to help with the search for the weapon, though it seemed more and more unlikely that it was still here. But as Chime put it, "We have to search every handbreadth of this boat. If the Hians who left didn't take it with them, we're going to feel awfully stupid."

Moon and Jade went up on deck when the warriors landed with Bramble, Kalam, and Delin. Setting Delin down, Saffron reported to Jade, "The wind-ship is following us, and the other groundlings are doing the thing they need to do with the moss to track the Hians."

Moon was glad to see that Bramble and Delin looked better than they had last night. Bramble's eyes were clear again and her scales were bright. Delin's face seemed less sunken and bruised, and he headed down the deck toward Chime with more of his old energy.

Kalam still looked furious. "They told us what you found," he said. "Stone is right, some larger air-going craft have small portions that can be steered independently. Dranam can still follow it with our moss samples, so unless the motivator on this ship is damaged, I don't know why they would take the smaller craft."

"The Hians we found alive were barricaded in a room, so we think the others had to take the small boat to get away," Jade told him as they started down the deck. "We need you to help talk to them, so we can find out what happened."

"The weapon is not here?" Delin asked. "You are sure?"

"We're still searching the hold," Jade said, "but it's more likely they took it with them when they left."

Jade led the way through the hatch and down the first set of stairs. Moon found himself beside Kalam and asked, "Is Callumkal any better?" They had left the wind-ship so quickly at dawn, Moon hadn't had a chance to find out.

"No. Not yet," Kalam said. "Ivar-edel and Merit said this morning that there hasn't been enough time for the poisons to wear off." It was an optimistic answer, but Kalam didn't seem as if he believed it himself. He added, "At least he is with us now, and cared for, and not in the power of that lying traitor."

Moon tried to think of something encouraging to say that didn't sound like he had no concept of reality. Ivar-edel, Merit, and Lithe might all be very good healers, but none of them had any experience with Jandera.

They reached the room with the captured Hians. Balm stood on guard outside. Inside, Stone leaned casually against the wall, the Hians clustered on the far side of the room. A big one was on the floor, cradling an injured arm. They stirred uneasily when Moon and Jade stepped in. The air was tainted with sickness and some Hians slumped against the wall, as if too ill to sit up straight. Jade glanced at the one with the injured arm, and asked Stone, "Something happen?"

"Idiots tried to rush me," he said.

Jade turned to Bramble and Delin. "Do you know anything about them?" She spoke Raksuran.

As first Bramble, then Delin looked in, the Hians seemed startled to see them. One turned to another and said in Kedaic, "It's the prisoners."

Bramble leaned in the doorway and eyed them thoughtfully. She pointed. "That one, the small male, served food to Vendoin. And that female, she was a guard on our cage sometimes."

Delin nodded agreement. "I have seen them in passing, only, when I was taken to the steering cabin to speak to Vendoin." He pointed to one. "She is called Vinat, and seemed to be in charge of the other guards."

Jade flicked a spine in acknowledgement and switched to Altanic to speak to the Hians. "Where is Vendoin?"

They stared at her with that same apparent lack of expression that had made Vendoin so hard to read. Moon shared an irritated glance with Stone.

Then Kalam slipped through the doorway past Bramble and Delin. "Do you know me?" he asked Vinat. He was trembling a little. The Hians might interpret that as fear or nerves, but Moon knew Kalam well enough to tell it was anger. "Callumkal, who you held prisoner, is my parent. You poisoned our companions, and killed five of them."

Vinat's gaze went to the fire weapon slung across Kalam's back, then strayed to Bramble and Delin, but she said nothing.

Kalam's fists clenched. "Where is Vendoin? Where is the artifact she stole?"

Vinat said in Kedaic, "Why are you with these animals?"

Moon was unsurprised, and Jade's spine flick showed bored annoyance. Kalam quivered, as if the desire to fling himself at Vinat's throat had just passed through him. He turned to Jade and said in clear Altanic, "If they don't answer, we should kill them."

Jade tilted her head, pretending to consider it, but Moon saw the doubtful angle of her spines. He didn't think that was the right path to take. The Hians expected Raksura to be savage and kill them. If that was the case, there was no motive for them to talk. On impulse, Moon said in Altanic, "Did you know they locked you in here?"

The Hians all stared blankly at him. He continued, "There were metal bars fixed over the door. Is there another way out? Because I don't see one. I don't see any way to control the boat from in here, either. It looks like they couldn't make you come out, so they took the small flying boat and left you to die on this one, trapped in this room."

Stone stepped out, then returned with one of the bent metal bars. He tossed it on the floor.

Jade said, "Who left you here? Was it Vendoin? We know it wasn't Bemadin. We found her dead in the corridor below the steering cabin."

Two Hians flinched. Moon noticed the small male had fixed his gaze on the corner, not reacting. Moon said, "Did you kill Bemadin?"

Vinat made a faint noise that sounded like derision, but the male seemed to shrink in on himself. Then the male said, "If you agree to release us, I'll answer."

Vinat sat up and said in Kedaic, "It will do no good. The animals mean to kill us anyway."

The male answered in the same language, "The others turned on us, killed so many, why protect them?" He waved at the bent metal bar. "They meant us to starve to death in here, drinking poisoned water."

Vinat leaned back against the wall. It was hard to tell if the argument had swayed her or not. The one who seemed the most ill stirred a little and said, "We owe them nothing, now. You're the highest rank. Act to help us who are left, not those who abandoned us."

"She is right," Delin said, watching them. He had lost enough weight that his features were sharper, and it made the degree of calculation in his expression more evident. "Vendoin has left you behind in this strange place. Did she know there was some power in the ruin that would take her flying craft to the cloudwalls?"

The response to this seemed to be blank astonishment.

From the doorway, Chime whispered in Raksuran, "They don't know where they are." There was a stir as Balm nudged him to be quiet.

"Yes," Delin said to the Hians' silent shock. "The darkness that fell abruptly was a magic, which has taken this ship up to the flying island formation called the cloudwalls. Our friends' ship was taken as well, and we have no notion how to return the same way, or if it is even possible for a flying craft to make its way down from here."

Vinat hesitated, apparently disbelieving. Kalam added, "It's true. And we don't care about you, or what you do after this, or where you go. It's Vendoin we want."

The male said, "Lavinat betrayed Vendoin and Bemadin." Vinat turned toward him as if she might try to stop him. Then she slumped against the wall, clearly realizing the words were out and nothing could call them back. The male continued, "Lavinat killed Bemadin."

Not that the words were that helpful. Moon remembered Lavinat from the confrontation in the bow, but he wasn't sure what it meant that she had betrayed Vendoin.

Jade turned to Bramble and Delin for an explanation. Brow furrowed in confusion, Bramble said in Raksuran, "That was the other Hian leader. I don't think she was here the whole time. I got the impression she wasn't with Bemadin when they caught us in the ocean."

Delin was nodding. "I agree, I think perhaps she was on the Hian ship—this Hian ship—that we met at the port city, when we left the original ship behind."

Jade nodded to the young male. "Go on."

He said, "After everything went dark, Vendoin and Bemadin were trying to decide what to do." He looked at Stone and Moon and lifted his shoulders in a gesture that conveyed wariness and fear. "They were afraid you would come back. There was a place they had to look for, but Lavinat said they should wait for daylight. I went to Bemadin's cabin to sleep. Then I heard weapons, I came out. I found her . . ." He looked at the others.

Vinat said, "Lavinat's cohort were moving through the ship, killing anyone they saw. We made it in here, and barricaded the door."

"Vendoin isn't here," Jade said. "Maybe she betrayed you too."

"Why?" The male asked. "She was leader, we followed her."

Jade eyed him skeptically. "Then what caused the fighting?"

There was another hesitation. Moon glanced at Jade, got a spine flick that told him to go ahead. He said, "We know about the weapon. We know Vendoin is going to use it to kill all the Fell, Raksura, Jandera, and any species related to them from here to the eastern sea."

The others all looked at Vinat. She said, "It was Fell, when we started this. It was all meant to kill Fell, that's what they told us. Then the Fell appeared and Aldoan had the weapon on the deck, and they took her, and . . . It killed Aldoan, and the scholar who was going to help Vendoin, and all her family. Bemadin and Vendoin became afraid that it meant the weapon would kill Hians as well. There seemed no other reason for Aldoan's death. Our physician examined her body and there was no wound made by the Fell. She said there was bleeding in the brain, but no sign of a break to the skull, nothing else that could have caused it." Vinat looked at the wall, her body going stiff and stubborn. "That is all I know."

Thoughtful, Delin twisted his fingers in his beard. "Does the physician live?"

Another Hian said, "We don't know. But she was in Bemadin's cohort, not Lavinat's."

The little male said, "Bemadin was angry at Lavinat."

The others turned to stare at him, but more in surprise at what he said than anger that he was talking. He continued, "Bemadin came to her quarters the night before—" He threw a clearly nervous look at Moon and Stone. "The night before all this happened, before we reached the sea. She said Lavinat had abandoned her senses. She wouldn't tell me why. That is all I know."

Jade waited, but none of the others spoke. She motioned for Bramble and Delin to retreat, and stepped back through the doorway, tugging Kalam with her. They went a few steps down the passage, out of earshot of the Hians. Moon followed, with Stone pushing off from the wall to stroll after them. Moon said, softly, "'Why' is a good question."

"If Lavinat and Vendoin disagreed over how or when to use the weapon, and it turned to violence, it could work in our favor," Delin put in, as Chime stepped closer to listen.

"It can't work in our favor yet," Jade said. "We've still got to find them."

Flicker called from the stairwell, "Jade, the wind-ship is here."

"We need to go." Stone's voice was an impatient growl. "We can't wait around here to figure this out."

"I know." Jade tilted her head at Kalam. "What should we do with them?"

Kalam didn't hesitate. "Leave them. It's Vendoin I want to find. But we should take the levitation packs they have aboard, and disable the ship's weapons. Rorra will know how to do that quickly."

"Go with Flicker and tell Rorra to get started," Jade said, and Kalam moved hurriedly to the stairwell.

Once he and Flicker had climbed out of sight, Jade turned to Bramble and Delin. "What do you two think we should do?"

Jade had given Kalam the impression she was letting him make the decision, but Moon knew she had only been asking for his opinion. Kalam wasn't the only one injured by the Hians.

Chime stood with Bramble and Delin, watching, while his spines flicked uncertainly. The other warriors were still by the door, keeping guard on the Hians. Only Balm had her head tilted in their direction, unobtrusively listening.

Delin glanced at Bramble, then said, "Not kill them, not on my account at least. I don't see how we can wrest the weapon from Vendoin without killing her and perhaps the others with her. That will be a necessity, this is not."

Bramble stared at the deck, flexing her foot claws. Then she said, "I'm not mad enough anymore to make it easy." She lifted her head. "So we should do what Kalam said, and leave them."

Jade met Stone's gaze. "Well?"

Stone lifted his brows at Moon. Moon didn't want to leave the Hians alive. Except then he pictured himself killing the little male, and knew that just wasn't going to happen. That one might be considered a mature adult by Hian standards, but there were too many things about him that read "fledgling" to Moon. And leaving him alone without the others was worse. Vinat seemed to be the only capable one left, and without her, the others would die. They might die up here anyway, but that was their doing for following Vendoin in the first place. He said, "Leave them."

Stone shrugged. "It's Vendoin I want."

Jade's spines moved in assent. "All right, we'll leave them."

Moon felt he had to ask, "What about Root?" He wasn't even sure if a warrior got any say in something like this.

Jade hissed in mingled annoyance and resignation. "He's in no state to give his opinion on anything, that's why I left him on guard on the deck. Come on, let's go."

Not long after, the wind-ship was underway, following the direction Dranam was able to tease out of the moss samples. Moon had heard her tell Rorra, "It's a relief. I was a little afraid it wouldn't work in this strange place."

While they were waiting for Dranam to work on the moss, there had been a discussion about how best to pursue the small flying boat.

Stone was in favor of flying ahead to try to catch it. Moon had to admit that it sounded like a good idea to him, too. The night had seemed long, but the little boat couldn't have more than a few hours head start.

But Jade had refused to consider that. "Not here. We don't know anything about this place."

Niran agreed. "There could be anything out there. And now that we have managed to retrieve everyone who was missing, I feel we should stay together."

Stone folded his arms. His expression would have still been opaque to most observers but Moon recognized the stubborn set to it. Stone said, "We don't know how far they have to go. If they get there ahead of us and use this thing, the first we'll know of it is when we drop dead."

Niran grimaced down the deck at the young Golden Islanders who were sorting through the fire weapons taken from the flying boat. They didn't know yet if the artifact would affect the Islanders.

Moon had to point out, "The Hians don't know how to use it. We don't even know if they know where they're going with it." Obviously the Hian scholar in the river trade city had been an important part of Vendoin's plan. Not having access to her or her writings had already thrown Vendoin into confusion. That was probably the reason that Lavinat had seized control, not any change of heart on Vendoin's part.

Rorra, who had been listening quietly up to this point, said, "Jade is right. You and Moon crossing the outskirts of Kish and the far south is one thing. But we've already seen one forerunner ruin and we know the forerunners and the foundation builders fought something terrible. Something could still be trapped up here."

Stone eyed her for a long moment, while Rorra glared at him. Moon could tell she was actually glaring this time, that it wasn't just her habitual frown. Then Stone said, "All right."

Rorra lifted her chin a little self-consciously. "Then will you come and tell the kethel to get away from the stern hatch so we can set up a weapon placement?"

"Sure." Stone followed her away down the deck.

Jade watched them go, brow furrowed. "What just happened?"

"He likes her," Moon said. Stone would have obeyed Jade, though there would have been more arguing and growling first. But while Stone listened to groundlings and gave their opinions weight, he had just given Rorra's fear for his safety the same consideration that he would have given to a queen. His queen.

Chime nodded agreement. "He does."

Jade stared blankly at them. Niran shook his head and turned for the door to the steering cabin. "Don't tell grandfather, he'll write a monograph on it."

As Niran left, Jade said, "But Stone wouldn't sleep with a groundling."

Moon snorted.

Jade turned to him. "What was that?"

"Nothing."

Chime was still thinking it over. "How would—I mean, what if your parts aren't compatible?"

Moon told him, "There are ways around that."

Jade was still watching Moon, scaled brows drawn down. Moon wasn't sure if it was Raksuran sensibilities being offended or the fact that Stone was a consort, even if he was a line-grandfather. He sighed and clarified, "In all the turns Stone's been away from court, wandering around, you don't think he's ever done that."

Jade had looked down the deck toward where Stone and Rorra had disappeared. "This is not something we're going to tell Pearl. Or anyone. Whatever happens on this wind-ship, it doesn't get back to the court."

Now Jade had gone up atop the cabins to take over the watch so Balm could get some rest. Moon thought it was also so she could see as much of this strange place they were traveling through as possible, to get some idea of the dangers. It was why he was out on the bow deck.

As the wind-ship angled further from the ruin, it was more apparent the structure stood on tall narrow pillars that stretched up out of a lake. The mist still lay across the water, an indication that there wasn't much air movement near the ground. *At least finding water isn't going to be a problem,* Moon thought. It was a lack of game he was worried about. They couldn't even start looking for a way down until they got the artifact back, and they had no idea how long they would be stuck up here.

He heard a faint scrape of claws on the deck behind him, and turned. It was Root.

His spines drooped as he stared at the receding Kishan boat. Moon said, "You all right?" Moon hadn't really had a conversation with him since he and Stone had left the others to search for the Hians. Maybe since Song had died.

"Yes." Root absently dragged his claws over the deck. It left faint scars on the tough plant fiber.

"You don't look all right." Moon wasn't good at this. He hated to talk about what was wrong with him, and so never felt inclined to make other people talk about what was wrong with them. Stone was better at it, but he was down in the stern staring intimidatingly at their kethel. He wrestled with his reticence, and asked, "What's wrong?"

Root was quiet for a long moment, the wind playing with his frills. Hesitantly, as if he had to choke the words out, he said, "It's like no one thinks about Song but me."

Moon turned all the way to face him, startled. "That's not true."

Root's spines flicked. "I know it's because you're busy. But no one talks about her but Briar and that's just because she feels guilty."

Moon felt that needed to be unraveled. "So we don't think about her because we don't talk about her and Briar talks about her but that means she doesn't care?"

Root glared at him. "I'm not stupid."

"I know you aren't." Moon let out his breath, trying to think how best to handle this. Jade had said Root's behavior was uncertain at best. But he hadn't had to come over here and loiter around Moon, hoping Moon would start a conversation. Which meant Root wanted to talk, if Moon could just think of the right things to say. "Not talking about her doesn't mean we don't think about her. Jade and Balm . . . You know how they felt about Song. They trusted her like . . ." Jade had other favorites, but Song had been with her on her most harrowing trips away from the colony. Queens were always closer to female warriors than to the males, and Jade had trusted Song, been sure of her, in a way she wasn't with most of the others. And Balm had felt the same.

It was why Jade and Balm had gotten so angry when Song had challenged Jade back on the foundation builder city's island. And Moon knew how responsible Jade felt for Song's death, how Pearl might react when they got back to the court and Jade had to tell her how Song had died. Not in battle with Fell, but in a trap set by groundlings. "But Jade can't show things like that, and neither can Balm. Not while we're still out here."

Root twisted away, as if he couldn't bear to hear it. He stepped back from the rail. "I have to go. It's my turn on watch next."

"Root—" Moon called after him, but Root pretended not to hear, and leapt up to the cabin roof and disappeared.

Shade stepped out of the cabin doorway and moved to stand at the railing beside Moon. "Is he all right?" Shade asked.

"No." Moon let out his breath in exasperation, mostly at himself. He had made a bad job of that, but he had no idea what to say to make anything better for Root or anyone else. Shade was in groundling form, so Moon shifted to lose his scales and wings. The damp cool air settled on his skin and clothes. "He thinks we don't care about Song."

Shade winced in sympathy. "It's not as if you can have a ceremony for her until you get back to your court. Your Arbora would be furious." He shook his head a little, looking out over the view. "I don't think warriors that young really understand how queens feel about their warriors and Arbora. There's a connection that they just haven't lived long enough to feel and understand, yet. And Song was in Jade's bloodline, wasn't she? She looks—looked like Balm. Jade and Balm can't afford to show weakness now, no matter how upset they are. They have to be strong to show the rest of us that everything is all right, or at least under control. Even if it isn't. Especially if it isn't."

Moon wished he had been able to say all that to Root. Though he wasn't sure it would have helped. He said, "Are you all right?" He jerked his head toward the stern, where the kethel lurked under Stone's watchful eye. "After the thing with the . . . Last night."

Shade lifted his shoulders, uncomfortable. "Not really." He glanced down the deck. "I guess we can't just tell it to leave, since Malachite's made an alliance with the Fellborn queen."

"Telling it to leave doesn't really work," Moon admitted. "And it's hard to kill it when it's just standing there looking at you. And it keeps talking." He hesitated, then asked, "What did you think about that alliance, about what Malachite's doing?" He wanted to ask what Shade thought of Consolation, if he and Lithe had seen her for themselves. There were other half-Fell at Opal Night, the rescued children of the Arbora who had been captured by the Fell at the same time as Moon and Shade's father Dusk. But Moon was wondering if Shade would have felt any special connection to Consolation. Thinking about it, it felt like a completely stupid thing to ask. Shade was more of a Raksuran consort than Moon was.

From Shade's expression he was contemplating a much more complicated question. "I don't know. It's not like I want the other half-Fell to be . . . If they're really going to ally with us and help us . . ." He leaned heavily on the railing. "Lithe thinks it could work out for the best."

"But you don't want to be near Fell," Moon guessed. Considering what had happened to Shade when they had been captured by the Fell flight northwest of the Reaches, it was only rational.

"No, I don't." He looked at Moon hopelessly. "Is that weak?"

Consorts were supposed to be weak and delicate and to need everything done for them, but Moon and Shade were different, and nothing was going to change that. And "weak" wasn't really the right word for what Shade meant. What he was trying to say was harder to express. It was giving in to feelings other people thought you were supposed to have about things that shouldn't have happened to you in the first place, but were not like the actual feelings you did have. There wasn't a word for that in Raksuran or Altanic or Kedaic or any other language Moon knew. Moon said, "It's not weak."

The wind-ship moved out over the plain of gorges and the rushing sound of waterfalls became audible over the wind. The cliffs were thick with deep green foliage, and there was no sign of any other ruins. Shade twitched a little, and said, "I'm glad we have Dranam. At least we know where we're going."

Moon nodded. But they didn't, though. They only knew the direction.

CHAPTER EIGHTEEN

In the Eastern Reaches

Heart waited in the greeting hall, trying not to pace. She was going with Pearl and Malachite to talk to their new half-Fell allies, and she was trying to pretend as if this didn't frighten her. Though it wasn't the idea of the half-Fell that was the problem. Malachite had made it clear most of the flight were Fell, subordinate to the half-Fell queen.

The shared dream and visions of Fell attack had been bad enough. Heart took a deep breath to calm herself. This was different.

"Are you all right, mentor?" Celadon asked her. The Opal Night daughter queen waited a few paces away with three of her warriors. Floret had just arrived with Vine and Sage and Malachite's warriors. Celadon herself would remain behind, since leaving a court without a queen present just wasn't a good idea, especially under these circumstances.

No one smelled as nervous as Heart, which didn't help. She said, "I'm fine, thank you. It was just . . . I was held prisoner by the Fell once, when they attacked our court to the east. Moon saved us."

Celadon's spines flicked in sympathy. "I haven't heard that story. Will you tell me when we get back?"

For some reason it was easier to remember that Malachite was Moon's birthqueen than it was that this sober, capable daughter queen was his clutchmate. Distracted, Heart dipped her spines in assent. "I will."

Heart sensed movement overheard and looked up in time to see Pearl and Malachite launch themselves off the queens' hall terrace. Apparently they had solved the question of precedence by simply going at the same time, though Heart somehow doubted if Malachite cared. Heart said, tentatively, "They're getting along very well." She wasn't sure Celadon and the Opal Night contingent understood what a revelation that was for Indigo Cloud.

Celadon lowered her voice. "No one speaks to Malachite like that, especially not another reigning queen. She's enjoying it."

The two queens landed on the greeting hall floor before Heart had a chance to take that statement in. Then Pearl said, "Come on, let's get this travesty started."

Heart clung to Vine as they flew through the cool damp air. It was a long trip but it had been a while since she had been flown through the Reaches, so she didn't mind. The sunlight that streamed through all the thick layers of the canopy was soft and green. Platforms made by the wild mountain-trees' branches were covered with lush grass, vines, and flowers. Many supported glades of smaller trees or the swampy overflow of water drawn up through the mountain-trees' roots. Heart caught glimpses of a dozen different grasseaters and predators that lived on the platforms, including the mottled gray-green tree-frogs bigger than she was, too shy to come near the colony tree.

Some of the mountain-trees were in strange shapes, bending down or curving around other trees, some were hung with curtains of moss big enough to drape over Indigo Cloud's main garden platforms. It was all a much-needed distraction, until Vine said in her ear, "We're nearly there. Can you scent them?"

With her next breath Heart caught the Fell stench laced through the air. It was like a thread of bitter rot creeping through all the intense green and flower scents. She tried not to react, but she must have tensed, because Vine tightened his hold on her.

Pearl abruptly signaled a landing and they banked down to a platform heavily overgrown with vines and small, purple-fern trees. Vine said, "This is one of our outposts. Well, one of Opal Night's outposts, but we helped."

Heart's eye caught movement, and she realized there were warriors and a few Arbora under the cover of the ferny leaves, waiting for the queens to land. Huge branches that had fallen down onto the platform had been hollowed out and made into shelters. Heart studied it avidly, trying to spot and memorize all the details. It was an excellent concealed camp, and Blossom and Rill and the other teachers would want to hear about every trick and technique.

Pearl and Malachite lit on the broken remnants of a fallen branch and the warriors followed them down. By the time they landed, a female Opal Night warrior was reporting to the queens. Heart only caught the last bit as Vine set her on her feet. "—more of them, maybe another flight."

Malachite said, "I need to see for myself." She tilted her head at Pearl.

Pearl twitched her spines in annoyed assent.

Heart steeled herself, set her jaw, and said, "I should see them. In case it sparks a vision."

Malachite tilted her head at Pearl. Pearl considered it, her spines flicking. She said, "Come here, then. The rest of you wait here."

It wasn't long before Heart began to glimpse brighter sunlight between the branches and platforms ahead. "They won't be close," Pearl had told her, "but we need to be careful of dakti scouts." As they drew nearer to the edge, Heart found herself taking a firmer grip on Pearl's collar flanges. It was a different experience being carried by a queen of Pearl's size. It was like being carried by Moon, whose easy, unexpected strength in flight was always surprising, and so different from the warriors. Pearl was like that, except her larger body was more reassuringly solid.

Finally Malachite lit on a large branch on a mountain-tree sapling just at the edge of the wetlands. Pearl cupped her wings to land beside her. She didn't set Heart down immediately, and Heart found herself clinging like a baby. *You're a grown mentor, you can handle this,* she told herself, trying to settle her nerves.

"There they are," Pearl whispered.

Heart stretched to look. She was afraid of what she would see, but it was just the bright sunlight on the tall grass of the wetlands. Light played on stretches of open water between stands of reeds and the occasional copse of broadleaf trees. She had seen this fringe of the Reaches when they had first arrived here, when they had left the destruction of the old eastern colony and so many of their dead behind.

Floret had described the western fringe of the Reaches as a gradual change from mountain-tree forest to rocky plains. But here on the eastern fringe the change was abrupt; the wetlands turned into lush fields of short green grass, dotted with tiny white flowers and alive with glasslizards and insects, then it stopped abruptly at the line of mountain-trees. Standing on the grass and facing the forest was like looking at the impenetrable wall of a giant cliff face.

Heart had been afraid the Fell would be as thick on the wetlands as the myriad colors of the waterbirds. It was a relief to see the landscape empty. Then a dark shape moved in the distance. And then another, and another. *Kethel*, Heart thought, and felt a chill travel through the skin under her spines.

She counted at least twelve. They were mostly clustered over a group of low hills, some distance across the wetlands. "Is that an old ruin?" Heart asked softly. The ripple in the terrain of the marshes looked unnatural.

"Probably." Pearl hissed and said, "There's more kethel than there were before."

Malachite didn't acknowledge that, but after a moment said, "We should go."

Pearl turned and dove off the branch, snapping her wings out. Heart shivered against the heat of her scales.

They rejoined the warriors and Pearl handed Heart over to Vine again. As they flew toward the camp of the Fellborn queen's flight, Vine asked her, "Was it worse? Pearl looks like it was worse."

"We saw more kethel," Heart told him. She had been hoping it would spark a vision, but nothing had happened yet. She could still sense the potential for one in the awareness of uncertain movement just outside her conscious thoughts.

The Fellborn queen's flight was camped on a platform high in a mountain-tree. The tree's canopy bent toward it, the huge branches curved over, giving the feeling of a cavern or a vast green chamber.

The platform had been efficiently cleared to its grassy surface and the Fell had actually built shelters of woven leaves and stripped saplings. There were hearths, too, dug out of the moss and dirt. The big bones of several grasseaters, probably the furry hoppers from what Heart could see, were piled near the edge. Dakti peered out from under the shelters, watching their approach. Heart scanned the canopy and picked out two kethel, coiled on the upper branches, keeping watch. A growl built in her chest and she forced it down.

Vine landed with the others on a branch overlooking the platform. He said to Floret, "That's weird. It looks like a real camp."

"It does," she said, settling her wings. She eyed the camp critically. "I didn't think they knew how to do that."

Rise leaned over and told Floret and Vine, "We had to show the dakti how to build the shelters, and what grasseaters to hunt, but I was surprised they actually listened to us."

"Better you than us," Vine muttered in Heart's ear.

Malachite and Pearl waited further down the branch, Malachite as still as if she was a wall carving and Pearl flicking her spines impatiently. A figure ducked out of the biggest shelter and at first Heart thought it was a ruler. As it came further into the open she realized this was the half-Fell queen.

Malachite and Pearl launched off the branch and dropped to the platform, Pearl flicking a spine to tell the warriors to follow. Vine landed with the others and set Heart on her feet. He gave her wrist an encouraging squeeze. Heart took a deep breath, reminded herself she was a mentor, and stepped forward. The wet grass brushed her scales as she moved to stand just behind and to the right of Pearl.

The Fell queen, Consolation, picked her way toward them, a dakti in her wake. She said without preamble, "There are more today. You saw them already?" She spoke Raksuran but not as fluently as the other Fell. She spoke it like Delin did, just a little hesitantly, as if trying to remember words. Heart wondered if it was because the flight had no progenitor. The Fell's facility for their prey's languages might come from their connection to the progenitor or the rulers. It was something to talk to Merit about. *If Merit's alive*, Heart thought bleakly. *If Jade can find him and Bramble.*

Malachite said, "We saw them."

Pearl's gaze moved over the dakti, the two rulers who remained back near the bigger shelter. The way her spines angled told Heart she was acutely aware of the kethel in the branches above. Pearl said to Malachite, "We need to talk about this strategy of yours."

The dakti nudged Consolation. She said, "We know how to make the progenitor come to us. But we want something else from you before we do it."

Pearl's spines took on a flare that would have caused the warriors to bolt out of reach if it had been directed at them. Malachite tilted her head and said, "And what is that?"

The dakti ducked its head in a gesture Heart would have sworn was nervous. Consolation hesitated, watching them both warily. She dragged one set of foot claws through the grass and moss and said, "We had a consort."

Heart's lips peeled back to bare her teeth without any conscious volition on her part. Pearl's hiss was near soundless and the tip of Malachite's tail flicked almost imperceptibly. The cold, sardonic amusement was heavy in Malachite's voice as she said, "You say this to us."

Consolation's brow furrowed. "He was my sire. He named me. I can speak of him."

Heart made herself take a breath. Pearl's tail lashed. Malachite said, "Speak."

Consolation said, "Before he died, he said we were going to go someplace, just us and a few others, the nice ones. A big tree, maybe." She added defensively, "I didn't know what he meant until we got here."

Heart had to lock her jaw to keep her expression neutral. It was painful to think about, this long dead consort making plans for escape with his fledgling queen. She wondered if Malachite could identify the court. But she didn't see how a consort could be taken from a court within the vastness of the Reaches. It must have been an eastern court, one that told stories of their old mothercourt and its colony tree in the west.

Consolation continued, "But we had to learn to hunt grasseaters and grow things, like groundlings." The dakti risked a glance at the queens, then scratched the side of its head, somehow conveying mild doubt. Consolation eyed Malachite. "If you show us that, I'll help you with the plan. I can get the most powerful progenitor to come to me."

Heart could feel the skepticism rolling off Pearl in a wave. Malachite gave no hint of her own reaction. Malachite said, "How?"

Consolation settled her shoulders, her own spines moving, though Heart wasn't sure what that meant. She said, "I have secret information and she has to come to me to get it. Then she comes and we kill her. This will do what we want, make her flight and the others confused and easier to kill."

Pearl hissed in disbelief. "And you think that will work?"

The dakti tilted its head to look up at her and said, "It worked on us."

Pearl deliberately turned her gaze on it and it cringed and edged back a step.

The tip of Malachite's tail moved in a small circle. "One of the other progenitors won't take the lead?"

That was what Heart was wondering. The problem was that they had very little idea of how Fell flights cooperated, or didn't cooperate, with each other. They knew the flights shared knowledge, maybe through bloodline connections between the rulers. Maybe the same way that the rulers of a flight knew one of their own had been killed, and how they could locate the body unless the head was severed and buried. But Heart had never known of two flights cooperating. This idea of different Fell flights massing for a single purpose was new and horrible.

Consolation said, "None of the others are as powerful as her. They'll try to take the lead, but the others will resist, and they'll fight."

Pearl and Malachite looked at each other. Watching the accord between them, Heart realized she had never seen two reigning queens work in concert like this.

Pearl's spines moved in inquiry and Malachite moved one spine in response. Heart wasn't even sure what that meant, but Pearl hissed again and said to Consolation, "What secret information?"

Consolation seemed exasperated. "Can't I just tell them it's something secret?"

Pearl regarded Malachite again, her spines twitching in irritation. Heart read that expression clearly as *I can't. I'd have to kill her. You do it.* With the patience of a rock, Malachite said to Consolation, "Send a message, tell her you know where another Raksuran colony is, a small one, not well guarded, closer to the fringe. You won't lead her to it, but you'll tell her where it is when she meets you."

Pearl's spines moved in thoughtful consideration. "When the progenitor asks why she wants to meet instead of just sending the direction?"

Malachite tilted her head at Pearl. "She wants something in return."

"A big tree, but not like this, a better one," Consolation supplied. The dakti nudged her, but whether it was to urge her to be quiet or agree about the tree, it was hard to tell. "With an inside," Consolation added.

Pearl and Malachite ignored her. Pearl said, "The Fell aren't going to believe that."

This time it was Consolation and the dakti who exchanged a look. The dakti said, "Correct. They don't understand us."

It was right. The Fell would never understand the half-Fell's desire for a permanent home. Heart wasn't even sure if she believed in it or not, if it was a whim or if it was the Fellborn queen's real goal. It seemed an incredible thing to consider, and the Arbora had worried about the possibility of Fell influence being directed against courts inside the Reaches, even if the half-Fell didn't intend it consciously. But Opal Night's mentors had said that the lack of a progenitor meant the flight couldn't direct their attention toward Raksura like that, even if they wanted to.

Consolation's expression turned exasperated. "Then what do I say?"

Malachite said to Consolation, "Tell them you want a consort. From the spoils, after you kill us all."

Heart twitched and felt her spines flare despite her best intentions. The movement rippled through all the warriors, an instinctive response. Even the idea, even if it was just part of a trick, made rage pulse inside her chest.

Consolation's brow furrowed, as if she suspected a trap. She glanced at the warriors and said, "It's just a trick. We're really getting a big tree."

Pearl growled under her breath and twitched her spines at Malachite. Malachite told Consolation, "In the western Reaches, there are old abandoned colony trees in my territory, owned by Opal Night. I will give you one, and you will be shown how to live in it. But if you touch any Raksura, Aeriat or Arbora, or kill and eat any sentient being, groundling or swampling or skyling or other, if I find you have lied to me, I will kill every single one of you."

There was no change in her inflection but Heart felt the air turn just a little colder. She drew a sharp breath. *Malachite did that. That was not my imagination.*

Consolation eyed her warily. The dakti drew back a little. It poked Consolation and said, "This tree is good."

"You're not having this tree," Pearl growled. "It's the one in the west or nothing."

Consolation gave the dakti a gentle push to the head. "We'll take the tree in the west."

Malachite stood still for so long, Heart felt the nerves ripple under her spines. It was a predatory stillness, that seemed to affect everyone except Pearl. Consolation watched her with an uneasy air, and the dakti hunched down again. When Pearl finally demanded, "What?" Heart flinched.

Malachite said, "This needs something else." She turned to regard Pearl. "It's just her word that she knows where a court is. And these Fell will know by now that she helped destroy a flight in the sel Selatra. We need something more convincing."

Pearl let out a hiss and lashed her tail a little, but admitted, "You're right."

Consolation drew breath, clearly to protest, but the dakti said, "Correct." Then it added, "You know what they think of us. They will suspect." Consolation subsided mutinously.

Malachite said, "She needs a captive."

Heart hissed to herself. *She's right, the Fell will never believe it without some kind of proof.* Before she came to her senses, Heart said, "I'll do it."

"It can't be a queen, because the Fell aren't that stupid," Heart said. Pearl had picked her up by her frills and hauled her to the edge of the platform, out of earshot of the Fell, to discuss it. Heart didn't mind, because it was Pearl's version of discussing, which involved a lot of growling and veiled threats that Pearl had no intention of carrying out, so it was better to do it in private. "It can't be a warrior, because they don't want warriors. It has to be an Arbora." She wasn't even going to list the reasons it couldn't be a consort. They were just lucky Moon was with Jade and not here to volunteer.

"Heart—" Pearl put her hands on Heart's shoulders as if she wanted to shake her. Well, she did want to shake her.

Heart clasped her wrists. "You know this is best. You're just angry because you can't think of a good reason not to do it."

"I can't risk the chief mentor for this stupid plan," Pearl hissed.

"It's not stupid," Heart said. "It can work. It could save so many lives, if the Fell panic among themselves and fight, or leave. And Malachite is right, if Consolation has a prisoner, the progenitor is more likely to be fooled long enough for the plan to work." She met Pearl's gaze. "And I'm the chief mentor and I say I take the risk." As difficult as it was to do this, Heart knew asking someone else to do it would be worse. She added, "And I've done it before, for real. I can handle it."

Pearl growled in frustration. "If you get yourself killed—"

Heart did what only an Arbora or a fledgling could have done in this situation. She stepped forward and leaned against Pearl's chest. "Don't be angry."

Pearl stopped growling. After a moment, she said, "Stop that."

To the Far South, On the Cloudwalls

As the wind-ship flew, the cool wind turned colder. Moon stayed up in the bow, resting and keeping watch.

The gorges still wound through the plain but the low hills looked as if they were moving off toward the east. Literally moving, as Moon realized they weren't hills, but enormous creatures with gently curving backs. They had legs like the trunks of mountain-trees, stepping with ponderous deliberation. Not long after, Chime spotted a flight of wingless birds that were flying anyway, slipping through the air like fish in a stream.

It was cold enough for the groundlings that the Golden Islander crew had to get out extra clothing. Shade came up to sit on the deck with Moon, bringing some of the extra garments the Islanders had loaned them. He gave Moon a loose shirt, made of a very soft fabric woven from the fibers of a plant that grew on the shallow seabed near the Golden Isles, dyed a soft blue. Chime wore one similar to it but an undyed yellow. Moon wasn't that cold yet but the cloth still carried the scent of the Golden Isles: a hint of the spices they used on their food, and the salt and sun scent of the wind that crossed the Yellow Sea. He had already changed into the other clothes he had brought, the shirt and pants of dark-colored silky material woven by the Arbora at Indigo Cloud. He had left them with Jade and the others as too fine to blend in with the groundling crowds at the trading ports and settlements he and Stone might have had to stop at. But the sleeves were long and the pants went all the way down to his ankles, and they provided more protection from the cold. He pulled the borrowed Islander shirt over his head.

Bramble and Delin came out to join them, Bramble squishing herself between Moon and Chime for comfort and Delin sitting nearby, sketching the landscape in one of his books. He had been almost as happy to see his papers, carefully saved with his pack from the sunsailer, as he had been to see Niran and Diar and the rest of the Golden Islander crew.

Rorra and Niran had followed them out with Kalam, and taken seats nearby on the sun-warmed deck. It was clear they were trying to get Kalam to take a rest from anxiously watching his parent. It was hard to tell with Jandera, but Kalam's eyes looked sunken, a sign of fatigue, and Moon thought he had probably stayed up all night with Callumkal. Watching Rorra and Niran, two people not known for their cheerful demeanor, clearly trying to make Kalam feel better about his parent's prospects was awkward.

Maybe that was what made Bramble wriggle out from under Moon's arm to change the subject. She asked, "Do we know why the Fell are attacking the Reaches now? I mean, they've always hated us, so why now?"

Chime said, "The Fellborn queen told Malachite that the Fell are blaming us for what happened to the flights that tried to breed with Raksura."

Bramble snarled at the unfairness of it. "That's not our fault."

"It is not your fault. But it is certainly due to the Fell's lack of understanding of Raksura," Delin said. He looked down the deck toward the kethel, who had moved up to the mid portion of the wind-ship. It sat back against the cabin wall with its head tilted up and its eyes closed, apparently enjoying the sun. "Do the Fell practice controlled breeding, as the Raksura do?"

That got Rorra's and Kalam's startled attention. Rorra said, "The Raksura do what?"

Delin explained, "When Arbora mate in order to breed, it is only with a great deal of consideration of their lineages and what traits they wish the offspring to have, and if they wish to produce Arbora or warriors. They try to anticipate what the court will require anywhere from twenty to forty turns in the future, since maturity rates for Arbora and Aeriat are different. There are no clutches created without careful planning."

"He's right," Niran said with a sigh. "The teachers talked a great deal about their bloodlines and prospective clutches when I was there. In exhaustive detail."

Moon had never thought of it in those terms, but he knew that was what Raksuran courts did. Indigo Cloud was breeding for survival, Opal Night breeding for war.

Chime said, sourly, "Sometimes it doesn't work out the way you plan, no matter how well you've taken everything into account."

Bramble nodded in resignation. "We ended up with way too many Arbora for a while, and not enough warriors." She looked up at Moon. "Or consorts." After a moment, she added hesitantly, keeping her voice low, "I know you weren't serious when you said—"

"I was serious," Moon told her. "If you want." He couldn't remember if Bramble was one of the Arbora who had said she meant to try for a clutch later this turn. "If you don't want a clutch—"

"I do." Bramble bounced happily and squeezed his arm.

Rorra was saying slowly, "I'm still not sure I understand—" Kalam looked baffled and dismayed.

Delin smiled. "Sex that is not for procreation is a different matter, and done only to please the participants."

Niran added, "That matches what I observed." Rorra and Kalam turned to stare at him. Niran kept his expression carefully blank.

Moon said, "I don't understand." Chime, drawing breath to speak, broke off to stare at him in astonishment. Moon said impatiently, "No, I understand all that, but I don't understand what it has to do with the Fell."

"Oh, right." Chime turned to Delin. "I'm not sure if the Fell plan their breeding like we do. I don't think anyone knows. We know the progenitors breed with the rulers, but the dakti and kethel aren't fertile. Or at least that's what the mentors have always believed." He frowned. "If the Fell don't exchange rulers between flights . . . No, they must, or it wouldn't work. I guess we could ask our kethel."

Niran grimaced. "I'm not sure I want to be there when you do. Grandfather, what are you getting at?"

Delin said, "So the Fell's controlled breeding, if they practice it at all, would be a simple affair. Whereas a Raksuran court's controlled breeding is an elaborate weaving, all the threads considered and carefully placed by both the queens and the Arbora, with new thread judiciously spun from other courts as needed."

Bramble stirred and said, "That would be a lovely drawing, if you knew more about weaving."

"I've seen weaving done," Delin protested to her. He made a gesture toward Shade, who leaned on the rail, listening with an expression almost as confused as Moon's. "Fell and Raksura are two different species who share the same common ancestor. Yet Raksura are experts at breeding for beneficial traits, for the good of the whole court." He shrugged. "If the Raksura had a way to manipulate the breeding of the Fell by some trickery, to add new bloodlines, they could turn the rulers and the progenitors into something else, more like the Fellborn queen, or like Shade. They could allow the kethel and dakti independent thought and let them develop naturally. Left to their own devices, the kethel and dakti might become more like the Arbora, able to provide and create, with no need to steal and destroy other species. No need to kill and consume each other in times when no other prey is available, or when the progenitor wishes to reduce their number. They would be ruled not by a progenitor with absolute control, but a being more like a Raksuran queen or consort, for whom the welfare of each member of the flight is of primary importance."

Then Shade hissed in startled fury. Moon snapped around to look, shifting in mid-motion.

Kethel stood beside the cabin, having approached in total silence. It stared at Delin, its gaze fixed but lacking the predatory glint that would have sent Moon for its throat. It said, "How? How would this be done?"

Everyone had tensed. In his peripheral vision, Moon saw Kalam touch the belt of the fire weapon slung across his back, as if making certain it was still there. Rorra put both hands on the deck, ready to shove herself upright. Niran carefully didn't look toward Diar, who stood in the steering cabin and had just picked up the fire weapon stored there. Shade had shifted and coiled himself around the railing, ready to strike.

Then Moon spotted Stone atop the steering cabin, sitting just at its edge. Moon didn't think the kethel meant to attack, but it was a relief to see Stone nearby.

Delin was the only one who seemed undisturbed. Watching the kethel thoughtfully, he said, "I cannot say. It is only a theory. And would of course require the cooperation of many Fell."

Kethel took this in, its large brow furrowing, apparently oblivious to the reaction it had caused. It said, "But not progenitors." Moon wasn't sure what was stranger, that it had been so excited by the prospect or that it appeared to be getting depressed as it considered the more practical aspects of it.

Delin lifted his brows. "You think there is no progenitor who would cooperate?"

"No." It shook its head slowly, reluctantly dismissing the idea. It looked around at all of them finally. Then it said defensively, "We changed. And it was better for kethel and dakti."

Moon made himself lower his spines. He exchanged a glance with Chime. It had occurred to him that Delin had seen the kethel approaching to listen and had been talking solely to it for the past few moments.

Shade was still braced for attack. Moon shifted to groundling and said, "Shade, come here."

Shade's tail lashed once, but he was far better trained in good Raksuran behavior than Moon, and too polite to resist when an older consort called him. Reluctantly, he shifted and climbed down from the rail, still watching the kethel with hostility. Chime scooted over to make room and Shade came to sit behind Moon.

Kethel watched this with curiosity, but said nothing.

Niran turned deliberately to Delin. "What does this have to do with the Fell striking at the Reaches, grandfather?"

Delin said, "Just that I think it isn't the rumors of the artifact from the foundation builder city which has caused this. It may have been the catalyst, when word reached the other Fell of the flight that had been destroyed in pursuit of it. But the Fell must have been attributing their decline to the Raksura for some time. Fell do not seem to exchange information with each other with much frequency, and ideas must spread between flights very slowly. But if I have noticed the Raksuran potential for breeding the progenitors' control out of the Fell, surely the progenitors have as well."

Still watching the kethel warily, Rorra said, "Whatever the cause, it's the artifact we have to worry about at the moment."

Then Kethel said, "Where do they take it?"

Moon glanced up at Stone, who shrugged and looked out over the plain. He read that as Stone not being able to think of any particular objection to sharing this information with the kethel. Moon couldn't think of any reason not to either. He said, "We don't know. And we're not sure if they know. The person who was probably going to help them figure it out died in that river trading town."

Kethel didn't respond, but moved to the railing, squinting as the cold wind gusted across the deck.

Chime hunched his shoulders, obviously still uneasy at the kethel's part in the conversation. He said, "The Hians have to have some idea. They didn't just head off at random. But if we're lucky, it's the wrong idea."

Kalam said, "Perhaps Vendoin spoke more to Callumkal than she did to you and Bramble. When he wakes—I'm sure he will wake—He can tell us more."

Faced with Kalam's hopeful expression, Moon tried to look like he thought this was a real possibility. But he saw Rorra look away toward the rail, her face creased with worry.

It was a relief when Merit and Lithe came out of the belowdecks hatch. At least until Moon saw their expressions.

Chime sat up, frowning. "What's wrong?"

Merit said, "Lithe and I had a vision." He glanced at her. "Not a joint one, but still . . ."

Lithe's expression was distressed. "The details were different, but it was the same central image. Metal buildings on a cold sea, so cold it made ice, like the top of a tall mountain. At least that's what I thought it was."

"That's what you saw before," Chime said to Merit. "Back home, in the joint vision with Heart and Thistle. Isn't it?"

Merit nodded. "I thought it was a city. But this time I could tell it was a huge boat, a water ship, like the sunsailer but much bigger."

Lithe let her breath out. "In those early visions, there was an image of a stone city in the clouds. We think now that was the foundation builder city in the escarpment. The feel of something powerful waiting must have been the artifact."

"This water ship must be up here somewhere," Merit added, making a gesture toward the plains below the wind-ship. In the distance, another flock of wingless birds rode the wind. "It must be where the Hians are going."

Moon pushed to his feet and stepped to the rail. It was cold enough now for frost to collect on the tall grass patchworked across the rocky plain, and it glittered in the sunlight.

They must be approaching the cold sea from the mentors' visions.

They spotted another ruin in the late afternoon, this one just a huge, partial circle of metal standing on its side, mounted in a stone base, with weather-worn designs embossed into what was left of the rim. It was so tall, the wind-ship could have brushed the top with its hull.

Leaning over the rail, Moon saw where the missing section of the rim had fallen, its outline still visible as a raised sickle-shape in the soil and grass.

"Are you certain that isn't where they went?" Diar asked. She made a gesture. "It looks strange enough."

Rorra lowered the distance-glass. "There's no sign of their craft," she said, but she didn't look entirely satisfied with that. She turned away from the rail. "Better have Dranam check the moss again."

Chime came to stand by Moon, squinting at the structures at the ruin's feet. "It doesn't look like it was made by the forerunners. It looks more like that building that was stuck in the middle of the forerunner ruin."

But Dranam reported that the moss still showed movement, and the wind-ship sailed on. By evening they had seen four more similar ruins off in the distance, but the moss said the Hians had passed them all by.

They spent a chilly night, and finished off the dressed meat that the Opal Night warriors had stored away in the hold. It wasn't as good as fresh, but the cold had helped keep it from rot. Stone took a portion to the kethel up on the deck. Bramble and some of the groundling crew had made a shelter for it behind the stern cistern, with some blankets and a tarp waterproofed with mountain-tree sap. Kethel seemed bemused by this gesture, but hadn't hesitated to crawl inside.

As the dawn light gradually grew brighter, Moon got his first glimpse of the cold sea.

It stretched out from a shore concealed under a coating of snow. The low waves carried chunks of ice and had built a white wall along the water's edge, so tall it was hard to tell if it was made entirely of ice, or if something else lay beneath it. The water washed against small ice-covered islands that spiraled out from the shore in a pattern that didn't look natural. Moon wondered what the ice and snow concealed, if the islands were pylons for a broken causeway, or foundations for long-gone structures.

In the bow, the freezing wind pulled at Moon's hair and stole the breath from his lungs. Even without their scales, Raksura weren't as susceptible to the cold as other soft-skinned groundlings, but he was glad of the Islander shirt over his other clothes. He was used to snow and ice in the valleys and slopes at the top of mountains, not on flat terrain, and the strangeness of it was unnerving. There was no scent of salt in the air, so it must be a freshwater sea.

He heard Jade's claws scrape the deck behind him. She wrapped her arms around him and he leaned back into her warmth. "Be careful," she said, "you don't want to get a lung sickness."

"I think that's going to be the least of our problems," Moon said, keeping his voice low.

Niran stamped out of the hatch, wrapped up in a blanket. He surveyed the cold blue water in horror, muttered a curse, then turned to stamp toward the steering cabin. "Diar!"

They gathered just outside the open wall of the steering cabin, watching Dranam tease more information out of the moss. Chime sat on the deck, helping to hold the chart that Diar was drawing. Kalam and Dranam didn't seem much bothered except by the wind, but the Golden Islanders were feeling the cold, even bundled up in all their extra clothes. They looked so uncomfortable, River actually stepped back and spread his wings to help block the wind. Delin had tried to come out on deck twice so far, and been unceremoniously bundled back below by the nearest Islander.

Lithe slipped up beside Moon, and he put an arm around her. Rorra shivered, her face pinched with cold, and Moon remembered that her clothes had always been much heavier than the Kish-Jandera's. She stood next to Stone, leaning on him.

"I wanted to make certain before I told you," Dranam said, "but the Hians are slowing down. I think we're only a few hours behind them at most. I can't be more exact."

Jade sat on her heels to look and for once Dranam didn't try to unobtrusively edge away. Jade's claw tapped the point Diar had marked on the mostly empty chart. "Can you show me how far this is? Compared to how far we've come."

Diar leaned forward to point. "It's about as far as it was from the ruin to this point here, where that big waterfall was."

Watching thoughtfully, Stone said, "We can reach that."

Jade nodded and pushed to her feet. "I think it's time we flew ahead."

CHAPTER NINETEEN

It would be a long flight in cold weather, so they made some quick preparations first. Jade told everyone to eat, so they had some dried fruit and fish paste from the boat's stores. Moon finished eating before the warriors and went to find his pack where it was stored in the sleeping cabin. He was bringing some food, a knife, a waterskin, flints, and a couple of extra blankets. Rorra was preparing some of the smaller fire weapons for the warriors to carry.

Kalam came in with a small pile of folded cloth. "Moon, please take these with you. For you or the others, or Jade, when she takes her smaller form."

"Are you sure?" Moon asked, as Kalam sat on the floor beside him. "Don't you need them?"

Kalam made a negative gesture. "Our clothes are mainly for show. Merit used some pots to make heat in the cabins for the Islanders, and they say they have enough blankets and clothing to stay warm."

If the Raksura had to spend the night on one of those ice islands, more clothing to wrap up in wouldn't hurt. Moon took the pile to hand out to the warriors, and asked, "Callumkal?"

"I think he's better." Kalam smiled a little wryly. "I know I keep saying that, but he swallowed water on his own and squeezed my hand. Ivar-edel thinks the poisons may be wearing off."

"That's good."

They looked at each other for a moment, then Kalam reached over and squeezed Moon's arm. "Be careful."

Moon said, "We'll try." There wasn't anything else to say.

Kalam left and Chime, Briar, and Saffron came in to make their own preparations. Bramble followed Jade, saying, "I know I could help. I know all about the Hians now. And I—"

"No," Jade said. She took Bramble by the shoulders and said, "We don't know what we'll find and I don't want to risk you. It's bad enough that we have to bring Merit, but we may need both mentors."

Bramble sagged in defeat. Then Root slammed into the cabin and demanded, "Why not me? I'm a better flyer than Chime, and I've been to more places than them." He made a gesture toward Briar and Saffron. Briar, pulling on a borrowed Jandera jacket, turned and stared at him, startled. Saffron's expression was already verging on the homicidal.

Chime was more shocked than offended and Bramble snarled. Moon hissed in reflex, too startled to do anything else. Root knew better than to speak to Jade like that.

Jade looked down at Root, her spines starting to spread and lift. Her voice hard, she said, "You've got your own behavior to blame for that. I can't use a warrior who won't obey."

"I should be there." Root barred his teeth. "I want to—"

Jade's spines flared and she suddenly had Root pinned against the wall beside the door, her hand curled around his throat. He shifted to groundling, staring up at her, his eyes wide.

Briar and Saffron twitched back a step, Bramble flinched, and Chime made a squeak of alarm. Jade ignored them all, and said evenly, "Root, you need to think very carefully about your behavior, because I will not tolerate this."

After a long moment, Root dropped his gaze and whispered, "I'm sorry."

Jade released her grip and moved back. "Go be sorry somewhere else."

Root slipped out of the room. Saffron turned and busied herself with her pack while Chime and Briar stared uncomfortably at each other. Moon controlled a surge of fury; it was every Raksura in the eastern Reaches and beyond they were fighting for, but Root didn't understand that. Maybe it was too much to get his head around and he was using Song as an excuse not to try. Whatever it was, they didn't have time for it. He asked Jade, "Are you all right?"

She settled her spines. "It's fine. We need to go."

They took flight, following Dranam's directions. As one of the stronger fliers, Moon kept to the back of the group, watching to make sure the warriors didn't have any trouble with the harsh gusts of wind. He also wanted to keep an eye on the kethel, who trailed them at a distance. In a way it was a relief that it was following them. Moon wouldn't have wanted to leave it on the boat with the groundlings and Bramble, with only the warriors left behind to guard them.

Before they left, Chime had said, "I'm hoping the Hians just stop out there. Maybe their moss will quit working, or they're lost and wandering."

Moon nodded, checking the fastening on his pack. "Sure."

Chime sighed, his shoulders slumping. "But you don't think so."

No, Moon didn't think so.

Jade had spoken last to Niran, Rorra, and Delin, telling them, "If it happens, if we don't stop them, I think you'll know immediately."

She meant that the Raksura still onboard and the Jandera would drop dead. Moon was trying not to think about that. Just the idea made him want to minutely examine every sensation in his body, wondering if that was it or not. That was a quick way to drive yourself mad.

Delin stepped forward and took her hands, wrapping his soft-skinned fingers around her claws, and looked up at her. He said, "If it happens, we will not stop. We will take the artifact from them and find a way to destroy it."

Niran had grimly agreed but Rorra had said, "It won't happen. You'll catch them."

Moon hoped she was right.

The wind was rough at first, whisking away any warming effect that the bright sunlight on Moon's scales might have. Lithe was being carried by Shade and Merit by Briar. Moon hoped they weren't suffering too much in the cold; being carried was never easy but it was worse in bad weather.

Below them, the icy islands were further apart, but still seemed to form a loose spiral, if Moon wasn't just seeing a pattern in a random arrangement. If it was really there, maybe the Hians had followed it to their destination, whatever it was.

As they flew, the islands grew more frequent and closer together. The larger ones were still surrounded by ice but shards and slopes of black rock were visible. They looked as cold and inhospitable as it was possible to be, but at least they were a place to land in an emergency.

It was late afternoon when Stone suddenly banked and turned aside. *He's spotted it*, Moon thought, his heart starting to pound. Jade signaled the warriors to follow and they curved down toward a cluster of islands. Moon circled once, trying to glimpse what Stone had seen. He couldn't make out the small flying boat but far ahead, there was a large gray shape on the water.

The others had gathered on an island, the warriors perched on the sharp columns of ice. Stone, shifted to groundling, stood on the gentlest slope with Jade. Moon rode a tricky draft down to the rocks below the slope and scrambled up to join them.

As he shook the icy spray off his wings, Jade said to Stone, "We can't afford to wait until dark. We have to get closer, see what we're dealing with."

Stone squinted into the wind. He wore an extra jacket over his own clothes that Moon recognized as one of Rorra's. "If we stay low, jump from island to island, we'll have a better chance of not being seen."

Moon flinched at a crunch near the waterline, but it was the kethel in groundling form. It climbed up to the rock just below the slope and waited expectantly.

Jade sighed. She told Stone, "You—and that—are the ones the Hians are most likely to spot. You'll have to go high, up to cloud level, and wait for us to signal you."

Stone grimaced but didn't disagree. The kethel said, "Groundlings never think to look up that high."

Everyone stared at it. Jade's spines lifted. Moon shared a look with Stone, who sighed and wiped the ice crystals off his face. Jade hissed. "Fine, let's go."

A large wave hit the other side of the island and cold water filled with ice flecks rained down.

Bramble leaned on the bow, wrapped in one of Kalam's extra jackets, trying to urge the wind-ship to go faster. After days and days of being trapped on the flying boat, she found it hard to stay in the cabins. She kept falling asleep and waking in a panic, thinking she was still in a cage. Even though the light woven walls were nothing like the flying boat's moss, and the scents were all of Raksura and familiar groundlings mixed with their strange kethel companion, it was still uncomfortable. She hoped she could get over it, but until then the deck was better, even with cold sharp wind and the strange icy sea.

She was so lost in her own thoughts it took her a long moment to realize that Root stood nearby. She slid a look at him, not pleased to see him. She was furious at the way he had spoken to Jade.

Trying to change a queen's mind about something was one thing; it was practically an Arbora's duty. But for a warrior to challenge a queen, and at a time like this . . .

She knew he was upset about Song. But so was everyone else.

As if her simmering anger had actually penetrated his thick skull, he said, "Are you mad at me?"

"Yes," Bramble snapped. "People die, Root, and sometimes it's like losing a limb. It always hurts and you never forget." As if any of them had ever forgotten about Petal and Shell and Branch and all the others killed in the Fell attack on the eastern colony. "But the court has to come first. We're fighting for all the courts in the Reaches and the east, and a bunch of Jandera groundlings in Kish, though none of them know it. If you can't understand that, then you're useless and you should fly off and become a solitary."

There was a long silence, then Root said, "They don't care because Song argued with Jade—You and Merit ripped her up because—"

Bramble turned on him with a snarl. He flared his spines. She took a deliberate step closer and said, coldly, "Think twice about that."

A fight between them would be a disaster. Bramble didn't want to think about what it would do to Jade, who would have to take the responsibility with Pearl. Stone would never speak to Bramble again. The entire court would be upset and there was no way she would be allowed to clutch with Moon. But Bramble had been helpless and poisoned and frightened for days and if Root touched her it would be a fight she intended to win.

A thump on the deck made them both twitch, then someone said, "Just what the shit is going on here?"

Root fell back a step and Bramble hissed out a breath. It was Spark, a female Opal Night warrior, and Flicker, Shade's favorite. Spark stepped up to Root. She was bigger than he was, Balm's size, and muscular across the shoulders in a way that seemed to follow the Opal Night bloodline.

Root barred his teeth at her, but his spines quivered with the urge to drop. "It's none of your concern. We're not part of your court."

Spark tilted her head. "Oh, it is my concern. If you saw a belligerent warrior threatening an Arbora, you'd just stand there and watch?"

Flicker took Bramble's wrist and tugged her over to his side. Flicker said, "We just chased the groundlings that stole her all across the Three Worlds, and you want to hurt her?"

Root fell back a step and dropped his spines. "I wouldn't hurt her!"

Flicker hissed in disbelief. "That's not what it looked like."

Bramble set her jaw against a well of emotion. She wanted to curl up in a corner and wail. She knew it was her fault, that she shouldn't have let it go this far. She had failed her court as a sensible Arbora. She choked out, "It's my fault."

"It is not," Flicker said.

Spark lifted her spines as a signal for quiet. Bramble held her breath. In the absence of a queen, the largest female warrior was in charge, and Spark would have been perfectly justified in beating Root senseless for threatening an Arbora. Bramble had lost her control over the situation when she had lost her own temper. All she could do was try to talk Spark out of it.

But Spark didn't attack. Eyeing Root critically, she said, "Go inside and get some rest."

Bramble let out her breath in relief. Fortunately for Root, the Opal Night warriors all seemed to be a fairly calm group.

Root, who finally seemed to understand that he had gone too far, took a step toward the doorway. He protested, "I'm on watch."

"And you're doing such a brilliant job of it," Flicker said. He glanced out at the water. "You haven't even looked at—Wait, what's that?"

Bramble turned, following Flicker's gaze. Arbora eyes weren't as sharp as warriors' at long distances, but the movement caught her attention. Something was alive on one of the rocky little ice islands. A figure stood there.

Root flung himself at the rail. "It's one of the others, they're hurt—"

"No!" Spark caught him by the frills and kept him from leaping off the boat. "The wind was pushing them to the west when they left. That's someone else."

"You're right." Flicker perched up on the rail, squinting into the wind. "It looks like a groundling."

Bramble turned and bolted for the steering cabin. "Niran! Diar!"

Bramble waited at the rail, trying to remember not to scrape at the deck with her claws. The wind pulled at her frills as Diar brought the wind-ship to a halt. Not far ahead, Spark and Flicker circled above the island, taking a closer look at the groundling who stood there. Flash was still up on the look-out post atop the tallest mast, on watch in case it was a trick. Spark had ordered Root to keep watch in the stern, and he had actually obeyed. Maybe the almost-fight had brought him back to his senses a little.

Bramble thought the presence of the groundling might be a trick. She had recognized the figure as the wind-ship had drawn closer, and it was either a trick or she was having some kind of hallucination.

Rorra came up beside her with a distance-glass. As she lifted it to study the island, Bramble said, "It's Vendoin, isn't it."

Rorra lowered the glass. Her mouth was a grim line. "Yes. And she's not armed." Despite the wind, Bramble caught a trace of her communication scent, and filtered it out. It was a sure sign that Rorra was worried. The only sign, since Rorra kept her expression hard.

The island was just a rock, washed by ice-filled waves. There was no place to hide anything that Bramble could see. Vendoin wore only the light tunic that Hians seemed to prefer; there was no way to conceal even a small fire weapon in it.

Niran stepped up behind them, watching the scene with a frown. "Perhaps the small moss-craft fell, and the survivors washed up here."

Rorra shook her head. "The current's wrong for that. And Dranam would have seen the change in direction."

Spark must have been satisfied it wasn't a trick, because she dove on the island and snatched up Vendoin. She rose on the wind again, Flicker pacing her.

Rorra and Niran backed away from the rail to allow them room to land. Niran said, "Bramble, go to the main cabin, please. Tell the others we'll bring her in down there. I don't want Kalam to be startled."

Everyone who wasn't steering the wind-ship or tending to Callumkal had gathered in the main cabin, waiting for the warriors to return with the castaway. Bramble reached the hatch in one bound and hurried down the stairs. She shifted to her groundling form in the doorway.

Delin sat on a stool, bundled up in several layers of Islander robes and shirts. Kalam paced in front of the stove. All the Islanders were wrapped up in extra clothes, though the room felt warm to Bramble. Everyone turned expectantly to her, and she said, "It's Vendoin."

Kalam's jaw set in a hard line. He still had a small fire weapon slung over his shoulder; a wise precaution for groundlings in a strange place. Bramble said, "Kalam, are you going to . . ." She didn't know how to put it without sounding insulting or condescending.

But he folded his arms and said, grimly, "I'm anxious to hear what she says."

From his stool, Delin told him, "I have listened to her for days on end, and I can tell you it will be a frustrating experience."

One of the Islanders snorted a laugh, and there was a relieved stir as the tension broke. Bramble felt the tightness across her shoulders ease a little.

Steps sounded from the stairs, light Raksura steps and the clunk of Rorra's boots. Then Spark pulled Vendoin into the room. Spark let her go and shook ice drops out of her spines. Vendoin stepped away from Spark, stumbling a little, as Niran and Rorra followed her in.

Vendoin gazed around at them all. She appeared to note Bramble and Delin without reaction. The gray skin between the rock-like armor plates was pale and tinged with blue, which must be a reaction to the cold. The light tunic she wore was torn and stained. She said, "So, you did follow us. I—" Then her gaze met Kalam's, and the words seemed to catch in her throat.

The room was silent. Rorra watched Vendoin intently, as if reading expressions that Bramble couldn't interpret. The deck creaked and Bramble felt the wind-ship move. It was fighting the wind to continue on its course.

As if the faint sound and movement had broken a spell, Kalam said, "My father still lives, despite what you did to him."

Vendoin drew breath. "It was not my intention—"

"I don't care," Kalam interrupted. There was a faint quiver in his voice. "Why were you on that island? Where are the other Hians?"

Vendoin looked at Niran and Rorra, her attention passing over Bramble. As usual. Bramble managed not to roll her eyes and hiss.

Niran said, "Obviously the Raksura don't abandon their own, and neither do we. We couldn't have followed you here without their help." He made a gesture to the other Islanders. "I am Niran, and these others are my family, and Delin-Evran-lindel is our grandfather."

Vendoin's gaze went to Delin. "You will not believe me, but I was taken from my moss-craft."

"We believe you," Rorra said, still watching her critically. Her self-control was almost queen-like, and Bramble found herself grateful for it. Rorra added, "We found it, and what was left of the crew. You seem to be making a habit of abandoning ships in distress."

"I wasn't the one who killed them," Vendoin said, still expressionless.

Bramble felt a growl build in her chest. Deliberately, in the Hian-inflected Kedaic, she said, "I told them it was hardly a surprise. You Hians aren't like the other Kish. You're uncivilized." She had meant to sound ironic, but found her voice rough with rage.

Vendoin turned to stare at her. "How long have you known our language?"

"Bramble is not here to answer your questions," Rorra said. "Did your companions drop you on the island because of your charm, or did they just not need you anymore?"

Vendoin looked around again, as if taking stock of them all. Fragments of ice slid down her legs to collect on the woven grass mat on the deck. Rorra said, "It's up to you whether you tell us or not. We have a horticultural tracking your moss and the others have already caught up with the pinnace."

Vendoin made a slight movement, maybe so slight the groundlings wouldn't see it. To Bramble's eyes, it looked like a movement of relief. Vendoin said, "I refused to cooperate with Lavinat. I assume Bramble has told you about her."

Rorra said, "Yes, go on."

"When I took the weapon-artifact from—from you, aboard the sunsailer, I did not realize what its abilities were. How flawed it was."

Delin said, dryly, "Even the fragmentary writings the foundation builders left said that the artifact was flawed beyond their ability to repair. They left it for the forerunners, hoping they could render it useful. The fact that it was still inside the city is proof enough that the forerunners never came for it. We are not fools, and kindly do not treat us as children. You knew it was flawed and you didn't care."

"I didn't know that it would kill Jandera." Vendoin's voice was hard, but Bramble thought she detected a faint tremor underneath. Then Vendoin admitted, "I knew it was a possibility."

Rorra glanced at Kalam, her expression sour. He looked incredulous. He said, "A 'possibility.' How many other species, how many other species in Kish, does it kill?"

"It kills Hians," Bramble said. She knew she was right. "It killed Aldoan, it killed the Hian scholar and her family. That's what made you afraid."

Vendoin didn't look at her, but the muscles of her neck tightened. "Lavinat insisted that it was the operation of the weapon that caused Aldoan to die. That it was not meant to be held by a living being, that it was the close presence of the Fell that had caused it to operate. She said the Fell killed the scholar. Bemadin and I were not convinced. But many of Lavinat's crew were aboard and we found it politic to pretend to accept that explanation, at least until we had more information. We never dreamed—" She stopped, cutting off the words.

"You never dreamed she would betray you," Kalam finished. "If my father was conscious, I'm sure he would say the same about you."

After a moment, as if Kalam hadn't spoken, Vendoin continued, "We believed that the weapon would eliminate the Fell in the east. If it worked, we could leave Hia Iserae and return to Hia Majora. We could go home. That was our only goal. My only goal." She looked away, her gaze on the wall. "I and others had worked for a long time for this, even before I joined Callumkal in Kedmar, ever since the message stones that described the weapon were uncovered in the foundation builder ruins buried beneath Hia Iserae. Lavinat had also worked on it. When she betrayed us she admitted that she had concealed things from the rest of us, that there had been warnings that the artifact could cause terrible damage."

Delin's expression was disbelieving. "And yet she still intends to use it? Has she lost her senses?"

Vendoin's mouth curled. "She believes it is worth it, to destroy the Fell. She believes that some of our people still in Hia Iserae, in our cities sheltered by layers of rock, will survive. That it is worth the sacrifice of those who live in other parts of Kish and the east, or are caught out without shelter."

Bramble met Kalam's gaze, and he shook his head incredulously. The Islanders murmured in shock. Niran's expression was appalled.

Hard and practical, Rorra asked, "How did you know where to take the artifact?"

"Lavinat had a map, found in one of the message stones that she concealed from us."

"The map led you to the ruin on the coast," Niran said.

"Lavinat attempted to use the weapon, and it caused the . . . transition here." Vendoin looked around again. "The existence of this place was a surprise."

Rorra grimaced. "How does this Lavinat know where to go now?"

"She said the artifact was telling her where to go."

A chill went up Bramble's back. Niran said, "Is she right? Or is it delusion?"

Vendoin said, "I don't know. When I said I wouldn't help her, she abandoned me on the rocks."

Rorra eyed Vendoin. "If you can't help us anymore, what should we do with you?"

Bramble thought it was another prod to make Vendoin talk more. But Kalam answered immediately, "Put her back on the island."

Vendoin said, "No. Lavinat let me look at the writings she brought with her, the ones she couldn't interpret. I was able to understand some of it, but I withheld the information from her." Her gaze met Rorra's. "I can tell you how to stop the artifact."

CHAPTER TWENTY

They flew low, not far above the floating ice, from island to island as the gray shapes grew on the horizon. The sea was relatively calm, though Moon felt windblown ice chips catch in his frills.

When they reached a narrow rocky ridge just above the waves, Jade signaled a halt. Moon crouched with the others on the frozen rock, and got a good look at their goal.

They had found the metal ship Merit and the others had seen in their visions, but it wasn't out here alone. It sat at what had to be the ruin of a forerunner docking structure.

It loomed up out of the sea, the flower-like pods for docking flying boats arranged around a central stalk, like the fluted curving bell of a flower. It was a mountainous structure that dwarfed even the great metal water ship moored at it.

Huge half-moon shaped sails stood on narrow pillars above a wide hull as big as a small city. The stern was high and square and the bow came to a curving point. Above the hull were dozens of towers like big spheres piled atop each other, with darker shapes in their discolored metal that might be doors or windows. Bridges connected the towers with other scaffold-like structures with a less obvious purpose. There was no sign of life or activity, and from the metal debris embedded in the chunks of ice surrounding it, bits had been falling off for some time.

Merit and Briar had landed further down the ridge. Moon saw Merit look toward Jade and signal assent with his spines. This was the place from the vision. *It better be the right place*, Moon thought. There surely couldn't be more giant ships on this frozen sea. He hoped.

Chime whispered, "It's so big. Maybe the mentors were right the first time, and it's a city. Was a city."

"Maybe." Moon didn't think it mattered what it was, as long as it was the place the Hians were looking for.

Shade crawled up on Moon's other side to say, "The ship doesn't look forerunner."

Chime leaned across Moon to tell him, "I don't think it is."

"How can you tell?" Moon asked.

Frowning at the ship, Chime said, "The shapes and the angles and curves aren't right. Especially when you compare the ship to the docks, or whatever that flower thing is. The curves and shapes on it definitely look like the forerunner ruins we've seen."

Moon asked Shade, "Do you understand that?"

Shade twitched his spines in assent. "Sure. The forerunners built the flower docks, but somebody else built that ship."

Moon gave up. Chime still had an Arbora's eye for this sort of thing, and Shade was the only Aeriat who was able to draw, at least as far as Moon had seen. Shade hadn't gotten the ability from his progenitor mother, so maybe it was a forerunner thing, like the way he had been able to open the doors in the forerunner city.

Balm scrambled up the rocks behind them and said, "Did you see it?"

Moon stared at her. Baffled, Chime pointed at the giant ship. "Uh, yes?"

Balm's spines flicked in exasperation. "The little flying boat! It's caught on top of that big flower dock, towards the middle."

Moon had been too struck by the water ship to see it. Squinting against the wind, he spotted the flying boat tied off to the top of a flower-shaped docking pod near the lip of the central stalk.

The little boat was a gray-green oblong of moss, with a small deck in front, one hatch, and several windows in the upper portion. About twenty paces long or less, it didn't look able to hold many Hians. Whoever was aboard had presumably used the Kishan flying packs to get down from it to the dock or the ship. The important point was that there was no large fire weapon mounted on it.

Balm continued, "Jade is going to check it out. She said for the rest of us to stay here." At Moon's expression, she grimaced, "I know."

Moon twisted around to look for Jade. She crouched atop a higher boulder at the edge of the ridge, shaking the ice out of her spines. She leapt upward, caught the wind, and flapped up toward the flying boat.

Moon hissed in pure nervous fear. Chime said, softly, "They might not even realize we're here, so they probably didn't leave anybody behind in the boat."

At least Stone was up there somewhere in the clouds on watch. Jade navigated the drafts and rode one above the central stalk, then dropped down atop the flying boat. She crouched there for a tense moment. Shade said, "I think Chime's right, no one's inside."

Jade slipped down to the deck, then disappeared into the hatch. After what felt like one of the longest stretches of time in Moon's life, she reappeared and signaled for them to follow.

Balm made a hiss of relief and turned to the warriors. "Let's go."

Shade hopped down to pick up Lithe, and Moon leapt into the air. He immediately slipped sideways and had to play his wings on the wind to rise toward the top of the dock structure.

The stalk loomed like a mountain, discolored and streaked by uncounted turns of weather and sun. It must be standing on the floor of the sea; the base was mired in an island of ice, washed by the freezing waves. Moon swept past a stained metal sail of the deserted ship and it vibrated with the wind, a low-pitched sound that resonated in his bones.

Moon banked and dropped to light on top of the Kishan flying boat. He furled his wings as Shade and the warriors landed around him. Jade perched on the railing, looking down at the curving edge of the docking stalk about fifty paces below. Moon hopped down to her side. A flat curved walkway ran around the fluted edge, its icy coating broken from the impact of several sets of feet. "They didn't care that they left a trail," he said, keeping his voice low. Maybe Vendoin and Lavinat had thought the magic had only worked on the Kishan flying boat. "They don't know we're here."

"We can hope," Jade muttered. She straightened and waved up at the clouds. Stone's dark shape appeared immediately and dropped toward them. Kethel followed at a respectful distance. Moon leaned out to try to see down the shaft as Chime came to stand near the rail. Like the flower the dock was meant to resemble, the interior twisted into a spiral, increasingly narrow and dark. There were ledges built into the inside, circling down, but it was an impossible entrance for ground-lings. If the Hians hadn't had their flying packs, there was no way they could have taken this route. And they had gone this way; fresh scrapes scarred the ice on the ledges all the way down.

Stone landed on the curve of the flower pod below the flying boat. The kethel caught the broad stem lower down and curled itself around it.

Jade raised her voice so the warriors could hear. "I'll go first. I want Stone with Merit behind me. Moon, I want you and Shade last."

Moon didn't argue. If the Hians, or something else, was down there waiting to trap them, Jade would be expecting him and Shade to keep the path clear for the warriors to escape.

Jade dropped off the rail. Stone reached out a hand for Merit to climb into, then followed. Balm, Saffron, and Briar dropped after them, then River and Deft. Moon nodded for Chime to go ahead with Lithe, then he and Shade jumped off the rail.

As Moon swept down to the land on the first ledge inside the shaft, he caught a dark shape at the edge of his vision. He almost yelled an alarm, then realized it was Kethel again, dropping to cling to a ledge not far above them. Shade hissed in exasperation. Moon considered telling Kethel to get out of here, but he doubted Kethel would listen. And if something awful was living in the ruin, maybe Kethel would be a deter-rent.

Jade had already leapt down the ledges to the spot where the shaft narrowed. There weren't a lot of perches down there, so Moon waited. He flexed his claws impatiently, noticing the material the structure was made of felt more like stone than metal. There were streaks of dark blue under the coating of ice and grime.

Stone slipped down into the narrowing shaft first, vanishing into the darkness in a way that made Moon distinctly uneasy. Then Jade and Balm. As the other warriors dropped down to follow them, Chime waited with Lithe.

The wall under Moon's claws shuddered. Below, Chime jolted forward and caught hold of the ledge with one hand. Lithe's head turned to look up at Moon, her frills catching in Chime's nervously flicking spines. Below them, Deft and River hesitated, still clinging to the ledge just above the twist where the shaft narrowed. Moon couldn't see the others, already vanished into the dark opening.

"The whole thing moved," Shade whispered. He was right, it felt like the whole structure, and whatever it stood on under the water, had jerked a few paces. "You think the Hians—"

The jolt was so hard it knocked Moon off the ledge. He skittered down the wall, his claws screeching on the surface until he caught a rough spot and managed to stop. He was only a pace above Chime and Lithe. Lithe had reached over Chime's head and hooked her claws on the ledge above.

The wall shook so hard it felt liquid under Moon's claws. He looked down for the others but River and Deft had disappeared. Shade shouted a warning as the shaft rippled like water, like a wave, and it was coming toward them. Moon yelled, "Go, go, Chime, up!"

It wasn't coherent but Chime obeyed instantly, scrambling up the shaft toward Shade. Moon climbed after him, sparing another desperate look down. The narrow part of the shaft buckled, the material bent and crumpled, closing off the opening. *They got through*, Moon told himself in horror. *They had time to get through.*

He made it up to Shade just as Chime and Lithe took the leap to the flying boat. Kethel had one clawed hand on the railing, holding the boat closer. With Shade, Moon leapt for it and felt the deck roll under him as he landed. He staggered into Shade, who had caught hold of Chime's arm and kept him and Lithe upright.

That was when Moon realized the sky spun overhead, that the whole huge docking structure below had started to turn. Kethel swung aboard the flying boat and clung to the bow, but the anchor lines gave way with a sound like something's spine snapping. The deck came up and slammed into Moon; he sunk one set of claws into it and held onto Shade.

The moss boat tumbled, bounced off something, then slammed into something else. Moon shoved himself upright, hooking his claws into Shade's collar flange to keep them together.

The wind roared in his ears and most of the flying boat was gone. The whole starboard side had sheared off from a few paces in front of them to the stern, only two walls of the upper cabin left. The stem-beams stuck out from the hull, bare and broken, and moss came off in chunks. The boat had hit one of the metal ship's huge sails. To Moon's relief, Chime and Lithe had managed to hold on, huddled against Shade's other side. Kethel's big dark shape still clung to what was left of the bow.

Everything was moving and Moon's sense of direction and of up and down was useless. He squeezed his eyes shut briefly, trying to center himself. No, it wasn't his sense of direction that was confused, it was everything else. The docking structure had started to rotate and was dragging the huge metal ship along with it. Moon's throat went tight and he thought, *did the Hians do this?*

The rest of the flying boat could come apart at any instant. They were lucky the moss hadn't unraveled yet and tangled in their wings.

Moon twisted around and spotted the curve of a wheel, attached to a mast. He tugged on Shade. "This way!"

Shade shoved upright and pulled Chime with him. Chime swayed, dazed, Lithe keeping him on his feet. Shade pulled her against his chest and passed Chime to Moon. Moon pulled him close and Chime instinctively clung to his collar flanges. "I think I hit my head," Chime muttered woozily. "What happened?"

"Tell you later," Moon said, as a crack appeared lengthwise down the deck. He leapt to what was left of the railing, then told Shade, "Go!"

Shade said, "Watch the sail," and dove off the boat. He snapped his wings out to get lift from a gust, then in again to miss the sail and land on top of the wheel just past it. He swung down to brace himself in the wide groove below the rim.

"He's been practicing," Chime said, then made an oof noise as Moon leapt into the air.

The wind caused by the motion of the ship and the docking structure made the air into a rapidly changing maze. Moon had to drop sideways twice, tossed like a puffblossom, before he landed on the wheel and swung down next to Shade. He clung there, breathing hard. Looking back, he saw Kethel push off from the flying boat, barrel roll past the sail and drop onto the lower part of the wheel. The shift in weight was enough to push what was left of the flying boat free. It hit the sail and burst into pieces, torn away by the wind. *It could have done that earlier and killed us,* Moon thought. They were lucky. *Sort of lucky.*

Voice raised to carry over the rush of air, Shade said, "Did you see what happened to the others?"

Moon moved his spines in a negative. "They were inside. River and Deft went after them." They had to be alive. He had to think that or he wouldn't be able to do what he had to do.

"What was it? What did this?" Lithe asked. Then answered her own question. "The weapon?"

"Has to be," Chime said, and his voice sounded stronger, less woozy. "The Hians must have figured out how to make it work."

Jade climbed down inside the narrowing shaft, tasting the air for any sign of the Hians. The ledges continued to wind down the sides, but the interior walls were embossed with flowing wave-like designs, that vanished into the darkness as sunlight from above faded. Dim blue illumination, part of the flowing pattern along the walls, provided just enough light to see. It reflected off slender curving pillars that supported the interior. *If they aren't too far ahead of us,* she thought, *we can—*

A sudden jolt knocked Jade into the nearest pillar. She snapped her wings in by instinct and caught herself, her claws scraping across the silvery stone. She lifted her head to see Balm hurtling toward her. Jade let go of the pillar and caught her. The force of it slammed them backwards.

But Jade had control of their fall now and landed them both on the curve of a lower pillar. She gripped it with her foot claws, supporting Balm, and looked frantically for the others.

She spotted Stone first, his tail and one set of foot claws wrapped around a pillar on the opposite side of the shaft. He had Briar in one hand and Merit in the other. Above him, Saffron perched next to River, who had Deft under one arm. Jade didn't see anyone else. And something had cut off the light from the top of the shaft. She hissed in terror, then tightened her spines down. Panic wasn't an option.

Balm clamped onto the pillar with her claws and gasped, "I'm all right." She shook her spines out as Jade carefully released her. "Are we moving?"

"Yes." The whole shaft, maybe the whole structure, was rotating, Jade felt it in her gut and the back of her head. She called up to River and Saffron, "Where are Moon and the others?"

River said, "They were above us." He turned and craned his neck to look up. "I think they were still near the top."

The constriction in Jade's chest eased a little. She said, "Saffron, can you get up there and see if the shaft is blocked?"

Saffron's spines signaled assent as she swung past River and started to climb.

None of the others seemed hurt. River set Deft on the pillar next to him, keeping a hand on his arm as the dazed warrior recovered. Stone curled around the pillar to set Briar on a perch. Merit climbed up his shoulder to hop over and sit next to her. Then Stone flowed up the pillar, following Saffron.

Jade watched him go, every nerve tight.

"You think the Hians did this, made it start moving?" Balm hooked her claws on their perch and leaned out to look down.

With effort, Jade made her voice sound even and ordinary. "They must have. This wasn't a coincidence." Below the shaft narrowed again, the pillars twisting towards each other, forming more of a climbing structure. The Hians had to be using their flying packs, which meant they had been able to move down through here almost as quickly as Raksura could.

Balm hissed in realization. "Delin said the Hians had magic that could make rock move. These walls don't feel like stone, but—"

Jade wanted to groan aloud and managed not to. "They caused this, they know we're here."

From above, Saffron called down, "Part of the wall came off, and it's wedged into the narrow part of the shaft. There's a lot of broken pieces around it. The line-grandfather is trying to push it free." A clanking noise echoed from above and a scatter of debris rained down. Saffron spread her wings and dropped to a pillar closer to Jade and Balm so she could lower her voice. "I didn't see or scent anyone. There's no sign anyone was in there when it happened."

Meaning she hadn't seen or scented any sign of blood or smashed bodies. Jade took a full breath to calm her pounding heart and moved her spines in acknowledgement. Moon wasn't crushed in the wall collapse, and Chime, Shade, and Lithe were with him. If there was any group of Raksura who could take care of themselves in a strange situation, it was them.

Balm stretched to look up, twitching back as more debris clattered down into the pillar. "Maybe we could use the fire weapons, but—Do we have time?"

"We could split up," River contributed from above. "Some of us stay here and try to dig out . . ."

Jade flexed her claws as she considered it. *We could already be too late.* The Hians were somewhere below them about to use the weapon. *And they already know we're here.* "We have to go on. Stone!"

After a couple of thumps and more debris, Stone dropped out of the shaft, caught the pillar above Briar's perch, and wrapped himself around it. He shifted to his groundling form and said, "I can't get through, not in a hurry."

Jade twitched her spines in acknowledgement. "We'll find another way out, once we stop the Hians. Briar, Deft, can you fly?"

Deft said, "Yes, queen, I'm all right," and unfurled his wings to prove it.

"Yes, Jade." Briar spread her wings cautiously, then picked up Merit.

"Then come on," Jade said, and dropped down the shaft.

Chime jolted forward and Moon grabbed a flailing arm to pull him back to their perch. The wheel shuddered like the whole ship was about to come apart.

Moon pulled himself to the upper rim. From there he had a view past the sail. As the whole docking structure turned, dragging the ship with it, clouds formed overhead. Below the water and ice chunks swirled into a vortex. He thought of the whirlpool that had pulled the sunsailer out of the foundation builder city. "This could be bad," he said.

"You think?" Chime gasped, then levered himself up a little to look. "Oh. Oh no, not again! No, wait." He hesitated, just as Moon felt the change in altitude in his stomach and the back of his neck. "We're moving down!"

From below, Lithe said, "This has to be the weapon. It's doing this!"

"We're not dead yet," Shade pointed out. "We still have time." The wheel jerked again and he added, "Maybe."

Kethel climbed up the wheel but stopped several paces below Lithe and Shade. Moon didn't think it was his imagination that it looked anxious.

I need to see what's happening below us, Moon thought. He let go of the wheel and stood up, clamping his foot claws to hold on. The wind gusted hard and he swayed with the motion but from this angle he could see the docking structure had moved down, pulling the ship with it. Below, the gray water churned, but there was something beneath it, something blue.

Sky blue, he thought, and caught a glimpse of brown and gold. *Grass, a grass plain*. A groundling might not have been able to see it, but Raksuran eyes identified it as a grass plain, seen from a great height. "It's a passage!" A massive jolt went through the ship and metal groaned, the wind rose to a shriek. The wheel shuddered again and Chime grabbed Moon's leg as he swayed. "It's a passage through the air." Moon dropped to a crouch to steady himself. "It's making an opening to someplace else, someplace below us, maybe so the Hians can use the weapon." That had to be it.

Chime's spines flicked in consternation. "That makes sense, sort of. Bramble said that they might need to be up high for the weapon to reach all the way out to the east. Like if you drop a rock from a height the—"

"I got it," Moon said. He just didn't know what to do about it. Something the Hians had done below was making the ship open a magical passage in the air. And if Jade and the others were dead down in the shaft, or trapped there . . .

Then Shade said, "We have to stop it, or—Can we move the ship? Make it drag the docks back up? Or maybe push it down to the ground, so the weapon can't get all the way to the Reaches or Kish."

"Yes! That might work." Chime steadied himself on Moon's arm and lifted up to a tentative crouch. "We need to find a steering cabin."

Moon gripped Chime's hand, anchoring him so Chime could stand. He tightened his hold on the rim and Chime as the ship jolted again and the wind pushed at them.

Shade had eased to his feet, trying to see. Then Lithe climbed down toward Kethel, ordering it, "Lift me up!"

Moon yelled, "Lithe, don't—" Shade snarled, "Lithe, no—"

Lithe yelled, "Quiet, both of you!" Kethel swung up toward her, clambered atop the wheel, and clamped on with its foot claws and tail. It closed one hand carefully around Lithe and lifted her up.

Chime dropped back beside Moon, and said, "She has to—I couldn't see anything." He added nervously, "I'm just glad I didn't think of it first."

Moon was too busy wrestling with his instinctive urge to go rip the kethel's eyes out. Shade's low frustrated growls said he felt the same.

Lithe scrambled up atop Kethel's hand as high as she could. The wind made her frills flare out. Both she and the kethel swayed as the ship spun even faster. They leaned far to one side and Chime made a faint squeak of alarm.

Lithe twisted around to look toward the other end of the ship and squinted against the wind, her face a grimace of effort. Then she dropped back into Kethel's hand. It lowered her to the wheel and opened its fingers so she could climb out. She pointed toward the far end of the ship. "I saw a raised chamber that way. It's the only thing that looks like a steering cabin!"

The people who had built this thing might be sightless and steer it from somewhere deep in the hold, they had no idea. But this was worth a try. Moon said, "Shade, you take Lithe; we'll follow you."

Shade swept Lithe up and crouched, then made a leap down to the next wheel. Shade had to partially extend his wings to make it, and slipped sideways on a harsh gust of wind with an easy competence. Moon glanced at Chime to make sure he was all right. Chime moved his spines in assent, and said grimly, "I can do it."

Moon dove after Shade. He landed on the next wheel and looked back. Chime fought the wind awkwardly through the leap but landed next to Moon with spines flared in tension. Kethel followed, swinging easily down.

After more jumps made dangerous with the increasing wind and motion, they reached the lee of the next giant metal sail. Moon spotted the big globe that Lithe had identified as a possible steering cabin. It sat just atop the center of a cone-shaped web of heavy metal cables and struts, and the light caught glints off large curving crystal windows. Moon felt a spark of hope. It looked as if it was connected to a large part of the ship, reminding him of the connecting tendrils of a Kishan water boat's motivator. Lithe was right, this might be it.

Shade reached it first and landed on the rounded top of the globe. Moon hit the side and slid down to hook his claws on top of a wide window. He pressed his face against it, trying to see in, but the interior was heavily shadowed. Chime landed on the side and scrabbled for a hold on the big cable just below the curve. He called, "Hey, I think this is the door!"

Moon pushed off from the window and dropped down to the cable. It was made of braided skeins of metal, jointed like armor, and attached to a conical base beneath the globe. Clinging to his cable, Chime pointed. Below was an elaborately twisted piece of metal that Moon realized was a staircase, very like the one inside the flower pods at the first ruin. He swung down to it, landed on a step, and saw the stairs led to a round doorway in the base of the globe. The stairs blocked the wind a little, and must be firmly anchored; Moon couldn't feel the movement of the ship nearly as much.

Moon retracted his claws to run his hands over the door's surface. "There's no lock." He dropped back down to a lower stair so Lithe and Chime could examine the door more closely.

"Wait, there's one of those forerunner flower locks here, but it's tiny." Chime clawed carefully at something set deep into the door frame. "Maybe we could pry it open . . ."

Lithe stepped aside. Shade dropped down and reached past Chime to put his hand on the lock. Moon craned his neck to see, but nothing happened.

Chime grimaced. "That would have been easy. We need a long metal rod—"

Then deep inside the door, something groaned. Chime twitched uneasily but Lithe said, "I think that's metal."

Moon snapped, "Chime, Lithe, get back from the—" and then the door opened.

Shade shoved his body in front of the opening, shielding Lithe and Chime, but nothing surged out of the door but a wave of cold stale air, scented of rust and rot.

Lithe dug in her bag and pulled out a glowing handful of Kishan moss. Shade took it and held it out as he stepped inside. "Here's another stair. And I think we're in the right place."

Moon pulled himself up and slipped inside after Shade. Instantly the motion seemed to cease. This chamber was protected somehow, stable no matter what was happening to the rest of the ship. The light gleamed on the dark blue of the walls and the flowing figured shapes of curves that might symbolize wind and water. In the center another set of the oddly-spaced stairs curved up toward the globe above. Even Moon could tell this was forerunner.

The cessation of the wind and the dizzying motion made Moon shake his spines and frills out in relief, shedding ice crystals. Lithe stepped in behind him.

Then Chime twitched. "Uh, I felt something. Heard something."

Shade stopped with his claws curled around the raised steps. He peered warily up into the chamber above. "Something dangerous?"

Moon asked, "Voices?"

Lithe touched Chime's arm in encouragement. Chime tilted his head, concentrating. "No, just . . . There's definitely something here." He hissed in frustration. "I'm not sure."

"Then we are in the right place," Moon said. And they couldn't stop now. He stepped onto the stairs and started up with Shade.

Moon carefully poked his head up into the next chamber. The discolored crystal windows had cracked and clouded. Only a little light shone through and the view out was barely discernible. It was oddly quiet, though Moon heard the howling wind through the open door below. The narrow sections of wall between the windows were blue and deeply figured. Moon climbed up onto a floor grooved with wave patterns, and looked for something like a steering lever, or a wheel, or anything.

Shade stood beside him, staring around, baffled, as Chime and Lithe climbed up. He said, "But there's nothing to steer with."

"This was built by forerunners to control this ship," Moon said, groping for a solution, "so . . . we don't even know how forerunners do anything."

"There has to be something here," Lithe said, and she started to feel the carvings. Chime hurried to help, poking at the crevices and angles.

Kethel, in its groundling form, appeared in the stairwell, startling a yelp out of Chime. Shade, crouched to search along the floor, growled but didn't object to its presence.

After what felt like a short eternity of searching, Moon knew this wasn't going to help. And the others could all be dead down inside the dock somewhere and he had to find out. He shook his spines and said, "I need to go back to the dock and get down to where the others are. You all stay here."

Chime looked up, appalled. "No, you can't—"

Shade turned away from the wall he was searching. "You can't make it alone. We barely got away from there alive. I'll go with you."

From the ripping shriek of metal outside, the ship might possibly be tearing itself apart. Moon wanted Chime, Shade, and Lithe up here where escape would be easier if the ship broke up. "No, stay with them. They need you. And you might be able to do something to help here."

"I'll take you there," Kethel said. Its dark eyes were stark against its pale skin, red bruises forming on its jawline from being thrown off the docking stalk. It looked frightened and that was almost more disturbing than anything else.

Shade hissed at it, then said to Moon, "We should stay together."

Moon flared his spines and snarled, "I don't have time to argue."

Shade bristled at him. Moon held his gaze and said, "The warriors and Bramble and the groundlings on the wind-ship are going to need you, and Chime, and Lithe." *If they're still alive after Vendoin uses the weapon,* he thought, and didn't say it aloud. He didn't need to. "You might be their only chance to get away from this place. If it gets worse, don't wait, get back to them."

Shade tried to stare him down. Moon had been in staring contests with queens and Stone; Shade wasn't nearly angry enough to win. Shade flicked his spines and subsided reluctantly. He said, "If it's too late, come back. Don't—" He stopped.

Don't die with the others, he meant. Just so Shade would let him go, Moon said, "I'll try."

Kethel dropped down the stairwell and Moon swung down to follow. Chime called out after him, sounding desperate. Moon's throat tightened and he didn't answer.

CHAPTER TWENTY-ONE

Jade led the way down as the shaft curved into another passage. The twisted pillars made climbing possible despite the motion that pushed her toward the walls. The jostling was deceptively easy to compensate for, but Jade hadn't forgotten that first jolt. She looked back to Stone not far behind her, and asked, "If it feels like this in here, what's it like outside?"

His claws hooked into Stone's collar flange, Merit admitted reluctantly, "Bad. We're at the center here, and protected. Outside . . . the dock might be tearing itself apart."

"Moon can take care of the others," Balm said, as she climbed along below Jade. "And they have a mentor with them."

"Shade's tougher than he seems," Saffron added.

Jade knew she should agree and pretend to be less worried, but she couldn't make herself say the words. She told herself to focus on finding the Hians. If they didn't do that, then it wouldn't matter what happened outside.

Then Stone flicked at her spines with one big claw. She stopped and tasted the air again. She hadn't been able to scent anything so far, just dry cold air tainted with metal. But now there was a trace of a familiar scent: the Kishan moss.

Jade signaled the others to move more cautiously, and started forward again.

At the next twisted pillar, she found a scraped off chunk of moss. At least they weren't on the wrong trail.

Further ahead, the shaft narrowed, but the quality of the light was different, more diffuse. "It opens out down there," Balm said, keeping her voice low.

As they moved into the larger space, Jade motioned for the others to stay back. She crept ahead.

The shaft ended in a large chamber where one pillar twisted around and formed a ladder-like climbing structure all the way down to the floor below. The chamber was more dimly lit, full of shadows, mostly bare except for the embossed wall panels. Jade spotted an open doorway in the wall, with something around it, some ornamental carving . . . And three Hians. Jade hissed in satisfaction.

Two had the smaller hand-carried fire weapons. The groundlings were always overconfident with those. And one was unarmed. Except that one stood with her hands out, eyes closed in concentration. The other two had their gazes locked on the shaft above them, obviously waiting for an attack.

The unarmed one has the magic, Jade thought. That had to be it. That Hian was waiting for the other two to sight the Raksura, and she was going to collapse the shaft again.

Balm, Saffron, and Briar had eased up beside Jade, River and Deft hanging back with Stone. Jade glanced at the three female warriors, gestured toward each of the three Hians in turn, and got spine twitches of assent. Then Jade rocked up on her heels and flung herself out of the shaft with the force of every muscle in her body.

A twist compensated for the rotation of the chamber and she hit the unarmed Hian with her foot claws before the others knew she was there. Jade slammed her to the ground, her claws cutting through the flying pack harness to contract around the Hian's throat.

Balm hit the next and the Hian's flying pack went one way and her head the other. The third lifted her weapon to fire at Briar and Saffron crashed into her from the side and slammed her into the wall next to the doorway.

That was when Jade saw the fourth Hian, who stood in the darkened space on the other side of the door. Jade crouched to leap but the Hian didn't lift her weapon, she reached to the side—

—and the rippled carving around the door began to spiral out and close.

With a snarl, Jade flung herself forward but she hit the closed door and bounced off the surface. Staring at it, she hissed in dismayed fury. The decorative border was made of petals formed of a hard white material, and now that it was closed, it looked like a huge flower. It was a forerunner door.

Beside her, Balm growled. "Is that—"

"Yes." Jade ran her hands over it, the material soft but impervious under her scales. There was no catch, no place to pry at it.

She felt the change in the air behind her as Stone shifted to his groundling form. He stepped up beside her and tried to work his hand between the petals in the center. He shook his head. "It's not there," he said, his voice grim.

"It's meant to open only for forerunners," Merit was telling the warriors. "The one we found before had a place where you could trigger the catch, Lithe and Chime figured out how to open it, but this one doesn't seem to have that."

"How did the stupid Hians open it—" River began, then answered his own question. "The weapon. It let them in because of the weapon."

Jade snarled again and slammed her fist against the impervious petals. This was why they had brought Shade, across half the continent, to open any sealed forerunner doors. And now she had no idea where he was, or even if he and Moon were still alive.

Kethel waited for Moon at the doorway, the wind tearing at his raveled braids. Moon's feelings toward Kethel were too complicated to sort out, but he had to warn him. He said, "You don't have to come. If the others can't stop it, we probably won't be able to help."

Kethel said, "I don't want to live without her and the others," and lunged out into the wind.

Moon climbed after him, up the stairs curving around the outside of the steering cabin. The cold cleared his head but the wind nearly tore him off the rungs. Ice pellets stung his scales and the shriek of metal tearing sounded like the ship was dying in terrible pain. Kethel shifted to its winged form and held out a clawed hand. Moon leapt to reach it, then scrambled up to just behind the horns on Kethel's head.

From here, Moon had a better view, not that it was encouraging. Walls of water stretched up all around them, the surface churning with storm waves. The metal ship skewed sideways, creating a vortex of air as the flower of the docking structure still rotated on its axis. Far below, through an obscuring haze of windblown water, Moon caught glimpses of the brown-yellow plain in bright sunlight. He had no idea what would happen once the docking structure got down there, and he didn't want to find out.

Kethel leapt down to the next wheel and the wind almost sent it off the ship toward the water wall. Moon flattened himself to its scales, trying not to throw off its balance. Kethel landed and scrabbled to get hold of the wheel, then climbed down toward the bulbous towers below. With some protection from the wind, Kethel made its way toward the bow.

They reached the point where the twisted skeins of cables connecting the ship to the dock were stretched tight. Moon wondered if it would help to break them, to set the ship loose. *No, it would probably just help the Hians*, he realized. Dragging the ship might be slowing the structure's motion, buying them time.

One of the leaf-shaped pods extended out over the cables. Kethel braced itself, then leapt for it.

Moon ducked down again to reduce the wind interference, for all the good that did. Gusts slammed into them like boulders and Kethel's claws scraped across the silvery surface. Then it caught hold and dragged itself up.

Moon flattened himself behind Kethel's horns to hold on, the wind singing in his spines, ice crystals peppering his scales like pebbles. As Kethel climbed, Moon realized the motion seemed to lessen, and when the wind eased, he lifted his head. Moon was so dazed by the constant pressure and sound that it took him a moment to realize that Kethel had just heaved itself over the outer edge of the central shaft and started down. Moon blinked and shook his head, the feathery protective membrane around his eyes reluctant to open fully with all the flying ice in the air.

As Kethel neared the blockage in the shaft, Moon was able to get a good look at the obstruction. He hissed under his breath. Part of the wall had broken loose and jammed across the opening. Moon climbed down off Kethel's back and started looking for gaps. Kethel dragged its big claws across it, searching for purchase to pry it up.

Moon circled the obstruction twice, digging at narrow crevices until his claws ached, but there was no point wide enough for him to wiggle through. He scrambled back as Kethel managed to dig out some of the debris on the side, but it only revealed how firmly the slab was jammed in. It made him remember what Bramble had reported about the Hians ability to manipulate rock; this had obviously been no coincidence.

Moon shook his head. "We're wasting time," he called up to Kethel. "We need to look for another way in."

Kethel didn't give any sign it had heard him, just glared at the obstruction. Moon had time to wonder if their unlikely partnership ended here. Then it held out its arm again for him.

On the way back up to the top of the shaft, Moon tried to decide where the best place for another entrance would be. Those petal structures had to be for flying boats, just the way the groundlings had used them in the ruins on the continent below. Even though the forerunners had been able to fly, they must have found flying boats just as convenient as Raksura did.

Just before they reached the top, he leaned down to Kethel's earhole and shouted, "Try to get inside one of the flower pods." Then the wind hit them at full strength and Moon had to huddle down behind its horns again.

He felt Kethel doing some fairly athletic climbing, then it swung down and the wind lessened again. Moon lifted his head to see they were in the lee of a set of pods. The one directly across had a dark opening deep inside, where the stem met the larger structure. Before the wind choked him, he managed to shout, "There, there's a door!"

Kethel reached the rim of the pod and Moon shook the ice out of his spines as they ducked inside. The curved interior was sheltered and compared to the outside it was like stepping into a warm cave. Moon jumped down from Kethel's back, and took a full breath of the icy air.

Kethel shifted to its groundling form, then staggered and sat down heavily. "Are you all right?" Moon asked, catching himself just before he reached to brush the ice off the top of its head. *It's a kethel*, he reminded himself.

Kethel shook the ice off and made a vague motion for Moon to go ahead.

The round passage at the back of the pod curved up toward the base of the central shaft. Moon started down it, and after a moment Kethel shoved to its feet and followed him. Moon's joints hurt and the skin under his hand and foot claws was numb. He guessed Kethel felt worse.

The gray light didn't fall very far, and Moon couldn't get a good look at the door blocking the passage until he was almost on top of it. It was a forerunner door, shaped like the carved image of a flower, the hundreds of petals folded into multiple spirals. But it was a crushed flower now, a twist in the shaft having broken it along the right side and detached it from the wall.

Kethel reached his side, dripping icy water from its braids and kilt. Moon said, "This is lucky. These doors only open for forerunners." Or half-Fell consorts, like the way the lock on the steering cabin opened for Shade.

"Not lucky." Kethel slid its hand in between the door and the wall and shoved the folded material down. "This flower is near the broken place in the shaft."

Moon flicked his spines. *Right, I should have thought of that.* He climbed the wall and used his weight to help the kethel pry the door open enough for them both to squeeze through.

Beyond it was a wide corridor, the floor rounded and the walls lined with vine carvings, as if it was meant for climbing rather than walking. Light glowed faintly from apparently random spots on the carving, and there was a crack along the ceiling, more damage from the collapse in the shaft.

278

Moon tasted the air but couldn't scent Hians or Raksura. He started down the passage with Kethel behind him.

Chime turned reluctantly away from the door, forcing his spines down to neutral. It wasn't easy. Moon had gone off alone with a kethel. They had no idea what had happened to Jade and Stone and the others. Their numbers were dwindling and there was nothing they could do in this steering cabin to help. Panic rose in his throat and it took everything he had to choke it down.

Shade brushed against his arm, and squeezed his wrist. "It'll be all right, Chime. Moon knows what he's doing."

Chime's laugh came out as half-sob, half-growl. "You don't know him like we do."

Shade snorted but didn't argue. "All we can do is keep looking."

So Chime continued to search the cabin with Shade and Lithe for anything that looked like a steering lever. Just because it wasn't obvious didn't mean it wasn't here. He forced himself to slow down and check every dark crevice.

Through the protective cushion of the cabin he felt the ship shake continuously. Their altitude was slowly dropping and the wind sounded like the worst gale Chime had ever experienced. It was making his spines itch and the muscles that controlled his wings twitch in reaction, even through the heavy walls of this chamber.

And the fact that it was still happening meant none of the others had been able to get to the weapon yet. Part of him wondered what it would be like when it happened, if they would just fall down dead suddenly or if it would hurt. The thing he was most afraid of was that it wouldn't affect them at all because of some protection the forerunner structure would offer, and they would return to the wind-ship to find everyone else dead. Then there would be the struggle to get back down to their own continent, then the long trip to return to the Reaches, knowing what they might find . . .

Examining the sill of the crystal window Chime had already looked at, Shade hissed and said, "Someone's out there."

"What?" Chime pushed to his feet, bumping into Lithe as they both tried to see.

"It's a Raksura, not sure who." Shade pushed away from the window and dove for the ladder.

His heart pounding with hope, Chime swung down after him with Lithe on his tail. She said, "Maybe Moon found the others."

If he had, Chime couldn't think why they would come back here. The rotation of the structure hadn't slowed any yet so he didn't think they could have found the weapon.

Shade climbed out to the stairs, clinging to the rungs as the wind buffeted him. Chime stepped out on the platform and leaned between the climbing bars, squinting to see as the wind tore at his frills. But it wasn't Moon, or Jade, or any of the others who had gone down the shaft. The figure fighting the wind above the ship was the Opal Night warrior Spark, and two other Raksura were with her. One carried a shape that was clearly a groundling. As they came around to approach, Chime recognized Root and Flicker. Flicker carried Rorra.

Chime hissed, and dropped back to the platform to report this to Lithe. She said, "Why would they fly ahead?"

"Probably not a good reason," Chime said. A thump sounded as someone landed hard on the roof and Chime and Lithe scrambled back inside to give them room. Root swung in first, breathing hard and covered with ice crystals. "What are you doing here?" Chime demanded.

Root shook his spines and turned to help Flicker and Rorra inside. Rorra wore one of the flying packs, but it would have been useless in the wind. Flicker stumbled and started to sink to the floor and Rorra held him upright. She was bundled up in an extra Kishan coat, but her skin was still gray-blue with cold. Her voice hoarse, she gasped, "We found Vendoin."

Shade pulled Spark inside, saying, "You're lucky you found us, you could have been killed in that wind."

"They found Vendoin," Chime told him.

Shade stared. "What?"

Rorra's teeth chattered as she tried to talk. Lithe stepped up and wrapped her arms around her to share her body heat. Rorra hugged her back, groaning gratefully. His voice rough from the cold, Root explained, "The Hians left Vendoin behind on a little island. She told us things about the weapon the others don't know."

Spark had gotten her breath enough to continue, "It was the Hian called Lavinat, like the others on the big flying boat said. She's taken over but Vendoin didn't tell her everything she knew about the weapon."

Lithe looked past Rorra's arm to say, "What do you mean? What did she not tell Lavinat?"

"She didn't tell her how to make it work in this place." Spark waved a hand, indicating the giant dock.

"That's why I brought this." Rorra eased away from Lithe, her voice a little stronger. She tapped the large fire weapon strapped next to her flying pack. "There's a large component in this place, that the artifact has to have nearby to work. We think if we destroy it, the Hians won't be able to use the artifact the way Lavinat wants."

Chime hissed out a breath. It made sense. There was a reason the weapon had to be brought here, a reason it had killed the Fell and Jandera inside the trading town but reached no further. Obviously Lavinat had been able to do something with it, or the dock wouldn't have started forming the passage down toward the lower continent. But maybe the reason they were still alive was that Lavinat didn't know what else to do.

"We have to find it." Shade looked toward the open door.

"Where is everybody else?" Root asked.

Lithe told him, "Jade and the warriors were following the Hians down the shaft in the center of the dock, but when the spinning started, the passage collapsed and we were thrown off. Moon and the kethel went to try to find them."

"Collapsed?" Flicker said, aghast.

"Moon and *the kethel?*" Root said, horrified.

Spark began, "We have to—"

"Quiet," Shade said, and all the warriors shut up. Chime blinked and managed to clamp his jaw shut on the comment he had been about to make. At the moment, Shade's resemblance to Moon was even more obvious; he wasn't a shy, delicate consort either, not anymore. Shade said, "Rorra, can that fire weapon get through whatever's blocking the shaft?"

"Metal, or whatever this place is made of?" Rorra made an uncertain gesture. "Maybe."

"We'll try that first." Shade tilted his head at Lithe. "You and Chime stay here."

Chime exchanged a look with Lithe. At the expression on her face and spines, he swallowed back his protest. This was no time to argue. Lithe said, "Maybe we can still do something here."

"We're going to have to stay low, try to use the docking flower things as wind-breaks," Shade said. "I'll carry Rorra. Can the rest of you make it?" His hard gaze faltered as he looked at Flicker. "Are you all right? You should stay here."

Flicker twitched his spines in denial. "I can make it."

Chime thought Shade wasn't convinced, but Shade said, "Let's go."

Rorra stepped to Shade. He put his arm around her waist and lifted her without effort, then swung out the door.

Spark and Flicker followed immediately. Root glanced at Chime, grimaced and said, "We'll find Jade. We'll stop the Hians."

He leapt after the others into the howling wind, and Chime felt his heart sink.

Moon followed the passage as it wound down through the structure. Kethel was so close he kept bumping Moon's shoulder, which made Moon want to bite but was also weirdly reassuring.

He couldn't catch any hint of Raksura, which had to mean the shaft that Jade and the others had followed down probably didn't intersect with this passage. Which meant this passage probably didn't intersect with where the Hians were and he and Kethel were just wasting their time, but he didn't know what else to do.

Kethel said, "Where did the forerunners go?"

Moon half-snarled, but it wasn't Kethel he was angry at. "They didn't go anywhere. They died out and left us and you."

Kethel hissed back at him. "I know that. The ones who came here in that boat, but didn't bring the weapon. Why come here? Where did they go?"

It was a good question. "They decided not to use the weapon, that's why it was still at the foundation builder city." He added, "I don't know what happened to whoever brought the ship here. We don't know it was forerunners."

Kethel didn't seem happy with the answer but then Moon wasn't either.

Ahead the corridor met another shaft. Moon cautiously leaned out to look up and down it. In the dim light he saw it had rippled walls, as if the material had been poured out like liquid metal and the little waves and rivulets formed had frozen in place. Kethel poked its head in too. "Up or down?"

"It's parallel to the big shaft," Moon said, keeping his voice low. "We'll go down."

Moon's claws found easy purchase, and though Kethel had to shift to climb, its big body fit easily into the space. It was a relief to be able to move faster. Moon tasted the air, but the odor coming off Kethel overwhelmed anything else. He tried to filter it out as best he could.

A few turns down and the tube turned horizontal. As Moon dropped into the junction he got a scent of cold outside air in the draft. He thought they had to be very close to the bottom of the structure, where it had sat on the sea floor before the air passage had started to open below it. He turned to the tube leading inward. Kethel dropped into the junction, then shifted back to its groundling form. That was a relief; its scent was easier to deal with in its smaller form.

Then Moon caught a trace of scent and stopped abruptly. Kethel stumbled to a halt behind him. The scent was moss, Kishan moss. *It has to be the Hians.* The warriors had carried a few of the fire weapons in their packs, but if that was the Raksura ahead, Moon would have been able to scent them by now.

Moon crept forward, very aware of Kethel's big presence behind him. But as he reached the last bend in the tube, he forgot everything else.

A crack in the wall gave a view of a huge round chamber, and Moon controlled a hiss of satisfaction. They had found the Hians.

More tubes like this one curled down toward the chamber floor, many with cracks or whole chunks broken away. Dark discolored walls curved down, covered with the figured designs of the forerunners, but stopped above the etched floor to leave an open gap. And through that gap Moon saw the swirling edge of the air passage. The bottom part of the chamber was suspended above the storm, though the howl of the wind was still muffled and there was no harsh flow of air.

Several Hians stood spaced around the center part of the room, holding heavy fire weapons, warily on guard. Above their heads hung a heavy slab of dark polished stone, and below that a nest or cradle of curved silver bars. One Hian turned and Moon recognized Lavinat. She held the artifact close to the cradle.

Moon went cold with horror and grabbed the edge of the crack. But it was too narrow to cram his body through; if he tried the Hians below would have plenty of chances to burn him.

Then the Hian next to Lavinat said, "It just isn't working."

Moon froze in hope. Beside him, Kethel snorted a breath.

Lavinat said, "There has to be a reason it didn't open like the others. The weapon has allowed us to get this far. Navin, put it back in the cradle."

The other Hian took the weapon, handling it carefully. One of the others said, "Perhaps it is for safety. If only a foundation builder can make it work, it prevents the weapon from being used against their will."

Lavinat made a negative gesture. She said, "The weapon opened the other doors for us, and the passage started to form as soon as we brought it into this chamber. There is no point to opening the passage if the weapon doesn't work." Navin laid the weapon in the cradle and stepped back. Lavinat reached up to touch the flat plate of stone overhead, and continued, "I think the door will open when we reach the correct position."

Moon wasn't sure what door she meant. Then he realized the floor wasn't just etched with a flower petal design, the whole thing was one of the large flower petal doors.

Moon eased back from the crack. He didn't know why Jade and Stone and the others hadn't gotten down here yet. He hoped they were ust stuck in the blocked shaft, but whatever had happened, he couldn't wait for them. Keeping his voice to a bare whisper, he said, "We can't count on her being wrong about that. Before the door opens, we need to get down there and get the weapon."

Kethel whispered, "We both attack at once."

It was a tempting plan, but Moon could see one big disadvantage right off. This tube curved down to open into the chamber, but the opening hadn't been designed for kethel-sized beings. "You're too big to get out of the tube fast enough. They'd burn you to death before you got close to the weapon."

Kethel grimaced, showing his clipped fangs. "I know that. You get the weapon then."

A kethel bursting onto the scene suddenly, even in its groundling form, would certainly be a distraction. But Moon didn't think he would have time to get around to where the weapon was and remove it from the cradle before the Hians saw him. "Then they burn me and take the weapon back. One of us has to stay alive long enough to hide the weapon somewhere they can't find it."

Kethel stared at the crack, its big brow furrowed in frustration. Moon thought it was going to argue, but it said reluctantly, "Maybe so." Then it cocked its head. "What about the thing they put the weapon in? If one can get close and destroy it, then it doesn't matter if they kill both."

Moon considered it, stepping close to the crack again to look at the cradle the weapon was nestled in. The curved metal vines looked jewel-like and vulnerable. It would be better to get the weapon out of the chamber entirely, but if that was impossible . . . "That could work."

Jade snarled in frustration. Stone had tried to push the door in, shoving his entire weight against it. They had tried to burn it with the Hians' fire weapons until the moss canisters stopping working and the fire ran out. It hadn't weakened the door at all. She had sent the warriors to explore the tunnel above again in case she had missed a doorway or opening in their haste, but there were no branching passages.

Balm growled but said, "At least we aren't dead yet. Maybe something went wrong and the Hians can't use the weapon."

Jade glared at her and Balm added in frustration, "I know we can'
count on that."

Balm was right, though. Maybe making the weapon work was a longe
and more involved process than they had assumed. "This thing is still mov
ing down, though," Jade said, mostly to herself. She could feel the continu
ing drop in altitude. They were going toward the continent below, some
how. But if they had been given a temporary reprieve, they couldn't wast
it standing here beating on this immovable door. "Stone, stop!"

Stone whipped around and all the warriors and Merit flinched back
Jade bared her fangs and Stone shifted down to his groundling form
Breathing hard, he covered his face with his hands and ground out th
word, "Sorry."

"It's all right," Jade said, and tried to sound as if she meant it. Th
last thing they needed was to turn on each other. "We have to go bacl
up, get past the block in the shaft, and look for another way down." Sh
ignored the agitated twitching of the warriors' spines. *Yes, I know it's*
bad idea, but it's the only idea left, she snarled to herself.

The crash from above made her twitch. Stone shifted to his winge(
form and River grabbed Merit as all the warriors braced to flee or fight
Jade pinpointed the source of the sound past the confusing echoes
"That was from the shaft. Someone got through the block."

"It has to be Moon and Chime," Balm said, hopefully.

Jade said, "Balm, Saffron, with me. The rest of you stay here." Sh
didn't want to leave the door unguarded, just in case the Hians openec
it from the other side for some inexplicable reason.

Jade leapt for the tunnel entrance, the rush of Balm's and Saffron';
wings behind her. They made it only partway up before she detectec
Rorra's distinctive scent wound through with familiar Raksura.

Moon whispered, "Now."

Shifted to its winged form, coiled awkwardly in the too-small tube
Kethel roared.

It staggered Moon and deafened him; he just hoped it had a simila
stunning effect on the Hians. He took a deep breath and flung himsel
forward, rolling down the tube and falling out into the chamber.

He hit the floor and rolled, shifted to his groundling form and let himself land in an awkward sprawl. He got a quick view of the astonished Hians. Across the chamber two Hians shot their fire weapons ineffectually at the tunnel mouth. Kethel roared again, then retreated up the tube, thumping and scraping its wings on the walls to make as much noise as possible.

Moon held his breath. This was the point where the Hians might just burn him, and Kethel would be on its own. He knew he looked wounded; the bruises and scrapes from being knocked off the docks transferred to his more vulnerable groundling body. He had hurt the skin under his claws and his hands and feet smeared blood onto the silver-veined petals of the floor.

Lavinat stepped toward him and said, "The Fell?"

Moon shoved himself up on his elbows, and gasped, "They're all over this place. They followed the Golden Islanders' wind-ship."

Lavinat's fingers curled around the stock of her fire weapon and Moon got ready to shift and leap. He couldn't make it to the cradle from here without being hit by one of the others' fire weapons, and he wasn't sure he could damage it enough on his own. No, he needed Kethel. But he wasn't going to lie here and let her burn him.

Then Lavinat said, "Two of you, go up that tunnel and see if there are rulers coming."

Moon dropped his head to conceal his slump of relief. *That might be even better,* Moon thought, as two of the Hians lifted up in their flying packs and cautiously advanced on the tunnel. If Kethel was able to pull off the deception.

The other Hians watched Moon nervously and Lavinat made a gesture, apparently telling them to pay attention to their surroundings. She said, "I have never seen a Raksura like you close up, before. You're very different from the Arbora, but not as much like the rulers as I've heard."

Moon eyed her warily. "If you do this, I might be the last one you see."

As if it was nothing, as if they were discussing what she planned to eat that day, Lavinat said, "I don't expect to survive this either." She added after a moment, "I regret the other damage this will do. But it's necessary."

"We're never going to agree on that." Moon made his voice hoarse. "Has it started yet?"

"Not yet." She stepped back. Without moving the nozzle of the fire weapon away from Moon, she nodded toward the slab of slate-like rock above the cradle. "That's how we know it will work. It was unrecognizable at first, then I realized it was a map. But the hills, valleys, even the rivers and mountains it marks have all changed over time. It's a map of the world below as it was, when this place was constructed. I've adjusted the cradle so the passage will open there, on the plain just outside the western border wall of Imperial Kish." Her mouth thinned, an expression of annoyance or anger. "I couldn't make it go any closer."

"You want to kill the Jandera. You don't have to kill us." It was a terrible thing to do, to try to offer the Jandera up in place of the Raksura, but desperation made Moon say it. And if they were lucky, no one would have to die. No one except the Hians in this chamber.

"I can't control the spread." Lavinat seemed distracted, but Moon wasn't willing to chance it. She had the concentration of a careful predator. "But unless we destroy the Fell in the east as well, and in the outer Marches and the plains and the drylands, then this is all for nothing."

There was a shout from the tunnel and the two Hians in flying packs floated out. The figure they shoved along could have passed as a groundling, a big soft-skinned one with braided hair and a kilt that was much the worse for wear. Kethel staggered, clutching its head. The bruises it had collected since they arrived on the docks stood out dark against its pale skin.

Lavinat's stare was concentrated enough to be a furious frown on any other groundling. "Jendon, what is this?"

"He says he's from a wind-ship," Jendon reported. "It must be docked above us, if they're in these tunnels."

Out of the corner of his eye, Moon saw Lavinat look down at him. *She's suspicious.* Moon rasped out, "Tlar, you should have run the other way!"

"The Fell are everywhere," Kethel sobbed on cue. Moon found it unconvincing, but he hoped the Hians found other groundlings as hard to read as he found them. Kethel at least kept its head down, hiding its fangs.

Navin said, "Lavinat, we are running out of time. How much longer before—"

Lavinat snapped, "Get him out of here. Throw him back in the tunnel. Kill him."

Kethel looked up, making its eyes widen in dismay and horror. Some of that was probably real. This was not going the way they had hoped; they were still too far from the cradle. But Moon gathered himself to leap at Lavinat. They had to do this now, Lavinat wasn't going to let Kethel get any closer.

A Hian reached for its arm and Kethel pushed to its feet, swaying away from her and a few steps closer toward the cradle, faking unsteadiness. "Please," it rumbled.

Moon shifted just as Lavinat shouted, "Kill him!"

Kethel flowed into its huge scaled form and shot across the chamber to slam into the cradle. The blow shattered the silver lattice and sent the weapon flying. Moon hit Lavinat and sunk his claws into flesh. As they hit the floor he felt the metal of the fire weapon against his scales and had an instant to know she had turned toward him just as he struck her. That the little disks the weapon used to direct its fire were on his chest. Then blinding heat washed up between them.

Moon shoved away from her. For a terrible instant he was numb, but the stench of burned flesh choked his throat and lungs and he knew what had happened. The wave of pain hit a heartbeat later.

He rolled over, desperate to cling to consciousness, to his scaled form. It felt like hot coals buried beneath his skin, like something was in his chest trying to claw its way out. The floor vibrated as Kethel collapsed, fire washing over its scales. The artifact clattered to the floor just past its body.

Kethel spasmed and lost its scaled form, its large groundling shape coalescing with bloody red and black patches instead of skin. Lavinat shouted a desperate command and a Hian ran forward to grab the artifact. But as her hand closed on it she pitched forward and fell to the floor.

The other Hians stared at her, then Lavinat. She took a breath, flexing her hands on her fire weapon, the blood from Moon's claws running down her arms and chest. Moon had a bitter moment of satisfaction.

But the slate surface of the map was almost above him and he saw spots of red light form on it, like glowing drops of blood. The light started to grow, then to spread in rivulets.

Lavinat said, "It's still working, it's working," her voice thick. Her hands tightened into fists. "Finally."

Moon tore his gaze away from the slate. He couldn't watch any more. They had been wrong about the cradle, wrong, and they couldn't stop this. He met Kethel's gaze where it sprawled on the floor. Its expression was torn between despair and rage. It tried to shove itself up and collapsed again.

CHAPTER TWENTY-TWO

The flower door opened at Shade's touch. Jade flung herself through but no Hians waited beyond. It led only to a corridor winding down in a spiral. It was barely fifteen paces wide, too small for Stone's shifted form.

Hissing under her breath, Jade went first, with Stone and Rorra and the others behind her. A tight sensation grew in her chest, the feeling that the delay had been too long, that they had lost their chance.

As she rounded the third turn down, a wooden disk from a fire weapon clattered against the wall barely half a pace from her head. Jade snarled a warning to the others and dove below the stream of fire, then leapt forward into the legs of the Hian with the weapon.

The Hian screamed and went down, the weapon's fire flowing over the ceiling. Two more Hians stood behind the first, and one tried to run and the other tried to trigger her weapon. Balm, Saffron, and River leapt over Jade and slammed into them. Jade ripped her claws across her Hian's throat and pushed to her feet.

"They know we're up here," Balm said grimly, shaking the blood off her claws.

"Then we have to hurry." Jade flung herself around the next turn. The corridor opened into an empty round chamber with an opening in the floor. Painful doubt made Jade freeze for an instant. There were no doors. But the Hians had come this way . . . Or at least, had thought this chamber worth guarding.

She motioned the others to wait, then stepped to the opening.

It was a short vertical shaft. A climbing bar spiraled around it, but the bottom rungs had been broken or melted away. She couldn't see into the chamber it led to, because it was blocked by a dark flat shape suspended in the air not far below the end of the shaft . . . Jade leaned closer, squinting to see. It was a stone, like a piece of slate, and red spots of light glittered on it, flowing across it like water. Aside from the red lights, it looked like the thing that Vendoin had described to Rorra and the others. She drew back. "That has to be it."

Spark stepped forward to look, and her spines signaled agreement.

Jade pushed away from the edge and turned to the others. "We need to—" She caught sight of Merit's face and froze. Merit's expression was like someone had gutted him. He met her gaze and looked away, but his flattened spines didn't even twitch.

He's had a vision, Jade thought. *A bad one.*

Stone saw her and turned to Merit, but Rorra handed him her fire weapon. "Hold this, please."

As Rorra pulled the flying pack off her shoulders, Jade forced her spines down and tried to make her expression neutral. *We're not dead yet,* she told herself.

Rorra was saying, "I used most of that canister getting through the blocked shaft." She opened the flap at the top of the flying pack and the acrid scent of the moss flooded the room. River winced and Briar sneezed. Rorra pulled out a ceramic container, a tall thin jar with a stopper on both ends.

"Is that more moss?" Shade asked, stepping closer.

"Yes, this tool and the pack work off the same sort of canister." Rorra handed him the flying pack, took the fire weapon back from Stone, and began to fit the canister into place.

Jade waved her forward. "If you can lean over the edge, I can hold onto you."

Rorra stepped forward to peer down the shaft. "I want the best angle I can get. Can you hold me out over it?"

Jade wrapped her arm around Rorra's waist and crouched. She leaned down and caught the top bar, and dangled Rorra directly over the shaft. The others gathered around.

Then below, someone shouted in Kedaic, "They're above us!"

Jade hissed, "Now!"

Rorra swung the weapon up and pulled the first trigger. Wooden disks shot out and clattered against the stone surface below. Jade heard thumps as something struck the wall beside them. It was the Hians shooting up at them. But Rorra hit the second trigger and the shaft below disappeared in a wash of fire.

Rorra held the trigger down, fire flowing out of the weapon, her face a grimace of effort. Then the fire slowed and cut off. Rorra gasped, "That's it!"

Jade hauled her up and dragged them both out of the shaft. Stone caught Rorra's arm and pulled her away and Jade rolled onto the floor. Balm hissed with alarm and wiped something off Jade's shoulder. She held her palm out, eyes wide. It was a wooden disk. Jade hissed and looked at Rorra in time to see Stone pluck one off her forehead.

River and Shade leaned over the shaft, trying to angle for a view. Saffron grabbed Shade's frills and bodily hauled him back, snarling, "Careful!"

River reported tensely, "The slab's still there. I didn't see any difference."

Jade held her breath to keep from snarling with fury. Rorra spat out a curse in Kedaic and reached for her pack again.

From below, a voice shouted in Altanic, "Raksura, we have your consort Moon here. If you stop, we will leave him alive."

Jade went still, rage and terror constricting her chest. Stone's furious growl vibrated through the floor. Rorra, jamming a new canister into the stock of the weapon, froze.

"She's lying," Balm whispered, aghast. "He's not down there."

River looked at Merit and started to apeak, then let the question die as he registered the expression of horrified resignation on Merit's face.

Jade twitched her spines in a negative. Of course the Hian wasn't lying. *For all Moon knew, we were dead in here,* she thought in anguish. *Of course he would look for another way in, would try to get to the Hians.*

Stone grated out the words, "She's not lying."

The warriors all stared at Jade. She forced her jaw to unlock and made herself say to Rorra, "Go on. We'll try again." *We have to,* she didn't say, *they'll kill us all, they'll kill the Reaches.* It was effort enough to get those words out and if she tried to say more her control would shatter.

She saw Balm's throat work, but Balm didn't protest. Shade's spines wilted in despair.

Rorra jerked her head in assent, fixed the canister into the weapon. From below, the Hian said, her voice more urgent, "Your Fell ally is here too. Stop and we will spare them both."

Stone hissed and pressed his hand over his eyes. Jade didn't understand. *Fell ally* . . . Then she snarled under her breath. *The Kethel.* It was more proof the Hian wasn't lying. Rorra grimaced in dismay and pushed upright again. She looked at Jade and nodded.

Jade took a sharp breath. The Hians were ready for them so there would be no other chance, no matter how many canisters of moss Rorra had brought with her. Jade caught her around the waist. Rorra lifted the weapon as Jade fell forward and swung them both out over the opening.

The fire from Rorra's weapon filled the shaft. This time Jade felt a vibration through the climbing bar, a reverberation as though something large had snapped. The fire ceased and Rorra shouted, "That's it!"

Jade dragged them both back, her burden lifting as Stone pulled Rorra out of her grip.

Then the whole room jolted and Jade hit the opposite wall, Balm on top of her. The floor rippled like a wave moved through it. The structure's steady downward motion turned into a headlong plunge. Beside her, Balm gasped, "You did it!"

Jade pushed away from the wall. "We need to—" Above her head, with a sound like screaming, the walls started to come apart.

Chime kept searching the cabin with Lithe, looking for symbols, looking for anything. Feeling the groove along one of the lower windows, and thinking how odd it would be for anyone, even a mysterious forerunner, to put something needed to steer the ship there, Chime hissed at himself in sudden realization. He sat back on his heels and told Lithe,

"We're doing this wrong. This is forerunner, and we're treating it like the foundation builder city."

On the opposite side of the chamber, Lithe turned, her brow furrowed. "What do you mean?"

Chime waved his hands. "We shouldn't be looking for symbols. There weren't any in the other forerunner places I've seen."

Lithe considered it, her spines flicking in thought. Then she stood and stepped to the center of the room, facing Chime. "Maybe that's because the forerunners don't need symbols. Maybe they were all like mentors."

Chime thought it was the only real option. "So you should try to . . . find their magic." The chances that they could control anything the structure was doing from here were dim, but at least they could try. "Try to think 'stop.'"

Lithe shook her head. "I've been trying that already, since we first got in here, but I don't have the right kind of magic. You do."

Chime's spines flicked in frustration. "I don't, I'm not a mentor any—"

"You do," Lithe said. "I've seen it." Chime shook his head, dropped his spines to a negative, but Lithe didn't stop. "You've got magic, Chime. Turning into a warrior didn't take it away, it just changed it. Just try."

Chime dug in, stubborn. "My abilities are—I can only hear strange things—"

With the firm patience of a good mentor, Lithe said "Strange *magical* things. Everybody in Indigo Cloud knows you have it, they're just confused because you keep explaining how it's not good for anything. Just try."

Chime hesitated. "It didn't work in the foundation builder city. I mean, it opened the door so we could get in . . ."

"From what Kalam said, those symbols were probably meant for forerunners, coming to the city after the foundation builders left. Whoever built the rest of this ship, this steering cabin is forerunner," Lithe said. "Just try."

Chime had thought of about three other uses this place could have besides steering cabin, but outside this bubble of calm he could sense the ship's movement getting faster and faster, and they didn't have time to look for another option. With the wind risen to terrible strength, he was terrified of what was happening to the others.

Lithe took his wrist and squeezed gently. Her claws were different than an ordinary Arbora's, longer and thinner, like an Aeriat's. It was a reminder that she was half-Fell, and it surprised him that he had forgotten, that at some point the darkness of her scales just meant that she was Lithe, and not anything else. She said, "It's just the two of us, Chime. If you try and nothing happens, I won't blame you and we won't tell anybody."

She didn't add that if no one could stop the weapon, there wouldn't be anybody to tell, and that they probably wouldn't be around any more to talk. Chime took a deep breath and pushed those terrifying thoughts away. He stepped to the wall and put his hand on it, hoping the symbolic connection to the ship would help. "Think 'stop,' right," he muttered. He pressed his eyes closed.

For a long time there was nothing, not even the drifting sensation that he had felt when they found the right symbols on the foundation builder city's door. There was nothing else to do so Chime kept trying. *Please stop*, he thought toward the ship and through it the docks. Reaching toward them, the way you needed to reach into someone's head to look for Fell influence.

He was distantly aware that Lithe had put her hand on his shoulder, that she must be reaching through him too, trying to use her mentor's skills to help.

Then something light and sharp flowed through the carving under his hand, a sudden shock, like sticking his hand into a fire. He hissed in startled fear as Lithe flinched. Then it was gone, leaving only a fading memory of the brief pain. He opened his eyes, still frowning in concentration. "I think I felt something. Or heard something. But—"

A metallic groan rose outside, so loud it overwhelmed the roar of the wind. Chime stepped to a relatively clear patch of window. All he could see was the top of the nearest wheel structure. He snarled and scraped at the crystal, then froze. The wheel was moving, falling away from them . . . No, the whole ship was falling. Whatever protected the cabin kept them from feeling it, except for the sense of their altitude rapidly dropping. He said, "Something happened!"

The floor moved underfoot and he jolted forward to bang his head against the crystal. It must have knocked him out for an instant because in his next moment of awareness he was shoved up against the window. Lithe lay crumpled in a heap beside him. The view through the crystal swam back into focus and he saw swirling water—He took a sharp breath, the spike of fear clearing his head. The wall of water towered above the skewed stern of the ship, looming over it like a mountain. He croaked, "I think we made the ship move. We hit the side of the passage."

Lithe braced an arm on the window and pushed herself up with a groan. "Do you think that helped?"

"Maybe," Chime began. Then another jolt rocked the cabin and metal screamed like a dying grasseater. "Uh, that sounded—"

"-like the ship is falling apart," Lithe said and pushed up off the wall, dragging Chime with her.

Once on his feet the floor swayed. The whole cabin was unsteady, as if some of the pillars supporting it had given way. "I think we have to get out of here," he said.

They made it down the climbing bars to the lower cabin. The view out the door confirmed Chime's worst fear: the outer stairway was sheared off and the unobstructed view was of the sky, the blue mottled with gray in cloud patterns Chime had never seen before.

Breathless with nerves, he said, "We'll need to climb out. Hang onto me."

Lithe wrapped herself around him and hooked her claws in his collar flange. Chime swung out the door and scrabbled up the side of the cabin to the roof. Out here the sway of the ship was terrifying, the wind pushed at him with the force of a slap from a kethel. He had to keep reminding the part of him that was still Arbora that he could fly.

Once atop the cabin, he looked toward the dock and hissed in astonishment. The ship had snapped free of its mooring, the big cables whipping dangerously in the wind. The jolt must have been more than the ancient structure could stand, because the whole central flower-stalk column of the dock was breaking up. Sections slammed away into the wind, the curved stems and the petals of the pods breaking and tumbling out and away. He gasped, "Did we do that?"

Lithe twisted to look and tightened her hold on his collar flange. "Maybe?"

"But where is everybody?" Chime said, all the implications dawning on him. *They were inside there . . .*

Then Lithe said, "There's the wind-ship!"

Chime turned and spotted the Golden Islander boat. It waggled back and forth in the tumultuous wind in a way he had never seen a wind-ship move before. It couldn't be good.

He looked back at the dock as another graceful petal gave way with a tearing shriek. They couldn't stay here. "We have to go to the wind-ship. Hold on."

Lithe ducked her head down and buried it against his shoulder so she wouldn't affect his balance. Chime braced himself, wrapped one arm around her, and thought, *you can do it, you have to do it*. He leapt into the wind.

It shoved him back toward the docks but he kept control of his wings and didn't let it tumble him. He fought his way up but it was like scaling a cliff wall that rippled continuously. He told himself he wouldn't give up but the words *I'm not going to make it* were in his head. At least there was no fancy flying trick that he had failed to learn; he just wasn't strong enough to beat this wind.

Then something shot past them. Chime flinched away and fell sideways. Then Lithe shouted in his ear, "It's a rope, from the boat!"

Chime caught the movement again in the corner of his eye and saw the rope whipping in the wind. He ground his teeth in effort, and tilted his wings. It sent him back the other way across the rope's path. Lithe let go with one hand and grabbed, her claws sinking into the skeins.

Chime wrapped his hands around it, managed to pull his wings in, and climbed the rope. They swung wildly around, the wind still buffeting them mercilessly, but at least they knew where the wind-ship was. Then he realized the rope was pulling them up, that the wind-ship was reeling them in.

The elegant and extremely welcome shape of the bow appeared abruptly and Chime freed one hand to grab the railing. A scaled Raksuran hand caught his arm and then Lithe's and yanked them both over the rail.

Chime collapsed on the deck, looking up at the Opal Night warrior Flash. Niran stood beside nearby, beside a winch device that had been clamped to rings on the deck. Bramble crouched on top of the rail, her claws sunk into it to hold her steady. All of them wore harnesses attached to ropes secured to the rail along the steering cabin.

"Tlar, Beran, we need harnesses!" Niran bellowed over the howl of the wind.

"Don't get up yet," Flash said, keeping a firm grip on Chime and Lithe. "You need ropes or you'll be swept off the boat."

Chime nodded, too tired to flick his spines, breathing too hard to talk. Lithe said, "Where are the others? We split up."

"Don't know yet," Bramble said, all her attention on the sky as she scanned it anxiously. He couldn't tell if her spines were flared or it was just the wind.

Tlar hurried up carrying two bundles of harness straps, already roped to the rail. She gave one to Lithe and handed the other to Chime, saying, "It doesn't fit over wings and spiky things, but if you put it on backwards, it works."

Chime hastily shrugged it on and figured out the way to buckle it across his chest. He fastened the strap that went around the back for Lithe, then turned so she could do his. "This is a good idea," he managed to croak.

"Before we got everyone fastened on, Flash had to catch several people," Tlar said. "It was very frightening." She yanked on the ropes to make sure they were attached correctly.

Lithe pushed to her feet and gave Chime a hand up. He stumbled to the rail, his joints still trembling from the effort of fighting the wind. Then he looked down and gasped in dismay.

More pieces peeled away from the dock, circling it like dirt and grass running down a bath drain. *The others are still in there,* Chime thought, shocked to numbness. He hadn't really believed it before. He had thought he would see them in the air, fighting to reach the windship.

Below the docks the ground was visible, the yellow-green of a field of tall grass. It looked nothing like the frozen sea that the dock had rested in. They really had moved through a passage from the world above all the way back down to the lower continent. The wind was warmer, free of the stinging ice crystals.

Then the giant metal ship swung away into the maelstrom. Everyone on the rail screamed and ducked, but it shot back up to disappear in the roiling clouds above. Chime eased to his feet again, staring after it. If the wind-ship had still been above it, it would have smashed it like a gnat.

Beside him, Niran said grimly, "That's one messy death averted."

"One down, how many to go?" Flash wondered.

Someone yelled from further down the deck and Chime whirled around. Lien hung over the rail and pointed frantically. "There! I saw wings!"

Chime reached her in one bound and gripped the rail so tightly his claws scored it. He spotted the movement among the swirling debris immediately. It was in the lower part of the structure, where a whole section with attached petals had just sheared off. "It's them! There!"

From the bow, Niran called directions to Diar. The wind-ship angled down but Chime doubted it could get any closer.

Bramble and Lithe stood on the rail beside Chime, while Flash helped Niran and the other Golden Islanders with the winch. At the steering cabin wall, Tlar was attaching more harnesses. Chime realized Kalam was beside him. He said, "The direction is wrong for the rope."

Distracted, Chime looked toward the bow, thinking about the angle of the wind. "Right, we have to get around the other side—"

Bramble tensed. "Maybe not! That's Stone!"

She was right, it was Stone, his dark shape fighting its way out of the flying debris.

Chime tightened his grip on the railing, watching as Stone's wings beat powerfully up away from the docks. "He doesn't see us! He's going the wrong way," Kalam said in alarm.

"No," Flash corrected him before Chime could, "he's following the wind, he's going to use it to get around the docks and back to us—Here he comes!"

Stone hurtled toward the wind-ship and everyone on deck scrambled to make room, either plastering themselves against the rail or flinging themselves through the nearest doorway. The wind-ship had closed its masts to protect the sails from the wind, and Stone swept in and caught one, curled his body around it. The warriors clinging to his body scrambled down. Deft lost his grip and tumbled. Flash hissed in alarm and leapt straight up to pluck him out of the air. Bramble and Lithe grabbed Flash's harness line to reel them back in.

Balm, with Merit tucked under her arm, bounced off the cabin roof and Chime leapt to catch her. They landed on the deck in a heap. Out of the corner of his eye he saw a dark shape with Rorra clutched against its chest swing down from the roof, and his head swam with relief. But when he pushed up on his arms, he saw it was Shade, not Moon.

Above, Stone shifted to groundling, Jade caught him, and climbed down the mast to the cabin. The wind-ship's deck swayed as Diar turned it away from the docks and the flying debris.

Chime pushed up away from Balm and Merit, and found himself facing Jade. "Where's Moon?" he asked.

She met his gaze, and the raw despair in her expression froze his heart.

Then the wind-ship shook, the wind stopped abruptly, and they were floating over an open grassy plain. In the distance a cloud rose as the docks collapsed and fell to the ground.

Chapter Twenty-Three

The eastern fringe of the Reaches

It took time to set the trap, and Heart had spent most of it with various people trying to talk her out of participating. Finally the Arbora finished making their preparations at the site, and now Vine and Sage waited with Heart at the half-Fell camp.

Consolation had sent three dakti to take the message to the progenitor. When all three returned, Heart saw the relief that swept through the flight. The other dakti, the big hulking kethel looming around in the back of the camp, even the rulers had been afraid they wouldn't come back alive. "They are different," Heart said quietly to Vine.

Malachite and Pearl had already gone ahead with the others to set the trap. It was late afternoon, well before nightfall, and they were hoping the progenitor would be overconfident. Vine flicked his spines and said, "It's unnerving."

Sage added, "Everything about this is unnerving."

Heart couldn't disagree.

Consolation spoke to the dakti, then came toward Heart and the warriors. As they pushed to their feet, she said, "It's done. She will come to the meeting. So we should go. I'll carry you."

"I know," Heart said. She made her spines neutral and her voice hard. It was the only way she was going to get through this. She felt the warriors' tension behind her. "It was what we decided."

"But you should be a soft skin," Consolation added. "It would look better."

Heart eyed her. "Why would I do that?"

"I might make you." Consolation scratched the skin under her scales almost diffidently. "It might be better if the progenitor thinks so."

"Can you make me?" Heart asked, trying not to flex her claws. If Consolation could, it would be like a nightmare repeat of the attack on Indigo Cloud's old eastern colony.

"I can make the rulers change," Consolation admitted. "Not the others. But the progenitor won't know that."

Heart didn't want any part of a Fell touching her groundling skin, but it made sense. She shifted, flowing into her groundling form. She had worn work clothes, a plain shirt and pants in a gold brown fabric, the hems stamped with designs in a lighter pigment, and some copper bracelets. The dakti nearby stared at her as if they had never seen anything like her before. Heart bared her teeth at them.

"Most of them haven't seen Arbora before, not close," Consolation said. She looked at the dakti and said, "They have seen now and are over their surprise."

The dakti took the hint and stirred, all looking in different directions. Heart stepped forward and let Consolation lift her up. Vine and Sage followed them, but broke off to wait on the branch of a last mountain-tree as the Fell and Heart flew out of the Reaches.

The place they had chosen was in the wetlands, though still within sight of the rampart of mountain-trees. The apparently empty spot was a low mound surrounded by a scatter of large rocks, the whole covered with a heavy carpet of grasses and flowers. From the shapes and the position of the boulders Heart knew that it was the foundations of a ruin. The stretch of open water nearby had an outline that was too regular, though it was softened by the water plants that clustered thickly along the edges.

One kethel coiled itself on the lower part of the mound behind Heart, and two others retreated a distance to keep watch.

It had been a while since Heart had been outside the Reaches. The sun felt good on her groundling skin, sinking down into her scalp and her bare arms, but the open sky made her feel exposed in a way it hadn't before.

Consolation talked to, or maybe consulted with, the dakti for a time, then began to pace absently in a circle in the middle of the mound. The dakti spread out over the ruin, some taking up positions behind Heart, as if preventing her from running away. But one sat next to her, its scales scraping on the moss.

It was part of the group that always seemed to stay near the Fell queen. Heart eyed it sideways, and said, "If you touch me, I can make the grass you're sitting on burn through your scales." *Then I'll rip your face off,* she added mentally.

The dakti held up its hands, claws partially retracted. "No touching." Its voice was rough and husky, more so than when shifted Aeriat spoke, as if its throat and mouth hadn't been designed for talking. "You're a mentor."

"Yes. What are you?"

It shifted. Heart had seen dakti in groundling form, usually dead ones, and they could be mistaken for Raksura. They were usually covered with dirt and grime and sores, which disguised the paleness of their groundling skin from a distance, and could make them look like an Arbora with a lighter complexion. Their hair was dark and straight like a ruler's, without any of the variations in color and texture common to Raksuran bloodlines. Their features looked like a carving someone had forgotten to finish, their eyes flat and dark.

But this one had coppery skin and curling light-colored hair, a narrow face and eyes as brown as Blossom's. It was wearing a scrap of cloth wrapped around its waist, like the kilts Arbora wore for outdoor work, but not well-made, and not decorated. Heart tried to conceal her surprise, though it was hard not to blink. She said, "You're half-Fell." It wasn't what she had been expecting. Lithe's groundling form looked no different from any other Arbora and her scaled form was a combination of Fell and Raksura. But there had been nothing unusual about the dakti's scaled form.

It said, "How did you guess?" Heart bared her teeth, fairly sure it would understand the gesture. It dropped its gaze, its brows drawing together. "I meant, what do I look like? Like you, a mentor?"

Now Heart understood. "An Arbora." She hesitated. "You haven't seen many Raksura."

"Not close," it said. "Our consort, your consort. Your warriors. The blue queen, the gold queen. The big green-black queen." It shuddered, apparently at the memory of Malachite. "Not the Arbora, unless from a great distance." It gave her another sideways look. "You."

The Fell queen had tried to take Moon in the sel-Selatra. Malachite had told them about it, but it hadn't seemed real until now. A ball of rage built in Heart's chest, so intense it seemed to be coming from outside her body, from her connection to the court. She ground out the words, "You tried to take our consort."

The dakti pulled back and stared at her. It said, "It was a mistake. I told her. She knows, now." It added, "She was afraid that she couldn't keep us alive without help."

If Malachite felt a tenth of what Heart felt, Heart couldn't believe she had left the Fellborn queen alive. She said, "Don't make mistakes."

"Raksura are always angry," the dakti said, and tried a small smile.

"Because Fell exist," Heart said.

The dakti regarded her a moment, then sighed. "I'm First."

Heart tried to parse that and couldn't. "What?"

"My name," it said. "I'm First. I was first, the first one born." It tilted its head at her. "It wasn't easy, until Consolation came."

Heart drew breath to speak, and the words fled. The vision struck her like a blow to the face.

She came out of it to warm sunlight and a circle of agitated dakti. Consolation knelt in front of her, pointing at First, still crouched worriedly next to Heart. "What did you do? Tell me exactly," Consolation demanded.

"It wasn't him," Heart gasped. "I had—I saw—It was a vision." She wasn't certain how much Fell knew about mentor's sight. None of the half-Fell in this flight appeared to have inherited any mentor abilities. *They were falling, all falling, and something tremendous fell with them, and there was burning ice, and fire burning through scales, and nothing could stop it.* "Something terrible is about to happen. Merit's there." She had a clear sense of him through the vision. "Jade's there. And Stone, and Moon."

The dakti stirred in alarm. Consolation's spines flicked wildly. First said, "And someone else? Who else is there?"

"The warriors are there, others . . ." The brilliant images slipped away. She shook her head. "I don't know, I don't know."

Consolation stared at First, and it stared back, its brow knit in consternation.

Then a dakti landed with a thump on the ground behind Consolation. She flinched around, suddenly on her feet. All the others twitched.

The newly arrived dakti pointed to the east. Consolation turned to the others. "They're coming," she hissed. The dakti scrambled into position and First shifted back to its scaled form. Heart almost shifted with it, then remembered not to just in time.

As Consolation moved away, Heart spotted the dark shapes against the blue of the sky, arrowing down toward them. She shuddered and wiped at her face. She was sweating all over her groundling skin, but the chill she felt went bone deep. At least she was going to look convincingly distraught for the progenitor.

Two kethel landed on the outer edge of the ruin. Then a scatter of dakti and rulers. Then a huge dark figure dropped to the ground in front of Consolation.

Terror seized Heart like a predator's teeth. She froze, her chest too tight to breathe. There was no mistaking the progenitor, though Heart had never seen one before. She was larger even than Malachite, maybe at least a head taller and more broad, the largest progenitor Heart had ever heard of. Her scales were as black as the rulers, but with a softer texture, and she held her leathery wings angled back.

Heart thought, *you're just here to look like a terrified captive, remember that*. She shouldn't have any trouble playing that part. But something built behind her eyes, a confused urge to flee or throw herself at the progenitor's throat, and she struggled to control herself.

The progenitor didn't seem to notice anything except the Fell queen, but Heart knew she was aware of every movement. The progenitor didn't make a gesture, but one of her kethel turned suddenly and plunged into the pool. It sloshed through the stagnant water, searching, then turned and flung itself out. It shook itself, sending torn vines and waterweeds flying. Heart kept her gaze on the ground. Malachite had said the Fell would be alert for that deception. Beside her, First made a restless movement.

The kethel settled into a guard position. The progenitor said in Raksuran, "The little abomination knows where a colony is." The progenitor's gaze fell on Heart, pretending to notice her for the first time. "The little abomination has a captive."

Fell always spoke in the language of their prey, and the progenitor's attention made Heart's skin creep.

"Proof I don't lie," Consolation said. The kethel behind Heart stirred restlessly. Consolation added, "Don't come any closer."

The progenitor's gaze fixed on Consolation. "Stupid to take an Arbora. They will know you are close."

"They know you're close," Consolation retorted. "You're all over the fields."

There was a moment of silence. Heart realized the progenitor was trying to impose herself on Consolation's mind, the way the rulers could on groundlings and unlucky Raksura. Consolation didn't look away, but she let out a bored hiss. "Satisfied?"

The progenitor drew back as if repulsed. "Abomination."

Consolation's spines moved and she made a noise that might have been a laugh. "That's what my mother said before I killed her."

Heart bit the inside of her cheek and thought *Careful*. They didn't want the progenitor's mind to go to traps. Beside Heart, First's claws sunk into the moss, a gesture of anxiety that Heart fully sympathized with.

The progenitor apparently decided there was no point in more games. "Tell us where the colony is."

Consolation shook her mane of frills. "You haven't heard what I want. You agree first."

"I don't bargain with an abomination."

Consolation stared at her, her spines trembling. She turned abruptly. "We're going." First reached for Heart's arm. She twitched away from him in startled reflex.

The progenitor didn't betray any anger. "You play with us like prey."

Consolation snarled, "I want what I want. You give it to me or I don't give you what I have."

The silence stretched. Two of the progenitor's rulers moved forward to flank her, the dakti and kethel drawing closer. The kethel behind Heart reared up. She felt it towering over her and quailed convincingly, though she was mostly relieved. The Fell had finally been lured into the right positions.

The progenitor said, "Then bargain."

Consolation seemed to brace herself. "The tree. When they're the dead, the tree. And a consort, alive."

"No."

Consolation did a convincing imitation of mortal offense. "What, no? Why not?"

"You wish to breed, breed with your rulers."

Where is she? Heart wondered. *What is she waiting for—*

That was when she realized one of the rulers was on the ground and Malachite stood beside the progenitor.

First and the other dakti near Heart squeaked in unfeigned terror and the kethel jerked back. The breath caught in Heart's throat as she stared. *I knew she was there, and I forgot. She made us all forget.* Heart concentrated, reaching for the memory of the last few moments, the way she did for sudden visions. She realized she had seen Malachite come up from between the rocks that blocked the view of the pool. That Malachite had walked between Consolation's dakti without alerting them, up to the progenitor's ruler and slashed his throat.

Consolation flinched and dropped into a crouch. The remaining rulers keened in startled fear and leapt backward. Consolation's kethel moved closer, within pouncing distance of Malachite but also near to the progenitor's kethel.

The progenitor snarled, "We know you, Malachite of Opal Night. Have you come to join us?"

Malachite flared her spines with predatory deliberation as she circled to the left, delicately stepping around the choking ruler. "Always the same offers, always the same mistakes."

The progenitor drew back, gathering herself. "You were foolish to come here alone."

Malachite stopped. She bared her fangs in amusement. "There is a question you should ask yourself."

The progenitor braced to leap. "We know the abomination aids you. We expected a trap. Others come and you cannot kill us all."

Unperturbed, Malachite continued, "The question is: was this mound here yesterday?"

The progenitor went still. She started to turn and Malachite leapt forward.

And the other side of the mound exploded. Dirt rained down as the kethel hidden inside stood up and surged over the progenitor's kethel. A gold form flashed out as Pearl appeared and a storm of Indigo Cloud and Opal Night warriors followed her into the air. Then the half-Fell leapt on the progenitor's dakti and kethel and everything collapsed into claws and fangs and growling.

In the hours of darkness, the Arbora had crept out here and transformed this spot, removing the turf, digging the hiding chamber and the shafts to allow in air for the warriors, Pearl, and the single kethel, then replanting the grass and weeds. Malachite must have dug in somewhere too, though Heart wasn't sure where.

Heart should have stayed out of the battle as Pearl had ordered but she lunged into the center of it, bloodlust whiting out conscious thought. A dakti raced for Malachite and Heart shifted in mid-leap and landed on it. It tore at her chest but her heavier claws ripped through its throat as she rolled. She shoved upright and shook the mutilated body off her.

Pearl's golden form flashed overhead, the warriors fought the dakti in snarling knots. Kethel battled in the air and a struggling cluster of them bounced off the edge of the pool. Malachite and the progenitor slammed across the hilltop, a fury of scales and claws that rammed through a scatter of dakti. Consolation wrestled with a ruler but Pearl hit them both from above, peeled the ruler away from Consolation and ripped his head off.

Consolation staggered free, then leapt to land on the progenitor's back. But the progenitor was too big, too strong. She rolled and crushed Consolation under her weight combined with Malachite's. As the combatants rolled away they left Consolation in the flattened grass, stunned. Heart leapt toward her to guard her from the progenitor's dakti.

The progenitor broke away from Malachite and they faced each other. Malachite's scales bore slashes and streaks of blood, hers mingled with the progenitor's. Malachite bared bloody fangs in a predator's smile and said, "Finish it."

The progenitor snarled back, "I intend to."

Heart crouched, watching wide-eyed.

Malachite said, "I wasn't talking to you," just as Pearl leapt atop the progenitor's head.

Consolation shoved unsteadily to her feet, but a ruler leapt at her. Heart lunged forward to help her but staggered sideways as another dakti slammed into her. Heart swung it around, bit into its throat. A ruler grabbed her from behind and she clawed at its arms, too enraged to feel terror.

Then First and a swarm of half-Fell dakti landed on them. Heart bit into the ruler's arm, aware of the strange sensation of a half-Fell dakti prying the ruler's claws out of her frills. The ruler wrenched away, snarling. Heart staggered to her feet and saw Pearl with her foot claws buried deep in the progenitor's neck and Malachite tearing at her stomach and chest. The progenitor tried to extend her jaw, then Malachite widened her own and bit down into the progenitor's face.

Then a dakti grabbed Heart's arm and she nearly shredded it before she recognized it as First. It pointed toward the east. "There! There!"

Heart squinted into the distance. A dozen kethel and a cloud of dakti shot through the sky, coming this way. "Pearl!" she shouted. They had to go, now, the progenitor was dying and . . . The kethel weren't coming. They were falling. Falling out of the sky.

Vision struck again and Heart saw a cold wave from somewhere out of the southeast, moving over the plain like a wall of ice, destroying everything in its wake. She felt the pressure of it already, in the places in her head that sensed direction, that controlled her mentor's skills, that allowed her to shift. She shouted, "Pearl, Pearl, we have to go! It's coming!"

The progenitor flung Malachite away, and staggered back. The other Fell screamed at her and she stared toward the east and the dark shapes dropping out of the sky. The quiet spread like a pool as the others felt it, Fell and half-Fell and Raksura alike, everyone staring into the east. Pearl landed beside Heart and snarled, "What is it?"

"Death." Heart shook the vision off. "We have to run, it's almost too late!"

Pearl grabbed Heart and whirled around. "Go! To the trees!"

The nearest warriors were all Indigo Cloud. They snatched up their wounded and dying and bounded away to leap into flight. Floret, Aura, and Sand landed beside Pearl. The Opal Night warriors waited, watching Malachite.

Malachite shoved to her feet but the progenitor snarled and leapt away. She landed further down the mound, then sprung into flight. Rulers, dakti, and kethel curved up to follow her.

The half-Fell were left behind, confused and hesitating. Consolation stumbled to her feet, blood dripping down her side. First keened in fear to see her hurt, but Consolation shouted and leapt upward. First and the rest of the half-Fell flight launched themselves after her.

Malachite took a step forward as if she meant to follow the progenitor. Loud enough to make Heart's ears ring, Pearl bellowed, "Malachite, tell your warriors to run for the trees if you don't want them all to die!"

That got through to her. Malachite turned back, flicked her spines, and all the Opal Night warriors were suddenly alight. The jolt when Pearl flung herself into the air after them took Heart's breath. She managed to wrench her head around to get a look back.

The wave of death crossed the wetlands toward them. In the distance another flight of Fell exploded up into the air, a cloud of frantic black dots, then slowed, and dropped like stones. "Hurry," Heart hissed, "faster." She felt Pearl's wingbeats in her own chest as they shot into the green shadow of the mountain-trees. Their path became erratic as Pearl dodged branches and kept flying. All around them were warriors, the half-Fell dakti and kethel.

Then a wave of pain took Heart's senses, and she saw—

—red light on a dark slate surface, fire washing against it, cracking, splintering, dissolving, falling—

Heart gasped in a breath. "It's stopped, it's stopped," she managed.

"Are you sure?" Pearl's voice said in her ear.

It had stopped and there was death behind them, across the plain. "Yes. They did it." She had a clear image of Jade and Balm, falling back from an opening, and someone else, a strange groundling woman.

Pearl's body jerked as she adjusted her course, and she called out to the warriors to stop. Floret and Sand and the others echoed her, then the unfamiliar voices of the Opal Night warriors.

Pearl landed and Heart lifted her head to find them crouched on the broad branch of a stunted mountain-tree. The birdsong and hum of insects and other life, silenced by their wild flight, was just starting to return. Pain coursed through Heart's legs, her arms, her back, but it was fading. Their own warriors had landed on branches above and below, and near Pearl was Consolation and First. The Opal Night warriors and the half-Fell dakti and kethel were scattered through the group.

Pearl rose up a little, and said, "Floret? Is anyone hurt?"

On the next branch Floret pushed upright. She shook out her frills unsteadily, her claws gripping the bark. "Aura, Sand, Spring, Drift, Band, Coil, Fair . . . Who has Serene, I know she was hurt . . ."

"Coil's dead," Aura reported, her voice rough with shock.

Pearl hissed and Heart winced. Answering calls came as Rise tumbled down from the branch above and began collecting Opal Night warriors. The dakti chittered above them and a kethel rumbled.

Malachite dropped down onto the branch on the far side of Consolation. Consolation twitched and First flinched right off the branch, falling down to the one below. Pearl said, "What was that?"

"I don't know." Malachite's spines didn't move.

Pearl snarled, "You do know."

Consolation looked from Pearl to Malachite and back, spines flicking.

"I have a suspicion," Malachite admitted. "I need to see." She jumped straight up to the branch above, then took flight up through the mountain-tree's canopy.

"I hate you," Pearl muttered, and followed her.

Heart shut her eyes as they hit the curtains of leaves in the upper canopy, then blinked as they came out into sunlight. Malachite lit on a bare curving limb stump that spiraled up out of the green sea of mountain-tree crowns. Pearl landed on the branch collar just below her. The blue sky curved over them and they had a view of the wetlands.

Malachite stared toward the east and Heart followed her gaze as Consolation belatedly scrambled up below them.

All over the wetlands, the dark shapes of Fell, some single and some in groups, were taking to the air and flying away. They moved slowly, like they were in pain. Like their joints and gut ached like Heart's did. It wasn't a coordinated effort, their courses were scattered, some directly east, some northeast, some south along the edge of the Reaches. They were fleeing in confusion.

Heart said, "Some of the Fell are dead. Maybe a lot of them." The vision still lingered in her thoughts, and she could see bodies strewn in the weed-choked ponds and reed-grass. Her brow furrowed as she turned over a stray image, another body lying in a different field, the dry grass more yellow than green . . .

"But not the progenitor," Malachite said. "She got away."

"She's just one progenitor," Pearl said. "I'm sure we can find some dead ones for you out in the marshes—"

Malachite turned on her with a hiss. "She was the one who brought the others together. You don't think she'll blame us for this? She will regroup, with even more power now that other progenitors are dead. She will do this again."

Pearl hissed. But below, Consolation said, "She's right. I don't want her to be right, but she's right."

Heart felt Pearl's throat move in a soundless snarl. Pearl said flatly, "You want to follow her?"

"Yes."

"And what if that happens again?" Pearl demanded. "Whatever it was?"

Heart touched the last image of the vision, the details scattering into dust as she tried to gather them. But the sense of finality was still there. "I don't think it will. I'll have to consult with the other mentors, but . . . I think it's over."

Pearl said, "Heart, keep your visions to yourself for the moment," but her tone was more disgruntled than angry. She sounded exactly like herself. Shaken to her core by what had just happened, Heart hugged her in relief.

Pearl absently patted Heart's head. She said to Malachite, "I can't stop you from going. And I admit it's exactly the sort of mad exploit you excel at."

Malachite still stared toward the east. She looked down at Pearl. "I don't need anyone to tell me to go. But perhaps I need you to tell me when to stop."

Silence hung in the air, just the wind in the leaves and the distant cry of a cloud-walker. Consolation had climbed up far enough to watch them with more fascination than wariness. Heart suspected progenitors didn't talk to each other like this. She was a little astonished to hear Pearl spoken to like this.

Pearl hissed out a breath of mingled exasperation and weariness. "Back to the colony first. We have wounded."

Jade couldn't stand to be near anyone but Balm.

The storm caused by the ruin's fall had thrown the wind-ship some distance from the site of the structure's final collapse. Now it was late afternoon and the sun warm on the deck as the clouds cleared and a column of smoke rose on the horizon. Jade stood at the rail, Balm beside her, a hand around her wrist as if Balm thought she needed to tie Jade to the deck. Maybe it was needed; Jade might have flown away, except her back muscles were strained from the effort to reach the wind-ship. She had shifted to her Arbora form, but it still felt like spikes had been jammed into her back.

This is what happened to Pearl, Jade thought. Even her secondhand experience with that devastation through Pearl's connection to the court, even her own grief for Rain, was nothing to this. She suddenly understood Malachite all too well.

The warriors were exhausted, sick, injured when they had struggled out of the debris, and their two mentors weren't in much better shape. She could hear muffled wailing from one of the belowdecks cabins. Jade should be taking care of them, instead of letting Bramble take charge.

An Arbora, a hunter, who should never have been in this situation in the first place.

But she couldn't make herself leave the rail. She was going to have to return to the Reaches and look at her clutch, at the three baby consorts that might grow up to have Moon's eyes.

Behind her she heard soft steps on the deck, then Delin said, "Balm, can you tell Jade that Stone is flying ahead?"

That shocked Jade into movement. She turned. "Stone's hurt." He had had to dig their way out of the collapsing passage.

Delin's brow was furrowed with concern. "Rorra cleaned and bandaged his hands. He said he doesn't need them to fly."

He shouldn't go alone, Jade thought. She should go with him; she couldn't fly but he could carry her. No, she couldn't leave the warriors and Arbora now. Before she could think who to send with him, who wasn't injured or exhausted, she felt the wind-ship tremble and Stone's dark form dropped off the stern. He slid sideways and caught the wind, flapped for altitude and shot off toward the column of smoke in the distance.

Jade started to hiss but lost the will for it midway through drawing breath. If Stone wanted to fly ahead, let him. Her gaze fell on Balm, who was in her groundling form. The sleeves of her borrowed Kishan jacket were ripped and her arms were scratched and bruised. Her cheeks were hollow and a bruise darkened on her temple. Jade said, "Balm needs some tea."

Balm's nod was serious. "So do you."

Delin lifted a hand and one of the young Islanders hurried forward with two cups. Delin took them and handed them to Jade and Balm. Jade drank hers, barely noticing that it was an Islander tea and already cool. It had been a mistake to speak, since once Jade had started, she couldn't just stop again. She handed Delin back the cup and said, "Who's that below?"

Delin probably couldn't hear it but he seemed to know what she meant. "Chime is badly off. So is Shade. The others . . . are not so well, either."

Jade twitched her spines in acknowledgement, then winced at what that did to her wing muscles. She made herself say, "I'll go down there."

Shade might not appreciate her presence, but Chime would, for now. Until someone told him what had happened in the ruin.

She pushed away from the rail and followed Delin, Balm trailing behind her.

Jade hadn't intended to sleep, but at some point she must have. She lay on the floor in one of the belowdecks cabins, and flinched awake when Balm leaned over her. The mentor's lights in the cabin were starting to fade and the air tasted of early dawn. The bruises on Balm's face had had time to discolor but her eyes were alight and her expression made Jade's heart seize up. Balm dragged at her arm. "Stone's back! Come on!"

Jade shoved upright and followed her. Her back still ached and the little food she had been able to eat sloshed unpleasantly in her stomach. But the wind-ship stirred around her, more movement and voices than she had been conscious of in hours.

She stepped out onto the deck and saw Diar holding up a lamp, its light falling on the circle of Raksura, Golden Islanders, Rorra, and Kalam. In the center stood Stone, with the kethel beside him, crumpled on the deck. Jade caught Chime's expression of painful hope and her mind went blank.

The kethel's pale skin was mottled with dark bruises, raw burns, and bloody cuts and scrapes. As Jade stepped forward, it looked up at her. "Groundlings took the consort," it said, its voice a harsh rasp.

Jade forced the words out, "Was he alive?"

"It doesn't know," Stone said. His clothes were torn and covered with dust, smeared with blood where he must have been carrying the kethel. "When it woke, it saw Moon on the ground next to a pile of debris, but a Kishan flying boat was coming. It crawled away through the grass and hid under a piece of wall, and pretended to be dead. It saw groundlings in flying packs come down from the boat and carry Moon and at least three Hians away. I searched, and there were some dead Hians left near that spot. They must have taken anyone they found still alive."

A flutter of anxious spines went through the warriors, and Bramble shook Chime's arm. Shade turned and buried his face on Flicker's shoulder. Jade couldn't trust herself to speak. Balm said, "It saw which way the flying boat went?"

"Northeast," Stone said.

Diar nodded sharply. "If my calculation of our position is correct, we're at the edge of Kish-Jandera. North is the territory of Kish-Majora, and the city directly to the northeast is Kish-Karad."

Kalam took a sharp breath. "The Imperial seat."

Jade found her voice. "Get the kethel some water. Stone, Rorra, Kalam, we need to make plans."

CHAPTER TWENTY-FOUR

Moon woke struggling to breathe, the stink of smoke overwhelming light and sound, nothing but dry grass and acrid metal and burning flesh. He had the bad feeling the flesh might be him; his skin felt like fire. He heard hushed voices, speaking some variation on Kedaic. Then footsteps, coming closer.

That penetrated the haze enough for him to realize the dirt and the scratch of grass was on his bare skin, that he was lying here in his groundling form, probably surrounded by dead Hians. *Lavinat used a fire weapon on me,* he remembered. He would have blood on his teeth, his hands. He knew what he had to do, pretend he was a groundling, come up with a story. He got his arms under him and tried to heave himself upright, but pain ran out of his chest like blood and water, and he slid down into burning darkness again.

The next time he woke slowly, drifting back up to an awareness of an unfamiliar place. He knew he had been almost awake before, that several dramatic things had happened while he was semi-conscious. He remembered flashes of intense searing pain between times of cool relief. Someone giving him water, and broth with just enough of a taste of meat to make him alternately sick and ravenous. He remembered trying to flex his hands and realizing his fingers were broken, held immobile by splints.

Now the skin of his chest felt tender and tight, but it didn't hurt nearly as much as he remembered. He heard movement from another room, the sound bouncing off stone walls, and voices, none familiar. He took a deep breath, keeping his eyes closed, and tasted the scent.

Sun-warmed air, incense caught in the folds of fabric, Kishan moss, though not nearby, strange groundling bodies, a trace of sweet oil, water running over stone and metal. And somewhere, the confusion of dust and sour/sweet scents that suggested a groundling city.

No Raksura. There was no scent of Fell, either. Kethel might have survived the fire weapons and the crash into the plain, but it wouldn't have survived being found by groundlings. It was either dead in the ruin somewhere or escaped.

Now Moon just had to figure out where he was.

He managed to get his gummy eyes open to see a high domed ceiling of gray-white stone, embossed with half circles, all set with chips of glittering blue and green glass. Morning sunlight fell through stone-latticed windows just under the dome. Figured bronze lamps hung from the ceiling, and the walls had more embossed images, repeating square designs. The bed he lay on was a stone platform built against the wall, but it was made comfortable with cushions and drapes in soft fabrics.

Moon started to lever himself up and subsided with a gasp at the stab of pain in his chest. He squinted down at himself and saw a lot of patchy new bronze skin in between bandages and red healing burns; the muscles underneath ached with every movement. All the fingers on his right hand and three on the left had been broken and mostly healed straight. He moved his feet and added several toes to the total. He had a dim memory of digging his way out from under smothering debris, breaking his claws in the process. Nothing was broken or strained in his back; it didn't hurt except for a dull ache. It meant his wing joins weren't damaged, which was a relief.

Someone had taken care of him, obviously. Someone not a mentor. There was no scent of the simples that Merit or Lithe would have used, and he could tell he hadn't been put in a healing sleep.

The door in the far wall was an open arch to another room. The groundlings he could hear were somewhere past it. He shifted to his scaled form.

Tried to shift. Nothing happened.

Moon tightened his throat against a snarl. *They know what you are.* He knew what being caught felt like. But it wasn't Fell poison; there was no scale pattern on his skin. He tried again but it was like there was a wall between himself and whatever power he needed to shift, a wall he couldn't break through. *Kishan shamen*, he thought. This had to be why the Fell were so wary of them.

He tried to sit up again and his arms trembled with the effort of pushing himself upright. There was no sign of whatever might have been left of his own clothes, or anything else he had been carrying with him.

Footsteps sounded from the other room and a small blue groundling appeared in the doorway. It squeaked with alarm at the sight of Moon awake and bolted out.

Moon waited, his heart pounding, but nothing drastic happened. There were agitated voices at a distance, then soft footsteps in the next room again. After a moment, the steps pattered hurriedly away, and it was quiet.

Moon climbed off the couch and stumbled, then lurched across the floor of polished stone tile toward the doorway. He leaned heavily on the doorframe, shocked at how weak he was.

This was room was larger, with stone-latticed windows taking up most of the far wall. A bench with cushions stood near the doorway, a drape of fine dark blue fabric across it. He picked it up and found it was a piece of clothing, a combination of a wrap skirt and pants. The idea of being trapped in groundling form and naked in front of strange people who were holding him prisoner was unnerving, so he got it on and tied at the waist. Then he headed for the windows.

Halfway there, he stepped in water and staggered sideways. There was a shallow round pool with a mosaiced bottom, apparently just there to decorate the room, since it was barely a fingerwidth deep. *That's a stupid thing to have*, Moon thought, reaching the windows. He leaned against the stone lattice, shaking the water off his foot.

The openings were easily wide enough to fit his head through. In his shifted form, he might have to dislocate a shoulder to get the rest of his body out, though it would be hard to force even his folded wings through. But he couldn't shift, so the point was academic at the moment.

The city spread out below was massive, the buildings made of golden stone, their domed roofs covered with carvings and painted designs, colorful banners hanging from open galleries and balconies. Broad streets wove between them, though most of the foot traffic was on the bridges that criss-crossed between the upper levels. He blinked and realized the large bridge curving away between distant buildings was actually an aqueduct, small boats sailing along it. He could spot the tower of a flying boat dock not far past it.

He had never seen a groundling city this massive in the east. This was what a city looked like that had never been destroyed by Fell or other predators, that had never had to move and leave half itself behind.

Behind him, quiet steps approached. Whoever it was seemed much calmer than the last groundling. He said, "What city is this?" He spoke Kedaic, matching his accent to the way Callumkal and Kalam had spoken it.

There was a moment of startled silence. Then the answer, "This is Kish-Karad, the western principal city and Imperial seat."

Moon turned, leaning on the windowsill to stay upright.

The groundling who stood there was short and round, with roughly-textured gray skin and a boney head crest like a crown across the skull, dark feathery hair sprouting behind it. The long sleeveless robe was shaped to indicate at least two breasts, so he assumed she was female. Her features were broad, her eyes large and dark, and she had that look that groundlings sometimes got, as if she hadn't expected him to be able to speak, at least intelligibly. Or just not expected him to speak first. Experience suggested it was mostly the former. Moon said, "Did you find any others like me?"

"Not like you," she said, obviously still regrouping.

They weren't dead in the wreckage. Moon didn't let his relief show, though he broke out in a sweat all over.

She watched him carefully. "You're a Raksura, correct?"

"You should know, since you're keeping me from shifting." If the Kishan had thought he was a Fell, they would never have let him live, much less healed him.

A sideways motion of her head seemed to concede the point. "It's a precaution. You were badly injured and not aware enough to be reasoned with." She added, "So what were you doing in a burning ruin that fell unexpectedly from the sky?"

At the city where the sunsailer had come to port, Kalam had told the Kish about the Hians; there had been plenty of time for that information to be carried deep into Kish via flying boat. "I was with Kalam of Kedmar, and Captain Rorra, helping them look for Callumkal, Master Scholar of the Conclave of the Janderan. Callumkal, and Delin-Evranlindel, a scholar from the Golden Isles, and two Raksura were stolen by Hians. They attacked Callumkal's ship and killed our friends."

He thought she had registered recognition at both Callumkal's and Kalam's names. She said, "Why were you helping Jandera?"

It was an odd question to ask, unless you already knew at least some of what had happened. "Because Callumkal is my friend."

She hesitated, the feathery hair on her brows lifting and expanding. "He lives, then?"

Moon wondered who had claimed that Callumkal was dead. "When I last saw him. He was sick. The Hians gave him poison." They seemed to be trading answers, so he added, "How long have I been here?"

She stood silent for what felt like a long moment, considering what Moon had said. "We found you fourteen days ago."

Moon managed not to twitch. *Fourteen days.* Long enough for the others to find him, if they were alive? They had to be alive; he couldn't handle the thought that they weren't. But were they here or trapped up on the cloudwall? And he knew he had done as much as he could to get this groundling to think of him as a person, getting her to answer his questions, referencing Jandera friends; it was time to ask the hard question. "Am I a prisoner?"

Her brows moved again, in what Moon thought was uncertainty. "You are too injured to leave here, and there are others who have questions. I am Ceilinel, Chief Arcanist of the Imperial Conclave. Will you tell me your name?"

Not the most encouraging answer, or lack of answer. He had been right about her being a shaman, at least. "I'm Moon of Opal Night, consort to Jade, sister queen of the Court of Indigo Cloud." He had to see if he could get a message to someone. He didn't know where the others were and he couldn't ask for a message to be carried to the Reaches, which might be under attack by Fell. He struggled to remember every groundling he knew who might owe him a favor and was still alive. Kalam had sent the survivors of his father's expedition back to Kedmar to get help, and it would surely be easiest to reach them. "Can I send a message to—" Then the world slid sideways and his vision narrowed to a dark tunnel.

He was suddenly on the floor, doubled over, struggling to breathe.

Ceilinel stepped forward, demanding, "What is it? The burns?"

Moon took a deep breath and the cramp subsided. He managed to sit up. His voice came out as a harsh croak. "It's been too long since I had food." From bitter experience, he knew he could go without solid food for some time, but the cramps and spasms would become less sporadic and far more painful.

Ceilinel asked, "What do you eat?"

Moon snorted a bitter laugh at the idea that it might be a trick question. "The same things Kishan eat."

Ceilinel's steps moved rapidly away. Moon eased himself into a sitting position and leaned his head back against the cool stone of the wall. Returning footsteps and the scent of cooked meat startled him awake; he had slid into a light doze, still sitting up.

Ceilinel returned with three more groundlings. One carried a low table and the other two had trays of food. Ceilinel gestured to them to put it near Moon, who faked another cramp just to hide his relief. They could have refused him food to get what they wanted, though he had no idea what that was.

One of the groundlings set a cushion beside the table and backed away. Moon slid over to it, his legs shaking, and got his first good look at the food.

The trays held a bowl with clear broth and cut roots and cooked fish pieces, and plates with fried balls of a yellow grain with red specks, little round cakes, puffy square bread things with a sweet paste, and cooked meat pieces in a dark sauce. A lot of it was wrapped in big leaves and sprinkled with little white flowers, and it was scented of a dozen different spices. A cylindrical pot emitted the smoky fragrance of Kishan tea and there was a flask of plain water.

At the moment Moon didn't care if it was all stuffed with Fell poison. He had been in the outer edges of Kish territory before, and some of this was familiar; the grain had been a staple for the Jandera on the expedition. He drank the tea first, then started on the food. He made himself eat slowly and use his best groundlings-are-watching-you-eat manners, so he wouldn't make himself sick or terrify the Kishan. Except for Ceilinel, they had retreated to the archway, watching with wary curiosity. Two were the same species as Ceilinel, but smaller, and one was the blue one, who had a curly mass of silvery hair on its head and very large, expressive eyes. They seemed to have every expectation that Moon would do something terrible, and it was a relief when Ceilinel gestured them out of the room.

She gave him time to eat half the food, then said, "Would you tell me how you came to be in the wreckage of that ruin, or great machine, whatever it was?"

He still wasn't certain how much she knew, if she was testing him. But calling it a "great machine" rather than just a strange stone-metal thing that had inexplicably fallen from the sky meant she knew more than she had implied. "The Hians stole an old weapon from the foundation builder city that Callumkal wanted to explore. They wanted to use it to kill Fell, but it also killed Jandera and Raksura. And Hians. They knew that, and didn't care. They put it in an old forerunner ruin to make it work. We tried to stop them." He kept the explanation short. Ceilinel might be trying to confirm someone else's story, or maybe catch Moon in a lie. He wanted to ask about Niran's wind-ship, but he didn't want to betray its existence if the Kish didn't already know about it. "Do Kalam and Rorra, or Delin, know I'm here?"

"I don't know," she said. "But the Jandera who speak for Kedmar in the Imperial councils do." She watched him for another moment. "I've been told consorts never leave Raksuran colonies."

She had used the correct Kedaic word for colony, not "hive" or anything else Moon had heard. It fed that spark of hope. She had spoken to somebody who knew about Raksura; it didn't necessarily mean it was Delin or Rorra or Kalam, it could have been some Kishan scholar Moon had never met. He said, "Not often. But consorts travel with their queens as . . ." He wasn't sure about the multiple meanings of the word he wanted in Kedaic, so settled for Altanic. " . . . envoys." The food was already making him feel less weak, making it easier to think. It wasn't a good idea to lie, since he had no idea how much Ceilinel knew. Which was a problem since Moon was much better at lying than telling the truth. "I was raised outside a colony, so I've traveled more than most consorts." Putting it that way sounded better than saying he had been what a Raksuran court would call a feral solitary for most of his life.

"What makes consorts so . . . in need of protection? Is it because you're male?"

Moon looked up at her. Two turns ago he wouldn't have been able to answer this question. "Because we carry the court's bloodline."

Ceilinel said nothing, though Moon could feel her watching as he cleared the last plate of little cakes. She said, "Is that enough food?"

He looked up at her. "That depends on how long you're keeping me."

"At least until you're well enough to travel. And food will be provided whenever you wish." She glanced at the empty plates. "Is there anything else you want now?"

"Do you have books in Altanic?" Moon asked on impulse. It was partly strategic; he had to keep her thinking of him as a person and not a dangerous if wounded animal. But if he was going to be stuck here for a while with no idea what had happened to the others, a distraction would help him keep his sanity.

Her brows moved in a way that made him think she was trying to conceal unflattering surprise. "I'm sure some can be found." She hesitated. "Anything else?"

"Why is there a pool of water in the middle of the room?"

"To cool the air," she said, and walked out.

Moon took the opportunity to lick the plates, then tried to stand. He had to haul himself up on the window sill and once upright, he swayed, shaky and sick. He didn't think they had drugged him. There just weren't that many drugs that affected Raksura that weren't Fell poison, and this didn't feel like it. It was more likely that his battered body had reached its limit for the moment. He barely made it back to the couch in the other room, climbed into it and burrowed down into the blankets, sliding back into sleep.

Jade and Rorra crossed a bridge beside an elevated canal, heading toward a clump of domed stone structures like small mountains. Below them, more ordinary paths, paved with flat river stones, wound through a garden and a grove of trees, linking more modest buildings of white limestone. There were groundlings and their draughtbeasts and carts everywhere. It wasn't as noisy as the section of the city near the trade portal or any of the markets, but it was still enough to get on what was left of Jade's abraded nerves.

Jade was in her Arbora form, wearing a set of Kalam's clothes, an open Janderan jacket, pants, and sandals on her feet. It was uncomfortable and just felt odd, especially the sandals, but it would keep anyone from suspecting she was a Raksura.

"Is that it?" Jade jerked her chin toward the biggest structure. "I need to stop so I can try to catch the scent."

"All right, I'll pretend to be tired." Rorra leaned on the parapet looking into the canal. A small boat was sailing by, and Rorra flicked her blunt claws in the water.

"Are you sure you're pretending?" Jade leaned on the rail beside her. There were canal boats and wagons driven by the Kishan moss that offered transport around the city, but they were enclosed and made it nearly impossible to scent anything.

Rorra's expression was wry. "A little. Kedmar isn't nearly this large. Kalam was surprised, too."

Jade knew how much gratitude she owed to both of them, for leaving Callumkal to the care of Golden Islanders and Raksura, for coming here to help search for Moon. Considering the reception Kalam had gotten in isl-Maharat, Kalam and Rorra had decided not to appeal to any officials of Kish, not until they had help. Their plan was to search for Moon on their own until Niran and Diar arrived with reinforcements from Kedmar.

Their knowledge of Kishan cities was invaluable, and they also gave Jade someone to talk to, since Stone was barely speaking to her.

Jade hadn't wanted to bring Rorra and Kalam at first, and it had added to the coldness between her and Stone when he insisted on it. As soon as she had seen the city, she had known she was wrong, and her effort to conquer that irritation had made things even worse.

This place made the port city they had stopped at on the way to the sel-Selatra look like an outpost. Even with Stone, Jade wouldn't have had any idea how to find Moon. Rorra and Kalam had never visited here before but they seemed to know exactly how everything worked. Rorra had found a caravanserai and Kalam had paid for it with the little tokens the Kish used for barter. His supply came from Kedmar, originally brought along on the expedition by Callumkal, and he was able to buy food and anything else they needed. The only problem was that Rorra had to keep her fire weapons carefully hidden, since they weren't permitted inside the city.

When they had first arrived, Rorra had explained that there was a place called the trade portal where all the boats had to go before they could navigate freely within the perimeter of the city walls. While they waited at the caravanserai, she had gone there to get word of any survivors from the forerunner docks.

"We should search the cadashah, depending on what Rorra discovers in the trade portal," Kalam had said while they waited for her to return. It was a Kish word Jade didn't know, and he had explained, "That's a place with physicians where anyone can go at any time, for treatment or medicine or to stay, if they're very ill and it takes time to cure them. If the people who found Moon didn't realize he was a Raksura, they may have taken him to one. The cadashah don't ask for payment, or anything, so it would make sense to take an injured, unknown traveler there for help. If it's the same way here that it is in Kedmar, the problem will be that everyone who doesn't have a private physician uses cadashah, so they're all over the city."

But when Rorra returned, it was with rumors of survivors found in the burning ruin and taken to conclave leaders. "They'll want to question them," she had said. "Obviously. Giant things don't just fall out of the sky every day."

So they had divided up the sections of the city that had public buildings for the conclave's use, and were checking the cadashah near them as well. Apparently the conclave had dwellings on top of structures used as libraries and meeting places, which made it easier for Jade and Stone to get close enough to try to pick up Moon's scent. Kalam was out with Stone today; he and Rorra switched between their two Raksuran companions in an effort to keep anyone from noticing and marking their movements. They met at the caravanserai every night and crossed off sections on Rorra's maps.

Now Jade tasted the air deeply, sorting out Rorra's scent, and the blended scents of all these busy groundlings. It helped that this city was almost as clean as a colony tree, with relatively few scents of rot or sewage. But no scent of Raksura, either. "Nothing. I'll try again once we're closer." Rorra was also asking questions of the people who took care of the buildings, telling them she was searching for word of a missing Jandera flying boat that she feared had been destroyed in the strange ruin's collapse.

Rorra pushed away from the parapet and they started down the curving walkway toward the domed building. "How long are you and Stone going to be angry at each other?"

Jade suppressed a jolt of irritation, feeling her spines press against her coat. It was followed immediately by a jolt of guilt; Rorra helped search for Moon with the dedication of a favored warrior and it couldn't be easy for her to walk all over this city, no matter what she said. "I didn't think it was obvious." It had to be obvious. She and Stone could barely look at each other.

Rorra glanced at her. "It probably wouldn't be, if I hadn't been living in your laps for so long."

Jade shook her head. "I'm angry at him because he's angry at me. When we find Moon—" She cut herself off, forcing the bubble of fear down. "—we'll talk." *No, we won't. Because I've come as close to killing my consort as if I snapped his neck myself, and Stone hates me for it, and I hate him for not stopping me.* Even if—when they found Moon alive, that wouldn't change. "It'll be all right."

"I hope so," Rorra's voice was uncharacteristically soft. As they drew near the smaller walkway that curved off toward the first building, she straightened her shoulders. "All right, remember, you're my friend the mineral hunter from the port of Ked-kalabesh."

When Moon woke next it was night, and the bronze lamps above had lit the room with a warm light that came from the Kishan moss. He struggled out of bed and went to the other room to look out the windows at the city. It blossomed with light from the open terraces, windows, from hanging lamps along the bridges and walkways. Snatches of voices were carried on the wind, with threads of music and drums. He tasted the air. Again, no hint of other Raksura nearby, though that didn't necessarily prove anything. *They got away*, he told himself. *That's why they aren't here.* Even if they had been trapped in the docks somewhere, they would have escaped when the structure had started to come apart.

At least he felt more awake than he had earlier, his head clear. He was weak, but the deep ache of abused muscle under the burns was less, and his newly growing skin itched. He tried to shift again, just in case Ceilinel had decided to trust him, but he could still feel a barrier keeping him in his groundling form.

Someone had been here, taken the dishes away, and left more water and tea, and more of the little cakes, and he hadn't even woken. There were new garments lying on the bench, another skirt-pants and a knee-length shirt of dark material with a soft brocade across the shoulders. A second low table had been carried in, and it held several Kishan-style books. Wincing, Moon sank into an awkward crouch on the floor to examine them. All were in Altanic, though one had Altanic text on one side of the page and Kedaic on the other. It was a history of Kish, and he set it aside to read first. While he was down there, he crawled over to the other table and ate the rest of the cakes.

He shoved to his feet and took the fresh clothes. Across the room was a door to a smaller space, the scents coming from it suggesting it was a bathing room. It was, with the basins for washing and elimination similar to the ones on Callumkal's flying boat, just larger and of richer materials. He used both, careful of all his burned patches and the bandages, then dressed again and continued to explore.

There was a door over the next arch, carved wood heavily reinforced with chased metal, but it was standing open. He slipped through into a curved hallway with one wall open to the chamber below. Everything was richly polished stone, sometimes carved but more often just showing off the natural colors of the different minerals. He followed the waist-high stone balustrade, tasting the air, looking for the source of the strong draft.

On the other side of the dome he found a gallery in the outside wall with floor to ceiling stone latticed windows, open to another view of the city. The breeze flowing along it was strong, and it had a better view of the aqueduct and a four-level building supported on multiple bridges, with open walls and walkways. It was brightly lit, and from the stalls he could glimpse and the groundlings moving around inside, it might be a market.

Moon carefully tore off a piece of bandage, then went to the gallery's far corner and found a place where he could knot it around the support for a stone drainage pipe just outside the lattice. The effort left him a little weak and he went back to lean against the wide doorway, the warm wind ruffling his hair. It would be better to put something on the opposite side of the building too, in case the wind changed. He refused to think about the fact that there was no one left, no one looking for him.

He pushed away from the wall and followed the hall around to a curved, serpentine stair that reminded him a little of the colony tree. Downstairs he wandered the lower floor and found two hallways blocked by locked metal gates. One had a draft that carried the faint scents of oil and spices, and he could hear distant voices occasionally. It probably led to the kitchens and the area where the groundlings who took care of the house lived. The other hall was quiet and he suspected it might lead to the stairwell down to the lower parts of the structure. It was confirmation that he was a prisoner, though a pampered one.

When he wandered back into the main stairwell hall, the little blue groundling walked out of a wide doorway, saw him, and let out a squawk of alarm. Before it could panic further, Moon said, "Where's Ceilinel?"

It took a breath, steadied itself, and said, "This way."

It led him back through the doorway, through a couple of antechambers, and out into another large domed room. Pillars of a gleaming jewel green surrounded a seating area with curved stone benches with thick cushions. A carved stream of water wound its way across the floor, decorated with bronze and gold insets of water plants, insects, and frogs. Ceilinel sat on one bench, facing two other groundlings. One was of a similar species to Ceilinel, with gray skin and a headcrest, but larger, more heavily built, and its hair was light-colored. The other was slim, smaller, its head of an oddly triangular shape, the rest of it mostly concealed by the silky drapes wrapped around its body.

Moon's unwilling guide went to Ceilinel and said, "He's awake again."

Ceilinel glanced up and spotted Moon. "That's all right, Vata."

Vata retreated hastily out another doorway.

The other groundlings faced away from Moon, and hadn't looked around. The big gray one said, "Surely you realize how dangerous it is keeping that creature here."

Ceilinel's brows lifted and spread. "I'm not sure why you seem so certain of that, Gathin. The Raksura are a relatively unknown species, but the Jandera seem to find them peaceful enough."

Gathin made a noise Moon could only interpret as skeptical. The other strange groundling said, "The Jandera who seemed to find them so are all missing or dead." Its voice was low and deeper than Moon had been expecting.

Ceilinel regarded it. "That's inaccurate, according to the messages we've received from the coast."

"But none of them are here to speak for themselves," Gathin said.

Since there was apparently no objection to his presence, Moon went in, his bare feet silent on the cool tiles. He stopped at the first bend of the carved stream, tempted to put his toes in the shallow water.

The slender groundling said, "The only difference between these creatures and Fell is that we know less about them." It leaned over. "You are putting yourself and your retainers in danger by allowing one of those things, no matter how injured, to remain in this house. You should release it from the conclave's custody so it can be contained."

Moon let out a silent hiss of derision. Ceilinel clearly wanted him to hear this, though he already understood just how precarious his situation was. He waited for Ceilinel to indicate that the creature was in the room, but she said, "I don't feel that I or anyone else is in danger. Should we not take this opportunity to find out more?"

Gathin said, "We don't have the leisure for that kind of inquiry."

Moon couldn't tell what Ceilinel's game was, but he didn't want to participate. He said, "Why not?"

Gathin twisted to look at him, surprised. It said, "Who is this?" The other turned more slowly. Its eyes were huge blue circles above a small nose and a thin-lipped mouth. Something about it reminded Moon of that brief glimpse of the carved face in the foundation builder city.

Ceilinel said calmly, "This is Moon of Opal Night, consort to Jade, sister queen of the Indigo Cloud court." She added to Moon, "This is Gathin, she is the speaker of the Imperial Boundaries, and Utreya-cal Doyen, who has taken on the duty as speaker for Hia Iserae."

Gathin stared. Her expression seemed to be conveying both horror and chagrin. It was always chancy reading the expressions of unknown species, but Moon thought this was a pretty safe guess. Doyen blinked slowly, the lids coming from the side of its eyes. Ceilinel said, "Moon, please sit down. You aren't recovered yet."

Moon stepped over the stream and went to the bench between Ceilinel and Gathin. His legs quivered at the last instant and the movement pulled at all his new and half-healed skin. He winced and settled on the cushion, trying to breathe slowly. Ceilinel took in Gathin's expression with some impatience, then asked Moon, "Were the books to your liking?"

He wasn't sure if she was testing him or showing off the extent of his civilized skills for Gathin and Doyen. Moon said, "The *Natural History of the Kish Imperial Origin* looks interesting."

Gathin had managed to recover a little from the shock. She said, "You are the Raksura found in the ruin." Doyen didn't react in any way that Moon could see, but there was something about its gaze that he wanted to interpret as predatory, even though its slim hands and delicate fingers were as unthreatening as possible.

"Are there any other Raksura here?" Moon asked.

"I hope not," Gathin said, sounding aghast at the idea.

It had the unmistakable sound of the truth. Moon hadn't really kept a hope that Ceilinel was lying and the others were locked up here somewhere, but it didn't hurt to be sure.

Doyen asked Ceilinel, "Will he cooperate with the conclave?"

"Let's ask him." Ceilinel turned to Moon. "A claim has been made by a group of Hians that Callumkal attacked their ship in a dispute over a valuable foundation builder artifact. They say this dispute was what made the ruin fall from the sky and that it caused the deaths."

Moon didn't understand. "The deaths? You mean the Hians who were in the ruin?"

"No. The ruin fell into the border area between Kish-Majora and Kish-Jandera, near the city of Kedmar. Though it fell in an empty plain, many Janderi and Janderan in nearby towns were struck ill, and at least fifty-three were reportedly killed outright. There were probably more. They are still attempting to ascertain the extent of the damage."

Moon was frozen for a moment, too stricken to react. Two thoughts hit him simultaneously: *did it get as far as the Reaches?* and *they meant to bring it down right on top of Kedmar.* He managed to say, "Callumkal can tell you that's a lie. So can Kalam and Rorra and the Jandera who were with him."

"The Hians claim Callumkal is dead, killed by Raksura. A flying craft will be arriving tomorrow from Kedmar-Jandera and the speaker for Kedmar has asked the conclave to wait for its arrival before formally hearing the Hians. I'm hopeful Callumkal, or some other representative, is on the craft." Ceilinel leaned forward, suddenly intent. "Whoever the craft brings, you will be asked to tell your story to the speakers in the conclave. Will you be able to do this?"

"Yes," Moon said, because there was no choice. He was the worst possible person for this. Did the Hians making this accusation know who had accidentally brought the artifact out of the foundation builder city? And would anybody believe it was an accident?

"Why would Raksura attack Imperial Kish?" Gathin asked suddenly.

Moon managed not to hiss, though he could feel the muscles in his throat work. "Raksura wouldn't, because they're completely indifferent to its existence."

Ceilinel's brows quirked. Gathin glanced at Doyen, then asked Moon, "You don't trade with other species?"

"Only some of the swamplings who live in the Reaches."

Doyen turned to Ceilinel to ask, "And what did the Raksura gain from this encounter with the Hians?"

Moon answered, "Nothing. We were trying to keep ourselves and the groundlings with us alive. We didn't completely succeed." Song. Magrim and Kellimdar and the other Jandera. Kethel. Hopefully not Callumkal, since it sounded as if he was the only one whose word the Kish would take. Doyen clearly didn't believe Moon.

"What do you want?" Gathin asked.

"I want to go back to my family." Moon was getting tired of stupid questions. "Why do you care?"

Ceilinel said, "Gathin will be your speaker in the conclave."

Moon stared at her. "You're joking."

Gathin looked offended. Ceilinel said, "She is pledged to uncover the truth for the conclave."

It was funny that they thought he was naive enough to believe that. "Is anybody uncovering the truth from the Hians? Are they locked up somewhere?"

Ceilinel turned to Doyen, who looked away. Gathin lifted a hand and said, "No, but they are members of the Imperial Agreement."

Moon didn't know what that meant, except that no one was going to believe his side of the story, no matter how well a speaker told it. He got up to go back to his cell.

He had passed through the doorway, and Doyen clearly thought he was out of earshot, when it said, "He should be restrained, Ceilinel. If he kills you all, you will be to blame."

CHAPTER TWENTY-FIVE

Moon waited for armed groundlings to show up and drag him away to a more secure cage, or possibly just to chain him up here. But no one came, and eventually he fell asleep.

He slept off and on through the night, waking in the late morning to the scent of more food in the outer room. After he ate, he took the Kish history book and left his cell to explore some more.

He avoided the chambers on the upper level where the faint sounds of movement and voices indicated that Ceilinel and at least two or three other groundlings were present. The wind had changed direction, so he found a lattice window on the opposite side of the tower from the gallery, and attached another piece of bandage to an unobtrusive spot. Moon didn't know if it was possible to trace a Raksura by scent in a groundling city this size, even with the help of cloth soaked with sweat and piss. But he knew how acute Stone's senses could be. If Stone was still alive.

He found a sitting room with latticed windows looking out onto the market structure. Beyond it was a canyon formed by domed buildings lining what seemed to be a major street. The room had cushioned benches and couches centered around another shallow floor pool, but Moon carried a cushion over and took a seat in the corner of the wide windowsill.

As the afternoon light deepened across the city, Moon slept off and on, and read the book while keeping an eye on the bridges and walkways. Large numbers of people came and went from the market. He couldn't see much of the inside, just occasional glimpses of bolts of gleaming fabric or tall urns and large pieces of pottery.

He tried to keep his attention on the book, tried not to think about where the others were or what might be happening in the Reaches. There were no maps in the text, but there was a description of the principal cities of Kish and their relations with each other, which told him where Kish-Karad was well enough to plan a rough route back to the Reaches, if he had to escape on his own. Or if Ceilinel kept her word and released him.

Finally the sunset washed the domes with gold, and lights began to gleam on the streets and bridges. The hanging bronze lamps in the room and the attached hall began to glow. During the day at least three groundlings had come to the door to peer at him and then retreat, probably to report to Ceilinel. The next one who came was Vata, and she said, "Ah, excuse me, but Ceilinel has asked to speak to you."

Moon sat up and folded the book back into its cover, taking one last glance out at the market. This time his eye was caught by a stillness in the river of movement on the walkway along the lowest level. A lone figure stood in a patch of fading sunlight, a tall shape in the kind of loose robe groundling traders from the southern drylands wore. The scarf wrapped around its head was a gold pattern, very like the one Niran wore to protect his hair on the wind-ship. Most groundlings sitting where Moon was wouldn't be able to see that much detail at this distance, and the figure standing there shouldn't be able to see Moon.

Moon set the book on the bench and pushed to his feet, as flushed and weak as when he had woken the first time. Hope was painful. He might be mistaken or hallucinating. He had seen more groundlings of different species stroll along that walkway this afternoon than he had ever seen in one place in his entire life; some of them were bound to be the size of an Aeriat and wear head scarfs like the Golden Islanders. It might actually be an unusually tall Golden Islander.

He took a deep breath, got his expression under control, and pushed away from the window to go to Ceilinel.

Vata led him to a room off the upper level gallery, where another groundling was helping Ceilinel into a robe with a lot more brocade than the one she had been wearing before. Ceilinel sent that groundling away and turned to a polished metal mirror to brush back her feathery hair. She said, "I've been called to the speakers' assembly and it will be better if you come with me. If the Hians present any claims tonight, Gathin may need to ask you more questions."

Moon hesitated, most of his attention still focused on that waiting figure near the market. Maybe leaving the house right now, giving himself another chance to be seen, wasn't a bad idea. "So you believe me?"

"My duty in this dispute is to find out the truth of what happened and I intend to do that." She turned and gestured at him. "Is it acceptable to your people for you to appear in public like this?"

Moon looked down at himself. He was dressed about the same as some of the other groundlings in the house, so it didn't worry him. She wanted the truth, so he said, "My people will be so furious at a consort being held prisoner by groundlings that it really doesn't matter what I'm wearing."

Ceilinel's brows twitched in a way he wanted to interpret as annoyance. "Well, I'll deal with that when—"

Moon lost the rest. A cry of pain and a crash of wood and metal sounded from somewhere below the house. He tilted his head, turning toward the noise, and tasted the air. "Something's happened."

Ceilinel and Vata stared at him. They clearly hadn't heard it. Ceilinel demanded, "What is it?"

The draft had just changed. A door had opened somewhere. And the air carried a metallic taint. *That was Stone, he's breaking into the house* ... Except that didn't make sense. If that was Stone, he had seen Moon sitting in a window reading. He would have waited until deep in the night and then tried to get close enough to speak to him. There was no point in attacking a place Moon might have been able to walk out of on his own. Unless Jade was with him and she was just that mad ...

Then he caught the acrid scent of a Kish fire weapon. He snarled and ducked out of the room to the gallery. The big chamber below was empty but just beyond it he heard cries of alarm and the roar of more than one fire weapon.

Ceilinel and Vata ran to the railing beside him. From their reaction, this time they heard the screams. "It's the Hians," Moon told Ceilinel.

The Hians who were so determined to conceal their part in the deaths outside Kedmar, who knew there was a surviving Raksura to be dealt with. "Unless you can fight them with magic, you have to let me shift."

Ceilinel snapped, "Vata, run, hide." As Vata darted away along the gallery, she told Moon, "Follow her. She can show you a place to—"

Moon said again, "You need to let me shift or they'll kill us both." He tried to keep the desperation out of his voice. The idea of being burned by one of those weapons again was a cold lump of fear inside his chest.

Impatiently, she said, "They wouldn't dare—"

Wooden disks struck the balustrade. Moon grabbed Ceilinel's arm and dragged her with him as he flung himself back against the wall. She cried out and Moon managed not to yelp as the burst of heat and flame washed over the stone railing. "That was aimed at you," he snarled. "Now do you believe—"

Ceilinel tugged at a cord around her neck and pulled it out from under her collar. It supported a small stone, polished to a dull red. Looking at it seemed to still the air around Moon, as if the little object took up all the open space in the chamber. She snapped the cord and dropped the stone on the floor, then stamped on it.

Moon felt the block around him dissolve, like chains that had suddenly fallen away. He shifted, wrapped an arm around Ceilinel's waist, and leapt up to cling to the side of the nearest column. She didn't shriek but he felt her body go rigid with fear. "Hold on to the ridge above my collarbone," he told her. He scanned the chamber below and marked the location of the Hians scattered there. At least half were armed, and three had seen Moon's leap and angled their fire weapons up at him. Her fingers wrapped around his collar flanges and Moon leapt, timing it so the wooden disks struck the pillar just as he left it.

He caught the chain of the big hanging lamp, swung to the balustrade on the far side. He let go just as a crack told him the base had ripped out of the stone ceiling. It brought half the mosaic tiles down in a crash as Moon bounded along the balustrade. Ceilinel gasped, "The stairwell, the one on the western side."

The Hians not staggered under the onslaught of falling tile ran to this side of the chamber to aim at Moon. Two bolted up the curving stairs to the gallery to cut him off. He flipped over the balustrade, bounced off a column, and landed at the base of a pillar on the opposite side. As the Hians spun to aim their weapons, Moon dodged around the pillar and raced down the corridor.

Moon had been through here earlier and didn't need Ceilinel's whispered directions as he ducked through rooms to a corridor in the outer section of the dome. A heavy metal gate blocked the large stairwell but Ceilinel pressed her hand to the lock and it sprang open. Moon leapt down the stairs to the next landing. From there he saw a wide hall opening into a dimly lit tile-floored space. He couldn't hear any movement down there, and the scents were dry and clean, free of the acrid fire weapon moss. He asked Ceilinel, "Where does this go?"

"The colloquium archives." Her voice was breathy with fear and he could feel her pulse pounding through her body, but she kept a firm grip on his collar flange.

Moon leapt down to the bottom of the stairs. As he landed he staggered and half-collapsed against the wall to steady himself. Ceilinel let go of him and stumbled away. He thought she might run; they still didn't have much reason to trust each other, or at least Moon didn't trust her. But Ceilinel cast a worried glance up the stairs, and whispered, "Are you all right?"

Moon looked down at his chest. Blood leaked between his black scales, the delicate new skin underneath torn by too-quick movement. His legs felt weak and unsteady, his wings as heavy as if he had been flying all day and night. What he wanted to do was shift to groundling and lie flat on the cool tile floor, but that wasn't an option right now. "Where's the nearest way out?" This was a junction with five archways leading to large dark hallways. He wasn't scenting any outdoor air, which was worrisome.

"This way, the public entrance. It's our best chance." Ceilinel started toward an archway and Moon shoved off the wall to follow. She added, "They must have come through the private entrance, on the side facing the reservoir. They couldn't walk up to the public entrance carrying weapons without causing alarm."

Past the archway the light was just bright enough to ruin Moon's night vision. It came from little bronze globes mounted on tall stone shelves that held wooden boxes. From the dry weedy scent in the air, Moon guessed the boxes contained Kishan books. A narrow stream of water ran down a channel in the floor, and Moon kept his foot claws retracted so they wouldn't click on the tiles. It would have been faster and safer to carry Ceilinel and jump from the top of one row of shelves to the next across the chamber. Or better yet, from the heavy stone supports and arches dimly visible in the shadow above. But Moon's side and chest ached and he could feel the skin under his scales tear and strain. He needed to conserve what strength he had left.

Ceilinel muttered, "They must be idiots to think killing either of us will help their case. It's just going to make the conclave certain the Hians are at fault." She hesitated at another junction, then turned right, and Moon realized this lower part of the dome was much larger than the upper section that Ceilinel lived in. She added, "Unless that's what they want. But why . . ."

She let the question trail off, clearly talking to herself more than him. But she was assuming the Hians were all in this plan together, and Moon knew that probably wasn't true. "When we caught up with the Hians who took the weapon, most of them were dead, killed by a faction on their own flying boat."

Startled, Ceilinel stopped and turned to him. "What? You said nothing of this."

Moon nudged her to keep moving. "You didn't ask."

She continued on toward the end of the hall. "What were these factions?" she asked urgently.

"Vendoin was the one who stole Callumkal and the others. It was her plan to get the weapon. She wanted to kill Fell, mostly, and didn't care if some Jandera died. She wanted the Hians to be able to go back to Hia Majora. Lavinat led the other faction. She didn't care as much about killing the Fell as killing Jandera. Then Vendoin realized it was going to kill Jandera and Hians and every other species descended from the foundation builders. We think she started to change her mind. So Lavinat stole the weapon from her and killed half the Hian crew. Lavinat was the one who took it to the ruin and made it work." They reached a wide cross hall and Moon caught Ceilinel's arm to stop her. He tasted the air and took a careful peek up and down. "Which way?"

"There." Ceilinel pointed to another hall that branched off the main one. In that direction, over the tops of the endless shelves, Moon detected a glow of brighter light. "How do you know this?"

"I was there. I tried to stop Lavinat and she burned me with a fire weapon. I don't know what happened after that." Moon's throat went tight, thinking about that moment and who might and might not have survived it. If that wasn't Stone he had glimpsed near the market . . ." There were other Raksura there. They must have made the ruin fall, trying to stop the weapon."

Ceilinel whispered furiously, "Why didn't you tell me this? If you had—"

"Would you have believed me? Gathin's supposed to speak for me and she doesn't even think I'm a person!"

She didn't answer, and by the time they reached the end of another hall, he thought the conversation was over. He heard the faint sound of running footsteps, maybe the creak of a door opening, but from the echoes they were some distance away. Then Ceilinel admitted, "I don't know if I would have believed you."

He didn't know what to say to that, so didn't say anything. She added, "This Lavinat, did she care if she survived? Or those with her?"

"I don't think so. I don't even know if they thought about it."

Ceilinel made a distracted gesture as she considered it. "So . . . The point of this attack is not that you and I are killed, it's that we are killed by Hians."

She was probably right. Some Hians wanted the Jandera to attack them, either so they would have an excuse to fight or for some other less apparent reason. Other Hians didn't. Killing an important Kishan like Ceilinel might force a violent response from Kish-Karad and the Jandera in Kedmar and take the choice away from the other Hians.

They had been drawing closer to the area where the sunset tinge of natural light still shone. The hall opened out onto a broad balcony, with a wide stair leading down to a chamber below. Three big windows, all sealed with faceted crystal, stretched up the far wall, allowing in the last of the day's sunlight. The water channels ran out from the halls of shelves to become miniature waterfalls at the balcony's edge. The falling water sound covered small movements. Ceilinel lowered her voice even more, saying, "The public entrance is down there."

Moon caught the scent of outdoor air. "There's a door open." The Hians must have gotten here first.

"The main doors are kept propped open. It's symbolic, so anyone can enter the archives at any time."

The Hians still might have gotten here first. Moon held out an arm to Ceilinel. "We'll go fast." All he wanted to do was curl up in a corner and collapse. *Just get outside, leave her where she can get help, and find a place to hide,* he promised himself.

Ceilinel reached for his hand, then her face went still. "Someone's performing an arcana."

Moon hissed, thinking of the collapse that had blocked the shaft down into the docking structure. "Watch out for these arches. The Hians could bring them down and trap us in here."

Ceilinel turned to stare at him. "Hians don't have that kind of arcanic ability."

Moon snorted. "Hians lie a lot."

Something cracked overhead, a deep ominous reverberation. Moon grabbed Ceilinel around the waist and bounced to the balustrade. Below he caught a quick glimpse of the big foyer at the bottom of the stairs, the large oblong fountain pools to either side, and the heavy chased metal doors standing open just enough for a broad-shouldered groundling to step through. Someone shouted and just as Moon leapt the air moved around him, pushed by the sudden force of a heavy object's plunge. He twisted to avoid it and knew he was about to fall badly.

He shoved Ceilinel away at the last instant so he wouldn't crush her, then the ground slammed into him. Everything went dark.

He came to with a gasp, lying at the edge of a fountain. He could feel the damp cool stone through his clothes, on his groundlng skin, and realized he had shifted in the instant of unconsciousness.

Moon rolled over. The haze of rock dust hung in the air and chunks of a supporting arch lay scattered around them. Ceilinel stood beside him, bleeding from a scrape on her cheek, a sleeve of her robe torn. Five Hians confronted her, all armed with fire weapons. Ceilinel was saying urgently, "Avinan, you know me, you know whatever caused you to do this, it can be resolved—"

"We're not interested in resolution," Avinan said. She wasn't looking at Moon, but her fire weapon pointed in his direction.

"It's too late!" Ceilinel snapped. "I know what your plan is, I've told my retainers and they've gone to alert the conclave. You can kill us, kill yourselves for all I care, and it will be for nothing."

Avinan said, "It's not a very clever lie." She took one hand off the fire weapon to gesture to someone on the balcony above. "Viniat, bury these creatures!"

Moon hunched his shoulders in reflex. Ceilinel stood there, her fists knotted in fury. But nothing happened.

Then Moon caught a scent. It was anxious sealing mixed with familiar Raksura, and the coppery hint of fresh blood that wasn't his. He must have made a noise in his throat because Ceilinel glanced down at him, bewildered. Moon reached up and took her wrist. Someone had just opened Viniat's throat up there on the balcony, but they weren't out of this yet.

The other Hians kept their fire weapons trained on Moon and Ceilinel, but Avinan turned to look up at the balcony. "Viniat, what—"

The change in the air and the scrape of claws on tile were the only warning. Moon yanked Ceilinel down on top of him and rolled them both into the pool. He heard fire weapon disks strike the water. Then something huge and dark slammed into the Hians. Moon lifted his head to see one Hian still on her feet lift her weapon—Then Jade slung herself down off the stairs. The Hian collapsed in a heap. Jade had ripped away one of her arms and half her shoulder along with the weapon.

The other Hians had been flattened under Stone's huge scaled body. Moon rolled off Ceilinel. She sat up, sputtering and coughing, just in time to see Stone shift back to groundling. She froze in astonishment.

Stone glanced around at the sprawled Hians. He still wore the dryland wrap over his clothes and Niran's scarf tied loosely around his neck. He kicked a fire weapon away from one limp outstretched arm. "Any reason we need them alive?"

"Yes," Moon croaked, and dragged himself to the edge of the fountain. He waved back at Ceilinel, who was shakily climbing to her feet. "She needs witnesses for the—"

Jade caught his arms and dragged him out of the pool. She snarled, "You're hurt!"

"I know," he told her. "I was afraid you were all dead."

"I thought you were dead." Jade's spines flared in rage.

Moon went limp so she had to catch him and clutch him to her chest. This would keep her from killing anybody until he had a chance to tell her what was happening. He grabbed her collar flanges just to make sure she couldn't put him down. "Did the others get out? Chime and Shade and—"

"The others are fine." Jade stared down at him, her expression impossible to read, at least in Moon's current state.

Rorra ran down the steps, a small fire weapon cradled in her arms. She stopped where she could watch the door and guard Stone's back. "If we're going, we need to get out of here."

"We're not going," Moon said, because he had seen who was following Rorra. It was Kalam, who was going to be much better at telling their story to Ceilinel than Moon had been. "Where's Callumkal?"

"In Kedmar," Kalam said, hurrying down the steps. "Niran and Diar took him there, and we came here to look for you." He looked from Moon to Ceilinel, who was stepping out of the fountain, her hair and robes dripping onto the tiles. "Are you all right? Who is this?"

Moon said, "This is Ceilinel, a speaker for the conclave of something. Ceilinel, this is Jade, sister queen of the Indigo Cloud court, Stone, our line-grandfather, Captain Rorra, and Kalam, Callumkal's son."

Ceilinel nodded, looking around at them all and settling on Jade as the leader. "Thank you for your timely arrival."

Jade eyed her over Moon's head. In Kedaic, she said, "Was she the one holding you prisoner?"

Moon tightened his hold on her. "I was nearly dead. She brought healers here for me." Jade's gaze jerked down to him. The cold fury didn't leave her expression, but at least she was listening to him. He switched to Raksuran to say, "She had a Kishan magic to keep me from shifting. She destroyed it when the Hians came so we could get away." He added, "Don't kill her."

Jade's gaze went to Ceilinel again. It was a predator's gaze, thoughtful and implacable. Moon wasn't sure if Ceilinel knew how much danger she was in, but she said, "I think this can be resolved easily now, if you'll remain here and speak to the conclave with me. The meeting will be soon, when a Jandera craft arrives from Kedmar. You could be on your way by morning, and the Hians' lies would be exposed to all of Imperial Kish."

Stone looked at Rorra, who glanced at Kalam. Kalam turned hopefully to Jade. Jade's spines shivered with the effort of control, and she said, "No magics to prevent us from shifting. If you try to use one on any of us, I'll know it. I don't need to shift to kill you."

Rorra added, "And Kalam and I keep our weapons."

Ceilinel jerked her head in acknowledgment. "Agreed."

Moon was impressed with Ceilinel. She dealt with the arrival of what seemed a large number of frantic and angry people who had noticed the archives were under attack, directed the armed Kishan to take the Hians away, calmed her scattered retainers, threw on dry clothes while waiting for a healer for Moon, and got them all on the way to the meeting. Though Stone had driven off the healer and taken his bag of supplies, no one had objected.

The method of transport was an odd little moss-driven craft about the size of a couple of large wagons set end to end. It was lined with cushioned benches and chairs, and the outer walls were mostly large latticed windows, letting in the cool night breeze. Lights at either end lit its way, but instead of flying, it moved along a narrow bridge that wound through the city. There were apparently a lot of the things, but this one had been reserved for Ceilinel's use tonight. Vata stood in the front, guiding it with a steering lever.

Moon sat on one of the cushion-stuffed chairs while Stone bandaged the parts of him that were still bleeding. Jade, Kalam, and Rorra were up in the front of the craft with Ceilinel, and right now Rorra was the one doing the talking. Jade had shifted to her Arbora form, since it looked less threatening and the lack of wings made it hard to identify her as a Raksura, or willfully mistake her for Fell. She kept glancing back at Moon, and he thought there was more to it than just normal concern for him.

He asked Stone, "What's wrong? Is somebody dead?" Jade had said everyone had made it out, but not what had happened to them afterward.

"You were dead," Stone said with a grimace. He poked through the bag of healing supplies and pulled out another clean cloth.

"Right, but I'm not anymore." Moon lowered his voice, even though he was speaking Raksuran. "What about our kethel?"

"That's how we knew where to look for you. I found him in the ruin, and he'd seen the Kish take you away. He was gone the next morning. I'm guessing he headed to the Reaches to find the Fell queen."

That was a relief. At least Moon hadn't gotten him killed. "Do we know what's happening in the Reaches? Have the mentors gotten any visions?"

"Not before we left the wind-ship." Stone sat back on his heels, eyeing Moon critically. It was reassuring, because what might be going on in the Reaches was clearly a less fraught topic.

They were passing over a narrow valley or gorge filled with trees, lights glinting here and there under the canopies indicating houses and pathways. The sound of water flowing over rocks and the scent of a clean river rose up from it. The valley bisected this section of the city, domes and other structures rising up to either side. Moon asked, "If the wind-ship went to Kedmar, how did you get here?" The Kish protections against Fell would make traveling across it equally dangerous for Raksura. It was why Moon had never ventured much past the borders and outer trade routes.

"Flew at night, hid during the day, circled around any settlements." Stone squinted into the distance. "We got here four nights ago, maybe. It feels like longer."

Making their way through a strange, enormous, crowded groundling city, with Stone in his groundling form and Jade in her Arbora form, where even Rorra and Kalam must have been off balance. Moon didn't have to imagine how unnerving that had been. "Where are the others?"

He hoped they were hiding somewhere outside the city; it would give them less scope for finding trouble.

"Jade sent Balm and three warriors to the Reaches, to tell the queens what happened. The rest are with the wind-ship. Niran and Diar are trying to get help from the Jandera in Kedmar." Stone looked at Jade, a line between his brows. "Chime wanted to come, but Jade wouldn't let him. They all wanted to come."

That made sense, but Moon wasn't sure why Jade hadn't brought Chime. His erratic ability to sense groundling magic might have come in handy, and he was good around groundlings. "I was mostly unconscious until yesterday. You caught my scent?"

"Finally." Stone rubbed his eyes and yawned. "I picked it up in the morning, and followed it until I was sure which dome it was coming from, then sent Kalam to our meeting place to get Jade and Rorra."

"I wish the wind-ship was here. Having Delin would help with this speakers assembly." Moon was still worried about having to tell their story to a bunch of disbelieving groundlings.

Stone made a noncommittal noise. "Whatever happens, we're leaving."

Moon had been expecting something impressive, but the bridge curved toward a dome that dwarfed all the others they had seen. It was at least as big as the Indigo Cloud colony tree's canopy, though not nearly so tall. There were so many lights around it might as well have been daylight, illuminating the giant carvings of dozens of different species, climbing over, or maybe building, the walls of a city. Two openings big enough to guide flying boats through pierced the dome, with bridges and walkways leading to doors lower down. Even one of the water bridges for boats led to it, ending in a large pool on stilts with docks. Moon craned his neck to look down and saw multiple roads ended at the dome, that there was a plaza surrounded by smaller structures and trees down there.

Their craft rolled along its bridge directly into one of the big openings. Moon stood as it slowed and slid to a stop. Stone put a hand on his arm to steady him.

Inside the dome, several small Kishan flying boats were moored around the upper part of the chamber, where a walkway allowed access to their boarding ramps. Lights on tall poles shaped like flowers lit the big expanse of the mosaic tile floor. Small spiral stairways led up to the walkways around the dome's walls, and larger stairwells in the floor led downwards.

A number of groundlings waited near the moss wagon's track, including Gathin. Moon spotted a group of Hians standing under a lamp, but something about them suggested they were uncomfortable and embattled. They didn't have fire weapons, though some of the Kishan near them did.

Moon and Stone followed the others out of the wagon. Gathin hurried immediately to Ceilinel, asking, "Are you injured? When we heard—"

"I'm fine," she said. "Come, you need to hear this." Ceilinel drew her away a little.

Moon leaned against Stone's shoulder and yawned. The intense relief at being with the others again left him wrung out, like he couldn't feel anything else except exhaustion. He kept an eye on Jade, who stood a little distance away, flexing her foot claws. He said, "I just want to get out of here."

Stone put an arm around him. "I just want to eat. You'd think with all these people, they'd sell food here."

Gathin turned to look back at them a few times in a way that made Moon want to ripple the spines he wasn't wearing. He wasn't the only one who noticed. Keeping her voice low, Rorra said to Kalam, "We should insist on seeing the speakers for Jandera. We need someone to contact the others if we have to remain here and answer to the conclave."

Kalam said, "I can't believe it'll come to that," but he seemed uneasy, watching the Hians like he expected an attack.

Moon started to make plans. He didn't think he could fly yet, but he could hold onto Stone's collar flange, leaving Stone and Jade free to carry Rorra and Kalam.

Rorra turned and said softly to Stone, "Do you think we should try to leave?"

His gaze on the groundlings, Stone answered, "It might be a good idea."

Rorra nodded. "Do you want to ask Jade?"

Stone shrugged. Rorra gave him an exasperated punch in the shoulder. Before Moon could ask what that was about, Ceilinel turned and came toward them, trailed by an obviously reluctant Gathin. As she approached, Jade's spines flicked once and she said, "Well?"

· Ceilinel didn't flinch under Jade's steady regard. She said, "I've been informed of the reason the conclave wanted to summon your consort here. They have had a report of a movement of Fell along the eastern border of Kish."

It wasn't what Moon had expected to hear. Maybe the half-Fell queen had been wrong, and the Fell hadn't headed toward the Reaches, but toward Kish instead. But that didn't make any sense. It was the Raksura they blamed for the death of the flight that had followed Callumkal's expedition to the sel-Selatra. Stone muttered, "Huh." Rorra and Kalam exchanged a startled look, and Rorra reached into her jacket to pull out a folded fabric map.

Jade was the only one who didn't react, at least in any visible way. "That isn't our concern."

Still calm, Ceilinel said, "It appears they've been driven there by Raksura."

Jade's brow furrowed in confusion. It didn't make her look any less intimidating. "What do you mean?"

Ceilinel said, "A Kish-Nakatel border patrol craft sighted a Fell attack on a small settlement. They approached to give assistance but saw what at first appeared to be a group of brightly colored Fell driving the flight away." She glanced at Moon and the others. They were all staring blankly at her. At least, Moon knew he was staring blankly at her. "These brightly colored Fell harried the flight directly past the patrol craft and continued southeast. I'm told there are other reports of this group, or similar groups, attempting to drive the Fell toward the Kish border."

"Brightly colored Fell," Jade repeated, her voice flat. Moon recognized it as a determined attempt not to react. At least it meant the foundation builder weapon's influence hadn't gotten as far as the Reaches, if Raksura were chasing Fell this far south. He hoped that was what it meant.

Ceilinel turned one hand palm up. "Obviously, once the reports arrived at Kish-Karad, our scholars of winged predators determined these were more likely to be Raksura."

Gathin said, "Why are Raksura sending the Fell to Kish?"

Rorra blinked and muttered, "Is that person serious?" Moon hissed under his breath. He hated Gathin. He understood the questioning thing as a way to get to the facts and provoke people to speak, but he hated it and it was the absolute worst way to approach a Raksuran queen who was already angry.

Jade's head tilted dangerously. Before it got any worse, Kalam said in exasperation, "The Raksura didn't bring the Fell. The Raksura must know about the border defenses in that region. They're driving the Fell into the fire weapon emplacements."

Gathin turned toward him. "How do Raksura know of our border defenses?"

Kalam folded his arms. "I've never heard anything about it being a secret."

She eyed him. "Perhaps not in Jandera."

Rorra's brow quirked. "You know the weapon emplacements are in the open along the trade roads. Anyone can see them."

Especially if you made sure your warriors engaged a Kishan flying boat crew in conversation about those weapon emplacements and how they worked, just in case you ever needed that information, Moon thought. He was betting these Raksura had gotten the idea from Malachite. Then he wondered, *Could it actually be Malachite?*

"That aside," Ceilinel said, frowning at Gathin. She turned back to Jade. "We would like to ask for your help. You are a queen, you have a consort with you, we understand that that makes you a diplomatic envoy, for Raksura. If you could speak to the Raksura at the border—"

"Most of whom we may be related to," Stone said under his breath, fortunately in Raksuran.

The more Moon thought about it, the more likely it sounded. It didn't explain what the Raksura might be doing, but hopefully it meant Indigo Cloud and the colonies in the eastern Reaches were safe.

Jade still didn't betray any reaction. "What about the Hians?"

"They won't trouble you," Ceilinel said. She glanced at the group across the chamber floor. "A Hian faction, separatist or not, attacked a conclave speaker and a public archive, there is no explanation they can give that makes it your doing."

"What about our explanation?" Jade said. "Do your people believe us?"

Ceilinel looked expectantly at Gathin. Gathin said, "They will by the time you return."

One of Jade's spines flicked. "Give me a moment."

Ceilinel nodded and withdrew, pulling Gathin along with her. Jade waited until they had returned to the group of watching groundlings, then turned around and hissed. Keeping her voice low, she said, "It will be easier to escape from the border."

Moon had been hoping that was her plan. "Especially if we know who's fighting the Fell there."

Rorra whispered, "Can it be Malachite?"

Jade's expression was grim. "That's what I'm hoping."

Reluctantly, Kalam said, "Perhaps I should stay here, and make sure Gathin tells the truth to the conclave?"

Rorra didn't hesitate. "No. I'm not leaving you alone here."

Jade seconded that with a lash of her tail. "You're staying with us until I can hand you back to Callumkal."

Kalam didn't object, and Moon suspected he didn't want to stay here and argue with the conclave or the speakers or whatever anymore than Moon did. Kalam added, "We should still talk to the Jandera speaker, like Rorra said."

Jade shared a glance with Rorra. "I'll ask for that."

Stone hadn't said anything. Jade eyed him, almost warily, and asked, "Any objection?"

Stone said, "No."

Jade turned back to Ceilinel to tell her they would go.

The flying boat preparing to leave for the border was large and, like Lavinat's flying boat, burdened with four fire weapon stations, two in the bow and two in the stern. Jade and Kalam stayed behind with Ceilinel to talk to the speaker for Jandera, and Moon, Stone, and Rorra went with Vata, Ceilinel's nervous retainer, onto the boat. The one bright spot Moon could see was that they wouldn't have to talk to Gathin again.

They boarded from a ramp extending out from the walkway that circled the dome, following Vata across the deck under the gaze of a not quite openly hostile Kishan crew. Moon didn't notice any Jandera; most of the crew had tough grey-blue skin and headcrests like Ceilinel's, but their hair was long and thick, braided in different patterns. They wore mostly small scraps of dyed leather, with heavy belts around their waists and brief kilts, with harnesses for their weapons and flying packs.

Vata led them through the boat with three crew following. They would have seemed like guards, except they weren't armed and Rorra was, but they were intensely wary. Rorra asked Vata, "This is a Solkis ship, from the interior?"

"Yes," Vata admitted, with a cautious glance at Moon and Stone. "This crew patrols the western border. They have a . . . great deal of experience with Fell."

Rorra's brow furrowed. "Then they know Raksura and Fell are not the same."

Vata made an equivocal gesture which was somehow not reassuring. Moon controlled a hiss. Maybe he was out of practice at dealing with groundlings like this, but it was hard to accept the hostility without reacting.

The inside of the flying boat was different than the others, the corridors wider and higher-ceilinged. The center was an open chamber with a walkway spiraling up to different branching corridors. They were led up two levels to a suite of four interconnected cabins, with low beds in the center of the rooms. The moss walls were hidden by drapes of dark blue and gold fabric and the floor was a smooth surface that felt like tile. The attached bathing room and latrine was larger and had basins set at different levels, as if meant to accommodate different kinds of species. Most importantly, the two outer rooms had large windows, the crystal covers designed to lift up and slide aside. Having a quick escape route made Moon feel better about the whole thing.

As Moon dropped down onto the first bed, Stone said, "I'll be happy if we never see the inside of one of these things again."

"From the design, it's meant for personal travel for the speakers and conclave members," Rorra said, glancing around critically. The groundling who had greeted Vata had tried to offer Rorra and Kalam separate quarters, as if the two might have been looking for a chance to escape the Raksura. Rorra had ignored it. "It'll be fast, maybe faster than Niran and Diar's wind-ship."

"Good, then we can get this over with," Stone said, and stretched.

There was a cough outside the door, and Vata said in Kedaic, "If you need anything, please ask."

"Food and tea?" Moon asked, remembering the others had had a long day looking for him. "Like what you brought me at Ceilinel's house."

Vata seemed relieved at the commonplace request. "How much?"

Moon eyed Stone. "A lot."

Vata withdrew hurriedly. Rorra sat down heavily on the bed and took out the fabric map again. Moon crawled over to look over her shoulder as she estimated distance on it with her fingers. The scrawled writing on the cloth was in a language he didn't recognize, and Moon wondered if she had been keeping track of her route since she had first left Kedmar with Callumkal. She said, "The question is, did Malachite encounter Fell on the way to the Reaches and stop to attack them, or did she pursue them from the Reaches, or is this an entirely different group of Raksura and Fell?"

Stone sat down on her other side. "Sounds like too many warriors to be the first option. I'm betting on the second." Then he leaned over and nipped Rorra on the ear.

Rorra smiled at her map, distracted. Deciding to leave them to the conversation and whatever else they were going to do, Moon rolled off the bed and headed for the innermost chamber.

From that window he could see Jade and Kalam with Ceilinel, Gathin, and a Jandera. Everything looked calm, and Kalam gestured toward the Hians emphatically. It was tempting to stand here and watch the activity in the dock, but being horizontal again was also tempting, and Moon fell into the bed.

The next time he woke late afternoon light streamed in through the window, and the warm body against his back was Stone's.

Moon shoved upright. Stone growled in his sleep but didn't wake. The boat was moving and he climbed to his feet and padded across the floor to the window. The sky was streaked with clouds and the wind scented with distant rain and dust. They were traveling over lush open country marked by long stretches of planted fields, gardens, and orchards. In the distance were the tall conical rooftops of a small settlement, partially shielded by a stand of trees.

Stone had rolled over and buried his face in the cushions, suggesting he wasn't planning on getting up anytime soon. Moon went through to the next cabin and found Kalam asleep on that bed, and Rorra sitting on the floor, cleaning a disassembled moss weapon. Her boots were off, and her legs were folded, the stump at the end of her right leg propped on the remaining fin on her left. Moon asked, "Where's Jade?"

"She's asleep in the front room." Rorra glanced up at him, brow furrowed. "Are you all right? You slept like a dead body."

"Sure." He was still achy in places, and the burns still pulled at the muscles in his chest, but it was an improvement over the last couple of days. He stretched, wincing as his back protested.

Moon went into the front room and found Jade curled asleep on the bed in her Arbora form, her spines softened in sleep. His first impulse was to get in with her, but empty plates were stacked near the doorway and a carafe with some tea still in it sat on a low table. Moon had drained it and set it with the other empty dishes when Jade suddenly sat bolt upright, spines flared, already shifted to her winged form.

She stared at him as if she thought she was dreaming, then slumped back on the bed, burying her face in her hands. Moon went to sit beside her, asking, "Are you all right?" She didn't look all right.

"I'm fine. Just tired of talking to groundlings." She slid an arm around his waist, but he could sense the tension in her muscles.

He leaned into her warmth. There were things he wanted to talk about, like what had happened in the forerunner ruin, and where the wind-ship might be now, and how likely it was that Malachite was involved with these Raksura chasing Fell on the Kish border. But her scent overwhelmed him and all he wanted to do was nuzzle her neck. She didn't react, except to squeeze his waist.

There was a cough and an embarrassed rustle from the door. Vata, who must have been hovering in the corridor waiting for signs of life, said, "Ceilinel would like to speak to you, please."

It took them a while, since Stone and Kalam were slow to wake and everyone needed a little time in the bathing room, but Vata made it clear the summons wasn't urgent. They hadn't brought Moon's pack from the wind-ship, so he was wearing the clothes he had left Ceilinel's house in. Stone was still wearing the drylands robe over his own clothes. Rorra apologized for her scent and not having time to wash her clothes, and Moon managed not to tell her it was all right because she mostly smelled like Stone.

Vata led them up the spiral stair and forward down a corridor to a steering cabin. It had large windows giving it a good view off the bow, and from its position the two forward fire weapon emplacements must be atop it. Two doors opened to the main deck and the breeze, heavily scented with wet foliage and loam, was cool and welcoming. They were passing over scattered trees and gardens around another small settlement, but a river gleamed in the distance with a heavy jungle beyond it.

Three crew members operated an elaborate set of steering levers at the back of the cabin. Near the front, Ceilinel waited with a tall, heavily muscled Solkis. Ceilinel greeted them all formally, then said, "This is Captain Thiest. She has fought Fell before, mostly along the Karad border."

"It was some turns ago," Thiest said, her expression cool. She nodded to Jade. "The two males are also Raksura?"

Jade's spines, which had been resting at neutral, twitched in pure irritation. Rorra made an annoyed snorting noise. Her Kedaic icily correct, Jade said, "They are consorts."

Thiest said, "May I be permitted to see their other forms?"

Silence radiated off Jade in a cold wave, and her spines started to lift and spread. Ceilinel's brow was beginning to furrow and she said, "Perhaps this is not permitted."

"Jade." Moon said in Raksuran, "She's trying to provoke you to see if you can be provoked."

"I know that," Jade said, tightly, in the same language.

Kalam said, "I know it seems like a rude request," this was pointedly aimed toward Thiest, "but maybe it would help. All this talk of the resemblance of Raksura to Fell rulers is exaggerated."

"I agree," Rorra added.

Stone hadn't reacted. He said, in Kedaic, "I wouldn't fit in this room."

Thiest's mouth drew down, as if she suspected it was a bad joke. Ceilinel explained, "He is a line-grandfather, and his other form is . . . very large."

This was getting ridiculous, and Moon was torn between just shifting and possibly making Jade even angrier than she already was, or standing here while the tension with Thiest grew. He wished he had shifted earlier, before it became a battle of wills between Jade and the Solkis captain. Finally Jade said in Raksuran, "Moon, if you don't want to, you don't have to."

Moon shifted, snapped his spines out and partially extended his wings, then furled them.

Thiest blinked, though Moon couldn't tell if she was impressed or not. She said, "I see. Thank you."

Impatiently, Ceilinel said, "Now that that's done, can we move on?" She turned to Jade. "We wished to speak with you about the Hians, and what they did in the floating ruin to cause the deaths in Jandera."

Jade flicked a look at Moon and said in Raksuran, "Go out on deck." Her gaze went to Stone, but she didn't say anything. Stone was wearing his opaque face.

Moon didn't want them to look any worse in front of Thiest than they already did, so he shifted to groundling and went out on deck. Stone followed, and after a moment so did Kalam. They leaned on the railing in the bright sunlight as the Solkis on watch in the bow and the fire weapon stations studied them with wary hostility. "Rorra made me leave," Kalam reported, sounding annoyed. "She says I'm too emotional. I don't know what they could say that I shouldn't hear; I've been with all of you almost the whole time."

"There's a lot of that going around." Moon tried not to sound sulky. Jade was more tense even than what their current situation warranted, and he was beginning to think he knew what the problem was.

Moon knew he hadn't exactly made a smart choice to run off into the depths of the forerunner ruin with Kethel and get nearly burned to death trying to stop the Hians. But it didn't mean he had suddenly lost all ability to take care of himself. He and Jade had come to the understanding a long time ago that Moon couldn't pretend to be something he wasn't. This felt like she didn't trust him anymore.

Stone, leaning on the railing, just sighed.

CHAPTER TWENTY-SIX

Moon spent the day and night mostly sleeping, continuing to recover. This was helped by Vata making sure that food was brought to them every few hours. Even Stone was starting to get full.

In the morning, Vata, still not venturing any nearer than the door to the corridor, told them the boat should be close to the Imperial border, so they went up on deck to wait. The jungle below was deep now, covering low hills cut through with the occasional rocky gorge or silver stream. There was no sign of groundling settlements. As the trees below sloped down into a valley, Stone tasted the air. He said, "Fell, coming from the west."

Jade hissed, and Rorra checked the moss canister on her weapon. Kalam pushed away from the railing. "I'll tell Thiest."

From the number of armed Solkis on deck and in the large fire weapon stations, Moon figured Thiest already knew.

Soon they sighted a border emplacement standing up out of the heavy jungle. It was a cluster of conical towers with fire weapons mounted atop their roofs. A broad balcony and pier extended out from the side of the largest tower, with a stairway and scaffold on the end, presumably for docking flying boats. "There's Fell everywhere," Stone muttered.

Moon hissed in agreement. The stench hung in the air, a foul taste in the back of his throat. He would have thought that traveling with Kethel for so long would make him used to it, but obviously that wasn't the case. Kethel just hadn't smelled that bad compared to this.

Rorra tightened her grip on the handle of her fire weapon. "Should we send Kalam inside?"

Stone shook his head a little. "I want both of you near us, in case we have to get away in a hurry."

Kalam leaned around Moon's elbow, his own fire weapon cradled in his arms. "I don't want to go inside."

"Hush." Stone tilted his head, listening.

As the flying boat turned to ease down toward the emplacement, Jade went to stand with Ceilinel and Thiest. Moon stayed at the railing with the others. It was a better angle to watch Jade's back.

The boat angled down to bring itself level with the pier, a cumbersome process. Moon stepped sideways, just far enough to get a glimpse of the boarding scaffold. Three groundlings waited there, two with gray skin and headcrests, similar to the Solkis, and one a dark-skinned Janderi. All wore leather harnesses with fire weapons over their clothing. *So they're alive in there*, Moon thought. No one else was visible in the windows in the curved walls, or at the fire weapon stations atop the towers. With Fell in the area it made sense for the groundlings to keep inside. Moon didn't know why there were cold prickles of unease traveling up and down his back, his prey reflex making him want to twitch.

Someone called out from below and the flying boat shivered as its motivator thumped to a halt. The Solkis on deck opened a gate in the railing and fastened lines to the ramp that extended out from the emplacement's boarding scaffold. The three groundlings hurried across, their steps drumming on the wooden planks. They stopped on the deck, dumbfounded at the sight of Jade. Ceilinel moved forward with Captain Thiest, who said, "We've come from the conclave to view the situation and to render what assistance we can. Which of you is the warden of this march?"

"Our warden was killed," the larger gray groundling said, and cast an uneasy glance at Jade. "I'm Neline, and as her second, I've been given charge. These are Ualck," he nodded to the other gray groundling, and then the Janderi, "and Pathial. I hope you've sent more help than this."

"Two more ships are following," Thiest assured him.

"What's happened here?" Ceilinel asked. "We know of the sightings of Fell—"

Neline interrupted, "There's been more than just sightings. The Fell are all up and down this march, attacking settlements, border stations, and traders."

Thiest threw an opaque glance at Ceilinel. "We heard they were being driven off by Raksura."

The Janderi Pathial said, "They're allied with the Raksura."

Jade's spines twitched. "That's not possible."

Pathial and Ualck stared at her, obviously shocked that she could talk. Neline said, "We have a trader who's witnessed it." He asked Theist, "You have Raksura prisoners?"

"No." Ceilinel didn't bother to expand on that. "You have an arcanist in this station? Or an esoter? A horticultural?"

"The esoter was killed with our warden." Neline gestured sharply toward Jade. "It's dangerous to have these creatures aboard your ship."

Stone hissed under his breath, his gaze on the sky. He wasn't the only one. A number of Solkis were on the walk atop the upper cabins, handheld fire weapons aimed upward, guarding the larger weapon stations at bow and stern. "They're here somewhere," he muttered.

Thiest was asking, "How were the warden and esoter killed? Was the station attacked?" Moon understood the confusion. He couldn't catch any scent indicating a battle had taken place. No groundling blood, no rotting bodies, and no lingering scent of the discharge of fire weapons. The only sign was that heavy Fell stench. Someone else was coming up the boarding ramp, hidden by the angle of the boat.

Pathial said, "During the attack."

Ceilinel's frustration was clear. "When did this attack take place?"

Neline seemed offended by the question. "If you don't believe us, the witness is coming now."

"We didn't ask to see your witness," Ceilinel said, an edge to her voice. "I'm asking you for a coherent report."

Moon belatedly put together the idea of *confused groundlings unable to answer direct questions* and *single surviving witness*. He said, "Jade, it's a—" at the same time Stone said, "Jade, they're—"

"I know," Jade snapped. "Ceilinel, Thiest, back away from them."

"What?" Rorra whispered.

"Fell ruler." Moon eased forward in front of Kalam.

The figure who stepped off the boarding ramp was tall and lean, and very like the groundling form of an Aeriat, except for its pale skin and long dark hair. It made eye contact with Ceilinel and started to speak.

"It's a Fell," Rorra shouted, and lifted her fire weapon.

Moon wasn't expecting much in the way of help, but the difference between groundlings who had little experience with the Fell versus groundlings who had fought them before was immediately evident. Thiest yanked Ceilinel away and shouted an order toward the steering cabin. An instant later the flying boat dipped sideways and ripped itself free of the gantry.

Neline staggered as the deck tilted. "What are you doing?"

Ceilinel scrubbed at her eyes, clearly furious. "It's a Fell ruler, get away from it!" Rorra and Kalam aimed their fire weapons.

Thiest ordered, "Ceilinel, get inside."

Jade stalked toward the ruler, her head tilted, angling her approach to shield the retreating groundlings. Moon shifted, ignored the nervous jitter from the crew, and moved to flank her.

Ceilinel backed toward the nearest hatch but said, "Can you make it tell us what happened here? Are there more Fell inside the emplacement?"

The ruler braced itself against the railing. It ignored the groundlings and smiled at Jade. It said in Kedaic, "You have a fine consort, queen. My progenitor is pleased."

Moon fought a surge of fury and made his hiss sound amused. "Is that the best you can do?" He tried to keep his attention on the towers, knowing the ruler's job was to distract them. Whatever it said, it couldn't have expected to find a Raksuran queen on a groundling flying boat.

Jade snarled, "Your progenitor will be in pieces. She's nearby, is she? She put you in that tower for a reason."

From behind them, Thiest demanded, "What reason?"

Moon said, "They want to destroy this flying boat. They knew it was coming." He realized Stone wasn't on deck anymore. He hadn't shifted and taken flight, and he hadn't gone inside, so he must have vaulted the railing in the confusion. *He's right, if the Fell aren't above us, they're below us.*

"They want to escape." Urgently, Rorra said, "Thiest, you need to get this boat out of here, now."

Taking mental control of the Kishan garrison would have allowed the Fell to know a boat was on the way. If Raksura were really hunting Fell through this region, then this flight must want to capture or destroy the boat so they would have a clear path to escape through Kish. Neline and Pathial stood like confused statues, as if they had no idea where they were or what was going on. Ualck backed away from the ruler, his face set in a grimace of horror, as the Fell influence faded and he realized what had happened.

"What about the garrison?" Ceilinel asked from the hatchway.

The towers were ominously silent, no one observing the standoff on the flying boat. Kalam, backed up against the cabin wall with Rorra, said, "They may be all dead."

Moon kept his attention on the ruler. The fact that it wasn't talking was worrisome. It looked like it was listening. The ruler had been the Fell's first plan, and it hadn't worked, and they had abandoned it. They would be working on their second plan now. "Jade—"

"You need to go, now!" Jade snarled at Thiest.

The ruler shifted and surged toward Jade. It either hadn't thought Moon would interfere or the mental command from its progenitor had allowed no room for caution. Moon hit it from the side and Jade bounced upward and slammed into it from above. Moon rolled clear of its flailing legs as Jade thumped it down to the deck and opened its throat. Thiest turned toward the steering cabin and shouted, "Take us up!"

Then a deadly cloud of dakti shot out of the tower windows.

The dakti swarm fell on the boat like an avalanche. A figure slung itself off the nearest tower and shifted into a kethel in mid-fall. Fire weapons roared as the Solkis fired into the dakti and the boat's two big forward weapons turned toward the towers. Moon leapt up to slash the first dakti to reach the deck, then slapped the next two out of the air. Jade took down a second ruler, and Stone's dark form leapt out of the trees below to snatch the kethel and drag it down into the foliage.

Dakti swarmed Moon and he slammed them down to the deck, ripping at their throats and wings. They fled abruptly and Moon caught movement out of the corner of his eye. The tube of the big fire weapon at the top of the nearest tower jolted into hesitant motion. Moon's spines shivered as it swung down to point toward the flying boat. *That's wrong, that's definitely not supposed to happen.*

Then two Fell rulers came over the top cabin. One hit Ceilinel and the other struck Thiest, dragging both up and off the boat. Jade braced to leap but wooden disks from the big tower weapon hit the steering cabin with a patter like a sudden heavy rain. Moon yelled an incoherent warning to Jade and she changed direction in mid-leap.

Moon grabbed the nearest groundling, a random blue-skinned person, and flung it down the deck toward the stern. Jade snatched up Kalam and leapt toward Moon. Moon turned, pounced on Rorra, and bounced down the deck.

As he reached the stern railing, the boat bucked. A fire cloud belched up out of the weapon stations and heat stung his scales. Something hit him from behind and bowled him down.

Moon struck the thick moss of a cabin wall. For a scatter of heartbeats he couldn't move, then Rorra dug her blunt claws into his shoulder. Moon forced himself to lift his head.

He had Rorra clutched to his chest and the weight atop him was Jade and Kalam. Fire consumed the whole bow of the boat. The deck was an angled mountain now, a jagged crack across it. Something important in the boat's structure had snapped. Groundlings lay sprawled on the tilted deck, some trying to stand or groping for their fallen weapons. The stench of burned flesh and moss filled the air.

Moon realized the freezing chill in his chest was shock, that the sight of the fire and the stink of the weapon's discharge had frozen him in place. Jade let go of Kalam, who woozily fell over on the deck, then pushed herself up.

"Are you all right?" Moon croaked the words out with effort.

"Yes." Jade glanced back and bared her fangs.

Rorra turned in Moon's arms, and gasped in dismay.

The boat twisted and jerked sideways. Moon reached up to grab the railing. Her voice gravelly with smoke, Rorra said, "The motivator, they've lost steering."

Kalam levered himself up. "They got Ceilinel and Thiest," he said, his voice shaking from reaction. "Maybe—They wanted the patrol craft out of their way, maybe they'll go—"

"They'll want to feed before they run." Jade grated the words out as she uncoiled and came to her feet.

In the air above the boat the dakti swarm reformed, swirling back down toward them.

Rorra flailed and Moon gave her a push to get her upright. She pointed toward the stern weapon stations, still intact above the cabin. "I need to get up there, see if the weapons are working. Kalam, come on!"

The two groundlings headed for the nearest hatch. As Moon shoved to his feet Jade said, "You go with them."

Moon twitched his spines in a negative. The Solkis still alive on the deck fired handweapons up at the dakti, temporarily scattering the swarm. It made his burns scars ache with remembered pain. More groundlings staggered out of the hatch with big tube things, directing a spray at the flames still licking the steering cabin. He said, "We've got to get to that big fire weapon on the tower. If there's Raksura here, they can't get close while the Fell have it—"

Her voice rough with rage, Jade said, "Not 'we.' I can't let you, not again."

"You want to die, or you want to fight?" Moon snarled back. He could just leap into the fray and make her follow him, but even furious he knew that was a terrible strategy.

Jade barred her fangs. Above their heads the starboard stern weapon loosed a burst of fire, shattering the cloud of dakti. It was the perfect moment; Jade snarled and turned to leap to the railing. Then she flung herself across to the big tower.

Moon followed and hit the curved wall just below her. He clamped his claws on the weathered rock. Movement under him made him flare his spines, but the dark shape weaving through the heavy foliage below was Stone. His big form coiled around the base of the tower and vanished; he must be looking for a way in.

Jade dropped to the nearest windowsill and paused for a heartbeat. She might have been trying to taste the air, but the smoke and

Fell stench was so thick, scent was useless. As she jumped inside, Moon swung after her.

His scales scraped against a folded metal arrangement that was probably meant to shutter the window, then he landed in a crouch. The room was wide and high-ceilinged, the thick walls carved out with shelves stacked with pottery jars and casks. Jade stood still, her foot claws retracted to keep from making noise on the stone floor, her head tilted toward the door. From this angle, Moon saw it opened into a larger space towards the center of the tower.

The shouting and fire weapons outside covered subtle sounds, but there was movement somewhere past the door. Moon stepped up beside Jade, ready to work out a plan with silent gestures, when Jade bolted through the door.

With a growl of surprise, Moon bounced after her and slammed into three dakti. He ripped the first one apart almost before he registered that Jade rolled across the floor, her claws clamped into a ruler. The second dakti clamped onto Moon's head and ripped at his shoulders, opening gashes in his scales before he disemboweled it and tossed it aside. The third had almost reached a doorway before Moon caught it and snapped its neck. He turned, hissing, as Jade shoved to her feet, shaking the ruler's blood off her claws.

This was the central stairwell of the tower, a large round space with various doorways, the spiral of the stairs leading up to a trapdoor in the ceiling. Daylight fell down the open shaft, the heavy metal sliding door pushed to the side. A groundling lay in a dead crumpled heap by the wall across the way, one outstretched hand still reaching toward the stair.

A vibration shivered through the floor as the weapon above them worked again, and outside fire roared. Moon hoped that Stone had stayed on the ground, that he wasn't the target. Jade stepped toward the stairway. Her expression was a grimace of doubt. Moon knew why; there was no way they could get up through that opening without the Fell having the advantage. *They'll rip our heads off as soon as we stick them up there,* Moon thought grimly. Trying to distract them from the outside would be. . . . His gaze fell on the bulge of a large ceramic tank tucked up against the ceiling, right below where the large fire weapon must be. The flying boats had those same kinds of tanks for their motivator. Like those, this one had tubes leading up to it from the floor. And it had levers along the side.

As Jade eased forward, Moon tugged on one of her frills and pointed to the tank. She hesitated, then flicked a spine in agreement, in a way he interpreted as *it's worth a try*.

Moon started toward it, keeping his steps silent. Jade flanked him, her attention on the spiral stair. Moon swarmed up the wall to the tank and pulled the levers. Something inside gurgled and the tubes made a whooshing noise. Above them the weapon coughed again, then there was a thunk and a noise like something large gagging.

Moon shoved off from the wall and Jade hissed, "Go, go, get out—"

A progenitor dropped out of the trapdoor and landed beside the stairs. She was huge, and she had her clawed hand wrapped around Ceilinel's neck.

CHAPTER TWENTY-SEVEN

"There! There he is!" Heart said. She crouched on a flat rock half-buried in the heavily forested ground below the Kish towers, with First, the half-Fell dakti beside her. Vine and Serene perched in the branches above her. Parties of Indigo Cloud and Opal Night warriors hid all through the trees and heavy vegetation around them, trying to approach the Fell taking shelter in the emplacement. Heart called softly, "Stone, it's us!"

Stone's dark form flowed up on the rock and First retreated with a noise of alarm. Stone shifted to groundling and said, "I know it's you, what are you doing here?"

He looked just the same, weathered and gray, but dressed in groundling clothes that had seen hard use. Heart flung herself into his arms. "I'm so glad you're all right! We heard—And I had a vision—Is Moon all right?"

"He's fine, he's fighting Fell on the boat with Jade." Stone grabbed her shoulders and looked down at her, baffled. "What are you doing here?"

Vine began, "There are Fell in the towers—"

Stone snapped, "I know there are Fell in the shitting towers!"

Serene finished, "—and we chased them here from the Reaches!"

"Pearl let you do this?" Stone demanded.

"Pearl's leading us, with Malachite," Heart told him.

Stone stared down at her, then slowly grimaced, still half incredulous. "Pearl?"

Heart felt a tug on her tail as First whispered, "Ruler has a groundling."

Heart's gaze snapped upward. Through the trees she saw a dark figure climb the outside of the nearest tower, a struggling figure tucked under its arm. She hissed in dismay.

"That's Thiest, the groundling captain. I was looking for her," Stone said. He shifted and leapt upward to batter the tree canopy aside.

Heart took the opportunity to tell Serene, "Better tell Pearl we've found Stone and Jade."

Serene twitched her spines in acknowledgement and hopped into the foliage, disappearing with hardly a rustle. Vine edged sideways, his head craned to watch Stone.

Stone landed with the groundling in one hand and what was left of the ruler in the other. First sunk further behind the rock.

Stone set the groundling beside Heart and tossed away the ruler's crushed body. He shifted out of his winged form as the groundling Theist stared at Heart in blank shock. She was gray-skinned with dark braided hair, her chest and shoulders badly scratched, bloody furrows from the ruler's claws. She breathed hard and seemed stunned, though she clearly recognized Stone. He told her, "We can help your crew, but you have to tell them to stop the fire weapons so we can approach."

She shuddered, then her expression cleared as she gained control of herself. She glanced at them all, then nodded sharply. "I can do that. Just get me back to the craft."

Moon didn't move, his heart pounding in his chest, suddenly aware he was dripping blood onto the floor. Jade let out a slow hiss. Ceilinel was still alive, her eyes wide, her face darkening as she was half-strangled by the progenitor's grip. This was the biggest progenitor Moon had ever seen, towering over Jade. But he scented fresh blood on her, a smell that made his claws involuntarily contract with the urge to rend. She was wounded, terribly wounded, somewhere under the plates of her scales.

The progenitor said, "You attack us with consorts, too? You are so confident in our destruction."

Moon held his spines flared though his heart had just contracted in hope. *So there are Raksura here somewhere.* Jade snarled, and didn't correct the progenitor's assumption. She said, "This place was a trap and you flew right into it. You should kill yourself now to save us the trouble."

There's two of us, Moon was thinking, *we could take her. Maybe we could take her.* If they could do it before more rulers or dakti arrived. But it would get Ceilinel killed. Ceilinel wasn't his friend, but she was right there and still alive and Moon had seen too many groundlings torn apart by Fell.

The progenitor's head tilted and Moon realized the roar of the flying boat's weapons had ceased. Outside it was eerily quiet.

Then Pearl whipped down through the trapdoor and hit the floor in front of Moon and Jade.

Jade flinched back. Moon was so shocked he nearly screamed, but managed to keep the sound to a strangled gasp. Yes, that was really Pearl, facing down a progenitor, here somehow from across the Reaches.

Moon had never seen Pearl's fully extended spines from this angle; when she was this angry, he was usually in front of her. Her growl was higher-pitched than Stone's but it made his ears ring. Pearl was always impressive when she was fighting but the force of her presence now was hard and vital, the air around her charged like lightning.

The progenitor widened her jaw in a grin, revealing her fangs. "Where's your companion?"

Pearl's hiss was all sharp amusement. "Guess."

Beside Moon, Jade's growl was almost voiceless. A heartbeat later he realized Malachite stood behind the progenitor, that she had dropped out of the figured stonework above. Moon had a picture of it in his head, a dream image, but he couldn't actually remember it happening.

"You want the groundling alive?" the progenitor said, and her voice was warm and even, as if she couldn't give up the deception, the belief that they might still be seduced by her. She flexed her hand and Ceilinel made a keening sound. "What will you give me in exchange?"

Malachite said, "You're weary, and hurt."

Her power curled around Moon's heart and his breath hitched.

The graceful coil of the progenitor's body moved, turned to face Malachite. She opened her jaw to speak, but stopped, a sudden stillness in her body. Jade tensed to move but Pearl flicked her claws, a warning to be still.

Malachite's head tilted and the progenitor's head tilted with it. *This is what she did*, Moon realized, fascinated. When she had broken and killed the progenitor who had destroyed her court, when she had rescued Shade and Lithe and the others.

The progenitor's grip on Ceilinel loosened, its claws leaving livid streaks on the soft gray flesh of her throat. She slid to the floor and half collapsed, catching herself with bloody palms braced on the floor. She tried to crawl away and Moon crouched down and sidled toward her.

The progenitor said, "We shouldn't have run. We became prey."

Malachite said, "There was nowhere to go. There was never anywhere to go."

Moon caught Ceilinel's arm and pulled her further away from the progenitor. He tucked her against his side and stayed in a crouch, ready to bolt. Ceilinel clung to his side, shivering with reaction.

The progenitor twitched, breaking the hold, and lifted her arm to strike.

But Malachite was already in motion. The crack of bone snapping made Ceilinel flinch and gasp.

The progenitor's body slammed down on the paving and Malachite wrenched the head off with a single sharp twist.

"Finally," Pearl snarled, impatient and irritable as always. She straightened and shook out her spines, as if they were in the colony and the Arbora were agitated about the tea harvest, and not at all as if she was facing the terror of the western Reaches over the mutilated body of a Fell progenitor. "Are you happy?" she asked Malachite.

Malachite said, "I'm mildly gratified." She turned her attention to Moon, her cool gaze flicking over him.

"Then we can go." Pearl turned to Jade. "Who else is with you?"

Jade snarled so hard her spines rattled. "What are you doing here? What—The court—"

Pearl's spines rippled at Jade's reaction, equal parts amusement and annoyance. Moon let out a pent breath, feeling light-head with relief. If the colony was attacked and the court fleeing in remnants, he doubted Pearl would find anything funny, no matter how much she enjoyed making Jade angry.

Rise and a dozen more warriors dropped down from the trapdoor. Moon spotted Fair, Sand, and Spring from Indigo Cloud, along with others he recognized from Opal Night. Malachite moved one spine and they dove down the stairwell. Pearl answered, "Celadon." At Jade's expression, Pearl dipped her spines in irony. "Yes, I'm sure Emerald Twilight will be throwing it in our faces ten generations from now. Are the others with you?"

Jade took a sharp breath and settled her spines. "Just Stone, and two groundlings. The rest are with Niran on the wind-ship, which went to Jandera for help. I sent Balm with some warriors back to the Reaches to tell you where we were."

Pearl flicked her spines. "They missed us. We had news of you from someone else."

Moon shifted to his groundling form so his scales wouldn't poke Ceilinel. He stood and picked her up. He didn't care who Pearl had left in charge of Indigo Cloud, it was just a relief to hear that all had been well when she and Malachite left. He interrupted the queenly posturing to say, "She needs help. Did you bring any mentors?"

Pearl's spines angled with irritation, possibly because Moon was talking to her and thereby ruining her good mood. More Opal Night warriors poured down from the trapdoor, and Pearl said, "Heart will be below with the others, they came in through the lower level."

Malachite, still eyeing Moon, moved a spine and a dozen warriors broke off to surround him as he carried Ceilinel down the wide stairwell. The Fell stench was fading but the smell of groundling death hung in the air. The remains of the Kish garrison must be all through these rooms.

"Are you all right, consort?" a female Opal Night warrior asked.

"Yes," Moon said, having no idea how else to answer. "It's been a long day."

Ceilinel held onto his arm, and croaked, "Who were they?"

"The queens? The gold one was Pearl, Jade's mother, the reigning queen of Indigo Cloud. The big scary one was Malachite, reigning queen of Opal Night, my mother," Moon told her. She blinked up at him, not really comprehending. He added, "That was why it was a bad idea to hold me prisoner."

"We weren't holding you prisoner," she muttered, stubbornly. "The conclave—"

"This way, consort," another warrior said from below.

The stairs ended in a big space with double doors now open to the balcony and the boarding scaffold, or what was left of it after the flying boat had yanked itself free. Warriors were stationed around on guard at the windows and doorways, others dumped dead dakti out the window. Moon saw Heart first, hurrying toward him. There was a dakti behind her and Moon stopped short, startled, until he realized it wore a braided leather and red cord necklace that was clearly Arbora work. It must be one of the half-Fell dakti, wearing the necklace as a marker to prevent accidents.

Heart said, "Moon, we were so worried—" She shifted to her groundling form and pulled her bag off her shoulder, kneeling as he crouched to set Ceilinel down. "I'm so glad you're alive."

"Me too." Moon hesitated. Malachite would have told Heart and the others about Song. "This is Heart," he told Ceilinel in Kedaic. "She's a mentor, a healer, and she'll take care of you."

Ceilinel nodded distractedly to Heart, then asked Moon, "Can those queens speak for the Reaches?"

"Parts of it," Moon said. Ceilinel's focused determination was almost as bad as an Arbora's. He asked Heart, "Is the court all right? Did you leave any warriors there?"

"It was fine when we left. Celadon brought over two hundred warriors when she came. Plus Sunset Water and Emerald Twilight and the other courts were patrolling the fringe." Heart gently turned Ceilinel's face towards her, wincing at the gashes in the gray skin of her collarbone.

That was good to hear. Maybe Pearl and Malachite hadn't lost their minds after all. Moon caught a glimpse of Stone and Rorra outside and pushed to his feet again. "I'll be back."

He went out onto the balcony. Kalam stood with Stone and Rorra, watching the broken flying boat. It still hovered in the air, though the stern rested in the tree canopy. The Solkis scrambled around on the broken deck, putting out the still smoldering fire. Thiest balanced atop the stern cabin, injured but alive, pointing and shouting orders.

Moon squinted up at the towers. Warriors had settled all over the sides and conical roofs, familiar faces from Indigo Cloud and strangers from Opal Night. Spines flicked everywhere as they sighted Moon. "They brought half the court," Moon said, not sure if he was complaining or not.

Stone was not pleased. "And mentors. As if we don't have enough Arbora running wild out here."

Moon would hardly describe what Bramble and Merit had been doing as running wild, but Stone clearly wanted a post-battle argument and Moon had no intention of giving him one. He nodded toward the Solkis. "The mentors can help with their wounded."

"We asked, they said no," Kalam said, clearly not happy with the answer. He wiped a smudge of singed moss off his face. "It's stupid."

"It's Solkis," Rorra said with a glare at the boat. She asked Stone, "How did you get them to stop shooting so the Raksura could come in?"

"Took Thiest off the Fell ruler that had her." Stone's gaze was on the flying boat. Thiest strode across the cabin roof to stamp out another smoking patch of moss. "I wasn't sure if she'd keep her word."

That was a frightening thought. Moon rubbed his face, realizing he felt a little dizzy. He probably wasn't as recovered as he thought he was. Then Kalam pointed and said, "Look!"

Moon braced for more Fell. But a large Kishan flying boat loomed into view over the treetops. It was built more like Callumkal's ill-fated craft, with the ridge up the center. There were two more flying boats much higher in the air, their course intended to flank the emplacement.

"Reinforcements," Rorra muttered. "This could be good or bad for us."

A figure came out of the tower doors, the warriors parting for him with only a few growls, and Moon was startled to recognize Kethel. The skin of his chest now had a rippling scar pattern from the healed burns, but he didn't move like he was hurt or ill. He was wearing a braided cord like the dakti, but his was blue and brown.

"You live," he said to Moon. He glanced at Stone. "Old consort."

Stone eyed him. "So you found your flight."

Kethel scratched the scars on his chest. "It was easy. They were following a lot of Raksura."

Moon knew what he wanted to say and there was no point in delaying. "I'm sorry I nearly got you killed. It was a bad idea."

"I'm not dead. I had the bad idea too." Kethel appeared unbothered by the whole thing. "She thanks you."

Moon hadn't seen the half-Fell queen, but she had to be here somewhere. "For what?"

"For not killing me." Kethel squinted up at the top of a tower. Moon followed his gaze. A number of dakti huddled in the lee of the roof, out of sight of the groundlings, with some Opal Night warriors perched beside them. The braided cords were bright against their black scales. Kethel added, "She would tell you herself, but the big queen will kill her if she speaks to you."

Moon could imagine. "What are you going to do now? Chase more Fell flights?"

Moon had never seen a Fell look happy before, so it was something of a shock to realize that was the expression on Kethel's face. Kethel said, "The big queen has said we can have a place to live. A big tree."

"A big—" Moon bit his lip, turning that thought over. "That . . . will be interesting."

"In the Reaches?" Stone said, floored. "What have they been doing while I was gone?"

As Moon carried Ceilinel down the stairs, Jade turned to Pearl. "I need to speak to both of you in private." She knew she should ask to speak to Malachite alone, but even after all the turns of aggravation and distrust in their relationship, Pearl was still her birthqueen and Jade wanted her here.

Malachite eyed her without any hint of expression in her face or spines, then flicked her claws. All the Opal Night warriors leapt, scrambled, climbed, or bolted out of the room.

Pearl's spine flare and eye roll said eloquently what she thought of this display. She turned to Floret, "Take everyone outside."

Floret gathered the Indigo Cloud warriors with a glance and they dropped down the stairwell. Jade saw Serene cast a worried glance back at her and tried not to react. Then the warriors were gone and they were left alone in the stink of Fell and dead groundlings.

Malachite nudged the dead progenitor with a thoughtful claw, then fixed her gaze on Jade. "We had word of how Moon was injured, lost, and taken away by groundlings."

Jade's jaw tightened. "How?"

Pearl said, "The half-Fell flight is with us. The kethel that followed Moon and Stone rejoined it some days ago, and we had its story from Consolation." Pearl watched her critically, with a trace of impatient confusion in the line between her scaled brows. "I assume you retrieved your consort since he was just here. What is it? Just tell me, you know how I get."

The Kethel obviously didn't know about the bargain Lavinat had offered Jade, anymore than Moon did. The urge to pretend she had nothing else to say was for a heartbeat overwhelming; but Balm and Stone and River and the others knew. Shade, as close and loyal to Malachite as if she was his bloodline birthqueen, knew. And Jade couldn't ask them all to lie for her.

Jade didn't clear her throat though it felt like there were ashes on her tongue. "The Kethel told you about the weapon, how he and Moon were trapped by the Hian groundlings?" When Pearl flicked her spines in assent, she continued, "The Hian leader offered me a choice: if I let her use the weapon, she would spare Moon. I could save my consort or I could save the Reaches. I chose the Reaches."

Malachite made a noise, a huff of breath like something had punched her in the chest. Pearl met Malachite's gaze, and for once there was nothing of irony in her expression. The silence went on long enough that Jade was tempted to attack one of them just to break it. Then Malachite whipped away and was suddenly on the other side of the chamber, facing the stairwell, breathing hard.

Pearl let out a breath, but there was nothing tense in her demeanor. She seemed more resigned than anything else. With a sense of shock,

Jade recognized Pearl's *I hate dealing with your emotions* face. Pearl said, "We were on the fringe of the Reaches, fighting the Fell, when it happened. We saw it come over them in the wetlands, and Heart said it was a wave of death. We fled and it stopped in the fringe."

"So close?" Jade managed. Cold prickled her spines. If she had stood in that chamber for another moment of indecision, if she had tried to bargain for Moon, the weapon's effect would have spread further across the Three Worlds. It might have killed Pearl and Heart and everyone with them. How many more moments until it would have reached Indigo Cloud and the other courts of the eastern Reaches? It had been an excruciating decision but she had thought it the right one. Now she knew it was, but it didn't help. She turned to Malachite. "Even if you kill me, believe there was nothing else I could have done."

"She's not going to kill you and spoil all this fun we've had," Pearl said, dryly. Malachite turned her head enough to give Pearl a look that would have dropped a warrior dead on the spot. Pearl barred her fangs in amusement, then told Jade, "Go now and make sure the warriors aren't doing anything stupid."

Jade took a half-step away, the accord between Pearl and Malachite enough to make her reel. Then Malachite's voice rasped out, "Does Moon know?"

Jade's whole body went cold with dread. She made herself say evenly, "No." It came to her that it would be better if Malachite knocked her across the room. This restraint was somehow more devastating. She wanted to say, "I'll tell him," but the words dried up in her throat.

Pearl flicked her spines in a clear order to go, and Jade went.

The flying boats had dropped to approach low over the treetops, so it was hard to see any detail from this angle. "We're going to have to leave soon," Moon told Stone.

Stone threw an impatient glance toward the tower and growled with annoyance. "When they're done."

Kethel followed his gaze and said, "Your queens talk to each other a lot."

Compared to progenitors, they probably did.

Floret dropped out of a window to land beside Moon. She peered at him. "Are you all right?" He had shifted back to his winged form and the healed burns had left ridges on his scales.

Moon saw Stone tense but he was too distracted to wonder at it. "I'm fine. So . . . Pearl and Malachite like each other."

"It's terrifying," Floret confided, keeping her voice low. "But it's also kind of . . . attractive."

Stone muttered, "They could have gotten half the court killed."

Moon looked for some sign of Jade again and spotted her perched atop the roof of the next tower with Sage and Serene. He frowned, wondering why she hadn't come down yet.

Then Pearl and Malachite dropped abruptly to the pavement. Warriors scattered and Kalam stumbled into Moon. Kethel backed away immediately, but Pearl told him, "Tell Consolation to take the half-Fell and withdraw to the camp."

Kethel jerked his chin, a gesture of acknowledgement, then said to Moon and Stone, "I'm telling the others your stories." He turned, vaulted the balcony railing, and disappeared into the trees below.

Jade extended her wings to glide down from the tower. She landed neatly, glanced once at Moon, then reported to Pearl, "The wind-ship is with them."

Moon turned as Stone hissed in startled relief. The first Kishan flying boat had just angled down toward the towers' landing pier. As its bulk moved aside, he saw the Golden Islander wind-ship trailing behind.

Kalam waved wildly at it and Rorra clapped a hand to her head and swore in relief. She added, "It must have reached Kish-Karad not long after we left."

The sight of those three sets of fanfolded sails was more than welcome. That was Diar standing in the bow signaling to whoever was in the steering cabin. And Chime and Lithe at the railing with the warriors and crew. Moon let out his own hiss of relief. The two craft appeared to be in perfect accord, as the wind-ship turned to pull alongside the Kishan boat and dropped its own anchor cables.

Chime and Lithe saw them and called out, pointing. Bramble bounced into view, waving back at Kalam. Niran appeared on the deck, helping a tall Janderan . . .

Kalam gasped, recognizing that figure an instant before Moon did. It was Callumkal.

Moon shifted, grabbed Kalam, and bounced into the air. As he landed on the wind-ship's deck he realized a dozen Opal Night warriors had followed him, surrounding him like a fledgling taking its first flight. *That's going to get old quick*, he thought grimly, as he set Kalam on his feet.

Callumkal didn't look well and had to lean heavily on Niran. But it was a huge improvement over the half-dead body Moon had retrieved from the Hians' flying boat. As Kalam flung himself at his father, Moon was immediately surrounded by a noisy group of Raksura and Golden Islanders.

Chime wrapped his arms around Moon. "We thought you were dead," he said, his face buried in Moon's neck, his voice harsh with emotion.

Everyone kept saying that. Moon hugged him back, just enjoying the familiar scents. Over Chime's shoulder, he spotted Bramble and Merit, bouncing excitedly, and Root, who looked guilty. "I'm fine," he told them all. Chime stepped back, still keeping hold of Moon's wrist.

"You don't look fine." Shade turned Moon to face him and studied him intently. "We really thought you were dead."

Lithe stepped between them so she could examine the burns on Moon's scales. "What happened to you? Does this still hurt?"

Then Kalam called, "Moon! Please come speak to my father."

Moon gently pried Chime off and stepped away from his half-clutch-mates. He shifted to groundling and reluctantly went to Callumkal.

The others must have told him how the artifact had ended up on the sunsailer, and Moon was aware of a tight knot of guilt sitting in his stomach. They hadn't meant for any of it to happen but it had, and there was nothing to be done about it now.

Callumkal stepped forward to wrap his arms around Moon in a hug. Moon returned the embrace, partly to make sure Callumkal didn't fall. Callumkal felt even more boney than a Janderan should and his scent still had a trace of sickness. Callumkal said, "There is no way to thank you for everything you did."

Moon fought down a lump of emotion that tried to close his throat. He managed, "You know about the . . ."

"I know everything." Callumkal stepped back, still gripping Moon's arms. "I was the one who trusted Vendoin, who shared all my work with her, who brought her on the expedition."

Moon shook his head. "That was . . . Not something anybody could have guessed."

Vine landed on the deck with Rorra then, and Callumkal smiled to see her. "Captain! It's good to see you well!"

Moon stepped aside to give Rorra room. Delin appeared at his side to say, "Vendoin is alive, did they tell you? We found her while you were at the forerunner ruin."

"Alive?" Moon growled the word. "Are you serious?"

"We left her in Kish-Karad under guard, with the Jandera speaker to the conclave." Delin's expression was grimly satisfied. "It gave the Hians there much to explain. They said they didn't know about Vendoin and Lavinat's plans, and Callumkal and the others said it would take some time to decide what to do, if the Jandera were going to accept that. But the important thing is that the other Kish believed us." He waved a hand. "We will tell you everything you missed on the way back to the Reaches."

"Back to the Reaches?" Niran had arrived just in time to hear this, and looked aghast. He protested, "Grandfather—"

Delin waved a hand. "We must go back. Our friends are surely too tired to fly all that way."

Jade stood with Pearl and Malachite on the open balcony below the big tower. Heart was nearby, Ceilinel leaning heavily on her. Jandera in flying harnesses lifted off from the newly arrived boat and landed several paces away. After a moment's consultation, the lead Jandera came forward and said in Kedaic, "We wish to speak with the Raksura leader."

Malachite twitched a spine and said in Raksuran to Pearl, "This is pointless."

"For once I agree with you," Pearl said.

Jade felt her spines tilt but she controlled her annoyance. "We have a chance to make an alliance with these groundlings." Pearl's expression said she was clearly unmoved by that statement. "You can't ignore them because you don't like to talk."

"I can." There was nothing ironic in the angle of Pearl's spines.

Jade took a deep breath, all too aware of Malachite. "Pearl, I want Vendoin and her people held responsible for this. For Song. For—" Her gaze flicked to the wind-ship where Moon was. "For the groundlings they killed who were under my protection. For what they meant to do to the Reaches. If we leave, they will lie about us, about what happened."

Malachite stared down at her. Pearl looked away, growling under her breath, her spines flicking. But Jade knew the whole variety of Pearl's growls, and that one was the *I'm angry that your argument has swayed my opinion* growl. Pearl said, "Well, what do you want to do, then?"

Jade said, "Stay and talk. Make sure they listen to Callumkal, and Kalam and Rorra."

Pearl gave Malachite a considering glare, then said to Jade, "I'll agree, if you send your consort back to the Reaches with an escort of warriors."

Jade controlled an irritated twitch. She had intended to do that anyway. "Of course. He can go on the wind-ship. The Golden Islanders will want to return with us."

Pearl hissed, "Of course they do. We'll never get rid of all these groundlings."

Jade pressed the point. "Then I have your permission to speak."

Pearl flicked her spines and Jade turned to the Jandera, and said in Kedaic, "You can speak to us."

Moon finally got a chance to sit down in the common room with the others when Heart came aboard with Serene, and the greetings started again. No one quieted down until Heart told them the full story of what had happened in the Reaches.

Stone hissed when Heart explained about the plan to kill a certain dominant progenitor. Bramble bounced with nerves as Heart described building the fake hill in the ruin, and what had happened after, and how the queens had seen the Fell die.

That was too close, Moon thought, and felt all the tension he hadn't realized he was carrying suddenly unclench. The others seemed to feel the same relief. Bramble scrubbed her face and shook out her hair, and Chime muttered, "I need a nap." Moon squeezed his wrist.

As Merit told Heart what had happened to them, Rise appeared in the doorway. She signaled to Lithe, who went to her, then returned to say to Moon and Shade, "Malachite wants to talk to us."

Moon had figured that was coming. He pushed to his feet and followed Shade up to the deck.

Serene had said that Jade, Pearl, and the Jandera had gone into the emplacement to talk, so Moon wasn't surprised to see Opal Night warriors still keeping watch atop the towers. A second boat had come in low near the big tower, and groundlings in flying packs hovered around the damaged Solkis boat, poking in the smoldering ruins of the steering cabin.

Malachite waited for them in the stern, seated on the deck, and Moon sat down while Shade and Lithe enthusiastically greeted her. His half-clutchmates and Celadon had a completely different relationship with his birthqueen than he did, or anyone else did, as far as Moon could tell, and it was still strange to watch. He guessed it was a little like his own clutch would experience later, growing up with Pearl as their beloved reigning queen and having no idea why the older generation viewed her with such a mix of emotions.

Once Shade and Lithe had settled down, Malachite said, "You are all well?"

The question shouldn't be as fraught with intimidation as it seemed, with Shade tucked into her side and Lithe sitting beside her knee, but this was still Malachite. Moon said, "Yes."

"We're fine," Shade told her. Then added, "Whatever you heard, it wasn't as bad as it sounds."

Lithe agreed readily. "It was frightening, but Jade and the warriors kept us safe."

Malachite was trying to bore into Moon's skull with sheer force of personality. He tightened his jaw in irritation and said, "Yes, I was captured by groundlings and taken to Kish-Karad. But they didn't hurt me. It was my own fault."

Malachite's eyes narrowed.

"What?" Moon demanded.

Shade squeezed her wrist and stared up at her, his brow furrowed. Malachite met his gaze. His expression said he was making an entreaty, but Moon couldn't guess what it was. Of the two of them, Shade's behavior had been correct for a consort, except for leading the warriors into the ruin to help Jade. *Maybe that's what he's worried about,* Moon thought. He glanced at Lithe but she seemed confused, as if she didn't quite understand what Shade was asking either.

Malachite's gaze went to Moon again, and he was startled to read just a trace of hesitation there. She said, "If you wish my help with anything, you need only ask."

Moon found himself wanting to squirm with discomfort. He would have preferred to be castigated for almost getting himself killed. He rubbed at a claw mark on the deck and said, "Sure, I will."

Shade said, "Lithe was very brave. Lithe, tell her what you and Chime did to break up the ruin."

Moon had only heard this secondhand from Stone, so it was enough of a distraction to get past his discomfort. He still had the feeling he was missing something though.

With everyone telling him he looked like he was half-dead, and Bramble and Merit demanding his clothes because the cloth smelled like unfriendly groundlings, Moon gave in and retreated to their cabin. Surrounded by the familiar comforting scents that clung to the blankets, he fell asleep almost at once. When he woke, Jade was sitting next to him, holding his wrist.

He yawned hugely, feeling the first stirring of hunger. Stone was nowhere to be seen, but Chime and Merit were curled on blankets not far away. Moon said, "Are we ready to leave?" He could tell it was twilight, from his sense of the sun's position, and the scent of the air drifting down the corridor.

Keeping her voice low, Jade said, "I'm going to have to stay here with Pearl and Malachite. You'll go back on the wind-ship with an escort of warriors. I want to make sure these Kish hear our side of what happened. I don't think it'll have as much weight if I just leave Rorra and Kalam to speak for us."

Moon struggled to sit up, trying to wake up enough to make a good argument. "No, we'll wait for you."

Jade squeezed his wrist. She sounded calm but Moon could feel desperate intensity in her touch. "I was lucky to get Pearl and Malachite to agree to this much. We'll catch up before you get home. I just want you out of here."

Moon stared at her. He couldn't fault her reason for staying. It was better to settle this now, and maybe she could even get the Kishan to stop confusing Raksura with Fell. "Balm isn't here. You don't have a female warrior." It was frustrating that he couldn't stay with her, but he knew it would still be days before he was in any shape for long flights.

"I'm taking Saffron."

Moon settled back. It wasn't a bad choice, except personality-wise. But he wished Balm was here. "That'll be fun. You don't want Stone to stay with you?"

Her expression and her spines went neutral. "The only way this makes sense is if Stone stays with you and Shade. I can't leave two consorts with no one to protect them."

"Yes, but it's me and Shade," Moon said. And the mentors, the warriors, and Bramble, plus a crew of Golden Islanders armed with Kishan fire weapons. He couldn't be much safer anywhere outside the Reaches. "It's better if Stone stays with you—"

"You and Shade need protection too, whether you know it or not."

"I just . . ." He captured her wrist again. "I want you to be careful."

"I can be careful more easily if I know you're safe."

Moon let go of her and sat up to give himself a chance to control his expression.

But he looked at the signs of strain in her face, the tight angle of her spines. This wasn't an argument to have now, while they were still in unfriendly groundling territory. So he said, "Just be careful."

Moon got up to say goodbye to Rorra and Kalam, who had come aboard to collect their belongings.

Kalam hugged him and said, "Bramble has said we can come to visit. My father and I want there to be a formal alliance with Kedmar and your court."

Moon had no idea how that would work but it sounded like Pearl's problem. "Sure," he said. He told Rorra, "You visit, too."

Rorra gave him the frown that he knew by now meant that she was trying to hide how pleased she was. "Are you sure the other Raksura wouldn't be bothered by—" She waved a hand, and Moon knew she meant her communication scent.

He said, "Stone will tell them not to be bothered by it."

There was no one else to be left behind, since the wind-ship had left Dranam the horticultural back in Kedmar. It surprised Moon that the Kish had let the Golden Islanders keep the fire weapons. He had always heard that the Kish guarded those jealously. "Not the weapons, so much," Delin said, when asked. "It's the moss itself. We have no way to grow it, and no horticulturals to manipulate it if we did, so the weapons will cease to work as soon as it runs out." He scratched his beard thoughtfully. "If we encounter any remnants of Fell flights on the way home from the Reaches, they will certainly come in handy."

By the time Rorra and Kalam said their last goodbyes, it was full night. Moon sat up on the steering cabin with Chime as the wind-ship lifted away from the dark shapes of the towers and the Kish boats, and sailed away under the bright ocean of stars.

Chapter Twenty-Eight

After the next few days, Moon almost wished he could have spent the trip in a healing sleep. Waiting for Jade and the others to catch up made him edgy and there were too many things to worry about. And Stone was preoccupied, loitering in the stern, talking more to Delin or Diar than anyone else.

Once Moon convinced Chime that he was fully recovered, they started having sex late at night on top of the steering cabin. It was somewhat challenging, since they had to be quiet so Niran wouldn't hear them and yell and bang on the ceiling. They were curled up together one night when Chime admitted, "I can't stop thinking about the Reaches. If it got that far into Jandera territory, if Jade hadn't stopped it in time . . ."

"But she did," Moon said, and nipped his ear. He was pretending to be less affected by it than he actually was. Diar had managed to plot a rough map of the weapon's effect, and how far it might have extended if it hadn't been stopped. Stone had asked her not to show it to anyone else.

"I know, but—" Chime began, and Moon did something that distracted him from the topic for the rest of the night.

But by the next afternoon, Moon needed something else to think about, and he started to teach Shade how to fight like a groundling. Moon had been in many situations where he couldn't risk revealing what he was by shifting but still had to defend himself. There was no reason to expect Shade ever would, but there was no point in not learning, either.

Shade was bemused at first and then increasingly interested. He had been taught the rudiments of fighting and hunting at Opal Night, but not how to use his strength in his groundling form. He was good at it; he was still built like a slender Aeriat but reaching maturity had added a lot of lean muscle.

They soon ended up with an audience of the warriors and everyone who wasn't busy on the boat, with Delin sketching and taking notes. Bramble wanted to learn too, and Moon ended up teaching her, Lithe, and Merit. Chime got lessons too, though Bramble had to drag him down the deck. "I don't need to learn," Chime protested. "I'm never leaving the Reaches again!"

It helped pass the time and gave Moon something to think about besides Jade. He was worried about her for several different reasons, and wished they had had more of a chance to talk before the wind-ship departed.

She couldn't be happy about the fact that he had left Chime, Shade, and Lithe to run off with a kethel and try to stop the Hians alone. It hadn't worked, and he had almost gotten himself and Kethel killed, but since Moon hadn't known if Jade and the others were trapped or dead, he didn't see he had had much choice. But he was tired of worrying about it. They were on their way home, and he wanted everything to go back to the way it was. He figured if Jade was still angry when she got back, he could apologize and pretend convincingly to be sorry. He just wanted her to hurry up and get here so he could do it.

But they had come out of the jungles and crossed the grass plains, and were almost at the edge of the western wetlands before the queens and the rest of the warriors caught up with them.

When they were specks in the distance, Deft sighted them from the look-out post atop the mast. The larger group of Raksura continued on, but two specks broke off and flew toward the wind-ship. By the time they landed, everyone was on deck and Moon was trying not to vibrate with impatience.

"Are you all right?" he demanded as soon as Jade furled her wings.

"Yes." She seemed startled to be asked. She looked tired and her scales were dusty. "We're fine."

"What happened?" Delin asked anxiously, proving Moon wasn't the only one who had been worried. "Are our other friends well? Was there a resolution with the Kish?"

Jade said, "Yes. Pearl and Malachite are traveling with the half-Fell flight, so they're going straight on to the Reaches." Moon realized Malachite must not have wanted the Fellborn queen anywhere near him and Shade. Jade continued, "We have an agreement with the Kishan conclave, for what that's worth." She glanced at Saffron. "It was fairly boring." Saffron twitched her spines in fervent agreement.

Jade's spines were drooping a little and Moon thought she must be exhausted. He said, "You need to rest."

That got Bramble moving, and she hustled Jade and Saffron below to where Flicker was already making tea.

Once they were sitting down, Jade still didn't talk much, though Saffron gave more details. Stone sent River, Root, and Deft off to get a couple of grasseaters, then sat down on the edge of the group.

Moon, partly so Stone didn't have to ask, said, "How was Rorra when you left?"

"She was ready to go back to Kedmar. So was Kalam." Jade flicked a look at Stone, or at least in Stone's direction. "I told her if Callumkal really does mean to visit us, she should come. She would be welcome."

Stone didn't say anything and the lack of response made for an awkward moment. That was when Moon added up all the hints and realized something was wrong between Jade and Stone. Diar asked a question about the Kishan conclave then and the talk went on.

Moon caught Jade alone in the sleeping room after she had eaten. She was leaning over, digging through her pack. He slid the light wooden door shut and said, "Did you want to talk about what happened?" He wasn't sure what was wrong between her and Stone, but being angry with him probably couldn't be helping. He wanted to give her a chance to yell at him in private before he apologized.

She glanced up at him. "With the conclave?"

Moon had been hoping not to have to spell it out. He felt badly enough about it as it was. "No, with Lavinat and the Hians, in the ruin."

Jade burrowed deeper into the pack, not looking up at him. "I'd rather wait until we get back to the court."

Moon hadn't expected that. "You don't want to talk." He had rehearsed this moment and he just wanted to get it over with. Waiting would just make it worse; at least, it always had before.

Jade still didn't look up. "No, not now."

Moon set his jaw. "About anything?"

Frustrated, obviously trying to avoid having the conversation, Jade kept pretending to dig in the pack, which couldn't have more than three things and a blanket in it. "Of course not. We can talk about something else."

Moon folded his arms and tried to force down his irritation. "I told Bramble I'd have a clutch with her."

Jade gave up on the pack and started pretending to arrange her blanket. "That's fine. She's a good choice."

Moon had put off this decision for so long, out of a combination of inability to choose and nerves, and he was hoping for a little more excitement at finally having made it. The lack of it didn't make this situation any less exasperating. He said, "We're going to have five mentors. Maybe six."

"Good." Jade sat back on her heels, checking the blanket's arrangement.

"We're going to do it right now, out on the deck," Moon added.

Jade gave in, stood up, and gripped his shoulders. "Moon, I'm just tired. We can talk about it when we get back to the court."

Moon hated the image of the sullen spoiled consort who fled in disarray when he didn't get what he wanted, so he kept his face expressionless and did not shift and break the door into pieces when he walked away.

He stood out on deck, breathing the damp cool wind. Flicker and Deft, on watch atop the steering cabin, regarded him warily. Then he went to look for Saffron. He disliked Saffron as much as she disliked him, but they had been imprisoned by Fell once together and that did create some sort of bond. Sort of.

He found her in the stern, using a bucket of water to scrub dust out of her frills. Some Golden Islanders sat nearby, sewing up rips in the covers used to protect the windows in bad weather, and River was up in the look-out post atop the mast, so Moon kept his voice low. He said, "Jade's upset. Did she say anything to you?"

"We barely stopped to sleep and hunt." Saffron glared at him.

Moon stood there, waiting. After a long moment of trying to maintain eye contact, Saffron hissed and said, "She didn't like dealing with the Kish groundlings." She flicked her spines. "That was all. Who wouldn't be upset after all this?"

Moon couldn't decide if she was telling the truth or being a good warrior and refusing to carry tales about the queen to the consort. He hissed at her and left.

He tried to find Stone then, but Stone was hiding so effectively that he might as well not be on the boat. Chime, Shade, Lithe, Heart, and Merit were all asleep in a pile in one of the other cabins. Moon gave up and went to lean against the deck railing near Bramble.

The breeze held just a hint of rainy season coolness and was like silk against groundling skin. Everyone else was either asleep or up atop the cabins, enjoying the sun.

Jade was obviously unhappy with him, and he was worried that the root of it lay in what was improper consort behavior by any Raksuran standard. Jade had been tolerant of Moon's behavior, because the court had been lurching from one crisis to another and there wasn't much room for a consort who couldn't take care of himself. But before the dreams had started and Callumkal had arrived, things had been quiet. Maybe Jade had gotten used to that quiet and it had eroded her tolerance for a consort who couldn't stay out of trouble.

And he was very aware that a consort getting into trouble in the Reaches was a very different thing from a consort being captured or killed by official forces of Kish. That if Malachite had wanted to retaliate, everything could have been unimaginably worse.

It was a depressing thought. Queens and consorts who traveled frequently together weren't exactly unknown, at least in Indigo Cloud's history. Moon had heard all the stories about Solace and Sable, though their adventures were probably exaggerated. What he and Jade had done hadn't seemed all that different.

Moon glanced over his shoulder and saw Root coming out of the belowdecks door. Root saw him, twitched, and vanished back inside with guilty speed. Exasperated, Moon turned back to the view of the approaching wetlands. "Bramble, is something wrong?"

"With me, no," she said, sounding genuinely puzzled. "With everybody else, sometimes I wonder."

They were two days into the wetlands, the long prelude before the Reaches, when the warriors on watch called a warning. They had seen several figures flying at a distance, either Aeriat or Fell.

Stone climbed up on the steering cabin to shade his eyes and squint in the indicated direction. He jumped down from the cabin to report, "Warriors, coming this way."

Moon hissed out a breath. A scatter of warriors sounded like a planned patrol, not survivors fleeing another Fell attack.

Jade's spines twitched. "Can you tell who it is?"

"Not at this distance." Stone stood, waiting for Jade to make a decision. Their behavior towards each other was absolutely correct, but the obvious disagreement between them, whatever it was, hung in the air like a boulder.

Jade said, stiffly, "Will you go up and signal them?"

Stone nodded and turned for the stern. Jade's spines tilted in distress for an instant before snapping back to a firm neutral. Moon caught Bramble's gaze, and Bramble signaled bafflement. Moon had no idea either.

In the past two days, it had become obvious that some Raksura were not speaking to other Raksura but there were too many Raksura on the boat to make the configurations obvious. Stone was avoiding everyone, Chime and Lithe were as baffled as Bramble, and when Moon had tried to ask River, he had hissed, "I'm not involved in this!" and climbed up on top of the mast again. Shade had changed the subject so adroitly Moon couldn't figure out if he knew anything or not. Any attempt to pin down Merit just resulted in pointed questions about Moon's injuries and veiled threats to put him into a healing sleep. Delin and all the other Golden Islanders seemed oblivious to whatever had happened, which further confused the issue. To Jade, Moon said, "Scouting for Fell?"

Stone jumped off the stern, shifted, and caught the wind, rising high above the wind-ship. "Maybe," Jade said, watching Stone.

Moon waited on the deck with Jade, the air cool and as humid as a wet blanket. There were traces of rot in the breeze, but not nearby. As the strange group drew closer, River and Flicker went up in the air to question them. They landed back on the deck and River reported, "They're from Emerald Twilight and Ocean Winter. They say they have news."

Jade turned toward Moon. "It's better they don't see you."

Moon stared at her, baffled. "Huh?"

Jade said pointedly, "It's Emerald Twilight. You know how they are. They might start rumors. Tell Shade, too."

Moon had to bite his lip to keep from baring his teeth. Emerald Twilight was perfectly capable of starting rumors about him whether they saw him or not. But he made himself turn and go through the doorway. He met Shade coming up the steps, caught his wrist, and tugged him back down. "We have to hide."

"I thought they were just warriors," Shade said, confused.

Moon swallowed a hiss. "They are. Stone had sex with a sealing all over this boat but we have to hide because they might start rumors."

Shade pulled Moon to a halt at the bottom of the stairs by simply stopping. He said, with just a little exasperation, "Moon, you're a consort, but there are courts that won't treat you like one unless you act like it. Emerald Twilight is one of them. Believe me, I know."

Moon managed not to growl. He was right, which didn't make it any better. "I know."

So they ended up sitting in the cabin next to the main hold while Jade and the others spoke to the warriors. They kept the door open so they could hear, and Chime, Flicker, and Bramble sat with them. Delin sat in the doorway, trying to be part of both conversations. Moon had difficulty controlling his irritation, but at least it was good to get more recent news of the Reaches.

The two female warriors who led the group were Crocus from Emerald Twilight and Spin from Ocean Winter, and they had been sent to make sure the Fell had left the wetlands. Crocus said, "We've been finding half-dead stragglers, and scattered dakti. There was word of an almost intact flight still in the area, but it was gone by the time we got out here."

Spin added, "We could tell the further the Fell were from the Reaches, the worse they got it, whatever it was. The last day or so, we haven't seen anything but rotting clumps of bodies."

As Jade asked for more details about the situation, Moon tried not to think about what it would have been like to come home and find the Reaches like this. Colonies empty and silent, with nothing but the scent of decaying bodies. The Hians had come so close to succeeding.

Even with the recent news, it was still a relief to see the colony active and well when the wind-ship dropped below the Reaches' canopy and made its way through the mountain-trees to Indigo Cloud.

Moon stood at the rail with Chime as the wind-ship entered the clearing under the colony tree's immense canopy. Groups of warriors flew patrol circuits and the Arbora were out on the garden platforms. There were far more Arbora and warriors outside than usual in an afternoon, since Jade had sent River and Deft ahead to tell the court they were here.

Pearl and Malachite must have arrived a few days earlier so everyone had been expecting them. The first to greet them was Celadon, who swooped up and dropped down onto the deck, followed by a happy cluster of Indigo Cloud and Opal Night warriors.

Celadon said, "Balm told us you were captured by groundlings, you idiot," and pulled Moon into a hug. He must be more upset than he was willing to admit to himself, because he held on to her longer than he had meant to. Finally she squeezed his waist and pushed him back. "You're all right?" she asked, brows lowered in concern.

"Sure, I'm fine," Moon told her. He felt it was unconvincing, and Celadon eyed him suspiciously.

Distracted, Chime pointed to the opposite end of the clearing. "Is that what I think it is?"

Celadon turned and her spines flicked. "It's the half-Fell flight."

Moon stepped to the rail to look. There had been occasional drafts touched with Fell stench coming from this direction, so the presence of the flight wasn't a surprise.

A camp had been built on a cleared platform in a smaller mountain-tree at the edge of Indigo Cloud's canopy. There were tent shelters augmented with saplings and firepits, and it looked exactly like a Raksuran camp, except for the pale groundling forms of the rulers and dakti. Celadon said, "They're staying here until it's time to go back to Opal Night. Malachite's promised them a colony tree in our territory."

Chime turned to her, brows lifted. "I bet Emerald Twilight and the other courts are thrilled."

"It was an interesting conversation," she admitted. "But the mentors said the Fell queen can't breed like a progenitor, so there was no reason not to have them here. Pearl supported Malachite on it. They make a fairly unstoppable combination."

As the wind-ship tied off to a branch above one of the bigger platforms, Moon and the others flew to the knothole entrance and went inside.

Filled with warriors and Arbora, the cavern of the greeting hall was loud with happy greetings. The wash of familiar scents, mixed with the sweet clean scent of the mountain-tree, made it unexpectedly hard for Moon to keep his spines neutral.

And it was strange to see the Indigo Cloud mountain-tree so full of Raksura. It wasn't crowded by any stretch of the imagination, but almost half the balconies in the normally empty levels between the hall and the queens' level were now obviously tenanted. There was a profusion of new scents, far more sounds of movement and voices, and a lot more clothing and blankets hanging out to dry.

Balm arrived in a flurry of wings and spines, shifting before she reached the ground. She flung herself at Moon and he caught her. "Pearl said you were alive," she said, and nipped his ear, "I wasn't surprised, I knew—I knew—"

He nipped her back. Not very coherently, he said, "Me, too."

She let him go and turned to Jade. Bone grabbed Moon enthusiastically then and he lost Jade and Balm in the crowd. Ember appeared after that, pulling Shade along with him, the warriors nearby stepping aside for them. He looked as beautiful as usual, even when flustered and worried. He said, "Moon, Shade said you were all right, but—You're really all right?"

"Sure," Moon said. "How are the kids?"

Shade nudged Ember, an *I told you so* gesture. Ember watched Moon carefully, but seemed relieved. "They're all fine." With more assurance, he added, "And you'll be very proud of how Frost behaved while you were gone."

When the storm of greetings had died down, Moon found himself next to Chime again.

Chime stood near where Heart and a large group of Arbora had surrounded Bramble and Merit. He was looking up at the central well, smiling a little. "This must be what it used to look like," he said. "I never thought we'd see it like this."

Moon looked up again, watching warriors flit from balcony to balcony. "It's going to be quiet when they go."

Jade appeared, skirting the noisy crowd of Arbora. She told Moon, "I've got to go meet with Pearl and Malachite."

Moon pretended to believe that. "If you need me, I'll be down in the nurseries."

She hesitated, then said, "I'll go down there later," and then leapt up onto the wall of the greeting hall.

Moon had meant to spend some time with his clutch and the Sky Copper fledglings, and talk to the teachers. But after answering a storm of questions from Frost and giving her, Thorn, and Bitter an expurgated account of the journey, and playing with all the babies, he fell so deeply asleep he didn't wake for anything. Even with Blossom, Bark, and Rill standing over him and talking and occasionally accidentally stepping on him.

He woke the next morning in a pile of babies and fledglings, with Rill handing him clean clothes, pointing him to a bathing pool, and telling him the court was getting ready to do the farewell for Song, as well as Coil and the two Opal Night warriors who had died in the fighting. Moon hadn't meant to sleep like this. He had meant to talk to Jade, and make sure the Golden Islanders were settled and comfortable, and a lot of other things. He hadn't even known Coil had been killed.

Part of the reason for the long sleep had to be that he was still recovering from being injured, but most of it was probably just the feeling of being home again, and completely safe. He asked Rill, "Where's Jade?"

"Up on the queens' level," Rill reported, pulling him to his feet. "Balm came down to see where you were, but she said Jade said not to wake you if you were asleep. Now hurry!"

Moon staggered to the bathing pool and got ready.

The court sang for the dead, a blend of Indigo Cloud and Opal Night's song. Moon had come to understand Indigo Cloud's song over the turns, but Opal Night's was still the one that wrung his heart. He fled the greeting hall as soon as it was over.

He went up to the consorts' level, quiet since Ember and Shade were both still below with the others, and reacquainted himself with his bower. The Arbora had been in to renew the heating stones in the hearth and the snail shells that were spelled for light. Moon would never take this for granted, this room that was his alone, something he had never had until he had come to this tree with the court. But it didn't feel right, knowing something was still wrong with Jade.

Then the draft of rain-scented outdoor air told him Stone was up here in his favorite spot for brooding, and Moon found him in the room with the outer door. It was open to the green light of the canopy and the breeze and hum of insects, and Stone sat on the floor in front of it. Moon sat across the room, where he could lean back against the wall and still feel the air on his skin. He sat there a while in companionable silence, sorting out and identifying the rich green blend that was the scents of the Reaches. It seemed turns since he and Stone had sat here and argued before leaving for the sel-Selatra.

After a time, Stone tilted his head toward Moon. "You wanted to talk."

Moon frowned. He hadn't been trying to wear Stone down with silence. In fact, he hadn't thought it was possible. But maybe Stone wanted to talk. As an opening gambit, he tried, "I think Jade is mad at me because I got caught by Lavinat."

Stone grimaced. "No, that's not it."

Moon considered that for a moment. At least Stone was willing to admit there was an "it" and it wasn't just Moon's imagination. "Is she mad at you?"

"She was. I don't know now."

"Are you mad at her?"

Stone moved uneasily. "I was. Not now."

"Why?"

Stone turned enough to regard him with his good eye. "It's complicated."

"Complicated how? You've were traveling across Kish and staying in a groundling city together for how many days, and you couldn't figure it out?"

Stone sighed and looked away. "By the time I was ready to talk to her about it, we were a little busy dealing with you and your new Kishan groundling friend."

"So what changed . . ." Well, one big thing had changed. "You found me. You were mad at each other because I got caught by Lavinat? Why?"

Stone pushed to his feet abruptly. "She needs to tell you herself." On the way out, he gave Moon a shove to the head, part annoyance and part apology.

Moon felt he needed more information. Shade had been unresponsive before but maybe it was worth another try. He found Shade on the largest garden platform, swimming in one of the ponds with a mixed group of Opal Night and Indigo Cloud warriors and Arbora. The pond was in the center of a grove of fruit trees with long twisting branches and brushy canopies. Tending and pruning had made them much taller than they had been when the court had first arrived.

The Indigo Cloud warriors and Arbora seemed comfortable around Shade, even when he was in his shifted form. It probably helped that the Opal Night Arbora were happily splashing and playing with him, and that he and Flicker kept getting into mock wrestling matches, which Shade pretended to lose. Moon crouched at the edge of the pond and managed to deflect attempts to get him to join in. When Shade surfaced in a spray of water and shaking spines, Moon got him to climb out and retreat past the grove and out of earshot.

Shade plopped down on a ground fruit mound, still shaking his spines. "What's wrong?"

Moon perched on a trough of melon vines so they could be at eye level. "Do you know what's wrong with Stone and Jade?"

Shade squinted up at the heavy branch arching overhead. He admitted reluctantly, "Probably, but I can't tell you."

Moon flicked his tail impatiently, scattering the little flying lizards that were trying to settle on it. "'Can't?'"

"Uh, shouldn't and won't," Shade clarified. "Not if they won't talk about it."

This was frustrating. "I'm your half-clutch-brother, you have to tell me."

"Where did you get that idea?" Shade's spines flicked in amusement. Moon glared at him. After a bemused moment, Shade said, "Are you trying to think of a way to make me tell you?"

Shade had been raised by Malachite, there was nothing Moon could do to intimidate him. He tried, "If I guess, will you tell me if I'm right?"

Shade snorted. "No."

Moon let Shade return to the pond and tried Chime, who didn't know anything but was at least more supportive.

Moon found him on a balcony that overlooked the greeting hall, with pens, ink stones, and paper spread out around him. He had said he was going to write up an account of their journey to share with Delin, and Delin was off somewhere writing up one to share with Chime. Moon had no idea why they needed two different versions but it seemed to be making both of them happy.

When Moon told Chime his suspicions about Stone and Jade, Chime waved his pen in exasperation. "I noticed that too. It keeps getting worse. I don't know what it's about. They didn't tell you?"

Moon slumped in disappointment. "Stone wouldn't." He added, frustrated, "Shade knows, why don't you know?"

Moon hadn't meant it seriously. But Chime considered the question, then lifted his brows. "It had to be something that happened in the ruin, right? Lithe and I were in the steering cabin of the giant boat the whole time. But Shade left to help Rorra and the warriors get to Jade."

He was right. Moon sat up straighter, feeling he was finally close to an answer. "Bramble didn't know either, and she was on the wind-ship. River knew, but wouldn't talk, and he was with Jade. So anyone who was with Jade might know."

"That's it." Chime decisively wiped his pen and tucked it away in its case. "Root was with Jade."

Moon smiled grimly. "Let's find him."

All the warriors who had gone on the trip had been told to rest and stay around the court for the next several days, so they knew Root wouldn't be on patrol or out guarding the hunters. They found him in the third place they looked, hanging around with some of the younger warriors at the fringes of the teachers' hall, watching the Arbora peel roots for the next meal.

Everyone was talking and busy, but Root saw them and immediately looked guilty, which told Moon they were on the right trail. Moon motioned for Root to come to them, and Root reluctantly pushed to his feet and went to the archway. Moon took Root's arm and pulled him down the passage into a chamber currently being used to store baskets of root peelings. "We need to talk."

Root said quickly, "I know I've been a bad warrior, and taking it out on everyone."

It was good that Root had finally come to his senses a little. Maybe the ritual for Song had helped. "Good, but we need to talk to you about something else," Moon said.

Chime asked, "What happened down in the ruin? After you got there with Shade and Rorra."

Root seemed uneasy and surprised to be asked, but he said, "You know that Vendoin told them there was a stone plate down there and breaking it would stop the weapon." Chime motioned impatiently for him to continue. "Rorra had the fire weapon and Jade was helping her point it down where the plate was. The Hians down there heard them, and they told Jade if she didn't stop the fire weapon, they'd kill you. And she didn't stop, and they killed you. Or we thought they did."

Chime turned to Moon, aghast. "Is that what happened?"

"I didn't make it up," Root protested.

"We know, just be quiet," Chime told him.

Moon leaned against the wall, trying to sort out his memories of those moments. Most of it was obscured by a haze of pain. He knew the Hians had been talking, but couldn't remember the words. "I don't remember. I was already burned when that happened. Kethel and I knocked the weapon out of the holder it was in, but it was still working."

"So it was after that." Chime watched him intently. "Did Lavinat use a fire weapon on you again?"

"Maybe. I'm not sure." He was beginning to understand what had happened, or at least why Jade was acting the way she was. And Stone was right, it was complicated. "Did Stone try to stop Jade?" he asked Root.

"No, nobody did." Root lifted his shoulders, uncertain. "We didn't know what to do. It happened so fast, there was no time to think. I was mad because Song died, but the Hians were going to kill everyone in the Reaches and Jade had to let them kill you to stop them." He met Moon's gaze, worried. "Are you angry because we didn't—"

"No." On impulse, Moon pushed off the wall and pulled him into a hug. It turned out to be the right impulse, because Root wrapped himself around Moon and buried his face in Moon's shoulder. This also explained the conversation with Malachite, Shade, and Lithe. Jade must have told Malachite, and Pearl, what had happened. Shade hadn't wanted Malachite to interfere between Moon and Jade, and Malachite had given in to him, but had tried to let Moon know that if he wanted to leave Indigo Cloud, she would make that happen. It was an impressive display of restraint on her part. *She must have been . . . And Jade must have been . . .* Moon rested his chin on top of Root's head. What Jade had gone through was terrible. Moon thought how he would feel if their positions were reversed, and his imagination just didn't want to go there. He didn't think he would have been strong enough to make the right choice. He said to Chime, "I wish I'd figured this out earlier."

Chime's mouth twisted wryly. "Me, too. Right after it happened, I was just—" He waved a hand. "Upset, and then we found out there was a chance you were alive and Jade sent Balm and the others off to the Reaches and she and Stone left with Rorra and Kalam. Everyone was frantic."

Moon was still reeling. He had thought Jade was angry at him for getting caught, when she must have been blaming herself for his death. "Stone must have realized that she didn't have a choice."

Chime nodded slowly, still lost in thought. "Sure, he must have realized it, but . . . Knowing there was no other choice, and living with it are two different things."

He was right about that. Still clinging to Moon, Root nodded agreement. Moon let his breath out and said, "Stone and Jade need to talk. Jade and I need to talk."

Moon caught Jade in the greeting hall, where she was watching Bramble and Bone and a group of Arbora talk with Niran, Diar, and the other Golden Islanders. She stood at the outskirts of the group, a restless, unsettled air about her that would have been a clear signal that something was wrong, if everyone hadn't been so distracted. It was a noisy group, and so no one noticed when Moon stepped up beside her and said, "We need to talk."

Jade flicked a look at him. "Not now. I have to—"

Moon said, "Now."

That did it. Jade turned toward him, spines starting to lift. "Or?"

Moon folded his arms. As a former mentor, Chime had been very helpful with suggestions about what options were available if Jade resisted. "Or I'll ask Malachite and Pearl to arbitrate, with Heart as a witness."

Jade took a step back, caught by surprise and completely appalled. "You wouldn't."

Chime had pointed out that it wasn't often that a queen and consort's birthqueens were both available for something like this, so it would be a shame not to at least threaten to take advantage of it. "I would."

Jade barred her teeth. "Moon—"

"They'll love it. You know how much they like to help with things like this." This was pure sarcasm, because settling an emotional dispute was Pearl's idea of a nightmare and she was bound to offer a lot of extremely bad advice. Malachite wasn't much better, though she would just endure it stoically and be a hundred times more judgmental.

"I told them what happened," Jade snapped.

"You didn't tell me," Moon countered.

Jade snarled, grabbed his wrist and dragged him down a passage behind the fountain pool. They stopped in one of the unused bowers.

It had a balcony looking down the lower stairwell to the Arbora workrooms, and had probably been left empty because it was too noisy. Moon sat down beside the cold hearth bowl and watched Jade pace and lash her tail. After a couple of circuits of the bower, she calmed down enough to sit down and glare at him. "So talk."

Moon said, "You need to talk to Stone, because whatever it is you think he thinks, you're wrong."

It startled her, which made Moon wonder what else she had expected him to say. She said, "He told you what happened."

"No, Chime and I had to pry it out of Root." Jade looked away, her spines making an effort not to show chagrin. "I'm not angry at you. You had no choice. I would have done the same, if it had been me up there and you with the Hians."

Her expression was skeptical. "You would have?"

"Yes." That was a lie. He thought he would have tried to think of a way to trick the Hians, delaying while the weapon spread further into the Reaches to touch Indigo Cloud. He might have saved Jade only to return to a colony tree full of corpses. If he had managed to make the right decision, he would have wanted to flee, to never see another Raksura again, but he would have been tied to the court by his clutch. No telling how that would have come out, except badly. "It was the whole Reaches, Jade. I'm not sure the others understood that, not really. If you hadn't done it, I would have been angry. And dead, because Lavinat would have killed us all."

She was quiet, watching a tiny red beetle make its way across the floor. "I didn't understand it, either," she said finally. "I was furious when we found that first message and realized you and Stone had kept going south, with no idea if you were heading in the right direction or not, knowing there were Fell out there and at least one kethel following you." She shrugged her spines. "But you found the Hians and got the Arbora back and I wasn't going to say anything. Then when Lavinat had you, and it was you or the Reaches, that was when I understood it." She squeezed her eyes shut for a moment. "That's why consorts are kept protected, why they stay in the colonies, so queens won't have to make that decision."

Moon put all his conviction into his voice and said, "But it was the right decision."

Jade hissed a little. "Do you understand how I would feel if you weren't here to say that?"

"Yes, but I'm here."

Jade reached over and caught his wrist, and pulled him to her. She held him so tightly his ribs creaked, but her bite on the skin below his ear was gentle. His return bite on the scales just above her collar flange was much harder. Jade twisted and thumped him down on his back, and talking was done for a while.

Jade lay heavily on top of him. She pushed herself up and said, "That was hard. I don't want to do it again." She saw his lifted brows and added, "You know I don't mean the sex."

Moon rolled over and sat up on one elbow. There was another thing he wanted cleared up and this was a good time to do it. He wanted everything between them, anything that might keep them apart, to be dealt with. "You want me to stay in the court and be a normal consort."

"No. Normal is one thing you'll never be." Jade sighed. "I want you not to get killed. But after everything we've done, it seems ridiculous not to make visits to other courts, like Opal Night . . ."

"And to Delin, in the Golden Isles," Moon added. "And Callumkal said he would come visit and take us to Kedmar."

"I hate Kish," Jade groaned. She considered for a moment, then smiled. "Maybe after your clutch with Bramble."

Moon thought about five little baby Arbora or warriors with Bramble's curiosity and stubbornness. It would be more than enough to keep him busy. He nudged her foot. "You want to talk to Stone now?"

Jade sighed and pushed herself upright. "Yes."

Moon found Stone on the consorts' level and dragged him down to see Jade. The dragging was much easier than it might have been had Stone actually put up any kind of effective resistance, so Moon figured Stone was more than ready to talk.

It was early evening by that point. Moon looked for Chime, and found him sitting out on the big garden platform on the edge of a group of Arbora and Aeriat from both courts, and the Golden Islanders. This platform had a good view of the waterfall that rushed down from the knothole but was far enough away not to be drenched by the spray. Delin sat nearby, sketching furiously, while Bramble told the story of their journey.

"Did it work?" Chime asked, watching him hopefully.

Moon settled into the damp grass beside him. Spark bugs played between the trees of the fruit orchard on the lower part of the platform. "She's talking to Stone now." He nudged Chime's arm. "Thanks for your help."

Chime leaned over and nipped his shoulder.

Not long after, Jade and Stone came out, and they sat on the grass until the green light started to fail and Pearl sent Knell to tell everyone to come inside.

ACKNOWLEDGMENTS

I want to thank Nancy Buchanan for the title of this book, and for continued support through thick and thin. And I want to thank Jennifer Jackson, my agent, for not giving up, and Jeremy Lassen at Night Shade Books, for believing in a weird book about flying lizard people called *The Cloud Roads*. Thanks also to Janna Silverstein for editorial support and guidance on the Books of the Raksura series, and to Cory Allyn at Skyhorse, and artists Matthew Stewart, Steve Argyle, and Yukari Masuike for the beautiful art and cover design.

And thanks to everyone who offered support and encouragement when I really needed it, especially Troyce Wilson, Beth Loubet, Jessica Reisman, Felicia O'Sullivan, Lisa Gaunt, Megan McIntire, Bill Page, Nora Jemisin, Sharon Shinn, Kate Elliott, and all the people following the Raksura Patreon.

ABOUT THE AUTHOR

M artha Wells has written many fantasy novels, including *The Wiz-
ard Hunters*, *Wheel of the Infinite*, the Books of the Raksura series
(beginning with *The Cloud Roads*), the Nebula-nominated *The Death of
the Necromancer*, as well as YA fantasy novels, SF novellas (like *The Mur-
derbot Diaries* series), media tie-ins, short stories, and non-fiction.
  Her website is www.marthawells.com.